Possum Heights

Best Wishes!
Alan Cutler

Possum Heights

by
Arlene Cutler

Ivy House Publishing Group

www.ivyhousebooks.com

PUBLISHED BY IVY HOUSE PUBLISHING GROUP
5122 Bur Oak Circle, Raleigh, NC 27612
United States of America
919.782.0281
www.ivyhousebooks.com

ISBN: 978-1-57197-515-7
Library of Congress Control Number: 2012939461

© 2012 Arlene Cutler

Cover Design by Beth Oldham

Printed in the United States of America

Dedication/Memoriam

This book is dedicated to:
My mom, Bessie Cutler
My sister, Deborah Lands
My twin sister, Marlene Rue
My brother, James Cutler, Jr.

MEMORIAM
In memory of:

My dad, James Cutler, Sr.
My other brother, James Cutler, Jr., who passed on
before the four of us were born

My nephew, Danny Lands, Jr., whose brave fight with
Muscular Dystrophy ended at the tender age of 21

Acknowledgment

I want to thank Amanda Faber, my publishing coordinator, for helping bring Izzy to life. She was absolutely wonderful throughout this whole process and I'm grateful to her with all my heart.

I also want to thank Beth Oldham, graphic designer, for the incredible job she did with the cover design, a perfect depiction of Izzy's home in Possum Heights and the core of the story.

PROLOGUE

Darkness penetrated the horizon on this desolate stretch of southern highway, stringing her along. At the time Allie chose this route—or maybe the route chose her—it didn't matter where it went as long as it led away from where she came. Although some of the scenes from hours earlier that helped launched her on this path were sketchy, appearing in bits and pieces, she couldn't escape the last image she saw, an image branded so deep into her memory, it made her tremble to recall it. But there he was, the moment she turned her head, lurking outside the door of the building. Gasping, she felt her heart pick up speed, thumping louder with each beat. At first, she didn't recognize the intruder, but then his face took on a familiarity. It wasn't the same man she had met only weeks earlier. His transformation was, to say the least, horrific, going from charismatic to deranged. She blinked as if that horrendous vision would somehow disappear, but it came back more powerful than ever: the dark, distant eyes, the stained teeth, the strands of sweaty hair clinging to his forehead. And eerier still was when he spoke. He kept repeating the word "Miami." What was in Florida? Had he envisioned whisking her away to this famous resort? These questions only left her more confused. All she knew for absolute certainty was that fear had propelled her to run with no destination in mind. It became apparent that her destination would have to find her. Now, as she traveled on through the wee hours of the morning, she passed the time by reminiscing of the life she was leaving behind and the events that compelled her to run.

Chapter 1

Regal Woods, a small community situated along the eastern coast of North Carolina, exemplary of its name, harbored the elite, those whose statuses were not truly branded until they joined the enchanted community. Its quiet charm and highest standards allured folks near and far, those who could afford the massive price tag of even the smallest home Regal Woods had to offer, such as the home Allison Jones purchased last year when she saw her prosperity taking new heights. It was three bedrooms, two baths, the smallest within this exclusive development and the closest to her budget, perfect for a single career woman like herself. Surrounded by the mass array of successful and wealthy homeowners—among them doctors, lawyers and corporate executives—she often reminisced of the success that brought her here.

Allie never imagined herself in the competitive real estate world, much less starting her own realty, which she named A.J. Realty. The idea originally never appealed to her as she envisioned the grueling classes and intricate tests that followed. And if you managed to survive the course, thus obtaining the coveted Realtor's license, there was the broker's license to consider, a more difficult feat, but with higher rewards and sweeter returns, provided you had the stamina to continue on. *Why stop with the realty license?* she remembered thinking. Holding that initial piece of paper that legally declared her a real estate agent didn't put her on easy street, but it sure paved the way for better opportunities.

Here she was, a few months into a new decade, ending the eighties with profound success, beginning the nineties even better. Maybe it was the collards and black-eyed peas, the traditional New Year's Day grub, symbolic for money and luck. Perhaps, on a more realistic scale, it was the long hours and hard work that had finally paid off and earned her a spot in the prestigious neighborhood of Regal Woods, a dream come true. Although it translated that she had made it, had moved to a higher plateau in her career, she didn't think of herself as a snob and neither did those she lived among in the community. It wasn't a gated community like others, and the people were actually down to earth, friendly and compassionate, like those in more humble surroundings. The difference? Bigger bank accounts.

The prospect of residing in Regal Woods was unrealized years ago when she worked a meager job at a retail store. Dissatisfied with being a clerk, a position which had become redundant and less challenging over the course of time, she began to explore her potential. She wanted a career that allowed her to express who she was: dainty, sporting the best attire, the best jewelry, not in vanity, but for her own personal self-esteem.

But if she had to admit the real reason for seeking a career change, she supposed it stemmed from a dare made by her brother. Derrick seemed to relish presenting his sister with challenges, which she usually took on. Although it was her idea in the first place to venture out into the real estate field, she began to express doubt, admitting to Derrick that she didn't know if she could deal with the long hours involved, which included holding down a full-time job in the day while learning the mechanics of the real estate world at night. But Derrick turned this despair into a dare. It was his way of prodding her on. Deep down, he wanted her to succeed.

Derrick knew what it was to succeed. He loved selling cars and had dreamed of one day owning his own business. Allie had embraced his ambition and encouraged him to pursue his dream, which he did. Although it was initially small, he managed to establish his own dealership, "Jones' Auto Sales," and saw it grow into a larger and more lucrative business. He was able to display a wider variety of vehicles than before and his clientele was steadily increasing by the numbers. With the expansion of his business, he realized he needed more space. As luck would have it, the piece of property adjoining his was up for grabs and Derrick easily bought it at $5,000 beneath the asking price. Allie was exceedingly proud of her brother. He had found success in something he loved to do. He had also helped ignite her career with a simple dare and lots of encouragement. This was sometimes the topic of conversation whenever they got together, which was almost every Friday morning as she made her way to work. It had become habit to stop by her brother's place and enjoy a cup of coffee on the last day of the workweek. It gave them a chance to share their events of the week and have a few laughs.

"You're gonna make some lucky girl a fantastic husband," Allie doted on an early Friday morning. "With all your smarts and good looks . . . genetic, no doubt," she added, laughing, "you'd make an excellent catch. Only thing is, she's gotta get past my inspection."

"I'd end up a dirty old single man the rest of my life if they all had to wait for your stamp of approval, little sis."

"That's not true. I like that last one you took out . . . Brenda."

"Oh yeah, you would! She doted more on you than she did me. 'Ooooh, what a pretty outfit, what beautiful earrings,' and 'Oh, I just love your hair,'" he mocked, hyping his voice. "And then, she wants to talk real estate with you. I started to let you take her out."

"Oh, come on now. She just found my line of work intriguing. That's all. . . ." Allie, sensing what Derrick was thinking, added, "And yours, too."

"Don't patronize me, Allie. I hate it when you do that. At least my dates were normal. Why don't we talk about some of the fruitcakes you went out with?"

"Oh no, here it comes," Allie groaned.

"Remember Toady? The one addicted to Tootsie Pops? It was bad enough that he resembled Kermit the Frog, but watching him lap at that Tootsie Pop made it look more authentic." Derrick made quick in-and-out thrusts with his tongue for emphasis.

"Oh, stop that," Allie said, but she was laughing along with him. "You know I can't even remember his real name."

"Wait . . . it's on the tip of my tongue." Derrick once again mimicked "Toady" and Allie laughed harder, hitting him on the chest.

"You're terrible, you know that?"

"Rib-it . . . get it?" Derrick croaked, pointing to his rib cage where Allie struck him.

"Now you're getting corny. Let's just keep Mr. Toady to ourselves. That's what I get for going out on a blind date. And his name, I just remembered, was Walter."

"Well, it wasn't your only blind date. That's how you and Tim met. I know I set you up with him and I'm sorry it didn't work out, but at least y'all remained friends."

"Friends . . . it was more like sour grapes there for a while. But that was years ago and like you said, we are friends now. It's hard to believe we even dated. I remember the feelings weren't exactly mutual and he was a little hurt that I wasn't interested in him romantically."

"Well, sis, apparently it worked out for the best."

Allie glanced at her watch and quickly set her coffee down.

"Look at the time already. I'm gonna be late for work."

"You're the boss . . . remember?"

"Doesn't matter, Derrick. I need to be setting a good example." Grabbing her purse and keys, she rose and gave Derrick a hug as he, too, stood and saw her to the door. "Thanks for the trip down Memory Lane. I'll have a constant image of Toady . . . I mean Walter in my head all day long today."

"What are big brothers for? Oh, I just remembered. I need to stop by Tim's on the way to the dealership to drop off a set of jumper cables I borrowed. You mentioned earlier in the week about needing an oil change. If you want, I can ask him to set you up a time to do it."

"Yeah . . . I'd appreciate that."

"I can just see him drooling now when you pull up," Derricked laughed.

"C'mon, you know we're way past that."

"I wasn't talking about you, your humbleness. I was referring to your car. He'd buy that pony in a New York minute, at your price, if you ever wanted to sell it."

"Well, it's not for sale and I don't foresee ever wanting to sell it in the future."

Allie proudly sported a 1965 red Mustang Convertible that she promptly had restored once her business had begun to turn a profit. Bought secondhand, she had longed for the day when she could renew its original luster and refinish the interior, which was in grave need of new upholstery and carpet. The expense was enormous but Allie looked upon it as an investment, which is why she was particular with who she chose to service it. Tim donned a reputation for providing just that kind of service, treating each vehicle as if it was his own. Although the first few times were awkward following their breakup, Allie gradually began to feel at ease bringing her vehicle to him for service. Tim, too, had apparently gotten over his jilted romance, or lack of, and concentrated more on his repair shop.

"I think you take it there just to torment him," Derrick teased. "Seriously, I know he's backed up right now since his help left, but I'll see if he can squeeze you in next week."

"Thanks again . . . and thanks for the coffee. See you later."

"No, thanks." Allie politely declined the cup of coffee Amber held out to her as she breezed through the door and down the hall to her office. Amber followed her to get an update on the day's calendar.

"My cup of joe at Derrick's gave me my morning fix. He makes his way stronger than I do."

"You and Derrick have been doing this Friday ritual for a long time now, haven't you?" Amber asked, admiring the bond between Allie and her brother.

"Yeah, it's been quite a tradition. We don't get to see each other much so it's our chance to get to visit and talk."

"That's nice. So . . . what's on the agenda today?"

"I've got a showing at ten this morning," she said, flipping through her planner. "Not really expecting anything from it. After a while, you kinda get a sixth sense about your potential clients. And one o'clock this afternoon, I have a closing with Mr. Creech . . . hopefully," she added, crossing her fingers. "This has been a humdinger from the get go. But if all goes well, this could put a little extra padding on all our paychecks. Have you prepared the Daltons' paperwork?"

"All typed and highlighted." Amber gestured toward the tray on Allie's desk.

"Great! We're in business! Oh boy, could I use a vacation!"

"So take one," Amber said. "Frieda, Tess and I can handle this place while you're gone. You know that."

"That's sweet of you, Amber, really. But the timing's not right. There are too many prospects in the wing; I just can't get up and leave right now. These could be some major deals. I can't afford to not be here if and when they bite."

"Excuses, excuses. C'mon, Allie. You need a break. You're wearing yourself thin. You never go anywhere or do anything. As long as I've known you, you've never had a real vacation. You live and breathe this place. You're gonna burn yourself out."

Allie seemed unconvinced as she crossed her arms and shook her head. Amber continued on.

"Look Allie, Frieda's got her broker license, Tess has her Realtor's and I know how to do all the other stuff. There is no better time than now to go and get some R & R. I promise you, this place will still be here, intact, when you get back. So . . . what do you say?"

Allie smiled, as if pondering the idea of taking some time off, maybe to catch up on some projects around the house, do some gardening, her definition of R & R. She never cared too much for travel except for an occasional trip to the beach and even then, her mind was always focused on work.

"No. I can't," she said, dismissing the idea altogether. "Not now. But I appreciate you thinking of me."

"You won't reconsider?"

"Maybe later."

"You always say that."

"If I didn't know any better, I'd think you were deliberately trying to get rid of me."

"Just looking out for you, boss. That's all."

Allie flushed, feeling a wave of pride thinking how fortunate she was to have the staff she did.

"I know and I'm touched," she said. "But right now, I need to get my stuff together for the ten o'clock appointment."

Amber took the hint and wished her luck with the showing, then settled in at her own desk. She marveled at Allie's relentless amount of energy and wondered if she would still possess that same energy level in twenty years.

Derrick pulled into the parking lot of Tim's garage. He'd hoped his friend would be outside or at least near the entrance of the shop. The last time he walked in with a crisp white shirt, he walked out with a few grease stains permanently engraved, most likely from brushing against something in the garage. He tried everything imaginable to remove the stains. Nonetheless, the shirt ended up in the rag bin.

Vowing to be more prudent, he entered the shop and laid the jumper cables by the door. Not seeing any sign of Tim, he tiptoed further into the shop, subconsciously holding his arms up. Peeking inside Tim's office, which was close to the entrance, he saw no sign of him, which meant doing the "dirty dance" through the shop to find him. He had to maneuver around a Nissan up on racks, then a barrel of oil, and then a large metal cabinet, drawers pulled out, exposing various shop tools. A thief would love this, he thought. Just as he was wishing he'd just called him regarding Allie's oil change rather than risking cleaning the shop with his clothes, he heard a door slam. Tim, in his greasy attire, spotted him as he came out of the bathroom.

"Derrick, my man! How's my favorite auto dealer?"

"Great, dude! How's my favorite grease monkey?"

"Don't you look all snazzy, black slacks, blue shirt, black tie."

Derrick glanced down at himself, suddenly aware he still had his arms in the air. Quickly lowering his arms, he extended a hand to Tim, hoping no grease would be transferred.

"It's good to see you, Buddy. I guess you're still backed up since your help left, huh?"

"It ain't so bad. I just come in an hour early and stay an hour later . . . and pay myself overtime," he added, laughing. "It's just temporary until I can get a replacement. I got a 'Help Wanted' sign out front."

"Yeah, I saw it. Good luck in finding somebody. Oh, I brought your jumper cables back. They're out front by the door. And Allie wanted to know if you could give her an oil change sometime next week."

"Sure. Guess she still ain't interested in selling it?" Tim asked wistfully.

"Sorry, Tim."

"Couldn't hurt to ask. Well, actually, it did, but I'll get over it," he laughed. "How about Wednesday?"

"Wednesday's fine, I'm sure."

"How's she doing anyway? I only see her about every three thousand miles," he joked. "But I guess being in her profession, she keeps pretty busy."

"She's doing great, a real workaholic, but she loves it. We were just talking about old times this morning, how y'all dated and ended up being good friends."

"Yeah, friends . . ." he repeated, a hint of sadness in his voice, then cheerfully adding, ". . . funny how we're all still single, too."

"That could be a good thing, my friend." Derrick glanced down at his watch. "I gotta go, man. I'll tell Allie to bring her car in Wednesday. Let's have a beer soon and catch up."

"Yeah, sure."

Derrick maneuvered himself out the way he came, jubilant he had avoided contact with any grease, other than what Tim smeared onto his palm. Just as he rounded the rack to exit the shop, his tie got caught on something, yanking him backwards and somehow ripping his shirt.

"What a surprise," he muttered, continuing on to his car.

From across the street, a passerby stopped to observe the young man with the torn dress shirt and wondered if he and the rough-looking mechanic had had a scuffle. He had heard the mechanic could be hot-headed, especially when it came to women. He was insanely jealous. Maybe the young man with the torn shirt had hit on the mechanic's old lady.

The passerby watched the young man squall tires as he exited the parking lot, obviously mad. He didn't realize the car dealership man was actually late for work.

He, like Allie, was his own boss, but unlike Allie, skimped on help to keep overhead down. With no one there to open the doors, he hoped no one had gotten frustrated and left.

Chapter 2

Tim arrived early Wednesday morning to his shop, but not out of eagerness to dive beneath some hood of a car or toy with a rear suspension. The dreaded task of pencil pushing awaited him for days in his office and the longer he put it off, the worse it became. His desk lay cluttered with an assortment of paperwork, bills to be paid, quarterlies to be filed and so on. He thought many times of hiring a part-time secretary to assist him with office matters but knew, financially, that it wasn't feasible. He needed another mechanic worse than he did a secretary, although both would make his life so much easier.

Looking across his desk, he remembered the vow he made a couple of months ago, when he could at least see the top of the desk, that he wouldn't let it get this messy again. *So much for vows.* As frustrated as he was with himself at the moment, he kept in mind that his primary responsibility, working on vehicles, demanded most of his time. This somehow made him feel vindicated.

A light tapping on the glass of his front door brought him to his feet. *It's not even close to opening hours*, he thought as his eyes glanced at the large clock on the wall, its hands in the shape of screwdrivers. Edging closer to the source of the tapping, he found himself struggling to remember if he'd locked the door behind him when he came in. But before he had a chance to check it, someone had eased it open and was peering in.

"Yoo-hoo, anybody here?"

Tim recognized the voice at once as he poked his head out of the office.

"Hey Allie, c'mon in. I understand you need an oil change."

"Yeah, I do. I'm sorry, I thought you were open."

"It's all right. You saved me from a boring mountain of paperwork," he said, relieved to have an excuse for putting off the work at the moment. "Care for a cup of coffee?"

"Oh no . . . but thanks anyway. Amber's waiting in the car for me. Here's the keys," she said, offering the contents of her hand, which included the good ole lucky rabbit's foot. "Derrick tells me you've been extremely busy."

"Yeah, I'm hoping to hire someone soon," he said as he slid Allie's keys into his pocket. "Hard to find decent help."

"True. I guess I'm pretty lucky. I've got a great staff."

Tim looked past her at the Mustang and shook his head.

"It's still amazing to me to see what you've done with the pony. That's some set of wheels. It sure attracts a lot of attention around here whenever you bring it in. You ever want to part with it, best keep me in mind first," he said, emphasizing what Allie already knew.

"I know your obsession with my Mustang, Tim. And I promise, if I ever have an insane moment and want to part with my beloved pony, you'll be the first to have a shot at it."

"I guess that means I'm out of luck," he laughed. After a few awkward seconds, Tim continued. "I should have it ready this afternoon, by two at the latest."

"No need to rush. I won't need it today. I'll get one of the girls to drop me off after work. Thanks again."

"Any time. And don't worry, I'll take good care of her." *And I would've taken care of you, if you'd just given me the chance,* he thought. That warm feeling of déjà vu passed through him as he caught a whiff of her perfume, the same perfume she wore years ago. He could feel the remnants of a kiss, warm to him, cold to her. Unaware at the time that he was alone in that moment of passion, he had envisioned a life down the road with Allie, a life full of hopes and dreams. It wasn't until their next and last time together that he realized his vision was only a hallucination. The words still stung as he remembered her response to his admission of love.

"I love you, too, Tim, just not in that way. I love you as a friend."

He knew she had this long thought out, for the words seemed too rehearsed. Everything she said beyond those first painful words became lost in a gust of wind. Bottom line: her mind was made up. Nothing he said could or would change the way she felt.

With this heartbreaking realization, he simply said, "Fine. No need to prolong the evening." And with that, he left her house, the romantic itinerary for the evening shattered.

"I'm sorry," she had called after him as he headed toward his truck.

That was the icing on the cake. *Why do people say they're sorry, when they're really not?* he thought.

"Tim . . . Tim!"

"I'm sorry . . . what?" He wasn't aware that his mind had suddenly veered off course. What had happened? He hadn't had those thoughts in years. Again, he got a waft of her old familiar scent. That had to be the trigger.

"I was saying you always do . . . take good care of my car. Is something wrong?"

"No, I guess I just got a lot on my mind with all this work." Noticing her look of concern, he added, "But don't worry. Yours is no problem, Allie. It'll be ready when you come back."

"OK," she said, backing toward the door. Not realizing someone was about to enter, she turned and walked straight into him.

"Excuse me, sir, I'm sorry." She blushed as they suddenly locked gazes. She was mesmerized by his incredibly dark brown eyes, and dark brown hair and then, when he smiled, his irresistible dimples.

"My apologies. I snuck up on you."

Tim noticed the mutual exchange and quickly intervened.

"Can I help you?"

"Yes, I was passing by and, uh . . ." his eyes followed Allie out the door, where she slid into the passenger side of Amber's car, then turned toward Tim. ". . . saw your 'Help Wanted' sign."

"You a mechanic? Might seem like a dumb question, but you'd be surprised at how many people want to apply for a job such as this and don't even know what a wrench is."

"Wrench? What's that? Ah, just joking," he quickly added when Tim failed to see the humor. "Yes, I'm a qualified mechanic. I actually have my credentials with me," he said, handing the paper over to Tim.

"OK, Mr. . . ."

"Carter, Gary Carter."

"Tim Cooper," he said, offering a handshake, then inviting him into his office. "Would you like some coffee?"

"No, thank you."

"OK, just have a seat over there."

Tim studied the piece of paper Gary handed him and didn't have to read far before discovering how qualified he really was.

"This is impressive, Gary. So you're not working now?"

"No, I got laid off. Work was slow and I was fast. Not to be bragging. I just believe in productivity."

"I see. Well, I usually like to take a couple of days to check out an applicant but I've got a backlog of work here. Tell you what. I'm gonna give you a shot at it. You'll be on a probation period of three months. Can you start tomorrow?"

"I can start now!" Gary beamed with excitement.

"Oh yeah? Well, fine by me. I've got duds in the room next to the bathroom back there. Go ahead and get changed and then I'll fill you in on all that's got to be done."

"Thank you, boss," Gary said, shaking Tim's hand vigorously. "I won't disappoint you."

"Now about salary," Tim said, clearing his throat.

"That's OK. We can discuss that later," he said, already making a move toward the back.

"That's a first," he muttered to himself, knowing that was usually the first thing a potential employee wanted to know. Shaking his head, he walked outside and removed the "Help Wanted" sign.

Chapter 3

Weeks passed and Tim was beginning to savor the sweet waves of relief from not working the extra hours. He also no longer felt he had to keep second-guessing himself whether or not he'd made a mistake by hiring Gary. The evidence all around him was proof. The backlog of broken down vehicles had been reduced. His office at long last bore the "neat" seal of approval: every piece of paper in its proper place, no more searching the trashcan to see if the stapler had fallen in by accident because of the mess on the desk, which was mahogany, not cherry, like he originally thought. And best of all, he was able to return to his normal working hours. He could, at long last, go on that fishing trip he'd been putting off, now that things had turned around.

It was a good feeling, to say the least. But he readily admitted to himself that he wouldn't be enjoying that good feeling if he hadn't hired Gary. He had reservations at first because of the way he ogled Allie that day she dropped her car off. He couldn't help but feel a tinge of jealousy, but his need for a competent mechanic overrode his petty emotions. Was it fate or sheer luck? Regardless, Tim put aside any animosities he had for Gary the day he hired him. He quickly eased the load, relieving Tim from a load of stress.

Derrick paid Tim another visit about a month after Gary had been hired. His facial expression said it all.

"Wow, Tim! Am I in the right shop?" He backed out and checked the name on the outside of the building, then walked back in. "It's so clean and organized . . . for a repair shop."

"Thanks to Gary over there," Tim pointed, "it's cleaner than my own house."

Derrick strolled through the area, not even minding he had on his dress clothes. "Well, it sure looks a whole heap better. You could probably have a picture taken and put it in *Better Homes and Gardens* and call it 'Repair Shop of the Month'."

"Cute, but a little sissified. I have a reputation to keep."

"I hear you, dude!"

Derrick started to excuse himself when Tim called out to Gary, who was working close by.

"I want you to meet the man who made all this possible. Gary, this is Derrick Jones, a whiz at selling cars. Derrick, Gary Carter." As the two shook hands, Gary connected the name to the dealership down the road.

"Derrick Jones, as in Jones' Auto Sales?" Gary asked. Derrick nodded. "Nice assortment of wheels you got on your lot. Like them colorful pendants you got hanging out there, too. It draws attention."

"Yes, it does. Sounds like you know something about marketing." At first, Gary appeared offended, but then smiled, his dimples hiding a grease mark.

"Not really. I'm just an ordinary consumer. Any ordinary consumer'll tell you that colors attract and grab the customers and customers equal sales."

"Right you are! Well, my buddy here has been bragging on your work. I happen to know it takes a lot to impress Tim, so that says a lot."

"Touché! It's par for the course. When you have a boss like Tim, it makes coming to work more enjoyable." Tim couldn't help but beam from ear to ear, listening to Gary's token of admiration.

"OK. Enough of this mush stuff. I gotta go see if I can sell some wheels. Oh, almost forgot, Tim. Allie said when you changed her oil, you must have done something else. She used to have some kind of knocking sound, but now it's gone."

"I made a slight adjustment," Tim explained.

No, I did, you prick, thought Gary.

"Well, she's happy, whatever you did. See ya pal! Nice to meet ya, Gary!" he said, making his way to the door.

Allie, isn't that what Tim called the lady I bumped into the day I was hired? Gary thought. Could it be one and the same? He remembered her car, the beautiful vintage Mustang, and even remembered the advertising plate on the front, A.J. Realty. But Tim never mentioned her name to him or who she was or what she did. He seemed to be guarded in that area, letting him do the bulk of the manual labor while he took charge of the customers. But later, as guarded as Tim wanted to keep Gary, he soon realized he was beginning to make an impression on those who brought their business to the shop. Tim lifted the restrictions when he saw how well he mingled with people and how attentive he was to their needs and concerns.

Tim introducing Derrick as "Derrick Jones." Could the A.J. on Allie's car stand for Allie Jones? He wondered. It was then that he began to consider an awful possibility. She was married . . . to Derrick.

"I've gotta pick up a part, Gary. You need anything while I'm out?"

"No, I'm good."

"If you get any messages, just tack it onto the corkboard in my office."

"But you usually keep your office locked when you leave."

"Not anymore," he smiled, letting him know he had earned his trust.

"Say, Tim," Gary called out as Tim turned to leave. "That Derrick's a nice guy. He and Allie been married long?"

"Married?" Tim looked confused. "Oh . . . no, no. You got it all wrong. They're brother and sister. Neither one of them is married."

"Oh, OK," Gary said, pleased he got even more information than he asked for.

"Well, be back in a few," Tim assured him.

Gary grinned as Tim walked out into the sunshine. It was time to go house hunting and he knew just the perfect realty. But first, he needed to go see Derrick. Couldn't hurt to have a recommendation from dear brother.

Gary was thrilled Tim let him have the afternoon off. After all, everything was caught up and Tim felt he deserved some time off, with pay. Gary's first order of business took him to Derrick's dealership, where he patiently watched and waited while Derrick closed a sale. He saw him hand the keys to a customer, then shake his hand, commenting him on his fine choice of a vehicle. It could have been a clunker and Gary thought he probably would've said the same thing. He then waved and grinned, almost mischievously, as another satisfied customer pulled out of his parking lot. As soon as they were out of view, Derrick punched the air with his right arm and yelled, "Yes!" Then he crouched at the knees and did the "victory dance," twisting and jiggling from side to side.

Gary sat off to the side, obviously unnoticed, taking in the free entertainment. "What a nut," he whispered. "Hope his sister's a little saner."

Not wanting to embarrass Derrick but eager to get on with the business at hand, Gary got out of the car and slammed the door, hoping to attract his attention. He pretended not to see Derrick in his awkward position but rather tried to look occupied with some of the vehicles he had on display.

Derrick, suddenly realizing he had another potential bite, straightened up, pushing his hair back with his hands and strolled over to where Gary stood ogling a truck.

"So we meet again," Derrick said, as he saw who his visitor was. "Gary, was it?" Gary turned, pretending to be startled.

"Yes, yes it is. I was just admiring your selections of vehicles. Like I said, you have quite the assortment. I feel like a kid in a candy shop."

"You thinking of trading?"

"Just looking, although I really need to. Mine's got quite a few miles on it. But it's a good car and you know what they say. 'If it ain't broke, don't fix it.'"

"They also say, 'If you snooze, you lose,' and 'The early bird catches the worm.' You couldn't have come at a better time. I just slashed the prices down to make room for new inventory."

What a sap, Gary thought. *Does he really think I'm that gullible?*

"But are they slashed enough for my wallet?" Gary joked. But while Gary laughed, Derrick masked a look of concern. He wondered if Gary could afford a new car on his salary as a mechanic, especially considering the fact that he'd just started work there. Gary seemed to sense Derrick's concern.

"Tim's a very generous employer. I was lucky to have been in the right place at the right time."

"Oh . . . well that's good." Derrick laughed with relief.

"As a matter of fact," Gary continued, "I'm thinking of buying a house here. I sold my old house and I'm renting right now. But I'd really like to own again."

Without giving Gary the opportunity to ask Derrick about any reputable realties, Derrick reached into his shirt pocket and pulled out a card, handing it to Gary. He immediately saw the inscription on the card: A.J. Realty.

"My sister owns a real estate agency. She'd be glad to accommodate you on what you're looking for. I might be a little biased, but she's good. You really oughta pay her a visit."

"I will. Thanks!" Gary extracted his wallet from his back pocket and tucked the card in behind some twenty-dollar bills. It felt like gold to him at the moment. "I'll just bet she has some business cards advertising a good auto dealership here in town," Gary teased.

Derrick made a clicking noise with his mouth and pointed a finger.

"You got it, pal! We sorta look out for each other." In the distance, a telephone rang. "Will you excuse me a moment? I gotta go answer that. But take your time here, OK?"

While Derrick skipped over to his office, Gary made a beeline for his car. Mission accomplished. He got what he came for, big brother's card and recommendation. It would look better than if he had just happened upon her place of business, especially since they had already met. Hopefully, Derrick wouldn't be too disappointed that his potential customer decided not to buy after all. *Oh well, sometimes you bag 'em, sometimes you don't.* Before settling back in his own car, Gary did a jiggle of his own, then snuck off the lot the way he came in, only faster.

Chapter 4

Allie put on her best poker face upon returning from her one o'clock appointment. She knew the girls would be anxiously awaiting the news of the biggest deal all year. It had been one disappointment after another for the past several months and she was beginning to feel all hope fade with the closing of the Crenshaw account at hand. Even though this was to be the official closing, she knew from real estate deals in the past that nothing is truly secure until the very last detail is seen through with precision to the satisfaction of buyer and seller, and of course, the bank. And once those names are engraved on paper, paper that felt like gold to her, *that* would be the defining moment.

All eyes were upon her as she opened the door and set her briefcase down on the floor. She glanced at the anxious group huddled together in the corner, but expressed no sign of victory or defeat. She wanted to prolong the moment. Then, without saying a word, she shook her head and continued on down the hall toward her office, all the while hiding a smile. While the three of them exchanged looks of bewilderment, Allie was bursting within from giddiness. Amber finally broke the silence.

"Well?"

Allie turned to face them. Her somber eyes glared defeat, until she burst out laughing.

"We did it!" she shouted. "It's finally a done deal!"

"You faker!" Frieda jumped in.

"Had you fooled, huh? You guys have no idea how relieved I am to finally put this baby to rest. It's been a harrowing ordeal for me and Mr. Creech. I think this calls for a group hug!" As the four of them locked themselves in a victory embrace, Allie got the first glimpse of the strikingly handsome gentleman standing just inside the front door.

"Hi," she said, freeing herself from the huddle.

"I'm sorry. I didn't mean to interrupt."

"No, not at all. Please . . . come on in." Allie tried to hide her embarrassment as her huddle buddies left the cozy circle to reunite with their own private stations. "You look familiar. Wait a minute. Didn't I bump into you a while back at the repair shop?"

"Guess we bumped into each other. As a matter of fact, we might be doing that more often."

"Excuse me?" Allie asked, thinking he was being a little bit presumptuous and perhaps arrogant.

"I work there. Have been for a little over a month. He hired me the day I walked in, the day I saw you there."

"You're kidding! I knew he had hired somebody but I didn't know it was you." She recalled Derrick mentioning it to her on one of her Friday morning visits, unaware that she and Gary had already unofficially met.

"Yeah, I'd already left when you came to pick up your car. I'm Gary, by the way."

"Allie. Nice to formally meet you." As she shook his hand, she couldn't help but think that he looked less like a mechanic and more like a stockbroker. He didn't come across as someone who could work with his hands or who had automotive knowledge. But feeling the rough texture of his palm against hers seemed to validate his claim.

"Well, Mr.—"

"Carter, but please, just call me Gary."

"Right. What can I do for you, Gary?"

Looking into her eyes, he almost forgot what he wanted to say. He hadn't experienced this kind of magnetism for quite some time. His first encounter with her at Tim's place of business was nothing compared to this moment. For a brief few seconds, he felt compelled to be honest and reveal the true nature of his visit. But when he randomly snuck glances around him, he realized he wasn't alone and decided to proceed with his original idea, hoping it sounded convincing.

"I, ah, just moved here not too long ago and would like to pursue the possibility of having a place of my own. I'm leasing at the moment." *Which is true*, he said inside his head. "But I did have a house prior to moving here, which I sold." *Which is true*, he mentally repeated. For a brief couple of seconds, he felt choked up, remembering the house he let go as well as the memories he took with him. But he also realized that even though he had just told the truth, he was also stirring in a lie. His heart was not anywhere close to seeking another home. A home to him meant there was a significant other waiting for him, and maybe a cat or a dog, and down the line, when the time was right, children to call their own.

Quickly recovering, he smiled and continued on.

"Anyway, I got wind from a very reliable source that this is the best agency in town."

Allie laughed. "So when did you talk to my brother?"

"You're very perceptive. I'm impressed. I also happened to be out car shopping. Well, more like browsing. I haven't made up my mind about that yet." *OK, so I just told another fib.* "Anyway, I mentioned to him I was in the market for another house and he steered me in your direction."

Allie turned her head in time to see Frieda winking and grinning while the other two made similar "go for it" faces. She quickly diverted her attention back to Gary.

"I guess I owe my brother . . ." she started, then paused, not sure how it would sound on the receiving end ". . . let's just say, I'm glad he steered you here. I'm sure we can find something that's just right for you. Won't you come into my office?"

Allie could sense the gazes of her staff following her down the hallway. She didn't dare look back, knowing they would be casting insinuating eyes. Once inside the office, Allie handed Gary a brochure of her current listings. As he took a seat across from her, he found himself immersed in her perfume, not overpowering, but light and delicate. He imagined her touch was the same. Suddenly fearing she could see through his façade, he tried with forced effort to focus on the material in his hands.

"If you can give me an idea of what you are looking for in a home, I feel we can narrow it down a bit. For starters, I hate to be nosy, but is this for you or you and your wife? Kids?"

"Just me," he said, feeling that swell form in his neck again. "I'm . . . very much single," he smiled, his dimples showing themselves again, as they did the first time she saw him. While he managed to dissipate the lump that kept popping up at the mention of anything relative to his past, Allie fought to control a "hot flash" at his admission of being "very much single." She hoped the dim light of her office had hidden the sudden redness on her cheeks.

"Oh, I see. OK. So you probably want something on a smaller scale, so to speak."

"Three bedroom, two bath, throw in a maid and I'll be happy," he joked.

Allied laughed. "I can't do that, but I can probably recommend a good cleaning service."

While Allie continued to point out the potential houses that she thought would suit Gary, he began fumbling through the brochures, pretending to explore his own potentials, when he suddenly felt her eyes upon him. When he looked up, he caught her gaze and flushed with a moment of awkwardness.

"Ah . . . listen, you don't mind if I just take these with me and look them over, do ya? It's a lot to absorb right now."

"No, of course not. Buying a house is a big decision. I'm just here to help you with the process. Here's my card, although I'm pretty sure you already have one," she said, remembering Derrick's referral. "You'll find my office number on there, as well as my home phone number."

Gary took the card, which was identical to the card Derrick had given him, and it was the first time he noticed Allie's home number engraved onto the card as well. He smiled and tucked the card inside his shirt pocket, then slowly stood, with nervous anticipation. *If ever there was a moment, this is it,* he thought. He had to seize the opportunity while he still had her gaze. He'd deal with the rejection later, as if already anticipating the worst.

"Allie . . . can I . . . may I, may I take you out to dinner, say, tomorrow night? I mean, that is, if you're unattached." He'd already learned from Tim that she wasn't married but to hope she wasn't seeing anyone was perhaps too much to ask, for she was way too attractive to not have suitors.

When she hesitated, he started to apologize, not wanting to hear the fated words. But before he could speak, she smiled and gave him a flirtatious wink.

"I'd like that."

"That's great," he said, his heart beating in his throat. "How about The Steakhouse and I pick you up at seven?"

"How about I meet you at The Steakhouse at seven?"

Gary didn't take offense at her cautious nature. If anything, it only added to her appeal. She was bright, attractive, and obviously sensible.

"It's a date then. I'll see you there at seven. I'll be driving a light blue Honda Accord."

"And I'll be in a red Mustang Convertible."

"I know."

"Of course you do. What was I thinking?"

It was all Gary could do to resist the urge to grab her hand and place a light kiss thereon, but instead, he smiled while walking away with the brochures he knew he would probably never study.

As soon as he was out the door and into his car, Allie shouted so the members of her staff could hear.

"It's just a date! Don't go marrying me off yet!"

It'd been a year or more since Allie had been to The Steakhouse, or to any up-scale restaurant for that manner. Her subconscious decision to put business first put everything else on the back burner, including fine wining and dining. It was a luxury she hadn't really missed, ironically, now that she could afford it. She discovered quite by accident that she was just as happy nibbling on a grilled cheese sandwich in front of the TV. Her finances were better but her tastes had simplified. Funny how you crave things you can't afford and when you can, you no longer care.

But tonight, as she pulled into the parking lot of The Steakhouse, she had a renewed sense of appreciation for how far she'd come. All the hard work, all the long hours, all the sacrifices made it worthwhile and to think it pretty much started on a dare from her brother.

Almost as soon as she had parked, Gary pulled in beside her. Even through the car's window, barely visible through the evening's fading light, Allie caught a glimpse of his handsome features. He had chosen to wear a short sleeve pullover shirt, which enhanced his bulging biceps that she had missed the day before since he was wearing a long sleeve dress shirt. She found herself trying to envision what he wore at work, perhaps a sweaty tank top that went beyond showing off the biceps, but the 6-pack underneath.

Together, they abandoned their vehicles and met at the entrance to the restaurant.

"Wow! You look fantastic!" he said, noting her attire. She was just grateful he hadn't been in her closet as she wrestled with what to wear for the night. She'd finally decided upon a white silk blouse and a pair of black slacks. The hours she spent grueling with what to wear and the decision she'd finally agreed upon were all made worthwhile just hearing his praise.

"You don't look so bad yourself."

"Why thank you, madam," he said, bowing. As he straightened up, he made it a point to glance back at her car. "And that is one sharp ride you got there. I had a hard time taking my eyes off it that day you had it in the shop. Candy apple red, is it?"

"Poppy red, actually. Candy apple red was introduced the year after."

"And the engine?"

"It's a 200 c.i. at 120 horsepower with a one barrel carburetor. Not your average speed demon, but it's great on gas."

"Impressive. Were you an auto mechanic at one time?"

"No," Allie laughed. "I just like to know what's underneath the hood of my car."

"Well, I must say, mine sure looks sad parked next to yours," he said, staring at the cars parked so close together. As he shifted his gaze back to her, their eyes met and he was instantly mesmerized by her beauty. Then, as if suddenly remembering why they were there, he quickly regained his composure.

"Hungry?"

"Famished," she said.

Gary extended his elbow so she could loop her arm in his, then together, they ascended the steps of the restaurant. She felt a tinge of pride as the hostess guided them toward a secluded booth. No doubt, there were feminine eyes following them as she proudly strolled arm-in-arm with the handsome gentleman guiding her to their table. She was anxious to call Derrick yesterday and inform him of her ensuing date for the evening but then thought it better to hold off in the event it turned out to be a disaster, considering her past record. It was bad enough he kept bringing up her date with the "toad."

"You have a preference on wine?" he asked.

"Red, thank you." Gary ordered a bottle of merlot when the waiter came by.

"So. Gary, how long have you been a mechanic? I mean, you don't really look like a mechanic, if you don't mind me saying so. It's just that you come across as some type of corporate executive."

"Boy, you don't beat around the bush, do you? Actually, I've done this all my life. I've always been intrigued with working on automobiles. It's been my passion since I was a little boy, so don't let these preppy threads fool you," he said, tugging at his shirt. Then, wiggling his finger, he motioned for her to lean across the table.

"I changed your oil," he whispered.

Allie leaned back, suddenly quiet and looking grim. Gary sensed her concern and continued.

"I changed it. I didn't drive it. Tim wouldn't let me. He was very particular with your car, a little overprotective, if you ask me."

"Now *I'm* impressed," she said.

"Well, there's really nothing to it. You just get it up on the racks, remove the drain plug..."

"I don't mean that, silly. I mean that you do what you do and there's not a hint of grease on you, not even beneath your fingernails."

"I think there's a compliment in there somewhere. Or insult?" he asked, looking puppy-eyed.

"I really didn't mean it as either, but feel free to take it as a compliment."

The waiter returned to the table with their bottle of wine and as Gary poured some into their glasses, he proposed to make a toast.

"Here's to an enjoyable and, what I hope to be, a memorable evening. May there be many more."

Allie, slightly taken aback at his bold toast, yet still flattered, clinked her glass with his and both enjoyed a sip of wine while exchanging mutual looks of admiration.

The remainder of the evening was spent savoring their dinners, which consisted of prime rib, rice pilaf and salad, and engaging in more stimulating conversation. What was initial nervousness disguised by laughter and small talk had slowly evolved into a much deeper dialogue between two people.

With the idle chatter aside, Allie found herself more at ease and began sharing her ups and downs of her personal relationships, stressing the need for honesty and loyalty and trust. She briefly mentioned her few dates with Tim but disclosed as little as possible since Tim just happened to be Gary's boss. The less he knew, the less awkward it would be the whole way around.

Hearing this from Allie, Gary appeared to be a little surprised, given the fact that Tim had never mentioned seeing her, even when he mentioned that he and Allie were going out after work. But then he decided that their brief connection with one another was probably too far in the past to mention. Water under the bridge.

As the evening progressed, it was Gary's heartbreaking story of losing his wife that seemed to bond them emotionally. Although he failed to mention her name, as if saying it would be too painful, she had no doubt that he'd been deeply in love with her. According to Gary, they'd been married for three years before she was tragically killed in a car accident a year ago. He told her he was slowly adjusting to her being gone but it was still very painful at times, especially when he was living at the house he and his wife had shared for those three years. It was only after he moved out and sold the house that he began the slow process of healing.

"I miss the house but I couldn't bear another minute living there without her. I knew it would never be the same again. So now, I have an apartment which is becoming a little cramped," he said, trying to convince himself. But in reality, he liked being cramp versus being in a large vacuum.

"So that's where I come in."

"Excuse me?"

"The house . . . remember? You were looking for a house."

"Oh yeah, right. That's where you come in." He wanted to erase the thoughts of "wanting to buy a house" as if it was an intrusion to their potential relationship. But the seed was planted and Allie would not see it die. She was determined to find Gary the right home, at the right price, even if he never had plans of buying.

As the two made their way out of the restaurant, Allie wondered where this was going. She was not anxious for a steady relationship but her night out with Gary was much more pleasant than she had anticipated. As he escorted her to her car, she envisioned an awkward end to their wonderful evening together. Would he dare kiss her or would he shake her hand, as if closing a business deal, or would he just simply say "goodnight" and walk away? To her relief, she didn't have to wait for long to find out.

"I had a great time, Allie," he said, then instantly embraced her with a tight hug.

"Me, too," she said, reluctantly slipping out of the hold.

"I'd like to do it again sometime."

"Sure. You have my number. And it's not like we won't be seeing each other again anyhow, I mean, looking for a house and all."

Gary could feel his stomach tense. Was this the price he would have to pay to keep seeing her . . . a house he didn't want? He decided he'd have to sort it all out later.

Smiling, he casually and confidently strutted back to his own vehicle. He couldn't have imagined this night a year ago. After the accident, he merely drifted from day to day, existing, but not living. Every move he made was an effort in itself. Even the simplest of things, like tying his shoelaces or brushing his teeth or paying a bill, was too redundant. It had all seemed pointless. But, he reasoned, each day that came along would mean another he could put behind him.

And now, with a year tucked soundly behind him, maybe he could celebrate a new beginning with Allie. But with that thought came an awful pang of guilt for his deception. How and when was he going to tell her the truth, that he wasn't in the market to buy a house, but rather created this ruse to invite her out? *The longer the postponement, the angrier she'll be,* he thought. Then again, maybe she would be flattered, even honored, that he went through these lengths to be with her. Then just maybe . . . he could rid himself of the pills.

As Allie cruised along the highway, she reminisced about the evening. *Derrick will love this,* she thought. *I went from a toad to a prince.* She could still smell his intoxicating cologne on her. It was a scent unlike any other she'd ever breathed in, a clean, fresh, soothing kind of scent, a scent she vowed to take to bed with her, instead of the fragrance from her moisturizers. She wondered if it would still be on her in the morning, or would it have faded into the night? Then she wondered when he would call again. He had to call; he was buying a house. Would tomorrow be too soon? She tried to put those thoughts aside and enjoy the moment at hand for this indeed was her moment and she was going to savor every bit of it. Funny thing, though . . . he didn't seem interested in talking about houses, the sole purpose he'd dropped by her office . . . or so she thought.

Chapter 5

Gary checked his watch over and over again as he labored beneath the hood of a 1973 Camaro. Each moment seemed to drag by as he began to feel more anxious and less confident with what he wanted to say. He couldn't remember a call he'd dreaded more than this one but he knew it had to be done. Postponing it would only prolong the agony. At least this way, he'd know early on if he and Allie had a shot at a future together.

He'd wanted to admit his shortcomings over their dinner last night but feared it would somehow spoil the mood. They were having such a wonderful time and when she opened up about her feelings of trust and loyalty and honesty, it seemed to seal his fate for the evening. He decided he'd have to continue his farce until he could figure out a solution.

But lying in bed that night, he was no closer to an answer. Unable to sleep, he found himself pacing the floors, wrestling with his dilemma, writhing in anguish over his ruse. He'd just have to tell her first thing in the morning when she got to work. That's all there was to it. The words would not come easy and at this point, he wasn't sure he knew what the words would be.

Then, a more pleasant thought entered his mind. What if he was making too much out of nothing? After all, it was just a harmless little ploy to get a date with her. Maybe he was fretting over nothing. Maybe she'd laugh it off and they could continue what they started. Maybe she'd be that kind of person, the kind to overlook something so trivial. This thought brought a tinge of relief and an idea that would most certainly soften the heart.

Dropping the wrench he had been working with beside the Camaro, he made a mad dash for the office and retrieved a phone book from off the desk. Thumbing through the yellow pages, he searched for a florist that opened early. He wanted the flowers to be there before she arrived.

"Somebody must've made a good impression last night," Frieda sang out as Allie walked in Friday morning. Confused, Allie saw Tess, Frieda and Amber all grinning and elbowing each other by the coffee maker.

"What are y'all talking about? Did one of y'all spike the coffee?"

"Go check out your office," Amber said.

Still appearing puzzled, Allie cautiously walked down the hallway toward her office, glancing back at her comrades, who had decided to trail her. When she got to her doorway, a dumbfounded face replaced the confused one. Placed on the middle of her desk was a vase containing a dozen red roses, with a card attached. Meticulously reaching for the card, she picked it up and read it in silence. "Enjoyed last night, would love to see you again," it read. She smiled.

"Well?" Tess asked. "Don't keep us in suspense!"

"Like y'all haven't already read it, c'mon."

"Honestly, we haven't," Amber pleaded.

"All right. It just says he enjoyed our date."

"And?" Frieda probed her, knowing there was more.

"And he wants to go out again."

"You go girl!" Frieda yelled.

"Y'all are making too much out of this," Allie said, feeling more than she let on. "It's just some harmless dating."

"Yeah, but a dozen red roses after the first date?" Tess chimed in. But before Allie could respond, the phone rang. Grateful for the interruption, she snatched the receiver off the hook.

"A.J. Realty," she greeted. A smile began to spread across her face, clearly revealing who the caller was. After a few seconds, she spoke quietly into the receiver.

"Excuse me just a minute." Cupping her hand over the phone, she addressed the three standing in her office.

"Do you mind?"

Tess picked up on the hint first. "No, of course not. C'mon girls. Let's give her some privacy."

Shutting the door, Allie returned to her caller.

"Yes, I got the flowers, Gary. They're beautiful, but you shouldn't have."

"It just seemed fitting," Gary said from the other end, swallowing hard as he did. The words he'd practiced only minutes before were there, but stuck in his throat. He then realized he couldn't possibly do this over the phone.

"I . . . just wanted to let you know what a good time I had last night."

"Me too . . . oh, I'm glad you called. I have a couple of houses I think you might be interested in. Can you meet me after work, say around six?"

"Ah . . . sure," Gary answered, disguising the treachery in his voice. He wondered how many more flowers he'd have to buy before telling her the truth, not to mention going broke.

"Good. Meet me here."

"OK. See you at six."

Gary hung up the phone feeling worse than ever. The last thing he wanted was to look at a bunch of houses but he owed it to her, despite his intentions not to buy. At least he'd see her in person and he could finally clear his conscious.

"How's the Camaro going?" Gary jumped at hearing Tim's voice from behind.

"Almost finished. Just a few more adjustments and she'll be done."

"Nice work," Tim said, curious over his phone call. "Looks like you were in deep thought. Something wrong?"

"No. Just a little tired, I guess. Didn't get much sleep last night."

"Know what you mean. My neighbors down the street partied until the wee hours of the morning, keeping me up. Someone finally called the cops and they broke it up." Tim had a feeling that Gary hadn't heard a word he said. His mind still seemed to be preoccupied on something or someone. Not wanting to pry but anxious to know what was going on, he invited him out.

"How about a beer after work?"

"No, I can't. I have plans."

"A date?"

"No, I'm actually going to look at some houses. I'm thinking of buying," Gary lied.

"No kidding. You going through a realtor?" Tim asked, sure he'd bring up Allie's name.

Gary fought to hide his annoyance at his boss's intrusive questions. He wanted to say, "Yeah, you idiot, ain't that how it's usually done?" but he refrained.

"Yeah, if you must know, I'm meeting Allie at six." Tim couldn't help but sense the apathy in his voice as he spoke.

"You don't sound excited."

"It's complicated," Gary said, reluctant to divulge anymore.

"What's wrong? Maybe I can help," Tim offered, more anxious than ever to hear Gary's story.

"You knew I was going out with her last night. Didn't it bother you?"

"Why should it bother me?" Tim asked, pretending he didn't understand.

"I know you dated her."

"C'mon, Gary. That was a long time ago. She and I are close friends now."

Gary let out a sigh of relief. He knew if he was to continue seeing Allie, that is, if she didn't blow him off after confessing his scheme, Tim needed to know in advance.

"I wasn't sure how you'd feel about us dating."

"Is that the complication you're talking about?"

"Well . . . no." Gary hesitated. He was about to reveal his deception to his boss, an old boyfriend of Allie's. He wondered if that might be stupid but he was this far in. Might as well go all the way. Besides, he tried to reason within himself, maybe Tim could offer some useful advice.

"Thing is, I'm not really interested in buying a house. I just pretended to be to work up the nerve to ask her out. Now I gotta go look at some houses I have no intent on buying. I feel terrible and I know I have to say something but I don't know how she's gonna react."

"You dog, you actually did that?" Tim smirked, trying to decide between sympathy or contempt for Gary. He did, after all, date his former girlfriend, or whatever it was he had with her.

"I'm not proud of it by any means."

"Well," Tim seemed to relish being the one in control for a change "If you want my opinion, just do it and get it over with. Tell her the truth. She ain't gonna like it, losing a potential sale and all. I mean, she is a businesswoman, after all. You can't keep her combing the market for houses you ain't interested in, can you? After a while, Gary, she's gonna get suspicious."

"I know, I know. I thought about telling her tonight. I'll tell her before we leave the realty. And if she never wants to see me again . . . well, you know. Better now, than later."

"Yeah, been there, done that." Gary overlooked the fact that Tim was actually referring to his last date with Allie.

Gary sighed, relieved to have it out. Talking to Tim and hearing his input put him in better spirits and oddly, made him appreciate his boss all the more.

"Well, enough of this. I gotta finish up on that Camaro. Don't want the boss to fire me."

But as he turned, he couldn't repress his gratitude for the one who'd hired him when he needed a job, but more importantly, for the one who had miraculously given him words of wisdom, advice he didn't have to offer, but did out of his own unselfish nature.

"Thanks, Tim. I appreciate it. I appreciate everything, man."

"Any time, buddy."

Tim eyed him as he skipped over to the Camaro, sensing his relationship with Allie was about to end . . . but he wasn't going to be the bearer of bad news, the messenger of gloom. *Let him see for himself.*

Allie sat in her office for a long time after her phone call with Gary, browsing through the same brochures she had given him. The two houses she had picked out seemed to be ideal for him and she was sure he'd be elated once they saw them. The tough choice: which one? Although he was vague in what he was seeking, she found these two particular houses to be charming as well as affordable. They were both an easy commute to his work as well. But she was still puzzled that he hadn't mentioned any prospects of his own given the chance he had to study the brochures. But then again, he had gone through a tragedy and maybe that had to be taken into account.

Rubbing her forehead, she looked up to see three pairs of eyes peering back through the glass in her office. Shaking her head, she walked over and swung the door open.

"Just in case you're wondering, I have a date with him this evening at six . . . to look at houses. Now that that's out of the way, let's all get back to work."

Laughing, she closed the door while Tess, Frieda and Amber, their curiosities satisfied, cleared the area in front of her office. Picking up the phone, she started punching in numbers.

"Jones' Auto Sales, Derrick speaking."

"It's Friday, big brother!"

"Hey Allie, good Friday morning to you!"

"Sorry I missed our Friday morning get together."

"Yeah, I got your message. No problem. I was in the shower when you called. So. What's new in the real estate world?"

"I closed that Creech deal. Major headache, but major moolah. Say . . . thanks for sending me that new client."

"You must be talking about Gary Carter. I thought he stopped by to buy a car but the ole buzzard took off when I got a phone call. But at least you got a nibble."

"I ain't so sure."

"What do you mean?'

"I went out with him last night and he didn't once mention an interest in buying a house. It's almost like he forgot he was looking."

"You sly rascal! Since when do you date clients?"

"You're starting to sound like my staff. It's no big deal. I just happen to find him attractive, that's all."

"I don't know, Allie, mixing business with pleasure. That's not a good combination. You know where he works, don't you?"

"Yeah, over at Tim's shop."

"You don't mind that?"

"Are you saying that I'm arrogant, that a little grease is beneath me? Are you forgetting that I dated Tim?"

"That was a long time ago. I just kinda pegged you for a 'suit and tie' kinda gal."

"I don't care what a guy does for a living as long as it's an honest living."

"Hello, is this really my sister, Allie, talking, or is this an imposter?"

"Oh, give me a break . . . oh, shoot, looks like I got a call on the other line. I had better take it. I'll catch up with you later."

"OK, sis. Just be careful. Love you! Bye!"

When Gary pulled into the lot of the realty, he expected to see just one car: Allie's. But apparently, one of her employees opted to work late to catch up on some paperwork, not in his favor, he decided. Allie saw him through the window as he drove up and went outside to meet him.

"You guys work this late?" he said, pointing to the other car.

"That's not unusual. Sometimes, I'm up here until nine or ten at night."

"That could be dangerous, Allie. You never know what lunatic is lurking around at those kind of hours." But at the moment, he was disappointed they didn't have the place to themselves.

"It's OK. I pack a .38 Special, not that I anticipate on using it. The crime rate here is pretty much narrowed down to petty theft. And even that's an exaggeration."

"Oh."

"Well, shall we go? I'll drive. I know you've been wanting a shot at my Mustang. At least this time, you won't be beneath it, with oil and grease; you'll be in it, with me," she winked.

Gary managed a smile and slipped into the passenger's side, disappointed that they weren't alone. He could talk to her now before she drove off the lot, but the woman inside would know that something was wrong when Allie would react to his admission, probably lashing out at him. No, that would be too humiliating. He saw no other choice but to take the trip to the first house as slated on her agenda.

"I think you'll like this first house. It's small, but cozy, and close to your job."

"Good," was all Gary could think to say.

"And it's within your price bracket, I'm sure."

Gary nodded, thinking if and when he finally spoke his peace, she'd probably take those brochures and shove them down his throat, then leave him for stranded, but it was a chance he had to take.

"And the second house is similar, just a smidge bigger and a little further out, but not by much."

As Allie rambled on about the two houses, Gary heard very little, but she didn't seem to notice.

When they reached the first house, Gary, again, was disappointed to find that there were people there, obviously the current owners. Upon getting out of the car, they approached the soon-to-be former owners. Allie made the introductions and then proceeded to give Gary the full tour of what lay within. True to her profession, she guided him step by step on the layout of the house, narrating the whole night-marish scene, "wall-to-wall carpeting, lots of closet space, vinyl windows," though he had to admit he liked the vinyl windows; his other house didn't have that.

At the end of the excursion, Allie tried, without success, to get a sense of feel about the house as they got back into the car.

"So, what did you think? Nice, huh?"

"Ah . . . yeah, it was. I guess I'll know more when I see the other house." *Oh crap, did I just say that?*

"Well OK. Let's go!"

Allie drove further down the road, making a couple of turns, then finally stopped at their second destination, a rather small house, similar to the first, as she had indicated. Gary glanced around and realized that for the first time tonight, they were alone, that it was just the two of them, affording him the opportunity to explain himself and hope that she'd understand. How he wished it could have been at the other house, though, for it was a little closer to walking home—should the unthinkable happen—and less confusing with fewer turns.

But as he opened his mouth to speak, he was startled that nothing came out. He had rehearsed this speech a thousand times but now he sat stupefied, totally aware that he'd forgotten all of what he wanted to say.

"What's wrong?" Allie asked, concerned.

"It's just that . . ." Gary felt his heart racing and beads of sweat popping out all over his forehead, giving salute. If he could form any words of any kind at the moment, he thought of Ralph Kramden of *The Honeymooners* saying, "Hubba, hubba, hubba," but not even that could find its way to his lips, fortunately for him.

"Are you OK?" Allie asked, with a hint of impatience in her voice.

"I . . . ah . . . no, actually, I'm not. I think we better go back. Must have been something I ate."

"Well, OK."

Gary silently reprimanded himself for being a coward, for losing the courage to come clean with Allie. Then, as if trying to assure himself, he decided that maybe he just needed a better setting, a cozier atmosphere . . . the restaurant . . . again.

"Sorry about this. I know you went out of your way to do this," he admitted with remorse.

"No, not really. Although I did put off a client until tomorrow. No big thing," she said, smiling. *Oh boy, the ole guilt trip,* Gary thought.

"Well, how about dinner with me tomorrow night to make amends?" He was surprised at how easy those that request had spilled out, considering he couldn't form a word earlier, much less a sentence.

Allie smiled, taken aback by his forwardness; she supposed this was what drove her to him to start with, along with his good looks and figure.

"Sure. I'd love to."

"Six o'clock and I pick you up?"

"Perfect. Here's my address," she said, scribbling neatly on a small piece of paper.

When Gary returned to work Saturday morning, he found a note left by Tim, informing him he wouldn't be in. He and Derrick had decided to do a little fishing. Derrick had left his dealership in the hands of a competent and experienced part-time salesman. It felt good to be able to leave and not worry about who was running the business, he once told Tim. Tim, apparently, had expressed that same sentiment to Derrick regarding Gary, or he wouldn't have left him in charge.

As Gary wandered around, he suddenly felt a sense of power. It was the first time Tim had left him totally alone with the business, as far as the opening and closing, even if it was just for half a day. The shop closed at twelve, which was fine by him. This would give him time to catch up on some chores before his date with Allie that night. *Tonight will make or break us*, he thought. It was a matter of saying the right thing, in the right way, at the right time, and he felt this time around, he could do it.

Chapter 6

Allie tripped and nearly fell trying to grab the phone before it hung up.

"Derrick, hey," she said, panting, "how did the fishing trip go? Catch anything?"

"Nothing we could keep. What little we snagged could fit in a sardine can. Why you breathing so hard?"

"I was just getting out of the shower when I heard the phone ringing."

"Um . . . hum."

"I know what you're thinking. Get your mind out of the gutter."

"I didn't say a word."

"You didn't have to."

"So, whatcha up to?"

"I was just getting ready for my date tonight with Gary."

"Oh. So you two are all right then?"

"What do you mean? Why wouldn't we be all right?"

"I mean, Tim told me that Gary was going to have a talk with you yesterday about what he did."

"What he did? What are you talking about?"

Derrick realized, too late, that no talk had taken place. He also realized he had just stuck himself in the middle of something he couldn't get out of.

"I just assumed . . . maybe you better let Gary tell you."

"I think *you* better tell me. I need to know what's going on before he gets here. So spit it out!"

"Well, all right. You see . . ."

Five o'clock, nothing left to do but pick up Allie, Gary thought. He'd showered, shaved, put on his favorite cologne and now he found himself pacing the house. Several times he went to the bathroom, opened up the medicine cabinet and picked up his bottle of prescription pills, then placed it back down, then picked it up again.

"Do I really need the pills?" he asked himself in the mirror. "What would be the big deal if I skipped them just this once? I mean, I feel great, better than ever."

But he couldn't ignore what the doctor had told him. "The drugs serve a purpose; you need to keep taking them for a little while longer, even if you feel otherwise."

"I ought to know my own body. What does that doctor know anyway?" he said, jeering at his own reflection. Then he smiled, realizing how good life was now, with a good job, a decent place to live, and hopefully, he'd still have Allie after tonight.

"Oh, screw it," he said, placing the pills back inside the cabinet. Slamming the cabinet door shut, he abandoned the bathroom and headed for the kitchen to an awaiting brandy cocktail he had prepared earlier. Taking a sip, he pulled out a drawer, and scanned over a piece of paper laying just inside, a piece of paper with her address written neatly upon, not that he needed to see it at all. He knew where she lived before their first night out. It was on file inside Tim's office. He'd even driven by there after work one day and was speechless to see how well she had done for herself.

At precisely six o'clock, he pulled into her driveway, feeling a surge of excitement. As he stepped out of his Honda and started walking toward the door, he made the mistake in looking back. He saw how shiny and clean her Mustang Convertible looked in the driveway next to his beloved Honda, which was in dire need of a bath. He'd wish he'd at least taken a couple of minutes to run some water over it before he showed up here. It also looked out of sorts with the neighborhood vehicles, such as the BMW's and Lincoln Town Cars and Jaguars. At least a wash job would've helped it blend in a little.

Reaching the door, he gently pressed the doorbell and heard a musical lengthy chime. Just waiting for Allie to appear, he felt giddy all over despite what still weighed heavy on his mind. Hopefully, she would be in the right sort of mood, the kind of mood that's hard to taint with a little thing like deception. He fondly recalled his wife, how he could always predict her moods, even being married for so short a time. But he attributed that to a deep-seated love, a real connection some people never get to experience.

With Allie, he would just have to hope for the best. They were just beginning to know each other. He would have to pick the moment with careful precision to come clean. First would be the wining and dining and some casual conversation, and it couldn't hurt to throw in some dessert. Then he'd throw in a joke or two. Inserting a compliment here and there might not be bad either. And then . . . the heart to heart talk. Oh, how he wished it would be that simple.

A few seconds after sounding the doorbell, he heard the door unlatch. Feeling as if he was picking up his date on prom night, he stepped back with his hands clasped behind his back and waited for his prom night beauty to spring into view from the other side of the door. His heart seemed to pick up speed, anticipating the moment they'd be facing one another again, eyes locked, hearts melting.

He felt his jaw drop at the sight of her in full view.

"Wow! You look stunning!" Gary couldn't help but ogle her as he stood there, waiting for an invitation inside.

"It's just casual, nothing special," Allie said, straining to conceal her recent revelation.

"Well, maybe it's just what's in it, then," he laughed. Allie smiled, hiding her insincerity. Had he made that compliment earlier, before she'd last talked to Derrick, she would have been flattered.

"Won't you come in?" she said, trying to get past the moment.

"Thanks," he nodded, slipping through the doorway.

"Would you care for a drink?"

"Sure."

Allie went to the kitchen and came back with two glasses of wine.

"You really have a nice place," he commented, sipping on the wine. *I guess that counts as a compliment,* he thought. *Just got a few more to go.*

But Allie considered it the gap she needed and Gary had done just that.

"Thank you. It's one of the smaller homes in this community, but it's perfect for me. Speaking of homes, have you had time to look through the brochures? I mean, you must have seen something in there that interested you. Oh, and we never did get to view the second house I took you to. What did you think of the first house? Does it compare to any that you've seen in the brochures? That is, if you've studied the brochures."

Did I just open up a can of worms? Gary thought. He reached over for his glass of wine and took two sips, stalling, hoping and praying for words of wisdom at a time it mattered the most.

"Ah . . . I liked it, the house, that is, the one we looked at first. I'm just not totally sure yet. I really haven't had a chance to explore everything in the brassiere . . .

brochure," he quickly corrected, unaware his eyes had drifted. Allie, to his astonishment, didn't seem to notice his blunder or possibly chose to ignore it. Rather, she kept playing with the pamphlets, purposefully strewn all across the table. Although her eyes were scanning the listings, her mind was recalling Derrick's last conversation.

"We have a little time to play with before our reservation. Why don't we look at the brochures before we go?"

Gary appeared to be getting more and more uneasy as the moments dragged on. He found himself regretting not taking his pill. Allie, pretending not to notice Gary's fragile state of mind, continued to do a full layout of homes upon the coffee table. She pointed to ones she felt might be of particular interest to him, even going through the tedious details of each one's structure and maintenance. All the while, her senses kept in tune with his increasingly deteriorating attention span.

Allie reveled in the moment, as she kept on pouring over more brochures he hadn't seen. He anticipated her showing some picture slides before she was finished with her presentation, which is exactly what it felt like to him at the moment. He was relieved when she finally ended by glancing at her watch, noting it was time to leave for their night out.

"You don't mind if I drive, do you? It's such a nice night out and I feel like driving with the top down."

"Be my guest." Gary thought a little wind between the ears could help clean out all that talk of houses.

As they started out on the highway, the breeze rustling through their hair, Gary turned to say something but the words were lost in the wind.

"What did you say?" Allie shouted. "I can't hear you. You'll have to holler."

"I said, this is fun!"

Allie just smiled and nodded her head. For an instant, she was torn between her feelings of attraction and pain of deceit. He had lost the perfect opportunity to be honest with her as she went through her entire display of listings available and chose not to say anything. She felt in her heart that if he'd at least made an effort to tell the truth, she'd have listened and maybe forgave him. She might have even laughed it off and they could've continued on with their date. The cat would have been out of the bag and they could enjoy the rest of their evening together. But he deliberately led her on, pretending to be a client. She'd even put off a potential client to accommodate him. Did he really take her for a fool?

Gary noticed she had missed the turn that led to the restaurant.

"Uh, I think you were supposed to turn right back there!" he said, shouting so she could hear.

Allie turned to face him and for the first time, he saw something different in her eyes. Her intense glare brought to light a terrible realization. She knew. But how?

It was at that moment that he knew, without a doubt, he'd lost all hope of redemption. Even if he had planned to tell her later, it was now too late.

As she continued on down the road, driving in silence while pursing her lips, Gary accepted the fact that their date was officially over, as well as any chance of any future dates.

"Where are we going?" he asked, eager to clear the air.

But again, Allie only gazed back, her face tautly drawn. He began to see a familiarity in the location she was headed. She was actually taking him to the house they didn't get to explore yesterday. As she veered onto the last stretch of road, the house came into full view. Gary felt ill all over again, but this time for real.

Pulling into the driveway, she stopped and turned off the engine.

"You mind telling me what's going on?" he asked, pretending to be confused, but knowing he was just digging himself in deeper.

"You see," Allie said, halfway turning to face him, "you asked me out on the pretense you were looking to buy a house. I'm showing you a house on the pretense of going out with you."

Gary felt his face flush as he turned away, embarrassed to meet her eyes. Without turning back around, he inserted a question.

"Does this mean we're not going to eat?"

Allie, appalled at his lack of empathy, shouted. "Not now! Not ever!"

The words seemed to cut through Gary like a knife. He quickly turned to face her, feeling like a wounded animal, left to die, while she savored the scene. His own loss of words made the moment even worse.

"I had to hear it from my brother, who heard it from Tim. Everybody knew it but me. You could have said something before we went out looking at houses you knew you weren't going to buy. Instead, you made me look like a fool. I even rearranged my schedule with clients, real clients, to accommodate you. You were never interested in buying a house!"

"That's not true!" Gary pleaded, finding his voice. "I was interested, still am. Just not now."

"I liked you, Gary. I would've gone out with you without this whole charade." Allie forced back the tears. She didn't want him to see her vulnerability. "But after all that talk of loyalty and honesty and trust, I don't know how I could ever look at you without wondering how much is real and how much is fake."

Gary swallowed hard, searching for the words he'd originally planned to use that night, but once again, his mind failed him. His only hope was to express his good intentions and beg for a second chance.

"Please, Allie, I never meant to carry it this far. I just wanted to get to know you, that's all. Don't judge me in this way. I pledge with all my heart to prove to you that I'm better than that. I admit, I used poor judgment, and I will forever be kicking myself for doing so. But I can't begin to tell you what these past few days have meant to me. Please don't shut me out now."

Part of Allie wanted to believe him, to embrace his sincerity, but the other part still felt betrayed. His eyes, she knew in her heart, didn't lie. He seemed genuinely remorseful and sincere, but she suddenly felt emotionally drained and wanted to spend the evening alone.

"Let's go," she said, leaving him to guess their next destination, but he safely assumed it was back to her house. They rode together in silence. Only the wind seemed to speak, keeping rhythm with the roar of the motor. As she pulled back into her driveway, Gary made one last appeal to her.

"Allie, I'm truly sorry. I know you don't believe me, but I had intended on talking to you tonight at dinner. I had intended on talking to you before tonight but kept losing my nerve. It was stupid of me to keep putting it off like that but I was savoring every minute with you and I didn't want to spoil it."

"I'm tired, Gary," Allie said, oblivious to Gary's speech. "I'm going in and you need to go home. Don't call me, OK?"

Allie got out of the car without bothering to put the top up on her convertible. Gary reluctantly got out and slowly walked over to his Honda. He retraced his steps here earlier, remembering the anticipation and excitement at seeing Allie and looking forward to their date. And now, his pain overshadowed that memory.

Allie looked back and caught the disappointment in his face. She desperately fought the urge to run to him and hold him. Instead, she merely offered two words—"Take care"—before rushing into the house to release the wellspring of tears.

It would be a full ten minutes before she stopped crying and when she did, she went to the kitchen, where she found her unfinished glass of wine. Upturning the remainder of the wine, she gulped it down in one swallow, then tossed the glass across the kitchen where it shattered into several tiny pieces. Afterwards, she stumbled to the bedroom, where she fell face forward onto the bed and began weeping again, this time sobbing herself to sleep.

Allie squinted, trying to make out the time on the digital clock beside her bed. Peering through the small slits of her eyes, she managed to see the first number, an eight. Seeing the light streaming through the window, she deduced it must be eight in the morning. Still struggling with opening her eyes, she wondered why they were almost sealed shut.

Then it hit her in the pit of her stomach: the fight with Gary. She had cried herself to sleep, explaining why her eyes were almost swollen shut, with slivers for peepholes. As hurt as she felt over their severed relationship, short but very sweet, she found a ray of hope in that it hadn't happened during the week. There was no way she could've gone to work looking like this. There was no amount of makeup that could disguise those bags or swollen eyelids.

At least she felt better this morning, all the crying out of the way. There was still some inner pain that wanted to surface when she would allow herself to regress, but nothing a few cups of coffee and an afternoon at the mall couldn't cure. She decided that she would make that her mission as soon as she showered and hopefully, the warm water would return her eyelids to their normal size.

The phone rang, causing her to jump. At first, she hesitated to answer it for fear it might be Gary but after the third ring, she decided to pick it up.

"Hey sis."

"Derrick! Oh good, it's you!" she wailed, breathing a sigh of relief.

"Yeah, I just called to see how you're doing. From the tone in your voice, I'd say not too good. You sound stuffy. Have you been crying?"

"That noticeable, huh?" she said, relieved Derrick couldn't see through the phone.

"What happened? Are you all right?"

"Oh yeah, I'm fine now. Don't worry about me. It's Gary. I couldn't go through with the date last night. I sorta turned the tables on him. It just infuriates me to think he kept up his little ruse and I had to find out through you. He apologized and begged me to give him another chance but I said no. I told him to not call me anymore."

Derrick knew his sister well enough to know that she hadn't convinced herself it was all over. She still cared for him. He could sense it by the tone of her voice.

"Aren't you being a little hard on the guy, Allie?"

"What?"

"C'mon, Allie, it's not like he committed some sort of crime. Sure, he could've handled things better than what he did but a lot of guys resort to certain tactics just to get to know a girl. I think the guy really likes you, and if you don't mind me saying so, you really like him. Don't throw it away on something so trivial as this. You know I don't give you bad advice. Give him another shot. If you don't, you may always wonder what might have been."

"You know, sometimes you make a lot of sense, big brother. I admit, I do like him . . . a lot. I almost felt sorry for him when I think of those sad, dark, puppy dog eyes as he pleaded with me. So you really think I ought to give him another chance?"

"If you don't, I'm gonna look up Toady and tell him you're available."

"Stop that," she laughed. Derrick always seemed to cheer her up, no matter how down she was. And he always did seem to give good advice. It was almost as if he knew her better than she knew herself. Deep down, she knew what he was saying was true because she had those same thoughts.

"I gotta go, Allie. Gotta get ready for church, then afterwards, over to Tim's to watch the race. I'll tell the folks at church you're a little under the weather."

"Thanks. For everything. I'll talk to you later."

Talking to Derrick uplifted her spirits and helped make up her mind about Gary. It wasn't as if he'd committed a crime, as Derrick said, just a temporary leave of the senses. She decided she would give Gary a call later on in the day.

Feeling her way into the kitchen, her eyes still partly shut, she prepared to make some coffee. Her clothes were wrinkled from sleeping in them all night and her hair disheveled, but no one could see her through the confines of her tiny kitchen. She decided to make that a certainty by closing the curtains above the sink. Scuffling over to the window, she reached to pull the curtains when her vision suddenly became a little clearer. Seeing her car reminded her that she'd forgotten to put the top back up. But it was the inside of the car that made her gasp. It seemed to have been filled with dirt in the front and back.

"What the . . ." she gasped, unable to finish her sentence. Before she knew it, she was outside, standing beside her vandalized Mustang, staring in disbelief. The stench immediately told her it wasn't dirt, but manure. Holding her hand over her nose and mouth, she painfully took in the horrific sight of her beloved convertible trashed with poop, from who knows what kind of beast.

Her mind raced in all directions as she searched for someone to accuse. What kind of culprit was responsible for such a terrible deed? It only took her a few seconds before a name fell from her lips.

"Gary!"

She knew he was hurt and upset when he left her house yesterday and maybe this was his way of letting her know, by filling her beautiful Mustang with excrement. Her fury didn't go unnoticed as she raised her fist in the air and began punching at nothing visible.

"I'll get you for this! You'll pay dearly, I'll see to that! You wait till I see you, you just wait, you son of a . . ."

She held off on finishing her sentence when she realized she wasn't alone. Her neighbors had come out to see the show, many of them cupping their noses and mouths as she had first done. Some weren't as enthralled with the car as they were with her.

Embarrassed, she remembered she hadn't brushed her hair and still had on last night's wrinkled attire, not to mention her puffy red eyes, now redder with rage. Shyly, backing away, she turned to go back inside. Her first thoughts were to call the police, but she knew without witnesses, it would be a total waste of time. With shopping obviously out of the question—how do you go shopping with a bunch of turds in your car?—she teetered on the edge of calling Gary and giving him a piece of her mind.

But why? He would just gloat, whether he admitted to it or not. There was nothing left to do but change into some old clothes then find a bucket and a shovel. Her Sunday was planned for her with this act of bitter revenge. She would spend the day scooping who knows what kind of poop, but it would give her time to think and plan her own retaliation. Gary may have smiled and even laughed at his accomplishment, but she vowed that she would ultimately have the last laugh.

It was three in the morning. Most everybody in the lavish community of Regal Woods was asleep so he wasn't too worried about being seen. There was at least one person stirring around at that early hour and he could see her as she pranced in front of the window. *Why on earth*, he thought, *do people leave their shades up and curtains undrawn for perverts to peek in?* Peeping through the binoculars, he could see her even clearer as she waved her hands up and down. It then occurred to him that she had just painted her fingernails and was drying them. *An odd time to be doing nails*, he thought, *but maybe some manure got under them.*

"Sorry about that, Allie," he whispered.

She stopped waving and walked over to the dresser where she kept her perfume and makeup. Grabbing a bottle of perfume, she doused herself from head to toe, perhaps to help mask the scent of lingering manure. How hard she had worked, shoveling doo-doo out of her car, all day long, and then late at night, she had taken the hose and washed it out, then left it to dry with the top down, daring the culprit to do it again. He had watched her from a safe distance and ironically, wanted to assist her with this degrading task, but he couldn't. He was a party to the deed.

Finally, the lights were out and all of Regal Woods seemed to be asleep. Like a cat on the prowl, he slowly and cautiously emerged from hiding to inspect the property once covered in manure. Only a faint scent of the pungent waste remained. She'd done an excellent job in cleaning up.

Smiling, he placed a single rose on the front seat, perhaps an atonement for what he'd done, then quietly slipped away.

Chapter 7

Tim kept a vigil with his watch as he fumbled with the rear end of a car he had up on the racks. He opened at seven and it was going on eight. Gary hadn't showed up for work yet, nor had he called, and he could feel his agitation festering within. Although this was Gary's first time at being late, it still peeved Tim, what with all the mounting repair jobs coming in. It seemed like on Mondays, people were all in need of some kind of mechanical work for their cars. It made him wonder what stupid thing they did to their vehicles on the weekends.

Finally, around 7:45, Gary shuffled in. He'd already prepared his speech. He knew Tim would be infuriated with him this morning so he put together what he though was a plausible excuse.

"Hey boss. Sorry I'm late. I'm not gonna lie to you. I didn't get much sleep last night. I had a date with Allie but she got mad with me and called it off so I guess it's over between us. Anyway, I'm late cause I didn't get much sleep and when I finally did get to sleep," he yawned, "I didn't hear the alarm go off. I'm really sorry," he said, hanging his head down.

Tim had prepared a speech of his own, a simple speech: "You're fired." But after hearing Gary with his candid explanation, he changed his mind. Even if he thought deep down that Gary didn't really deserve Allie or even if there was a tinge of jealousy on Tim's behalf, he almost felt sorry for the guy. He didn't have to question the reason for the breakup. He already had an idea.

Feeling a bit of compassion for his jilted employee, he walked over and put a hand upon his shoulder.

"It's OK, Gary. Don't worry about it. You're here now. Once you dig into work, it'll take your mind off everything."

Gary looked up at his boss, and a thought suddenly occurred to him; Tim was partly responsible for his and Allie's separation. If Tim hadn't prematurely said something to Derrick, who in turn said something to Allie, he might not be in this fix. He and Allie might still be together. What should have been some sort of consolation offered little comfort but rather evoked an inner rage.

Despite his anger toward Tim at the moment, he decided to keep his feelings to himself. He also decided that his affairs of the heart were none of Tim's business. From now on, he'd leave his personal life out of their conversations.

"Give her time," Tim added, seeing doubt in Gary's eyes. "If it's meant to be, it will. Meantime, let's get a jump on the day. How about taking care of that lube job over there," he said, pointing to a jeep.

"OK," he said, walking away, his heart heavier than ever.

It had been a long day and Allie was relieved to finally be on her way home. Having not gone to bed until after three in the morning left her sapped of energy. She had seriously considered not coming in at all but there were pressing issues on her agenda that absolutely needed her attention. It meant drinking a lot of coffee and popping some NoDoz. Driving in with the top down helped, too. The wind in her face kept her alert, plus it helped to air out what was left of the poopy smell. To her dismay, she discovered that the seats were still damp so she had to place some bath towels on them.

That's when she had discovered the rose. It brought some old clichés back to her mind, "Putting salt on an open wound" and "Adding insult to injury," and that's how it felt. She had quickly discarded the rose and gone on to work, too tired to worry about Gary's unusual behavior. She'd briefly recapped her weekend with Gary to her staff and hesitantly mentioned the stinky "present" she discovered in her car Sunday morning, but spared them as much detail as possible. It was an ordeal she really didn't care to relive.

They didn't seem surprised at Gary's fake interest in buying a house, but they all agreed that the manure "incident" seemed out of character for him. Not knowing him that well, they supposed that anything was possible, but it just didn't seem to fit his profile, for some reason. Perhaps they just wanted to believe that the tall good-looking man with the darling dimples was an angel. She had also mentioned the rose she discovered this morning and they all wondered if they were dealing with a Dr. Jekyll and Mr. Hyde, or if she had two visitors within that time frame.

Allie arrived back at her house that evening just in time to see a florist's truck leaving her driveway. "Now what?" she said aloud. Parking her car, she saw the huge bouquet of flowers near the steps. Getting out of the car, she slammed the door harder than she meant to, attracting the attention of a nearby neighbor who stood outside watering his garden. She remembered seeing him Sunday afternoon as she shoveled buckets of feces out of her car. He had to be wondering what kind of whirlwind romance she was having, shoveling poop one day and receiving flowers the next.

Reaching into the bouquet, she pulled out a card that simply read, "I'm sorry."

"Yeah, so am I," she muttered. "Sorry we ever crossed paths, you psycho."

Crumbling the card and tossing it to the ground, she picked up the vase and carried it inside. It was a colorful array of carnations rather than roses this time. Allie smiled, thinking of her senior prom. That was the last time she remembered receiving carnations. Now that memory was tainted with the arrival of these menacing carnations. She stood near the trashcan for a minute, then continued on toward the kitchen table. *Such a waste to throw these in the can*, she thought, *makes a real nice centerpiece.* She just had to remind herself not to think of where it probably came from.

Back in the living room, she noticed the light flashing on her old but reliable answering machine. Somehow, she'd missed it on the way in. Reaching down, she hit the "Play" button, but no message. According to the machine, someone had called her three times, but left no message, only background noise. Listening closely, she could detect the unmistakable sound of tools clinking in the background, as if in a repair shop, perhaps a shop like Tim's.

"So, Gary's calling me from work," she said, tightening her jaw, "and too chicken to leave a message. Did he think I'd be home after yesterday's fiasco? Why else would he call me here, during the day, unless he thought I was going to be here? Why not call me at work?"

She glanced at the clock on the wall and realized the garage was closed by now. Oddly, she had misplaced his home phone number but decided it was just as well. What she had to say wouldn't be pleasant and all she really wanted to do was pamper herself the rest of the night by soaking in a hot tub with a glass of wine, then lounge in front of the TV. Then later, she'd head off to bed and curl up with a good book.

Gary had checked his answering machine when he came home Monday evening, not that he was expecting any calls . . . not from Allie anyway. The night seemed so oppressive with nothing to do except watch a little TV. But even after he turned it on, his thoughts strayed from the program he attempted to watch. Nothing seemed to hold his interest.

He got up and glanced into the kitchen where a pile of dirty dishes had gathered from two nights before. It was confusing as to how, since he hadn't eaten much, but then again, the past two days had been a blur in some areas. Normally, he was spotless. He liked the kitchen clean, the counters shining, everything put away in its rightful place. But tonight, it didn't matter because he didn't care. What might have been a simple task a week ago appeared cumbersome tonight.

He paced the hall from one end to the other, always stopping in the bathroom to ogle his pills. Much like an alcoholic who might consider his addiction as "nerve in a bottle," Gary named his prescription "crutch in a hutch." The months of anxiety that plagued him since his wife's death prompted him to seek help. The doctor gave him a prescription for lithium, which made an incredible difference in his demeanor. But it was never his intention to remain on the drug. He considered it a temporary solution until he felt emotionally stable again.

The only trouble was, each time he tried to wean himself off the miracle medication, the tragic scene would replay itself all over in his head, especially at night when he slept. Waking up in a cold sweat, crying out her name and bracing for the panic attack, was a pattern he was all too familiar with.

Maybe this isn't a good time to stop, he thought, recalling his devastating breakup with Allie. But he knew that he was only using her as an excuse. He felt he needed to summon the courage and the determination to do it. It was time to stop making excuses.

Touching the bottle of pills, then closing the door to the cabinet, he slowly backed out of the bathroom, taking a deep breath as he did. It was still early and with nothing here to absorb his time; the need to get out was overwhelming. He had no idea where he would be going or what he would be doing, but in the interim, he would figure it out. His thoughts kept wandering back to Allie and the weekend's horrible turn of events as he navigated toward the door. *If I could just see her one more time,* he thought, *I know I could make it right.* He wondered if that was ever going to be a possibility.

His thoughts were interrupted upon opening the door. From seemingly out of nowhere came a downpour of rain, appropriately mingling with his mood. Determined that the weather would not deter him from leaving the house, he grabbed his umbrella and decided to brave the elements of nature. Then, as an afterthought, he decided he didn't need the umbrella. Instead, he stepped into the pouring shower and gazed up at the sky, feeling the weight of the water soaking into his clothes, drenching through to his skin. Only when he felt himself shiver did he aim for the car, throwing the unopened umbrella into the floorboard in the back. Cold and wide awake, he started his car, then departed down the driveway, headed for a destination unknown.

Allie had just gotten out of the tub when the storm came. Putting on her robe, she observed the lights flickering as if trying to keep with the rhythm of the lightning streaking the sky. She found herself flinching at every streak and covering her ears, as if embracing for the thunder. Her fear of storms kept her familiar with her hallway. That was her comfort zone in weather like this. It was a torrential downpour she hadn't expected, but keeping up with the weather forecast was not a habit of hers.

A sharp flash lit up the sky and sent a powerful boom behind it, knocking out her power for good this time. In pitch blackness and stuck halfway down the hall, she muttered, "Oh great, I have no idea where the flashlight is." Feeling along the walls, still cowering with each thunder clap, she managed to reach the kitchen. A couple of high-powered lightning strikes illuminated the area just long enough for her to see the flashlight on top of the refrigerator. Soon, she had it in her hands, not taking the time to protect her ears. When the boom came this time, it shook the house, causing her to gasp.

Now that she had the flashlight, she could begin the search for the candles. Much to her relief, they were scattered in the first drawer she pulled out. She made a mental note to organize the drawer the first chance she got. Lighting one of the candles, she started back toward the hallway. Once there, she crouched in what she believed to be the safest part of the corridor. She noticed the wind had picked up speed, causing the branches of nearby trees to rustle against the house, producing an eerie intonation.

In between the booms and rustling branches, she thought she heard another noise, and the sound of footsteps. This propelled her to greater heights of fear. She struggled to remember if she had locked the door to the sunroom. That appeared to be where the noise was coming from. Too paralyzed with fear to check, she opted to stay where she was, wishing she had a glass of wine or even better, a shot of brandy. Suddenly, she let out a nervous laugh.

"I'm just trying to make myself go crazy," she said. "I'm letting my imagination run amok."

After an hour had passed, the storm had finally subsided and the power switched back on. Blowing out the candle, Allie slowly got to her feet, feeling the numbness as she did. She waited until the pins and needles triggered her blood back into circulation before attempting to take a walk. Still thinking about the noise or imagined noise she'd heard from the direction of the sunroom, she began her slow trek down the hall to the back of the house to the room in question. Peering through the glass door, she observed nothing unusual. The outside door was shut and appeared to be locked.

Breathing a sigh of relief, she went to survey the possible damage done outside by the storm. It was only when she turned around that she saw it. There, on the wicker table beside the door, was a vase containing a dozen red roses.

Chapter 8

Derrick was surprised to see Allie at his door first thing Tuesday morning since she normally came by on Fridays. He also sensed that this wasn't her typical social visit, judging by the wearied expression upon her face.

"Allie, what's wrong?"

"I think . . . I may have a psycho on my hands."

"What?"

"I'm talking about Gary. The guy's totally whacko!"

"Come in. Tell me what happened. I'll get us some coffee."

When Derrick returned with two cups of coffee, Allie filled him in on what happened Sunday morning after she had talked with him. He flinched at the thought of her car piled with manure. Then she told him about the rose she found inside the car the next morning and then the bouquet of flowers at her doorstep that evening. She mentioned the phone calls to her house but no one leaving a message, and that she suspected they originated from Tim's garage. Finally, she told him of the roses left in her sunroom the night before during the storm.

"I think he's stalking me. The guy's obviously obsessed with me and I don't know what to do about it. I've done everything I can to ignore him but it just seems to egg him on more."

"Are you sure it's Gary behind all this? I mean, you haven't actually seen the person doing any of this, have you?"

Allie seemed offended. "Of course I'm sure. Who else could it be? Not unless I've got a secret admirer who enjoyed filling my car with poop and then decided to send flowers. What sense does that make?"

"Have you called the cops?"

"No, and I don't want you to. That'll just make him mad and there ain't no tell-ing what he'll do then. Besides, what can they do? I'm sure they'd have to catch him in the act. Right now, I'm just going on assumptions and they're not going to arrest someone based on that."

"Yeah, but you can't keep living in fear like this. Let me have a talk with him."

"No! Absolutely not! That would be worse than getting the cops involved. I'm just hoping that he'll get tired of all this and move on. Maybe by the end of the week, he'll have it all out of his system."

Allie gulped what was left of her coffee, then got up to leave. Derrick walked her to the door and leaned over to hug her.

"You promise to call me if anything else happens or you get scared?" he asked, now more worried than Allie.

"Yes, big bro, I promise. But maybe I won't have to."

As soon as she was out the door, Derrick picked up the phone to call Tim's shop and began dialing the number. But after dialing all but the last number, he replaced the receiver. He knew Allie would be furious with him if he got Tim involved. *No sense in stirring the pot*, he thought. But he still felt a sense of obligation to pro-tect his sister. He also felt partially responsible for her whole ordeal. After all, it was he who had given Gary one of her business cards.

On the other hand, he knew Gary didn't need her business card. He had his own resources there at the shop. All he had to do was take a peek at the invoice from where she had her car worked on recently. Her name and address were clearly on the form. He could have looked her up any time without his unwitting help. Besides, the business card didn't have her home address, but it still didn't lessen the guilt that he had a part in steering him to her on the assumption that he really was in the market to buy a house.

Gary seemed somber as he strolled into work the next morning. Tim was work-ing beneath the hood of a Dodge as he quietly walked past him to see what was posted on the day's agenda.

"Morning!" Tim shouted as he walked by. Gary, barely audible, returned the greeting. Tim, shaking his head, thought that maybe he just had a rough night. Tim was too preoccupied with his quest beneath the hood to play the role of psychiatrist again. He accidentally let a curse slip as he struggled with the wrench.

"Why is it that they put things where you can't reach them?" he muttered to himself. He could hear the phone ringing as he fumbled with a bolt, not wanting to release his hold. After hearing it ring six times, he lost his patience and shouted at Gary.

"Answer the freaking phone, Gary!"

Tim paused with what he was doing to see if the ringing would stop and was relieved when he heard Gary's voice speaking to the caller. He could barely hear him as he strained to catch some of the conversation. He hoped that whatever Gary's problem was, it wouldn't spill over into his work. So far, he was pleased with both his mechanical skills and people skills. There were customers that actually bragged on him. It'd be a shame to see that ruined.

Although he still couldn't make out the conversation on Gary's end, he thought he heard him raise his voice before hanging up the phone. Making eye contact with him, Tim motioned for him to come over.

"Who was that on the phone?"

"Oh . . . just a solicitor. I handled it."

"Is something wrong, Gary? Are you still brooding over Allie?"

"No," Gary quickly answered. "Why do you ask?"

"Because you act like you're carrying around a chip on your shoulder."

"I'm all right," Gary lied. He had actually never felt more depressed. Maybe going off the medication wasn't such a good idea.

Tim decided, without commenting, that he was still upset over Allie. But he obviously didn't want to talk about it. "Well, OK. I just saw a customer drive up. Go take care of them while I try to get this clunker fixed."

Gary complied with a nod. Thinking of the phone call just a moment ago compelled Tim to stay within earshot of Gary as he attended to the customer who just drove up. The clunker would have to wait. He knew solicitors rarely called. What if it had been one of his best customers? Good steady customers were hard to come by.

Tim watched Gary from the side, recognizing the older gentleman, who had just driven up, as Mr. Phelps, a longtime client and friend. *Oh, please don't screw this up*, he thought. The elderly man produced a piece of paper from his pocket. It appeared to be a receipt from the garage. He pointed at the receipt while Gary took a look, studying it with intensity.

"I didn't request this but I was charged for it. I don't think I should pay for something I didn't ask for," the old man said.

"Sure you did. I wouldn't have done it if you hadn't asked." Gary felt the blood rushing to his face but fought to maintain control.

"No . . . I didn't. And I want a refund for it or I'm taking my business elsewhere."

"I distinctly remember you asking for it, Mr. Phelps," Gary insisted.

"I did not ask for it and I demand a refund," he said, his voice getting louder. "Where's Tim? He needs to know what kind of a crook he's got working for him."

"Look here, you old buzzard . . ."

"Mr. Phelps! Hey, good to see you!" Tim interrupted. The surprise on Gary's face let Tim know that he didn't see him sneak up. "Gary, how about leaving us? I'll handle this."

As Gary turned to leave, he wondered if the old man was right. Maybe he did hear him wrong.

"I'm so sorry, Mr. Phelps. I'll clear that off your bill and refund you the money. Also, next time you're due for an oil change, it's on the house."

"Now that's the way to do business," Mr. Phelps said, shaking Tim's hand. Tim didn't know about the job in question regarding Mr. Phelps' vehicle, but he did know Mr. Phelps. He had never been a problem customer and he intended on keeping him coming to his shop.

By the end of the day, Tim realized he was cleaning up more messes made by Gary than he was making money. As the complaints mounted, so did the promises of free oil changes. There was only one thing left to do and he hated the thought of it but at this point, he felt he had no other choice. He couldn't risk losing what took years to build up.

Upon slamming down the rollup doors at the end of the day, Tim summoned Gary to his office.

"Gary, we need to talk. Sit down."

Gary slumped back into the chair across from his boss. He immediately began to fidget with his knees as Tim seemed to search for the right words to say. Unable to come up with any to soften the blow, he decided to just tell it like it is.

"I'm sorry, Gary, but I'm gonna have to let you go. Too many customers were complaining today and threatening to go somewhere else because of you. And I can't afford for that to happen. You understand, don't you?"

Gary stopped fidgeting and stared at Tim with icy cold eyes. Tim wasn't sure what to expect once he let Gary know he was fired, but the frigid look in his eyes sent even colder chills down his spine. He still paused, waiting for a response and when there wasn't one, he went on.

"I'll go ahead and pay you for all the hours you've put in since your last paycheck, including the hours you worked today." He thought that was generous upon his part, considering all the free oil changes he had to commit to.

Gary slowly looked toward the ceiling, then closed his eyes, as if trying to remember where he went wrong, but then he surprised Tim by smiling and bringing his eyes level with him.

"OK, Tim. I understand. Can't have the customers balking to you about your number one mechanic . . . excuse me, only mechanic." Tim wondered if he was trying to make a point as he continued. "You gave me a shot and I blew it. No hard feelings."

Gary extended a hand and Tim, reluctantly, shook it. He was surprised it had ended on a rather good note, considering the mood Gary had been in. For a second, he'd even thought of giving him a second chance, then quickly dismissed the idea. He'd take his losses and carry on. He couldn't risk another day like today, financially.

Tim handed him his last paycheck and wished him well.

Wednesday morning on the way to work, Allie was more at ease than she had been over the previous four days. There hadn't been any more mystery phone calls or flowers popping up at her house. She figured if he was going to harass her any more, he'd have done it by now. Everything seemed to be returning to normal.

That euphoric feeling would soon be short-lived as she neared the agency. As soon as she turned into the parking lot, she sensed something was wrong. Tess, Frieda and Amber were all staring out the window, appearing somewhat somber as she pulled into her parking space. *I paid them yesterday . . . I think*, she thought to herself.

As she walked in, they looked at one another, then back to her, as if trying to figure out what to say.

"What is it?" she asked.

"Follow me," Tess volunteered. Allie glanced at Frieda and Amber, then started down the hall behind Tess. They stopped at Allie's office. The door had been opened, but not by anyone working inside the office. It had been jimmied open. On the desk was a vase holding two dozen red roses and an oversized Hallmark card conveying a simple message for all to see: "Love you, miss you." Next to the card was a box of chocolates.

"How did this get in here?"

"We don't know," Amber said. "We know your door was broken in but we can't see where or how he got into the building itself. The doors were actually locked when we got here."

"This has to stop!" Allie picked up the phone and started dialing.

"Who you calling?" Frieda asked.

"I'm calling Tim's shop. I need to nip this in the bud right now. Hello? Tim? Hey, this is Allie . . . well, I've been better. Is Gary there, by any chance?"

Frieda strained to hear the conversation on the other line as she inched closer to Allie, but it was too muffled.

"He isn't? You did? When? I see . . . no, we're not seeing each other anymore," Allie said, looking eager to get off the phone. "I'll have to tell you about it later, I got a call on hold . . . yeah, you have a good day, too. Bye."

"You don't have a call on hold," Frieda corrected.

"I know, I was just trying to get off the phone with him. I didn't feel like answering questions about something that's really none of his business."

Although Tim didn't elaborate on why he let Gary go, Allie couldn't help but speculate as to the reason. The timing made it all too obvious. It had to be his obsession with her that spilled over into his job performance. But now the magic question of the moment: where was Gary? The one place she knew how to reach him was no longer an option. She'd waited too late to confront him.

"Well? What did he say?" Frieda asked, anxious to know the story.

"Gary was fired yesterday."

Deep down, she thought she actually felt relief, relief that she didn't have to confront him. But now what? She still felt that she had to locate him and resolve the situation once and for all. The only problem was, although he had been to her house, she had never been to his, so she had no idea where he lived. Then, an idea came to her.

"Tim has got to have some paperwork on him since he hired him. I'll just go see him and get him to let me have his address. I have to find Gary and put an end to this, once and for all."

"You sure that's a good idea?" Amber asked, concerned for Allie's safety. "I mean, maybe now that he's fired, he'll move on down the road."

"That's no guarantee. If I don't do something, this could go on and on. But don't worry," she added. "He may be obsessed, but I don't see him as violent." Allie only hoped she could convince herself as well. "I'll go over there tomorrow. I just want to put this aside for now and concentrate on work."

Thursday morning, Allie sat in Tim's office, not believing what she was hearing. She had made sure she was there as soon as he opened.

"I'm sorry, Allie. I never got around to filling out the forms. I hired him on the spot so there's no application and as for the tax forms, I was more or less paying him under the table. I mean, I was writing him checks but I didn't note it as payroll. I wanted to see if he was going to work out before I went through the trouble of officially putting him on the payroll."

Allie couldn't help but think, *You idiot.* She couldn't fathom hiring someone without checking their background first, then getting the necessary forms filled out. It suddenly jarred her memory of why she and Tim never made it as a couple, or at least one of the reasons. He was too irresponsible.

"You don't even have a clue to where he lives?" she asked in frustration.

"Nope. Sorry."

"Yeah, me too," Allie said, annoyed with his candor. "Do me a favor, all right? If you happen to hear from him, please give me a call. Try to find out where he lives, too. OK?"

"I'll do my best. And Allie? I'm sorry."

"You already said that," Allie said, with a hint of agitation.

"No, I mean I'm sorry things didn't work out between you two."

Allie was somewhat touched by Tim's sentiment. Even if he had touched a nerve of hers with his inept office skills, he had managed to soften her heart with those few words.

"Thank you, Tim. That means a lot coming from you."

Tim smiled, but only because Gary was seemingly out of Allie's life.

Sleep had never felt so good as Allie drifted in and out of consciousness. The breeze coming from the open window added to the serene pleasure of slumber she easily succumbed to. Dreams wandered, then faded out like trailer clips of movies. All the nights of counting sheep had finally caught up with her as she surrendered to the night.

Never had she felt this exhausted, so exhausted, in fact, that she couldn't hear the commotion just outside the window. Or maybe she did and it incorporated itself into her dreams. She knew from experience that the more tired she was, the more apt her mind was to venture out on its own.

Suddenly, a shadow appeared beside the bed, a shadow holding an object of some sort. A quick dart of her eyes toward the window where the screen used to be forced a scream to the surface. The figure loomed larger as it eased closer to the edge of the bed and the object it held took the shape of a knife as it was raised into midair. Then, as quickly as it had appeared, it was gone, the figure and the knife. She discovered she was sitting up and drenching with sweat, and the window, as she cast a fearful glance, still had its screen.

"It was a dream, a nightmare," she gasped, her heart beating hard against her chest. Outside, the creatures chirped harmoniously and a dog barked somewhere in the distance. While most of the neighborhood slept, Allie thought she would be keeping vigil by the window, wondering what Gary's next move might be, or maybe this was it. Maybe the roses he had placed in her office were a farewell gesture. But realistically, she knew that was too much to hope for.

It was just a little after one o'clock in the morning but she was wide awake. The ease with which she had fallen asleep before was no longer there. Sighing, she slowly got off the bed and over to the window where she closed, then locked it for the night. She hadn't meant to leave it open but fatigue has a way of dulling your senses.

After a much needed trip to the bathroom, she shuffled to the kitchen for a glass of water. While sipping her water at the sink, she gazed out the window into the dark of the night. Although it was pitch black, the street lights out of all nights, she thought she caught movement out on the front lawn. But when she looked away and back again, it was gone.

Too tensed up to fall asleep, yet too tired to read, Allie wandered around the house sipping from her glass of water. Thoughts of Gary kept rushing through her head, good thoughts at first, then the overwhelming bad thoughts. She wished she could just keep the memories of their first time together at the restaurant and toss out everything beyond that. But even that precious memory was tainted with his deception.

Allie numbly walked toward the rear of the house and peered out the window overlooking the patio. While she enjoyed the last of her remaining water, she thought she detected some sort of movement again. This time, she was sure of something lurking outside for she heard it as well. Paralyzed with fear, she stood at the door, her heart pounding harder and faster than before. She knew the outdoor switch was only a few baby steps away, but it might as well have been several miles. Her feet refused to move.

As her eyes began to adjust to the dark, the object of her fear appeared smaller. Finally able to move, she stepped over just enough to switch the light on. There in the middle of her deck, a possum stared back, gnawing furiously on a steak bone he had retrieved from someone's garbage, possibly hers.

"Ugh . . . a possum. But you couldn't be more beautiful right now," she said, grateful that was all it was. But as she switched the light off and started to walk away, something about her patio looked different. Switching the light back on and taking a second look, she spotted the difference, an added décor. There before her eyes sat a large teddy bear and another dozen red roses.

"Oh, no!" she gasped. Slapping her right hand across her chest, she could once again feel her heart pick up speed. When had he come here and more importantly, was he still here? Her first instinct was to hide, but why? He'd probably find her. She had to face this head on or it was never going to end.

Reaching deep within, she summoned the courage to reach for the door, slowly unlocking it as she did. If he was still hiding in the shadows, there was no greater time than now to put an end to his fixation.

Tiptoeing through the door and out onto the patio, Allie saw nor felt any hint of him still being around. Not surprisingly, there was a card propped up against the bear. It simply read, "I love you."

Allie glared at the card, then back at the flowers and bear. *He's not gonna give up*, she thought. *I have to do something.*

She turned to go back into the house, twice looking behind to make sure she wasn't being followed. She was starting to feel the effects of sleep deprivation but when she crawled back into bed, she was more awake than ever. Whenever she closed her eyes in an effort to doze off, the image with the raised knife returned.

Frustrated, she leaped out of bed and started digging through her closet. After several minutes of unsuccessful searching, she gave up and grabbed a garbage bag from underneath the kitchen sink to pile some clothes and personal belongings into. It was then that she remembered she had loaned her luggage out and hadn't gotten it back. *Just great,* she thought, *the one time I really need it.*

After a quick change of clothes, she grabbed her makeshift suitcase and pocketbook, then headed out the door for her unplanned vacation. Loading up the trunk of her car, she commended herself on having filled up the gas tank earlier. A full tank would take her far without having to stop.

Realizing how late it was, she refrained from contacting anyone regarding her plans. Instead, she decided to stop by the office on the way out and leave a note letting her staff know what she was doing. After that, she'd be on her way to wherever. It was the first time she'd gone on vacation and had no clue as to where she was going. But as strange as it was, she discovered she didn't care. She'd figure it out as she was driving. Ironically, Amber had pleaded with her to take a vacation and she was finally doing it. *Won't she be surprised,* she thought.

The office was eerily isolated as Thursday night had rolled into Friday morning just a couple of hours earlier. With only a flickering street lamp illuminating the lot, she maneuvered her car as close to the front door as she could get. Her plan was to get in and out as quickly as possible.

Inside, she switched the light on, grabbed a pad off Amber's desk, and began to scribble with lightning speed. After proofreading it several times and making corrections, she tore the note from the pad and set it beside Amber's phone. Satisfied with her placement of the note, she switched the light off and slammed the door shut, sending a slight breeze over the note that caused it to float up and then gently to the floor, landing under the credenza.

She had been so busy concentrating on the note she'd prepared for Amber that she didn't hear the car pull up into the parking lot. It was only after she had locked the door behind her and turned around that she saw him standing beside her car. His hair was disheveled and oily, his eyes wide, his teeth . . . no longer white, and his clothes a shamble. If it hadn't been for that slight hint of a dimple, she wouldn't have recognized him as being Gary. But the instant she met his eyes, her mouth dropped, along with her keys. The car, all of a sudden, seemed a dangerous mile away, with him standing so close to it.

"Gary! You . . . you scared me! What are you doing here?"

His eyes were far away even as he stared coldly into hers. She felt chills trickle down her spine as she again attempted to communicate with him.

"Ga . . . Ga . . . Gary," she stuttered, "this, this has to stop, you hear? I mean, the flowers, the notes, the gifts . . . you can't keep doing this. I mean it, Gary. You need to move on. Am I getting across to you?"

Gary continued to stare at her like a puzzle that had to be solved.

"Are you listening to me?" she asked, more unnerved than ever. Suddenly, he opened his mouth to speak, but it didn't make any sense.

"Mi-am-i," he muttered.

"What?" she asked, confused.

"Mi-am-i," he repeated.

"Look," she said, bending down to get her keys, her eyes on him all the while. "I gotta go. Don't send me any more flowers, or gifts. OK?"

"Mi-am-i," he said again.

Allie crinkled her forehead, perplexed at his repetition of the word "Miami." What was the big deal about Miami? *No matter*, she thought, *he can go to Miami. I've got other plans.*

Allie quickly slid in behind the wheel of her car, half expecting him to stop her, but he didn't. He just stood idly by as she shut the door then locked herself in the car. Even as she started the engine and started pulling out of the lot, he still stood there, without moving, without expression. Glancing in the rearview mirror every few seconds, she could still see him in that spot, glaring back at her. She glanced for a final time when a curve in the road took him out of view. It was at that moment that it hit her how close she'd been to him, how afraid she had been of him, but she escaped with her life . . . and he hadn't even tried to follow. A cold flutter of shivers soared through her body as she tried to grasp all that had just transpired.

All of a sudden, she thought of Derrick. She knew he'd be expecting to see her later in the morning for their weekly Friday visit. But then she took comfort in knowing that she had taken the time to leave a note at the office. They could relate to Derrick what was going on. Meanwhile, she'd call him whenever she got settled into wherever she was going.

Looking across the seat, she'd forgotten she'd brought her pistol. *A lot of good it would have done if Gary had attacked me,* she thought, *with me on the outside and the pistol on the seat.* Even so, she was thankful that she didn't have to use it.

Reaching over, she picked up the pistol and placed it beneath the seat. Having a concealed carry license certainly was an advantage.

Chapter 9

Allie had been driving all night, a night where most people were comfortably sleeping in their beds after an evening of dining out or having a casual home-cooked meal. But for her, it was everything but that: an unplanned journey, provoked by fear, a fear she hadn't anticipated, and yet a fear that was strong enough to compel her to run.

Why did I have to take my car in that day, of all days, she thought to herself. *Why didn't I just let Derrick do it for me? He could have done it and I wouldn't be in the position I'm in right now.* But rehashing all the memories that led her to where she was didn't provide a remedy. Whatever had lured Gary to pursue her with such unnatural determination, she vowed, would surely not happen again. It was her first experience being stalked, and if she got through this alive, it'd be her last. She just hoped and prayed she could survive this ordeal.

Too tense and too frightened to be tired initially, she began to slowly feel the weight of her eyelids for the first time since being on the run . . . or on the lam. She even began to question herself; was she the criminal or the victim? But recalling the last few hours convinced her that she was definitely not the criminal.

Fighting the urge to close her eyes was becoming a chore in itself. She started experimenting with the good ole-fashioned technique of slapping herself every few seconds to stay awake, but that got old after a few whacks across her cheek, not to mention it was starting to sting a little. She then resorted to splashing some water from her bottle of Perrier onto her face, in hopes of a fresh revival, but that, too, also proved to be a temporary fix. Even with the windows rolled down, she had a hard time preventing her eyelids from drooping. As a matter of fact, it seemed to encourage her senses to want to surrender to sleep.

It also transported her to childhood memories, memories she hadn't thought of in years, perhaps as a result of being so transfixed in a non-stop world of buying and selling property. But now, those memories seemed to be some sort of solace as she envisioned herself on her grandma's front porch swing, with the cool summer breeze cooing her to sleep, her hair lightly tickling her face with each breath of wind. If it hadn't of been for the pothole in the road, she wouldn't be mentally sitting on her grandma's swing, but rather up a tree. The sudden jolt brought her back to reality. She was no longer in the safe haven of Grandma's porch. She realized that she had to keep the breeze that felt so good then, and apparently now, from snapping her out of consciousness.

With no toothpicks for a prop, she knew there had to be another way to keep her eyelids from wanting to sag. She remembered hearing from someone, somewhere that pulling over to the side of the road and getting out to stretch, walking around the vehicle a few times, generally rejuvenated the senses. But whether that was true or not, she resisted the temptation to try it. She knew she had to keep going and the further away, the better. With no better solution in mind, she resorted back to "slapping and splashing."

Although it was the onset of spring, her favorite season, she oddly found herself thinking of autumn, her second favorite time of year, as she traveled this unfamiliar road lined with trees. It reminded her of those months late into the year when she'd be leisurely working out in the yard, enjoying the cooler temperatures after a long sweltering summer. It was these simple memories brought to the surface that had her aching for what she'd left behind. Besides missing her brother and everyone else she knew, she missed the simplicity of the life she had, something as ordinary as walking among the scattered leaves while sipping freshly brewed coffee, embracing the serenity of the season. How far away that all seemed to her now as she still struggled to stay awake.

Daylight was starting to seep in and Allie found herself fighting harder than ever to resist the temptation to just pull over and grabs a few winks. It was all she could do to talk herself out of finding a quiet little path along the road to park and, with the headrest as her pillow, she could doze just long enough to make it to wherever she was going. But the thought of why she was running and the idea that he may catch up with her while she snoozed kept her drudging on. Yet she caught herself repeatedly drifting over the center line. Another couple of slaps on the cheek and a splash of Perrier brought back a tab of vivacity, far from the adrenaline rush she experienced hours earlier, but just enough to keep her focused for a little while longer.

Once again, she was drawn into obscured memories of the previous night. It seemed like a dream, a bad dream, one she didn't care to remember, but had to. It was at that moment that she began to question the validity of the events that led to her swift departure. Then again, why else would she be cruising an unknown highway, long overdue for repaving, at almost six o'clock in the morning? She concluded that this was definitely for real.

The sandman was once again closing in on her senses when a stray rock made contact with her windshield, jerking her awake.

"Where did that come from?" she shrieked.

The rock had made a perfect bull's-eye in the center of her windshield, nothing that couldn't be patched fairly inexpensively. She was actually grateful for the high-flying rock, for it kept her out of the ditches as did the pothole awhile back. It made her think of the Sundays she would doze off in church and her mother would nudge her to stay awake. Was this God's way of nudging her awake?

"Six o'clock," she mumbled, barely audible, eyeing the clock on her car. People all over the south were having their pancakes, sausages, bacon and grits. The thought of food woke up her taste buds while her stomach began to rumble. She'd barely eaten the night before and now craved everything that came to mind.

"Road kill would be good about now," she mused, "sautéed possum with a hint of butter and lemon juice."

Grabbing her stomach with her left hand as if that would stop the growling, she thought she saw the "Golden Arches" a few miles down the road. But when she blinked, it was gone, like a mirage in the desert. Having no idea where she was or how far she'd come, she tried to focus on the hour she'd left and add the time in between. It surprised her how something that normally would be so simple suddenly seemed complex. She also had trouble recalling when she had made the turn onto this particular road, this road with the fake Golden Arches. She did recall taking several roads, either veering right or left when one ended, but not having a destination, she was totally lost. *But under the circumstances, not a bad place to be*, she admitted to herself.

The first few signs of civilization began to emerge as she started to encounter other vehicles on the road. This brought about a wave of relief. Now that it was light, there was more to see besides the road. Very few houses could be seen and those that were visible were nestled comfortably off the beaten path. One house in particular stood out. It was a large two-story house with a wraparound porch and a white picket fence, the typical "dream house" of many first-time buyers.

It even has a porch swing, just like Grandma's, she fondly recalled. How she longed to be in that swing again, next to Grandma, as she would tell her endless stories of her own life as a child growing up. They were fascinating then and they were fascinating now as she plucked from memory the most vivid and chilling story.

"Back in the good ole days," as Grandma would begin many of her stories, "things were so much simpler. 'Tweren't no need to keep your doors locked, not even at night. Folks didn't have to worry about strangers coming into their houses and robbing them or trying to hurt them. Things like that just didn't happen in the good ole days. Why, folks could go off to church and leave their doors unlocked, even open, and come home, not worried that someone had been there pilfering through their belongings. And while some left their screen doors open, there were some houses that didn't have screen doors at all.

"Then something happened that changed people's mind about leaving their screen doors open or installing screen doors if they didn't have 'em. There was this couple that lived down the road . . ." Allie remembered all of Grandma's stories were about someone who lived down the road. ". . . that kept their main door and their screen door open all the time. One afternoon, in the dog days of summer, they were sitting side by side out on the back stoop when low and behold a snake slithered up the steps in between them. It slithered up the steps and into the house.

"The couple, horrified at what they saw, jumped up and ran down the steps. The man runs toward the shed and grabs a hoe while the woman starts screaming, 'The baby, Jeb! The baby's in the crib! Hurry, Jeb! We gotta go get the baby!' Her husband ran back to the house, with the hoe in his hand.

"But then he stopped, as if something didn't want him to go any further. Instead, he turned to her and said, 'Ella, something tells me we need to wait a minute. That was a black snake that crawled up the stoop and into the house. Black snakes ain't poisonous; they kill the poisonous kind. Let's just wait and see what happens. I think it went in there for a reason.'

"Sure enough, a few minutes later, the black snake came out, with a rattler clinched in its jaws. It slithered back down the stoop and into the grass and on toward the canal. The couple later learned that the rattler had harbored itself into the springs of the baby's mattress. The black snake had saved their baby's life. From then on, most people made sure their screen doors were shut, or their main door if they lacked a screen door."

Allie shivered involuntarily. It was a story that haunted her even into her college years and recalling it now didn't make it any less eerie. She never questioned the validity of the story from her grandma, but all her stories were told in such realistic detail that she assumed this could and probably did happen.

Shaking her head, she again tried to focus on the road. With no music to pass the time—no radio signal in Hicksville—she entertained herself with the notion of settling down in an area such as this.

"Where's the grocery store?" she laughed. "Don't tell me I'd have to kill my breakfast before I ate it. And the TV? If I can't get a radio signal out here, that means there's no TV signal . . . probably. And gas stations . . ." she stopped, gasping. "Oh no, I forgot about gas!"

Cautiously peering in between the steering wheel of her vintage Mustang, she observed the position of the gas needle, which miraculously revealed she still had a quarter of a tank of gas left. She knew her car could get close to thirty miles a gallon on the open highway, but would there be a station in sight before she found herself driving on fumes? This set off a major panic alert. As a rule, she'd set her trip meter after each fuel up, but she had forgotten to this time in her rush to get away. She'd stopped just on the outskirts of Regal Woods to top the tank off and never thought to reset the meter gauge. She knew she could estimate the miles from the previous time she'd fueled but was way too tired to fiddle with the numbers.

"Oh, dear Lord, please don't let me run out of gas," she prayed. The gas needle teetered between "E" and a quarter of a tank. It seemed to be jeering at her, daring her to go another mile without stopping. Beads of sweat popped out on her forehead and her heart seemed to take on a heavier beat. She wondered how much more excitement her "pump" could take.

There were no road signs hinting to what lay ahead. All she saw were fields and barns and houses set far back off the road.

"Dear Lord, please be my guide. Show me to a gas station."

Allie couldn't remember the last time she'd prayed and felt a tinge of guilt for calling on the Divine in her hour of desperation. All the same, it brought back the most vivid memories of her youth, attending Sunday School classes. So clear were the memories, in fact, that she could remember the songs they sung.

"Jesus loves me, this I know. For the Bible tells me so," she sang softly. "Little ones to Him belong. They are weak but He is strong. Yes, Jesus loves me. Yes, Jesus loves me. Yes, Jesus loves me. For the Bible tells me so."

When she wasn't singing Bible songs or reciting the Lord's Prayer, she was quoting famous words.

"We have nothing to fear, but fear itself . . ." To that she added, ". . . but you're not out here on the run, FDR."

Finally, just up the road, there appeared to be what resembled a miniature red octagon. Not wanting to be disappointed again, she pretended it was an illusion. But as she sped toward the illusion, she found herself squinting, as if the sign could better come into focus. The needle on the gas gauge hadn't dropped any, so that was good. She felt the urge to floor it but realized that would only end up burning more fuel, so she kept a calm and steady speed.

Before long, the miniature octagon had enlarged and she saw the most beautiful word attached to it: STOP.

"Yippee!" she shouted. "Thank you! Thank you! Thank you!" It was just a stop sign at the end of a long road, but to her, it was divine intervention, an answer to her prayers, for she could also spot the little green rectangular signs affixed to neighboring posts that pointed in both directions, indicating what lay ahead. She was still a little too far to decipher the words on the green signs, but just the sight of it was exciting to say the least.

The impulse flight from the previous night combined with the fatigue from the long and grueling early morning road trip, as well as the scarcity of traffic along this remote highway, made her vulnerable to any obstacles along the road. So what seemed to be "her" road for hours suddenly changed. About a hundred feet or more from the stop sign, a red VW Beetle, almost as bright in color as her Mustang, crept onto the highway, taking its sweet "country bumpkin" time shifting into gears.

"You freaking idiot . . ." Allie stopped short, realizing that this was totally out of character for her. She was tired and hungry and irritable, but nonetheless reprimanded herself for the outburst. She thought the early morning intruder on "her" highway would quickly step up the pace when it caught sight of a shiny red Mustang Convertible bearing down upon its bumper. But as Allie drew closer to the "turtle" on the road, it seemed to be slowing down rather than speeding up, almost closing the gap between the two. She was now close enough to where she could read the personalized license plate, which said, "IZZYSBUG."

"Figures," Allie fumed. "She's probably a dizzy Izzy."

The VW appeared to be struggling with the gears or maybe it was the operator of the Beetle that needed a refresher course in driving.

The VW finally managed to kick in the last gear right before it had to downshift into first as it closed in on the stop sign. By then, Allie could no longer hide her irritation. When the VW came to a near halt at the stop sign, she whipped around it, narrowly missing the rear of the sluggish Beetle. Just as abruptly, she pulled in front of it, pausing long enough to read the green rectangular signs, indicating which way went where.

No need to check for traffic, she thought, *ain't been no real traffic here in Hicksville.* A casual glance in the rearview mirror caught the image of an agitated woman, middle-aged perhaps. Her dark hair appeared to be disheveled and her eyes said more than her mouth, which was, fortunately, cut off from the limited view.

Not wanting a confrontation, especially in her state of sleep deprivation, she quickly diverted her attention to the signs on the pole again in order to get going in some direction.

"Possum Heights, three miles to the left, or Pine Cone, ten miles to the right," she muttered. She instantly knew what her choice would be, although she wished the names had been reversed.

"I can't believe I'm about to enter a town named after road kill."

Screeching tires, she veered left and bore down hard on her accelerator. She was still puzzled at the town's chosen name, wondering how it came about but also wondering about its townspeople.

"Who in their right mind would want to live in a town named after a marsupial? Did I jinx myself when I entertained thoughts of sautéed possum earlier?"

Glancing in the rearview mirror again, she saw the VW was still stalling, perhaps wondering which way to go as well. But even as she mounted a hill and rounded a curve further down the road, the Beetle still sat motionless. Allie wondered if she should go back and check on the driver but quickly decided that turning around would use up more precious gas, gas that may not get her to Possum Heights if she tacked on any more miles. She tried to reassure herself by thinking that someone would come along and help the lady, should she need a jump or tow or whatever. Somehow, that small amount of assurance did nothing to ease her guilt. She felt a bit of remorse for passing her the way she did, narrowly missing the car. Then, adding insult to injury, she left her stranded on a desolate road.

The tow truck barely missed the ditch trying to maneuver itself around the VW. If there had been any real traffic on the road, it'd been backed up in both directions.

Izzy stood on the side of the road with her arms crossed, wearing her trademark crinkle cotton, long-sleeve pullover shirt with the embroidered flowers on front and crochet trim, a relic from the seventies. When she wasn't wearing that, she liked to don her psychedelic tie-dye tops. Naturally, she kept her "Peace" necklace around her neck, tucked snugly inside her shirt. At least she surrendered the low riding bell-bottomed pants, as she discovered her figure no longer conformed to their fit. Instead, she wore plain faded jeans and sandals, another fashion statement from the sixties and seventies. In the cooler temperatures, she substituted her canvas shoes. A woman in her late forties, she still retained much of her shoulder-length, jet-black hair. Only when the sun aimed just right could you detect a few streaks of gray. And then there were those dark brown eyes that were daunting at times and menacing at others. Despite being of medium build and slightly on the heavy side, she was agile in every way, perhaps athletic at one time in her life.

"Isabelle, we have got to stop meeting like this," the tow truck driver joked. "The whole town's starting to talk. This is the third time within the past twelve months I've had to haul this thing. Why don't you ante up and buy something a little more reliable? I know you can afford it."

"Oh, shut your trap, John, and get it hitched up. That lady maniac! I was pulled off to the side of the road cause ole Barney was spitting and spurting. And when I got back on the road, I saw her in my mirror, speeding up like she wants to beat me to the stop sign. And she does, killing my Barney!"

"Your Barney was already on its last leg . . . uh, tire."

"Then she leaves the scene of the almost-accident!" Izzy continued, ignoring John's comment. "I know she saw me and my poor Barney stalled here, to fend for ourselves. Didn't so much as slow down! Can you believe that? Got to be one of them out-of-towners. A local wouldn't have done that. Well, anyway, thanks to that ding-a-ling, I gotta fork out a chunk of change to you for towing it to Ollie's and ain't no telling what he's gonna charge to get ole Barney going again."

John scratched his head, inwardly amused at Izzy's ranting but outwardly compassionate, to a degree.

"C'mon, Izzy, take this as a sign. It's time to trade in this heap of ju—" Izzy gave him an evil glance in mid-sentence, prompting him to re-word himself. ". . . this fine piece of machinery and get you something more dependable, say, another Barney, with low mileage. I know you got better than half a million miles on this baby. It's just lucky I happened by with nothing in tow. Stand back a minute."

John pulled a lever in the back and began to reel the VW up on two wheels. Upon securing it, he glanced underneath, then back at her.

"When's the last time you changed your oil?"

"When's the last time you changed your drawers?" Izzy shot back, still peeved with the driver of the Mustang. John shook his head again.

"Hop in. I'll drop you off at the house."

"Naw, better take me straight to the diner. I don't have time to go back and switch vehicles. I'm already late and Frank's probably having a hissy fit about now. I'll get someone at work to take me home when my shift's over."

"All right, to the diner it is."

Chapter 10

There was no mistaking the town if you were looking for Possum Heights. Many towns had signs of all colors and sizes proudly displaying their roots but Possum Heights not only boasted their small community with a sign, they also represented it with a carved statue of a possum on each side of the road upon entering town.

"I feel like I'm in the Twilight Zone," Allie murmured to herself. As it was too late to rethink her path, she eased through the entranceway to this unknown territory and cautiously cruised what she perceived to be Main Street. Main Street. *What a crock,* she thought, but not for long. All along side the streets, she encountered all sorts of shops, shops that pleasantly reminded her of her childhood days. Downtown shops like the Dime Store, the Malt Shop, the Pizza Parlor, even the old fashioned Barber Shop, like Floyd's in Mayberry, sent a rush of memories from a timeless era. She even captured the scent of what might have been an old-timey grill cooking hotdogs and hamburgers the way they tasted back then. It was especially hard not to notice the people, the casual way they dressed, which made her look down at her own clothes, a reminder that she fled in a hurry, putting on the same clothes she'd worn that day.

Despite the name of the town honoring its "Grand Marshal" at the entrance, she was actually starting to find it appealing. Other than a few stares from some of the sidewalk gawkers, she almost felt welcomed here. There was an air of amity about this town, an odd sense of belonging. *Is this an illusion brought on by fatigue,* she wondered, *or destiny unforeseen?* She needed some assurance and what better assurance than the view a block down the road. Situated in the heart of Possum Heights, was a gas station/diner next door to a motel. She couldn't believe her luck to stumble upon this package all rolled into one. Days before, this would have been so trivial, but this morning, it was a gold mine.

She coasted up to the full service lane at the gas pump—*Didn't know they still existed,* she thought—and noticed the needle on the gas gauge was resting directly on "E." It had also triggered a warning light on her dashboard, just as she had pulled in. An attendant immediately approached her on the driver's side as she rolled the window part of the way down.

"Fill 'er up, ma'am?"

"Yes, please . . . and could you also check my oil?"

"Comes standard, ma'am. We also check your other fluids and wash your windshield as well."

Allie suddenly felt stupid. It had been a long time since she'd seen, much less been to, a full service station. *Maybe I really am in Mayberry,* she thought, *and this is Wally's Filling Station and that was Goober or Gomer.*

"Oh, OK. Great. Thank you," she said, almost blushing. The attendant winked and continued to service her car.

Eyeing the motel next door, she decided a nice hot bath and a nap would be her first priority. Too tired to eat after a long night on the road, she decided she would check out the diner after a few winks. She also felt unprepared for the inquisitions of the locals in her present state of exhaustion. No doubt they would be eager to unearth her secret, as all strangers entering into a small town were bound to have secrets. This was no time to make mistakes. With no plan in mind, she focused on renting a room for the next few days. That would buy her more time to consider her options. But for now, sleep appealed the most.

"You have a tail light out, ma'am."

Startled, she turned to face Goober, who by now was leaning his arms on the roof of her car, talking through the window, rolled halfway down.

"I noticed it when you stopped at the gas pump," he continued. "If you'll let me into your trunk, I'll be glad to replace it."

"Why . . . thank you! I appreciate that, really," she said, trying to smile through her lack of sleep. She wondered if she should tip him or did full service cover it all? How much did a bulb cost anyway?

Removing the keys from the ignition, she passed them over to the attendant so he could open the trunk. In a matter of minutes, he had extracted the burnt out bulb and replaced it with a new one. The force of the trunk lid shutting jolted her a little. She eyed him curiously in the rearview mirror as he started around toward her window, wiping his hands on a rag as he did.

"That'll be twelve forty-five for the gas."

"What about the bulb?"

"No charge. Bulb doesn't cost much."

"Well, thank you again," she said, grateful for his generosity. She reached into her purse and pulled out the exact amount of money.

"You must've been riding on fumes, ma'am," he said. "Sounded like it was close to empty when I started putting the gas in."

"Yeah, well, I have a tendency to do that, go until the last drop," she said. Not wanting to engage in any lengthy conversation, she politely thanked him a third time and drove away. He watched her pull off and turn into the motel parking lot next door. He didn't think it strange for a woman traveling alone to check into a small town motel but he did find it peculiar that she had no luggage, just a large garbage bag with some personal items and meager clothing. Not only that, he caught sight of the butt end of a .38 revolver sticking out from under the seat of the passenger side.

Once checked in, Allie reparked her car in front of the room assigned to her. Leaning back against the headrest, she surveyed the quaint hostelry before her. *I don't know where I'm at or what I'm doing,* she thought, *but this may be home for the next few weeks.* Fighting the urge to close her eyes, she reached over to grab her purse, at the same time noticing her revolver poking part of the way out from beneath the seat. She wondered if Goober back at the gas station saw it and concluded that he probably didn't. Carefully removing it from beneath the seat, she placed it deep inside her purse.

"Thank goodness for large purses," she sighed.

Once inside the motel room, she quickly locked the door and pulled the curtains. She had paid extra to obtain the efficiency room, complete with refrigerator, stove and coffee maker, and now, looking about the room, she was thankful she'd made this choice. It made the room a little homier. Besides, at this juncture, she preferred seclusion and this room provided her with all the amenities she would need to keep her sustained, along with a quick trip to the grocery store, which she decided could wait until tomorrow. There were complimentary packets of coffee with cream and sugar, although she had no need for the condiments provided since she loved her coffee black. She once told her staff that she wanted to taste the aroma, not hide it with cream and sugar.

Her intentions were to shower first but on impulse, she grabbed the remote to the TV instead. After a little channel surfing, she settled on a channel that looked halfway interesting and dove backwards onto the bed. Once her head hit the cushiony pillow, she was pulled into sleep. Even the heavy traffic of feet above her and the slamming of doors all around failed to disengage her from the deep slumber she so badly needed. But with the sleep came dreams, and naturally, the more tired she was, the more she dreamed and the more realistic they were. But it was too easy to give way to the sandman after hours of being a zombie.

In a strange twist, she somehow found herself in a dark closet, tightly clutching a .38 revolver, in fear of what was on the other side of the closet door. There was silence, where she would have preferred noise. At least with noise, she could detect some sort of movement and have some idea of what her options were. But it was the dreaded silence and the darkness that offered nothing but fear. She rarely perspired, not even working in the yard, unless temperatures were extreme, but as she clutched her knees to her chest with the revolver clinched tightly in her right hand, she began to sweat profusely. The sting of the salty drops making contact with her eyes forced her to blink several times as they nervously darted back and forth trying to catch a glimpse of the intruder. There is no greater fear than the unknown, so she'd heard, and for the first time, realized just how true that was.

Without warning, the doors flew open as Allie, in vain desperation, made an attempt to scream, but her throat suddenly became constricted so all that could be heard was a rasp relative to someone with laryngitis. Although she couldn't see his face, as the room was dimly lit, she could feel his pleasure at seeing her fear, her body cowering there before him.

Noting the gun clutched in her hand, he reached to pry it away but her finger was already squeezing the trigger. The intruder gasped, then faked a shot to his heart before Allie realized something was amiss. Her revolver was no longer a revolver but a child's water pistol.

The intruder seemed amused by his performance and her misfortune; his evil laughter resonating throughout the room. She was sure she had bought a .38 revolver at Ray's Gun Shop but it turned out to be a toy pistol. *Fine time to find out I've been duped*, she thought.

Enraged, she threw the plastic pistol down. The jerk who sold her the fake revolver would be hearing from her attorney. The more she fumed over the gun, the louder the intruder laughed, shadowing her fear with more anger.

"Shut up!" she yelled, finding her voice this time. The intruder with no face yielded to her command, but then produced a weapon of his own, a .38 revolver, just like the one she thought she'd bought, or maybe it was the one she'd bought.

"My gun!" she yelled. "You stole my gun!"

As she lunged forward, no concern that the barrel was aimed at her, an explosion of gunfire filled the air. In the bright lights of the ammo being unloaded, she could almost see his face and then . . .

Drenched in sweat and breathing rapidly, she discovered herself sitting up in bed, the TV remote still clutched in her hand, just like the pistol in her dream. Dropping the remote, she patted her chest and stomach, feeling for blood that wasn't there.

"Oh, thank goodness, just a bad dream," she sighed, her breathing slowly returning to normal. Glancing around the room, she searched for clues as to where she was, as she knew this wasn't her home in Regal Woods. Then, as quickly as she had fallen asleep, she found her memory returning upon awakening. The TV was still on but the romantic comedy playing before she had fallen asleep was now a classic black and white thriller. It appeared that Alfred Hitchcock had crept into her room and seeped into her mind as she slept. As she sat analyzing the dream, a series of loud bangs from the parking lot startled her, eerily similar to the ones that jolted her awake.

Leaping from the bed, she dashed to the window. Cautiously, she peeled back the curtain to get a visual of the source of the ruckus. Just outside her window, a Monte Carlo idled, smoke billowing from its ragged muffler. It backfired a couple more times before its owner, in an act of mercy, shut it off. Between the horror movie playing and the rusted metal on wheels with the car farts, she quickly interpreted her dream. But she also wondered if Gary played a part in this dream as well. At least roses were omitted from the dream. This thought invited another. What if she developed a phobia of roses? Silly as it sounded, she knew the realm of possibility was there. Her love of flowers, especially roses, had been tainted with Gary's obsessive behavior.

Closing the curtain, she retreated back to the bed, still tired but not anxious to return to sleep. She picked up the remote and turned off the TV. Still no closer to formulating a plan, she lay there idle, her thoughts drifting back to all she left behind. Her girls would see the note she left and in turn inform her brother. And she would call them as well, when the time was right. *Time,* she thought. She hadn't thought of the time. Glancing over at the clock beside the bed, she was surprised to see it was already past noon. She wondered, had it not been for the car backfiring, if she would still be snoozing away.

Although her senses were a bit dull, her stomach was seeking attention. She was reminded of her hunger, probably enhanced by the enticing aromas stemming from the diner next door. She felt ravished and ready for some solid food but not without a much-needed shower, which she regretted not taking before she lapsed into a coma. Fortunately, the diner stayed open until nine o'clock, according to the motel clerk, so she had several hours to toy with. After a quick meal, she would come back and relax with the TV and begin some kind of strategy. If this was going to be her vacation, she was determined to make the best of it, even if it meant spending it in this quaint motel located in a remote town named after, of all things, a possum.

"She's late."

"I know she's late, Frieda. I can tell time," Tess snapped.

"This is not like her," Amber added. "She would've called or something."

"You don't suppose . . ."

"Gary's involved?" Amber finished Frieda's question.

"C'mon you two. You're getting carried away with your imagination," Tess said, trying to sound reassuring. "Any minute, she's gonna come crashing through that door apologizing for oversleeping. And y'all are gonna feel stupid." The phone rang and Frieda quickly reached over to pick it up.

"A. J. Realty. Oh, hey Derrick!" A pause and look of concern spread across Frieda's face.

"No, she's not here. And you say she didn't make her Friday morning stop at your place? And you've called the house? No answer, huh?"

Tess and Amber now wore the same worried expression as Frieda as they strained to hear Derrick on the other end of the line.

"Well, OK. Let us know what you find out. Thanks, Derrick." Frieda hung up the phone, appearing slightly flushed.

"Derrick's going to her house," she said. "He's calling me back to let me know what he's found or hasn't found."

"I hate to say this, but if Derrick's worried, there's probable cause for concern," Tess said, almost catatonic-like. Frieda and Amber looked at each other, fear heightened at this new revelation. The phone rang again, prompting all of them to jump in unison.

"A. J. Realty." Amber answered this time. On the other end, a voice spoke slow and deliberate.

"I . . . want . . . to . . . speak . . . to . . . Allie."

"Gary? Is that you?"

"Allie . . . I want . . . to speak . . . to her."

"So would we, Gary. She's not here. We were hoping you could tell us where she's at." There was a long pause.

"Gary?"

"Mi-am-i," he whispered.

"Excuse me?"

"Mi-am-i," he repeated even softer, then hung up. Amber held the phone out like it had just goosed her.

"What is it, Amber?" Frieda asked, holding her hand to her mouth.

"When Derrick calls back, I need to talk to him, should either one of you answer the phone."

The police department was only minutes away from Derrick's place, so rather than calling them, he drove the short distance to their headquarters. He didn't hide his fears or frustrations in talking with the police.

"She was supposed to stop by this morning, as is her habit every Friday morning. She didn't show up at work and she's not at the house. Something's not right."

Lieutenant Mims struggled with words as he often did when a concerned relative confronted him with worried thoughts of not knowing where their loved ones were.

"Look, Mr. Jones. I empathize with you, I really do. But as I've already told you, we can't put out an APB on your sister, not yet. It hasn't been twenty-four hours. And who's to say she won't be back before then? What's the urgency? If she left on her own accord, which by all probability is the case, we can't be trouncing about the country, patrolling the highways and byways trying to track her down."

Derrick looked down, shaking his head. There was no doubt in Mims' mind that there was cause for concern. He'd observed many subjects before and could almost anticipate their every move. But Derrick's behavior was definitely a signal that something was amiss.

"Mr. . . . I mean Lieutenant Mims, I wouldn't be here if I didn't think something was seriously wrong." He raised his head and looked the officer square in the eyes, his own eyes glaring with tears. "My sister's in grave danger, do you understand that? There is a nut out there after her! I'm afraid he may find her . . . if he hasn't already."

Lieutenant Mims tapped the desk with his pencil for what seemed to be an irritating length of time. Finally, leaning forward, he spoke in a softer tone of voice.

"Maybe we better start from the beginning, Mr. Jones. Come on, let's go somewhere where we can talk in private."

Chapter 11

The aroma, combined with the nostalgia of Frank's Diner, created a déjà vu for Allie. She remembered the dime store she and her mother would frequent as a child, a child teetering on the edge of the "good ole days," for most stores had modernized with the times and had lost that down-home touch. But as far as the dime store, it had kept its original décor, attracting the youngest of generations. As soon as you walked in, you could smell the mouthwatering hotdogs and hamburgers and see the people lined all the way down the counter on stools. People were friendly and acted as if they knew you, even if they didn't. The memory of it warmed her within, thinking of holding her mother's hand, walking across those hardwood floors and being hoisted up onto one of the vacant stools. It didn't seem that long ago, but it was. She was twenty-nine; that had to be at least twenty years ago. *It's funny*, she thought, *how the senses can take you back down memory lane . . . a certain smell, a certain taste, a certain sight, a certain sound or even . . . a certain touch.*

This place, Frank's Diner, definitely had the sight and the smell of the dime store back in Washington, North Carolina. The sudden memory brought a smile to her face as she waltzed in and took a seat at the counter. *We'll see if the taste is the same*, she thought. Her original plan was to order her food and take it back to Room 109, but she quickly found the atmosphere irresistible. She was captivated by the coziness of the diner, the familiar backdrop of happier times. It didn't matter that she was a stranger here, and perhaps overdressed as well, with her designer dress suit on. She felt welcomed.

"What dya' have, sugar?"

A woman with a pinned up hairdo stood before her, then reached for a pencil behind her ear and a pad tucked in her apron. Her name was June, according to the tag pinned onto her smock.

"A cheeseburger, all the way, and some fries. Oh, and a large Coke."

"You're new here, aren't ya, sweetie? It ain't often we see fresh faces, especially with the fancy threads and all."

Oh, brother, here it comes, the inquest, Allie thought. But to her relief, the kind and seemingly middle-aged waitress just winked, then wiggled—reminding Allie of Flo from the sitcom *Alice*—her way toward the kitchen with her order. *Phew, that was close, thought I'd have to tell her to kiss my grits.*

Happy she'd decided to eat in, she scanned the restaurant from one end to the other. In the back area was the kitchen where the staff was scurrying around, performing designated duties. She glanced at the patrons sitting at the counter, who she easily concluded were regulars with the way they carried on with the diner crew. A couple of people just sat there reading the paper and drinking their coffee. All in all, everyone seemed to be doing their own thing, not minding that an alien came to sit among them. *Maybe this is just the diversion I needed,* she thought to herself. But part of her still missed what she'd left behind, even if it was only less than a day ago.

Subconsciously, she rested her forehead in her left palm with her elbow placed on the counter. She was still suffering from lack of sleep but not near close to what it was several hours earlier. She surmised that the tension she had endured on the road had finally subsided and along with a few hours of rest, she had become almost completely relaxed, nearly dozing off at the counter. But every time her eyes started to droop, she'd be startled back to reality by what sounded like the laugh of a kooka-burra, most commonly known as a laughing jackass. Although slightly annoying in her weary state of mind, it was ironically comforting, considering what she felt hours earlier. Just being among people laughing, carrying on with their normal lives, was a much-needed transition.

Releasing the embrace of the hand against her forehead, she massaged her eyes then gradually turned her attention to the cooking area of the diner.

"For Pete's sake, break up this hen party! We've got customers out there!" Frank yelled.

Izzy rolled her eyes as her high-strung boss gently shoved the other two women back in the direction of their stations.

"You need to lighten up, Frank. Let go a little bit, let your hair down. Oops, sorry, ain't got none." She made sure he knew she wasn't intimidated by his orders, even gawking at his balding head.

"I'm serious, Izzy. I've had just about enough of this tomfoolery. I'm trying to run a business. . . ." Izzy ignored him as she started taking up the fries and then carefully placing them in the small paper sacks, counting the fries in pairs.

"Twelve, fourteen, sixteen . . ."

"Izzy, stop that! That's another thing. You have got to stop counting the fries. We don't have time for whatever that compulsion is of yours. You just need to take a scoop full and insert it into each bag. You don't count them. Nobody cares how many freaking fries are in their bag as long as it's full. Do you understand?"

"Dag blast it," she mumbled. "I've got to start all over again. Don't talk while I'm counting."

Emptying the fries back into the fry basket, she again meticulously began her ritual of sorting just the right amount of fries into the small paper sacks, this time counting off in fours. In between counts and Frank's nonstop ranting, she couldn't help from sneaking a peep at the young lady seated at the counter. She looked familiar, as if she'd just passed her on the street. But that didn't seem to be it. And then she remembered, the second they locked gazes. It was the unmistakable eyes, with saddlebags attached—less prominent now, perhaps due to a little sleep—that told her it had to be the idiot who narrowly missed her beloved Barney, causing it to stall. And for a second, she thought the maniac driver sensed who she was as well, when the stares were returned.

"Izzy!" Frank yelled. "Are you listening to me?"

It might as well have been filet mignon or lobster. For all Allie knew, it was the best burger and fries she'd had in her mouth in a very long time. The Coke even tasted better than she remembered. She wondered if it was a result of going without food for so many hours or perhaps it was the atmosphere, just like the good ole dime store where she grew up.

Careful not to appear famished, she ate with as much dignity as she could muster. Attracting attention was the last thing she needed right now. But somehow, she couldn't shake the eerie feeling that someone was watching her with every bite she took.

I'm just being paranoid, she kept telling herself. But when she stole a glance to the kitchen area, she very quickly eliminated her theory of paranoia. The laughing hyena with dark hair and piercing dark eyes, and coincidently, no longer laughing, wasn't just staring at her; she was staring straight through her. It was almost a sinister gaze. She didn't smile but kept that glued on look as if trying to read her mind.

"Izzy!"

Izzy broke away from her trance at Frank's second and louder command.

"Didn't I specifically tell you to stop counting the French fries? Do you see that crowd out there? Now here is what you do. You grab a scoop full of fries," he said, imitating a scoop in his right hand, "and then you place it in the sack, then you do the same with the next, then the next and so on. Got it?"

"There's gotta be thirty-two fries in each sack, Frank. For as long as I can remember, I put exactly thirty-two fries in each sack, no more, no less. You don't want somebody complaining cause I cheated them out of some french fries now, do ya?"

"No, there don't gotta be thirty-two fries per sack. I don't ever recalling anyone complaining because they didn't get thirty-two fries. And who, for Pete's sake, counts their fries before eating them? No one complains because no one cares. As long as you fill the little fry sack up, everyone's happy, especially me."

Izzy stared down at her scoop. *If only it were that simple*, she thought. At least Sam understood when he owned the diner, not that she expected the same of Frank, but she missed Sam's compassion and understanding and his willingness to overlook any strange obsession she had, instead praising her on all her positive attributes. She suddenly wondered why she was even there anymore, now that Sam was gone. She even speculated that Frank may have thought he had her over a barrel, when in actuality, it was the other way around.

Feeling a surge of anger, Izzy shoved the scoop at him, almost knocking him off balance, then shoved past him toward the dining area.

"Where do you think you're going?" he asked.

"I'm outta here. You handle the freaking fries!"

Frank, still clutching a greasy scoop to his chest, became eerily aware of the menacing eyes all around watching him. He knew his role had somehow placed him as the villain as soon as Izzy walked out. He was not only the villain, but the mean-spirited boss, the wolf among sheep and now, the butt of ridicule. Izzy had been a fixture at the diner for almost as long as the diner itself. She was Sam's first and longest-lasting employee, although rumor had it she didn't need the income. It was just a pastime, a hobby she enjoyed because it meant mingling with the towns-folk.

And the townsfolk were equally fond of her. Her combination of warmth, hospitality, wit and fire overrode any hidden flaws or peculiarities. In Sam's eyes, Izzy *was* the diner. Everyone who met her was enthralled with her, on one level or another, except, of course, for Frank. He didn't dislike her, but he wasn't totally enamored with her personality, considering the fact that it conflicted with his own. But even more than that, he harbored a bit of jealousy, something he'd never admit to Izzy or anyone else. She was getting all the attention, all the praise, all the glory, when it was his diner.

But despite his negative feelings when it came to Izzy, he was forced to face the awful reality of what it would be like with her gone, this icon of his diner no longer a part of his staff.

Allie was savoring the last of her burger and fries while an irate Izzy stormed into the dining area, narrowly missing the waitress that served Allie.

"Izzy, where ya going?" June asked, concerned for her friend.

Ignoring the confused waitress, Izzy continued on until she stood near the counter, facing Allie.

"I know who you are! You killed my Barney!"

Stunned and slightly amused, Allie almost choked on the last bite of her burger.

"Excuse me? I did what to your what?"

"You were driving out there like a maniac this morning, cutting me off and slamming on breaks, causing my Beetle to choke off! And now, now, he's in the shop! Ain't no telling what that's gonna cost me...."

"Whoa, whoa, there, hold your horses, missy," Allie interrupted. She wondered just how crazy this woman was, referring to her vehicle as if it was human. "I'm sorry about your car and all and I'm sorry if I did that to you. But don't blame me if you got a lousy means of transportation. Sounds like it needs to be put out of its misery, if you ask me."

Faint nearby giggles could be detected as an older man at the counter, apparently eavesdropping, came to Allie's defense.

"I've been trying to tell her that for years."

"Oh, shut up, Henry! You got a lot of room to talk with that beat up old jalopy of yours!"

The old man threw up his hands and went back to eating.

"Again, I'm sorry. Really. It wasn't intentional," Allie said, recalling her sudden maneuver around the struggling vehicle. "I was tired and not thinking. And . . . I'm willing to assist you with your car if you deem it appropriate." *Boy, I must be really tired*, she thought, *if I'm offering to help this lunatic with her "Barney" and I didn't even touch it.* "I mean, if you need a lift anywhere, I'll be glad to take you. I was just fixing to leave."

Although Allie did feel a tinge of guilt for what happened, her motivation to try and be the good Samaritan had less to do with that and more with avoiding further confrontation as more eyes turned their attention to the fiasco developing. Izzy eyed her curiously at first, then smiled.

"Well, now, Ms. . . ." Izzy waited for her to give her a name as she surveyed her from head to toe, while Allie mentally searched for a name to give her other than her own.

"Jenny."

"Jenny, huh. Well, well. Funny, I'd pegged you for a Sally. Mustang Sally."

Allie, her mind still a fog from the long drive, appeared confused. At the same time, it had just dawned on her that she'd registered under her real name at the motel, something she hadn't meant to do. As she flushed with fear and anxiety realizing her mistake, Izzy ranted on, oblivious to her concern.

"You know. Mustang Sally, better slow your Mustang down . . . Wilson Pickett? Oh, never mind, you're probably too young to remember anyhow. Just thought the name appropriate." Izzy paused long enough to realize that some of her agitation was probably unjustified as she had just been in a squabble with Frank and might have been taking it out on her. "Anyway, I'm Isabelle Riley. Folks call me Izzy, for short. And yes, I actually could use a lift, if you don't mind. I just live a hop, skip and a jump down the road there . . . well, on that stretch of road we first became acquainted. Don't mean to put you out or whatever, but yeah, a ride would be good."

Allie, despite her guarded demeanor, was impressed with Izzy's sudden sense of charm and delighted at the opportunity to make amends.

"I'd be more than happy to give you a ride. Just let me take care of my tab here and we'll be on the way."

Izzy held up a hand. "No, allow me. Hey, June! This little lady here, her tab's on me!"

June smiled, shook her head and scribbled something on her pad. Izzy sighed and offered a partial smile as she once again took Allie in from top to bottom. *Somewhere inside that skinny, prim and proper chick is a story*, she thought, *and perhaps I can be the one to unearth it.*

"Well, I'm ready if you are," Allie said.

Izzy leaned over and whispered loudly. "You ain't gonna drive crazy, are ya?"

"Probably," Allie whispered back, but was a touch offended by the woman dressed as a hippie. *At least she doesn't talk hippie.*

"Peace!" Izzy bellowed out as she left with Allie.

I take that back, Allie thought.

Henry and June watched them exit the diner, smiling.

"That girl's in for a treat," remarked Henry.

"Ah, finish your grub, Henry. I gotta go charm Frank into hiring Izzy back or find another 'Izzy' to replace her, and you know there ain't another one like her out there."

"Izzy's quit?" Henry asked. June nodded her head toward the kitchen where Frank was hoisting a fry basket out of the fryer.

"When have you ever seen Frank with a fry basket in his hands? She's quit, all right. Uh-hum."

Chapter 12

Derrick seemed a million miles away when Lieutenant Mims returned to the more comfortable and private room of the police station. He sat a cup of hot steaming coffee down in front of him but Derrick didn't acknowledge it or even flinch when Mims grabbed a chair near the wall and dragged it up to the table, with it screeching horribly as he did.

"Derrick," he said softly, "I need to know everything, as much as you can possibly tell me. I need to know who this nut is you're talking about and why you think he's involved with your sister's disappearance. OK?"

Derrick slowly turned his head and eyed Lieutenant Mims with uncertainty. He wondered if he was just wasting his time here when he should have been out looking for Allie himself. At the moment, all he could feel was the impulse to drive and keep driving until he found her. But drive where? Caught between the impulse to run and find her and the slow mundane task of police work, he felt helpless. His eyes told Lieutenant Mims everything.

"Derrick, I know you're scared and worried for the safety of your sister. But trust me, I've been in this business long enough to know that seconds can quickly turn into minutes, and minutes into hours if you don't have something to go on. And the more detail, the better. So take a deep breath, and tell me what you know. Everything."

Derrick looked down at the floor in an effort to hide his face. He was slightly embarrassed at being unable to restrain the tears now welling up in his eyes. He had made several attempts to speak and choked up each time. Finally, after the lieutenant handed him a glass of water, which he eagerly drank, he began to regain his composure. Clearing his throat, he looked up, aware Lieutenant Mims was staring at his glassy red eyes. Nonetheless, he found his voice again and began to talk.

"Allie first met Gary when she took her car in for service at Tim's garage. But they didn't officially get to know each other until he came by her real estate office on the pretense of buying a house. That's when he asked her out. But . . . it ended shortly after that. She was furious because he had deceived her. He didn't want to buy a house after all. But apparently, in that short period, Gary had fallen right hard for her because he would do things like call and not leave a message or send her flowers and gifts. It made her very uncomfortable and a little bit frightened.

"She decided it was time to have a talk with him but she had lost his phone number and didn't know where he lived. She contacted Tim to get his address off the employment form he presumably filled out. As fate would have it, Tim never got around to filling out any forms. I think he wanted to make sure he was going to work out before he went through the trouble of filling out any paperwork and then I guess he simply forgot all about it—"

Lieutenant Mims interrupted. "When's the last time you talked to Allie?"

"Tuesday morning. Anyway, we have a standing Friday ritual where she would drop by and have coffee with me before going to work. When she didn't come by this Friday, I knew something was wrong. I called her work and talked to Frieda and she said she hadn't showed up. That's when I really got worried. So I decided to go to her house. Her car wasn't there but I have a key to her back door.

"Upon reaching the deck, the first thing I noticed was the flowers, a dozen red roses, and a teddy bear with a card attached. It said 'I love you.' After searching through the house and coming up empty, I stopped by Tim's but he hadn't seen Gary since he was fired, nor Allie since that day she went by to get his address. I then went back home and called the realty. Amber answered that time. They said she still hadn't showed up but they got a surprise call from Gary. He was asking to speak to Allie, which I think was a cover up. I think he knows where she's at, maybe even holding her hostage—"

"OK," Mims interrupted again, raising a hand. "All you've told me is circumstantial stuff. There's no real proof he's done anything wrong. I can't go and arrest someone without some solid evidence. I can, however, have a talk with this guy, providing I can find him. And then, after twenty-four hours, if she doesn't show up, we'll put out an APB on her. Meanwhile, do me a favor. Go home. We'll take it from here. We will do everything within our power to resolve this. I promise."

Derrick appeared defeated rather than grateful as he struggled with what to say. Unable to find the words, he stood up and moved the chair to one side. He then sighed as he turned his back to the lieutenant and stood motionless with his hands on his hips. The lieutenant sensed he had more on his mind than he was telling. He'd sat down with many others at the same table and had seen some of the same language Derrick was displaying, but as always, he wanted to hear what the subject wanted to get off his chest. Mims leaned back in his chair, his hands clasped together to form a "V" shape, and waited. Suddenly, as expected, Derrick turned around.

"Miami!" he blurted out.

"Excuse me?"

"Something about Miami. When I called the realty back, Amber said he mentioned Miami twice, then hung up. Allie's never been to Florida, much less Miami. Why would he mention Miami?"

Detective Mims raised his eyebrows.

Chapter 13

"Nice set of wheels. I had a Mustang once," Izzy said, almost dream-like. "They evolved quite a lot over the years but you really can't compare today with what they had back then. You can't beat the original Mustang. They're hard to find, too, especially in mint condition, like yours."

Allie nodded in agreement, pretending to be interested. Her thoughts still lingered with the night before. While she tried to sort through the chain of events that got her here, Izzy rambled on and on and the more she talked, the more irritated Allie became. She chatted nonstop with her from the moment they left the diner and it was becoming increasingly difficult to hold what was left of her attention span.

Izzy, on the other hand, had her own hidden agenda. Her curiosity peaked with every moment she spent around Allie. On the surface, Izzy contemplated, she was successful, financially secure, and possessed well-defined mannerisms. Although a tad bit on the prissy side, she didn't detect any sort of snobbiness or arrogance about her. But Izzy couldn't resist testing her new companion.

"Ya mind stopping at the thrift store up here? I wanna see if they got some good baking pans."

"Ah, yeah, sure. Why not, we can do that," Allie consented, suddenly feeling compassion for Izzy. *Poor woman,* she thought, *probably can't afford to buy new pans, has to buy them used.*

"They have great stuff here. You wouldn't believe the stuff I got for near nothing. Bought a toaster oven here for five bucks recently. Bet it cost at least thirty brand new."

"Wow!" Allie kept her pretense of being interested, even astonished, but inwardly, she thought it would be nice to surprise Izzy with a new set of baking pans. Allie had never been to a thrift store, never even a yard sale. The thought of buying something someone else had used, even dirt cheap, repulsed her. But as she and Izzy cruised the several aisles of goods on display, she slowly changed her mind. Many of the items appeared new or barely used. She stopped to examine the assortment of irons on one shelf.

"I could use an iron," she commented, picking each one up and checking for scorch patterns underneath.

"And they all seem to be in good shape," Izzy added.

"Can't beat the price on them either," Allie said, smiling, grateful Izzy had suggested they stop here. She finally decided on one that seemed to be in almost perfect condition. It had the automatic shut off feature, which she really liked. Not even her old iron had that and she paid eight or nine times the price.

"Three dollars, I think I can afford that," she laughed.

"Oh, and there are the baking pans further down," Izzy beamed. She found the perfect baking pans with no scratches, no baked-on stains and they were only two dollars for a set of three.

"How do they do it?" Allie asked, peeking at the price tag on Izzy's pans. "How can they afford to sell stuff so cheap?"

"It's all donated. Haven't you ever been to a thrift store?"

"No," Allie admitted, with a hint of resentment in her voice. Izzy laughed, hyena style, then sized her up and down, just like back at the diner.

"Well, of course not. What was I thinking?"

"I just mean I never thought about it before. . . ."

"You don't have to explain. I was once a rookie. Had a phobia about touching other people's stuff, not knowing its background. You take that there iron you're holding. Someone could've used that iron to press a pair of dirty drawers."

Izzy watched Allie's disgusted expression as she looked down at her prized iron and let the hyena loose again.

"Bad example, sorry. I really don't think that way anymore."

While Izzy and Allie continued to cruise the remaining aisle, they couldn't help but overhear the conversation going on in the next aisle over. Allie grew increasingly uncomfortable as she could hear the man berating the woman, obviously his wife. But Izzy seemed to be tuned out as she continued to examine the variety of items on the shelves.

"You'll do as I tell you," Allie heard him say.

"Not in here, Bob. People can hear us," she whispered back to him.

"You think I care who hears us? It's no one else's business what I say to you," he said, speaking even louder. "When I order you to do something, it's not to be questioned or debated! You got that?" The woman cowered and tried to hide her face as her bully husband continued to rant on. "You can't even dress right when we go out. Look at you!"

"Let's go," Allie whispered to Izzy. "I can't stand listening to that jerk anymore."

"OK. You head on up to the counter and I'll meet you there shortly."

"Where you going?"

"I forgot something."

Allie stood in the short line clutching her iron. After a few glances back, she spotted Izzy coming up the aisle with an arm load of stuff, including a golf club. One customer stood between her and Allie. Curious about the club, she reached around the elderly patron and tapped Izzy's arm.

"What's with the golf club?"

"It was a good buy," was all Izzy said. Allie concluded that if the light bulb overhead was a good buy, she'd buy that.

Allie saw the bully and his petrified wife approaching the checkout, getting in line behind Izzy. She quickly turned back toward the counter, suddenly feeling a nervous twinge in the pit of her stomach. She wished the cashier would pick up some speed.

"Hey, Mary, this'd look good on you." He had picked up a Halloween mask and placed it over her face, laughing loudly and harshly. Allie stole a glance at Izzy but she still saw no change in her expression.

At last, after a few terrifying long minutes, they both were checked out and headed toward the door. Allie sighed a deep breath of relief as Izzy calmly placed their newfound treasures in the backseat of the car. As Allie opened the door on her side and slid in behind the wheel, she noticed Izzy moving at a slower pace, obviously in no hurry. She organized the backseat, and appearing displeased, reorganized it again with unusual intensity. She seemed to be stalling as she looked up and peered around the parking lot, clinging to her golf club.

"Hey, what are you looking for?"

"Just a second," she said, not looking at Allie.

Soon, the bully and his wife retreated from the thrift store, bearing bags of assorted goodies. They had lingered around inside after checking out. The bully had found some other items he wanted to taunt his wife with. Izzy eyed them closely as his voice got louder and his wife seemed to be on the verge of tears. Their vehicle, a beat up Dodge Ram, was conveniently parked close to Allie's car. When Allie realized how close they were, she pleaded with Izzy to get in the car.

"C'mon Izzy, let's go!"

But Izzy ignored Allie's pleas and smiled as the odd couple passed by her to put their bags in the rear of the truck. Once Mary was safely on the other side of the truck and Bob was just inches from where she stood, Izzy seized the moment. Just as Bob was stepping up to get in his ragged set of wheels, Izzy took one quick backward swing with her golf club, perfectly striking her target.

"Fore!" she yelled. The club caught Bob directly in the groin, precisely between the legs, crunching the "family jewels." He instantly hit the ground, writhing in pain, while Mary gasped in confusion. One lady, catching a free view from inside the store, dropped her bag of goodies and began clapping, as she had also witnessed his nasty behavior inside the store.

Bob, reduced to a wad of agony in a fetal position, managed to display his contempt for Izzy and her lack of knowledge on golf.

"You're a dead hippie!" he yelled, his voice an octave higher. Even the bully could see through his pain Izzy's beatnik attire. "I'll teach you some golf!"

Bob grasped for the club but Izzy was quick on her feet as she threw the club in the backseat of the car and she jumped in the front.

"Now we can go!" she shouted, slamming the door. Allie quickly thrust the gear into reverse and as she did, Izzy gave the bully's wife a subtle wink, letting her know she was her friend. Bob, too incapacitated to notice the exchange, lay whimpering like a wounded puppy.

Allie wasted no time hitting the highway, running over a curb as she did. Once she felt the safety of the distance between them and the bully, she glanced over at Izzy, then back at the road.

"You are nuts! You know that? You trying to get us killed?"

"I just did what that woman wished she could've done. Did ya catch that swing? Made me wish I had bought that mallet instead of the golf club. That would've packed even more punch." Izzy laughed, letting the hyena out of the cage, then stopped when she realized her friend was not amused.

"Relax, they don't know us. I couldn't just NOT do something."

"You hit him in the crouch with a golf club! You don't think he's not going to remember that if he ever sees us again? How much did you pay for the club anyhow?"

"Five dollars and worth every cent of it," Izzy said, laughing again, then quickly clearing her throat, seeing that Allie still failed to see the humor.

"You ain't worried you'll run into him again at the thrift store, or anywhere else for that manner?"

"Nope."

"Why not?"

"I know everybody in this town. Ain't never seen them before. Besides, I saw the license plate. They're from out of state. I seriously doubt he'll be sticking around just to get revenge on me."

Allie let out a sigh, then finally started laughing.

"Glad to see you do have a sense of humor," Izzy said.

"I was just thinking about your golf swing. I'm no expert on golf, but I think you're supposed to yell 'fore' as a warning, not as an afterthought."

"Well . . . he got what he deserved. That's what counts. I hope it swells to the size of a melon . . . oh, turn down that road up there to the right," she said, pointing to the road where they first came in contact with each other.

"Oh yeah, I remember this road," she said, smiling.

"You should," Izzy teased.

Allie pictured in her head a dilapidated old house, screens hanging out of window frames, paint peeling, maybe an outhouse out back. She didn't see how Izzy could afford anything much nicer, working at a diner and shopping at thrift stores and still wearing clothes from the sixties or seventies.

"You go down about three miles and you'll see my house on the left," Izzy instructed.

Allie started to feel déjà vu once she made the turn. This was the road she traveled in the early daylight hours, the road she remembered the most. She even remembered pieces of detailed scenery, but it was only when she passed the three-mile mark and saw the house with the wraparound porch that she recalled how in awe she had been. Even through weary eyes in those early morning hours, she was captivated by this beautiful house with the white picket fence and wraparound porch.

"Slow down, turn up here," Izzy told her.

Allie gasped. "You mean . . . this house, this beautiful house with the picket fence and wraparound porch is yours?"

"Well, yeah. It ain't much but yeah, this is the ole crib. This is where I play and sleep."

"Ain't much? It's incredible!" Allie squealed as they eased up the pathway to the two-story white house. "This is really your home?" Allie asked again in disbelief.

"Better be. I've been paying enough taxes on it."

"I remember passing this house before ending up in Possum Heights. You just don't see these houses anymore, especially in this good condition. They're almost obsolete. It kinda brings back memories."

"Watch out for the mud—" The left front tire dipped into an unmarked hole and out again, sloshing Allie's bottle of water all over her lap "—puddle," Izzy finished.

"Sorry." Allie made a mental note to check her front end later.

Once parked in Izzy's front yard, she marveled at the carefully arranged garden and neatly pruned trees and the fragrance of the magnolia trees in full bloom. She wondered how someone could afford such a beautiful house with an immaculate yard, just working at a diner.

"C'mon in. I'll give you the five cent tour," Izzy said, already out of the car before Allie could answer. "It might be a little messy. I had to work the double shift last weekend and, therefore, haven't had much time to clean like I wanted."

Allie followed her up the steps, embracing all there was to see on the porch as Izzy unlocked the front door. Izzy stepped aside, hinting at her to enter first. Allie moved toward the door, unaware her mouth was agape as she took in the view of the immaculate hardwood floors and not a speck of dust or dirt anywhere. She looked at Izzy as if reading her mind and reached down to remove her shoes. Izzy smiled approvingly and placed her hand on her shoulder.

"You coming in, honey? You're letting out all my flies."

Izzy closed the door behind them, removing her own shoes, revealing her bare feet and painted toes. Allie watched her as she picked up one foot and wiped it, then did the same with other.

"Can't stand grits between my toes," she said, noticing Allie's gaze.

"Oh. I rarely eat grits. Don't have time to cook breakfast," Allie said, taking Izzy literally.

"Ain't talking about grits out of the box, honey. Talking about dirt."

"Dirt?" Allie, slightly embarrassed but more surprised, thought maybe she heard Izzy wrong. It was the first thing she'd noticed when the door was open, the spotless condition of the floors. Izzy seemed to know her thoughts.

"You may not be able to see it, but you can feel it. C'mon, I'll show you around," she said, motioning for Allie to follow her. The large foyer was simply arranged with wicker chairs and tables. An artificial floral arrangement adorned a corner table. Trailing Izzy down the hallway, they veered to the right and to the entrance of a large, brightly colored kitchen. The walls were wallpapered in garden-themed décor. A butcher-block island was placed in the middle with pots and pans dangling above. Adjoining the kitchen was the formal dining room, separated by two paned-glass doors. A large mahogany dining table adorned the center of the room with eight chairs proportionately placed around it.

"This room doesn't see much action. I reserve it for special occasions," Izzy said, as if pondering an event in her past. "I'll show you where I dine."

At the end of the hallway and down two short steps, Izzy proudly displayed her favorite room in the house, the den, done in pine knot paneling. There, in the corner, was her television console and opposite that, her recliner. A sectional sofa graced another side and corner of the den. Old portraits, perhaps of relatives, adorned the walls and a "whatnot" table showcased a variety of ceramic figurines.

"What's that?" Allie asked, pointing to the ceiling where tarp covered a square hole.

"Oh, I'm having a fireplace installed. I thought it would add ambience to the room, an aura of comfort and relaxation. Plus, I have a surplus of wood out there in the barn and nothing to burn it in right now. I also got a great deal on some cheap labor. Catch is, they can only do it in between jobs, which means there ain't no telling when it'll be finished."

"I see. And what's upstairs?"

"Mostly bedrooms, but I sleep in one of the downstairs bedrooms." Izzy suddenly grasped her stomach, feeling it rumble. "I'm famished. Guess that mention of grits earlier got my stomach churning a little. Can I interest you in a fried grit sandwich?"

Allie grimaced, thinking at first she was joking, then realized she was totally serious.

"No, thank you."

"Well, you got to at least try a little of my dessert."

Afraid to ask what it was, Allie quickly had her mind put at ease.

"It's homemade apple pie. Just let me get the grits agoin' and I'll slice you a piece a pie. Got some grits left over in the fridge. Just need to put 'em in a pan and sauté 'em a bit."

Allie followed Izzy to the kitchen, sure she had to be teasing her. Who ever heard of a fried grit sandwich?

She complimented her on the breakfast nook and the farmhouse table and chairs in front of it. Izzy nodded her toward the table while she waltzed over toward the refrigerator. Humming cheerfully, she took out a bowl then emptied the contents into a pan once dangling above the island.

She's not joking, Allie thought. *She's really making a fried grit sandwich.*

"So, Ms. Jenny, got any youngins?" Izzy asked, seating herself opposite her. For a moment, Allie forgot she had given her a fictitious name, then laughed, hiding her deceit.

"Usually, people start by asking, 'Are you married?'"

"Right," Izzy laughed, mildly for a change. "But I know you're not married," she said, pointing to her hand. "Ain't no wedding band, not even a sign of ever wearing one."

Allie self-consciously covered her hand, at the same time knowing it was too late for that.

"You're very observant. And no, I don't have any rug rats. Do you?"

"Not unless you count my four-leggers, Claude, Clyde, Cecil, Caesar, Clare, Clifton, Cleo and Chloe. It's easier to remember their names if they all start with the same letter. They're my children to me. Coincidently, they're all tuxedo cats as well." Izzy got up to tend to the grits.

"Tuxedo cats? What's that?"

"Black and white, they are all black and white."

Sounds like a bunch of skunks to me, Allie thought.

"You've got to have a ride to the diner until you get your car fixed, don't you?" Allie asked, suddenly remembering Izzy's ride was in the shop.

"Well, about that. I guess you didn't hear the spat going on in the kitchen there at the diner. I quit."

"What? Please don't tell me I had something to do with that!"

"No," Izzy chuckled. "Let's just say it was a conflict of interest between me and Frank, the idiot owner. Ah, grits are about done. Sure you don't wanna try it?"

Allie shook her head and flinched as she watched Izzy spread the gritty brown mixture onto a slice of bread.

"Used to take the grits straight out of the pot and spread it onto the bread, but found out when it's fried, it ain't so mushy."

This chick has a serious crush on grits, Allie thought.

Before sitting back down, Izzy grabbed the apple pie from the refrigerator and cut a modest slice for Allie, setting the aromatic dish before her. Izzy quietly took in Allie's reaction as she picked up the fork, ready to sample the mouthwatering treat.

"Boy, this looks delicious!" she said, digging in with the fork. Upon bringing it to her mouth, she let the aroma seep into her nostrils before tantalizing her taste buds. "Mmmm, good," she said through a mouthful of pie.

"Thank you," Izzy said, pleased she could share her prized apple pie.

Allie was relishing the last of the pie when she noticed the beautiful plate beneath. Her own dishes paled in comparison, plain and simple. But Izzy's was colorful and bright, a cheerful painting of flowers engraved into the plate.

"Such a beautiful plate! I love the design! And what a shine!"

"Well now, I can't take all the credit for that. Caesar cleaned it this morning . . . got a right nice scouring pad on that tongue of his. Cat saved me a fortune on Brillo Pads."

Allie stared at the piece of pie she was about to put in her mouth, then put it back down. *Please tell me you're joking*, she thought. *Please tell me I didn't just eat pie off a plate cleaned by the tongue of a cat.* She waited for Izzy to let out that hyena laugh and remark that she was just joking but instead, she called out to her cat.

"Cae-sar! Where are you, my handsome little boy? Come here, you little darling. Oh, there he is. Come here, my precious baby boy."

Trotting his way toward Izzy, his tail high in the air, Caesar made a graceful leap into her lap and began what she assumed to be the ritual of welcoming his "human" home. Shortly after his entrance, several more of Izzy's "fur balls" followed, tails high in the air, purring and meowing. At the moment, though, Izzy was preoccupied with the "Brillo Pad" cat, Caesar.

"You can't have my fried grit sandwich, no you can't, my sweet little boy." Izzy cooed at him like he was a baby, rubbing her head against his, a meeting of the minds, Allie supposed. She could still feel and taste some remnants of the pie in her mouth. She decided to take this opportunity, while Izzy was busy pampering Caesar, to spit out what she could of the pie into a napkin.

"Just hold on, boy. Momma'll get your din-din in just a sec." Embracing him like a baby, she looked up at Allie. "Say hello to Caesar."

Allie faked an interest in the introduction while Caesar didn't bother to hide his irritation. He jumped from Izzy's arms and ran back down the hallway.

"So, what's your story, Jen? May I call you Jen?"

Totally caught off guard, Allie stared at her, unsure of what to say, but Izzy persisted.

"What landed you here in the middle of nowhere and where you headed?"

Allie sat stone-faced, feeling her cheeks flush. She was amazed at how Izzy could change channels, so to speak, so abruptly, from being absorbed in cat chat to being Barbara Walters doing an interview. Fortunately, Izzy sensed her discomfort and didn't give her a chance to answer.

"How about some more pie?"

"No, no," she said, quickly shaking her head. "I can't, but . . . thank you. It was good." *Or at least it was before I discovered her dishwasher.* It made her wonder how many other people were victims of Caesar's tongue. "You gonna be OK without your car until they can get it fixed?" Allied asked, remembering again that her car was at Ollie's.

"Oh yeah. I have a jeep in the garage. I mostly drive Barney, though. He's great on gas. I suppose, in an odd sort of way, it's lucky you pulled out in front of me, stalling my car."

"How's that?" Allie asked, surprised.

"John, the tow driver, said I had an oil leak. So maybe they can fix that, too, while he's got 'em."

"That's good. I mean, not that you had a leak, but that they caught it. I guess things really do happen for a reason." Allie reflected on what she had just said. Although it was unclear how she ended up here in this particular town, she felt this, too, happened for a reason.

After a brief pause, Allie glanced down at her watch and excused herself. "Well, guess I better get back. Thank you for the pie. It was delicious."

"You're welcome, kiddo. Thanks for the lift."

Izzy saw her new friend to the door and watched her bounce down the path in her shiny red convertible. As soon as she disappeared from view, she shut the door and latched it, unlatched it, latched it, unlatched it, then finally, latched it for a third time. Satisfied it was latched and secured, she mumbled to herself while taking the dirty dishes to the sink.

"Got to stop doing that, it's starting to drive me crazy," she said, then smiled, remembering Allie's expression when she talked of Caesar's dishwashing talent. "Maybe I shouldn't have kidded her about Caesar cleaning the plate."

Interesting character, Allie pondered on the way back to the motel. *A little on the oddball side, though.* It puzzled her how someone who worked at a diner could afford such a beautiful place, so immaculate and grand. Izzy must have been getting some pretty big tips, she decided. Then she sadly remembered that she no longer worked there and wondered how she would be able to maintain her home, let alone feed eight cats. All of a sudden, her own situation seemed so trivial. At least she had the option of going back to Regal Woods to her realty anytime she wanted, once she figured out the route back. But what would Izzy do now that she was unemployed? There couldn't be but so many jobs in Possum Heights. She began to feel a growing sense of compassion for Izzy.

Back at the motel, she scrambled in her purse for the map she'd bought at the gas station. Carefully unfolding it, she laid it flat out on the bed and tried to retrace her drive from Regal Woods to Possum Heights.

"If Possum Heights actually exists on the map," she said, "I'll eat it." But there it was, almost as soon as she scanned the eastern part of North Carolina. "Well, I'll be. Not only does it exist, it doesn't seem to be that far from Regal Woods!"

It then occurred to her that she'd been driving in circles only to end up less than three hours south in a town she'd never heard of. It was comforting to know she wasn't lost. At least now she had some idea of where she was and the options that surrounded her as far as other towns. Too exhausted to pursue other possibilities, she refolded the map, tucked it inside her purse, then changed into her night clothes. Crawling in between the sheets, she felt a little more back to normal. Hopefully, with a good night's rest, she could face tomorrow with a whole new meaning and perhaps get a better understanding of where she was going, if anywhere at all. She was a stranger in a strange town but in a sense, it was much friendlier than where she came from, not that Regal Woods wasn't friendly. But in Possum Heights, it was like taking a few steps back in time to where hospitality was in abundance. She could feel it everywhere she went.

Reaching over to the nightstand, she switched off the lamp, then closed her eyes, knowing sleep would come easy that night.

"A new day, a new dawn," she whispered, remembering the words of Nina Simone. With that, she was once again caught up in the rapture of the sandman.

Chapter 14

Twitching from side to side, Izzy lay dangling between consciousness and unconsciousness. It felt good to sleep in late on Saturday morning, but this morning the aches and pains in her joints kept her teetering on the edge of getting up or snoozing some more. The former finally gave in as she moaned to the ceiling. To make it worse, she was weighted down by one of her "fur balls."

"Oh, oh, oh, oh, Cecil, please get off of me," she groaned.

It took a few turns of rocking from side to side before the agitated feline "paperweight" took the hint. He jumped to the floor, displaying his contempt with a quick meow and a silent pass of gas.

"Oh, good one, Cecil. That, I could've done without."

She still struggled with getting out of bed even after Cecil had relented his hold on her. The occasional flare-ups from her arthritis, although mild, made it a little more challenging to get out of bed, but it was nothing a little Tylenol couldn't remedy. And sometimes, she used ointments as well. The combination always seemed to work.

"Oh great," she mumbled. "The one time I left the Tylenol in the bathroom." She remembered to bring water to bed with her last night, a habit for as long as she could remember, but she'd forgotten her pain pills. "I go to bed with Arthur and wake up with Ben Gay," she continued to mutter on the way to the bathroom. As she passed by the window, grunting, she took notice of the lawn, how it desperately needed a "haircut." Glancing back at the clock, she realized it was only six o'clock.

"Oh, what the heck. I haven't gotten on Richard's nerves lately," she said, thinking of her neighbor. "Time to get him up anyway." She considered it her life's mission to taunt him simply because she knew it aggravated him. But everyone who knew Izzy and Richard knew better. Izzy was the only one who could bring out the good— and sometimes the bad—in Richard. She had the means, the will and the guts.

And she enjoyed it.

After downing a couple of Tylenols, she scuffled down the hallway toward the kitchen, eight tails keeping pace with her.

"One of y'all needs to go out and get a job. Your groceries are starting to cost more than mine," she grunted while the cats, oblivious to what she was saying, strutted along side her. She put four cans down and refilled their dry food bowls.

"That oughta satisfy y'all for the next couple of hours. Yeah, right. Thirty minutes, you'll be begging for more."

Izzy opted to mow in her pajamas, knowing it would irritate Richard more. After unlocking the barn door, she hoisted herself onto the mower like she was straddling a horse. The Tylenol hadn't worked itself in yet so she was a little slower getting mounted.

"Here comes the fun part," she said, grinning. Choking the engine, then turning the ignition, it immediately turned over. It usually took a few turns but this morning it seemed to want to start.

"Maybe it wants to get out and get some fresh air . . . or better still, mingle with Richard," she shouted above the engine, laughing loudly. "C'mon, Mabel, let's get this yard looking good. Gotta keep up with the Joneses, or as in this case, the nitwit who lives next door." She lovingly called her mower Mabel back when she bought it about twenty years ago and stuck with it ever since. She loved her Mabel, but certainly not as much as her Barney.

Izzy backed the mower out, splintering the doorframe as she did. She wondered why someone would design a hole where a riding mower could barely squeeze in and out. Once free of the barn opening, she put it in forward gear and pushed it in full throttle. Lowering the blades, she began the trek across the yard where the grass seemed to be the highest. Although her back still throbbed a little, the medication brought some relief. It was only when she rode across the portion of her yard that used to be an extension of the garden that she grimaced in pain. She reprimanded herself for not leveling that part of the ground with her tiller. But even this didn't deter her from her work. Instead, she halfway sat up, going over the bumps and amusing herself by singing the theme song to *Green Acres*. That song always seemed to pop into her head whenever she mowed this part of the yard.

"Eddie Albert, or I should say, Oliver Douglas, eat your heart out!" she yelled, letting out that infamous hyena laughter.

She started around the side of the house where the grass was almost as thick as the back. *It looks to be the perfect spot to hide Easter eggs*, she thought, reminiscing of her days growing up, coloring the eggs with crayons, then taking turns hiding and finding the eggs. She was torn between which excited her the most back then, decorating the eggs or playing hide-and-seek with them. All of it was fun, including the excitement of having a brand new Easter dress to wear to church on Easter Sunday and the Easter meal, which spread from one end of the table to the other.

The memories began to swell within her as she guided the mower through the thick patches of grass. In a few months, those thick green patches would be brown with the turn of the seasons, spring giving way to summer, then summer to autumn, and finally winter. The thought depressed her. She decided that she preferred to stay in the present.

As she finished mowing beside the house, she rounded the corner to start on the front where she narrowly missed Richard, who didn't try to hide his anger.

"Jumping junipers, Izzy!" he yelled. Startled, she cut the mower off and yelled back at him.

"Hey, wanna count your toes there? I almost ran over the little piggy who went to the market."

"It's six o'clock in the morning, Izzy! Don't you think that's an odd time to be mowing the grass?"

"What's the matter, Richard. Cat pee in your corn flakes?"

"Don't start with me, Izzy. I have a ratchet kit and I know how to use it. You don't want to walk out one morning and find that antique horror on wheels disassembled, do ya?"

"You can insult me all you want, but I draw the line when it comes to Mabel."

"Boy, I would love to hear what a psychiatrist's take on you would be," he said, then added, taking notice of the way she was dressed, "and what's with the pajamas? Where's your hippie attire? I was just starting to get used to it. Never mind, don't answer that. I don't want to know."

Darn, not the effect I anticipated, Izzy thought.

"Just, please do me a favor. No more trimming the lawn at six o'clock in the morning, OK? It wouldn't be so bad but you got the loudest mower in this town and it rattles my house whenever you buzz by. . . ." *Not to mention that ancient Beetle Bug when it leaves the driveway,* he thought, but he decided he'd tackle that with her later on.

Izzy stared at him, her mouth agape for a few seconds, then simply replied, almost smiling, "Okie dokie."

Richard opened his mouth in preparation for a sassy comeback but her response caught him off guard, like Izzy knew it would.

"OK. OK, then. I guess I'll be going." He sighed, then started back toward his house in his trademark brisk walk, but stopped almost halfway.

"Oh, by the way," he said, with a devious smile, "please close the blinds when you're changing clothes. I'm sick of looking at your size sixteen bloomers."

"And I'm sick at looking at your purple polka-dotted boxers!" Izzy shot back.

Richard gasped and self-consciously looked down at his pants as if she could see right through them.

"Well! I never!"

Izzy let out the hyena again as she watched him turn about face and head to his house, resuming his awkward stride. Unable to resist one more poke at him, she hollered just as he reached his back door steps.

"Don't you ever get on your own nerves, Richard?"

As he slammed the door, Izzy laughed harder than ever. She'd had her fun for the morning. *Time to do a little shopping*, she thought, *soon as I turn in Mabel and take me a shower.*

Chapter 15

Tim sensed someone was in the garage with him, but every time he turned around, there was no one there. *Watching too many of them late night horror movies,* he thought. It felt odd working alone again, as well as having to extend his hours the way they were before Gary came along. But he felt that was a small price to pay for some peace of mind. He was, thankfully, able to salvage his relationships with the customers Gary had almost single handedly destroyed. He figured what good he got out of him in the time he was there didn't amount to a hill of beans with what he spent to get his good name and reputation back.

As Tim delved back into his task at hand—a brake job—a loud noise, like the sound of a wrench hitting the concrete floor, startled him. This time, it wasn't his imagination. Someone was in the garage. He jerked his head around and still didn't see anyone. But as soon as he turned back around, there stood Gary, on the opposite side of the car that rested on the racks.

"For Pete's sake, Gary! You trying to give me a heart attack? What . . . what are you doing here?"

As Tim gazed closer into his eyes, he saw traces of fatigue, from lack of sleep he supposed. His eyes were glazed but they showed no emotion. And his hair and clothes were unkempt as if he had lost his comb and slept with what he had on. He had dark stubbles on his chin and as he moved in a little closer, Tim was about ready to offer him a bar of soap.

"Gee whiz, Gary," he said, distorting his nose. "What happened to you?"

Gary swallowed hard before speaking.

"I miss her. What did I do to deserve this?"

Tim felt at a loss for words as he watched his ex-employee teetering on his feet and staring wildly at him, almost through him. He had never seen anyone have a nervous breakdown but if it was up to him to make a diagnosis, this had to be it. He actually started to pity him but knew, at the same time, he wasn't doing him any favors by coddling him in his hour of pain.

Setting his wrench down, he moved somewhat closer to him, forcing himself to breathe as little as possible to avoid the stench. Looking into his eyes, he placed a hand on Gary's shoulder and uttered the only words he could think of at the time.

"Gary, why don't you just let it go? It just wasn't meant to be. You gotta accept that and move on or it's gonna drive you crazy." *Or crazier,* he wanted to say, but restrained himself.

Tim realized, despite trying to give Gary what he thought was sensible advice, that he'd picked the wrong choice of words, especially when he found himself on his back on the cold concrete floor of the garage. His jaw stung where Gary had delivered a powerful punch. There was nothing Tim could do but lay there and feel around inside his mouth with his tongue for any loose or extracted teeth. After spitting out blood a few times, he wiped his mouth with the back of his hand and looked up at Gary with fire in his eyes.

"Man, you got a problem! I don't blame Allie for not wanting to see you. You're nuts!"

Gary drew his fist back in a gesture to punch him again, but somewhere in his odd frame of mind, decided to just let it go. Instead, he withdrew his raised fist and started for the door.

As soon as Tim felt he was really gone, he slowly pulled himself off the floor and limped to the phone. He dialed a number from memory, hoping it was the right one. The blow to his face had jarred him so much that he was having trouble focusing on the call. He let it ring several times and just about the time he started to hang up, the answering machine kicked in.

"You've reached the residence of Derrick Jones. If you care to leave a message, do so at the beep."

Tim debated on whether to leave a message or not but as soon as he heard the beep, he rambled off his message. He felt Derrick needed to know what happened here even if he had to convey it through a machine.

"Derrick, it's Tim. He was here . . . Gary was here. He's gone totally mad! If you talk to Allie, you need to warn her. I just hope that she's OK. Call me if you need me, man. Bye."

Chapter 16

The sun broke freely through the faded curtains as Allie rolled back over to face the wall, wanting to take in some more Z's on her first Saturday in Possum Heights. It just seemed so good to have the freedom to have that option, to go back to sleep if she wanted to. Anxiety and fear had controlled her every move just hours earlier, but she felt that burden lifted with every moment that passed by with no calls from Gary or gifts popping up everywhere. Her biggest burden now was a dreaded trip to the grocery store. She had decided overnight to stick with her plans of staying for at least a week and keeping a low profile as much as possible. One trip to the grocery store would be all she needed to do just that.

Despite her desire to be discreet, she wasn't really worried about the townspeople, especially Izzy. She realized that giving her a false name said otherwise, but even people as seemingly trustworthy as Izzy can slip and say the wrong thing to, say, another stranger in town. She doubted that Gary had followed her here or would in the future but desperate people often resort to desperate measures and as the old saying goes, better safe than sorry.

Izzy had curiosity. Allie had picked up on that from the start. But she never probed deeper than Allie would allow. It was almost as if she knew her boundaries. This allowed more room for trust and she unexpectedly discovered that despite their rough encounter at the beginning and Izzy's peculiar personality, she was actually starting to like her. Aware of her obsession with cleanliness, Allie wondered how she was able to keep her house so spic and span, especially with eight cats. An image came to mind of her running to the litter box with a scoop every time one of them pooped, just to keep the box poop free. She knew that was a stretch of the imagination but knowing Izzy, anything was possible.

Unable to nap any more, she glanced over at the clock and saw that it was no longer morning. It'd been a long time since she'd dozed into the afternoon, with the exception of her first day here, which of course, was the result of driving all through the early hours of morning. But this time around was different . . . no nightmares, just a few extra hours of peaceful slumber. As matter of fact, it felt so good, she was tempted to snooze a little longer but then she remembered her needed trip to the grocery store.

With that thought nagging at her conscience, she forced herself up and yawned till her eyes started to water. The world beyond had been awake for hours, judging by the sound of all the banging doors and chattering. She was sure the same was going on while she slept, but it didn't seem to disturb her sleep.

Her first cup of coffee since being on the run would be from a complimentary pack of Sanka left beside the coffee maker. She could hardly wait to savor it, only wishing she had a doughnut to go with it. Maybe she'd pick up some at the grocery store. Grabbing a pencil and paper on the nightstand, she put doughnuts at the top of the list, while it was fresh on her mind. After fixing her pot of Sanka, she'd sit down and complete the list.

The local grocery store was about the size of the diner, to her disappointment, but on the other hand, she found commodities there that the larger chains didn't carry, such as rubber boots, lanterns and even chamber pots. She was surprised that they still existed. It made her wonder if people actually still bought them and . . . used them. These were modern times. It was hard to imagine a house without a toilet but then again, this was Possum Heights.

She was impressed by the perfect display of canned goods, each can neatly stocked and labeled, facing forward. Not a bad place to shop if you could overlook the "pee pots" on aisle seven. Instead of the dread she felt earlier, she actually found herself enjoying cruising the aisles, grabbing boxes of rice, cereal, cans of soup, beans, peas and corn, and of course, doughnuts. Then, she browsed the deli and dairy area and stocked up on meats like hotdogs and baloney, cheese, bread and milk. She snatched up a few items on the snack aisle such as potato chips and nuts. Her real love was ice cream but she knew there'd be no room for that in the tiny freezer compartment of the refrigerator. There was barely enough room for ice trays.

Before heading to the checkout, she remembered she needed some coffee and coffee filters, which she'd omitted from her list. As a last minute thought, and also not on her list, she grabbed a bottle of merlot in the wine section. Satisfied with her shopping debut in Possum Height's only grocery store, she started down the aisle toward the checkout counter with her packed shopping cart. On the way, she accidentally banged another cart.

"Oh, I'm sorry, ma'am, I didn't mean to . . ." she stopped, looking dumbfounded as the stooped customer, wearing a psychedelic tie-dye shirt, stood upright. ". . . Izzy! What a surprise! Didn't think I'd be running into you again so soon. Literally."

Izzy peered into Allie's cart, then gazed back at her.

"You don't bargain shop much, do ya?"

"What?"

"You need to check out this here merlot." She picked up two bottles of merlot off the shelf and placed one in her own cart. The other, she handed to Allie. "It's on sale, two dollars off. What you got's fine, but this one is better and like I said, on sale."

Allie stared at her for a moment then reached for the bottle she held out. Studying the bottle in her cart and the one Izzy handed her, she sighed and nodded her head.

"You're right; this is the better deal. Thank you for that tip." She suddenly felt flushed with embarrassment. "I use it when I'm cooking." She felt foolish for explaining herself, especially since Izzy had put a bottle in her own cart.

"Don't we all, honey," Izzy giggled. "Sometimes I even use it in my recipes," she mused, enjoying Allie's awkwardness.

"That's cute, real cute," Allie smiled.

While she chatted with Izzy, she couldn't help but notice the difference in the display of wines to her left in contrast to the ones right of Izzy. The ones on her left were all neatly arranged, the labels out front, no bottle out of place. To her right, it was a disaster. Izzy quickly noticed her observation and offered an explanation.

"The bottles were all turned around and I couldn't read 'em. Before I knew it, I was straightening the whole aisle. And don't it just drive you crazy when they put the labels on crooked?"

Not really expecting an answer, Izzy continued to straighten the bottles of wine while Allie wondered just how deep Izzy's compulsions ran.

"You were in the canned goods aisle, weren't you?" she asked.

"Yep."

"Thought so."

"They won't let me mess with the produce section for obvious reasons," Izzy confided. "Some things you can't stack, you know. I found that out the hard way."

"Right," Allie said, wondering if she had actually tried to stack some cantaloupes. "Well, I need to be going. Good luck with what you're doing."

"Thanks. Before you go, can I ask you a favor?"

Oh boy, didn't get away quick enough, Allie thought. "Yeah, sure. What is it?"

"Barney, my Beetle, should be ready for pickup Monday. Can you take me to go get him? I'll pay you for the gas, of course."

"Nonsense. You don't have to do that. I'll be glad to take you. What time?"

"How about nine?"

"OK."

"I'll treat you to breakfast."

"No, that's not necessary," she said. *Especially if you're making fried grit biscuits and serving them on plates Caesar cleaned,* she thought.

"It would be my pleasure. By the way, merlot makes a great lamb marinade . . . I mean, in case you didn't know."

Allie smiled. "Yeah, I know. But sometimes I forget that when I grab the empty bottle." With that, she gave Izzy a quick wink and headed for the checkout counter, leaving the laugh of a hyena in her wake.

Chapter 17

Izzy's thoughts were miles away as she transferred her groceries from the cart to the back of her jeep. This "Jenny" girl seemed to be out of her element, like an Eskimo sunning on the beach. Not that she expected her to dress and talk like the locals, but to be so secretive, she wondered who she really was. She seemed like a normal woman in her late twenties, early thirties, but what normal woman her age would want to vacation in Possum Heights? What was the attraction? Maybe she was a student working towards her masters degree and this town was part of her project. Or maybe she was seeking a relative or friend and wanted to surprise them or . . . maybe she was running from something.

Izzy slammed down the hatch then slid into the driver's seat. She loved her jeep. It was so comfortable and easy getting in and out of, especially with her arthritis. Starting the engine, then shifting into gear, she eased onto the highway headed home, her thoughts still looming over the mysterious "Jenny." Ever since the first encounter with her at the stop sign that first morning, she sensed an odd aura about her. It wasn't just her erratic driving she recalled. It was what she saw when she passed her. Even in those brief few seconds, her eyes captured a chilling, unforgettable image, a woman with dark circles beneath her eyes, tousled hair and a glazed stare. It was a picture, she was sure, that had a story, a story "Jenny" may not volunteer without some coaxing.

Nearing the diner, she slowed down and pulled in. But instead of stopping there, she continued on through the lot and parked in front of the motel. She recognized the vintage Mustang parked close to the office entrance. The curtains were drawn to the room in front of the Mustang. For a minute or so, she just sat there, studying the car, curious about its owner, why she never answered her questions during their kitchen chat. But Izzy was smart enough to not probe too soon. She didn't want to ruin what friendship they had thus far. She figured she'd open up when she was ready.

"But, in the meantime, can't hurt to pry a little," she said, eyeing the front of the office. "Haven't talked to my pal, Bobby, in awhile."

Before she could change her mind, she found herself on the other side of the jeep, triple checking her locked doors, just as she did with her house. Not even the tension of the moment could keep her compulsive habits at bay.

Bobby looked up from behind the counter as Izzy entered and smiled with delight at seeing her. She knew Bobby's interest in her went beyond friendship. It showed in his eyes and in his words. He was also clumsy about who he talked to, his revelation often finding its way back to Izzy. She just hoped he wouldn't take it the wrong way by her stopping in like this, but she knew that he could be the key to some unanswered questions.

"Well, hello, Izzy. This is a treat. I usually have to go to the diner to see you . . . well, used to. Sorry to hear you're not working there anymore."

"Good news travels fast." She wondered if he knew what really had happened and decided she would play it as if he didn't. "I was ready to quit. Can't be slinging hash for the rest of my life. So, how's business here?"

"A little slow. But I had a lady come in here yesterday and rented a room for a whole week." Izzy could feel herself getting excited. "Kinda odd, but I don't ask questions. As long as they pay and ain't doing anything illegal, it's none of my business. Drives that pretty red convertible out front."

"Yeah, I met her at the diner. Oh, what was her name? I'm drawing a blank."

"Allison. Allison Jones," Bobby offered.

Izzy smiled. She couldn't believe it was that easy. Now she knew her real name.

"Yeah, yeah. That's it. Well, Bobby, it was good to see ya but I just came from the grocery store and I don't want my ice cream to melt."

She was glad she didn't have to resort to plan B, which was to lure Bobby out long enough so she could match the room number with the name on the register. But why would she use her real name at the motel and give her a phony one? Didn't she know how small this town was?

"Glad you stopped by, Izzy. Miss seeing ya at the diner," he said, saddened to see her walk away. "Promise you'll stay in touch!" he blurted as she slammed the door. She stopped dead in her tracks upon seeing the plate on the front of the Mustang.

"Now, why didn't I see that yesterday?" she asked out loud.

The plate bore the name "A.J. Realty." It matched her real name . . . Allison Jones.

"Well I'll be. She owns a realty." This only added confusion to the puzzle. She hadn't even bothered to remove the plate advertising her business.

Derrick couldn't remember the last time he'd felt this exhausted. After talking with police for hours yesterday and combing the town this morning to see if anyone had seen Allie, his energy level was at an all-time low. Even the thought of popping a TV dinner into the microwave sounded like too much effort.

"Too tired to nuke," he muttered. "Wow."

The bed seemed more appealing. Although his thoughts were constantly on Allie, he knew there was little or nothing he could do at this juncture. He and the girls at the realty worried because they saw Gary's increasing obsession with Allie. The only speck of hope Amber could offer Derrick was that she might have decided to take that much needed vacation. But without telling anyone, especially him, who ritually had coffee with her every Friday morning, it just didn't make any sense. That wasn't Allie at all.

Derrick bypassed the refrigerator, which was out of routine for him. It was his habit to explore the contents therein before going to bed. He'd grab a drink, maybe a snack of some sort. But on this night, he didn't feel the usual lure. He headed straight for the bedroom, also bypassing the answering machine, oblivious to the blinking light signifying he had messages unplayed.

With the shades drawn in his tiny little apartment, Gary sat motionless in his recliner, looking at the blank screen on the television. Nearby on the end table was a bottle of bourbon and an ashtray nearly overrun with cigarette butts. Except for the occasional transfer of the bottle to his lips with one hand and taking a drag off a cigarette with the other, he was motionless. Nothing seemed real, not the birds chirping outside his closed blinds, not the barking of a distant dog, not the vehicles passing by in succession. All were just noises that he couldn't connect with. But suddenly, he felt his lips parting, needing to utter the pain he bore.

"Mi—am—i, Mi—am—i, oh how I miss Mi—am—i."

He trembled as he upturned the bottle of bourbon, then let it down with much steadier hands. Releasing the near empty bottle, he clutched his heart and closed his eyes, trying to rid himself of whatever thoughts were torturing him, and was relieved that no one knew where he lived—thanks to Tim—so that he could endure his pain alone. He then fell asleep.

Chapter 18

Derrick awoke Sunday morning with a sense of dread. He and his sister shared an almost-telepathic bond, like twins. When she hurt, he hurt, and vice versa, but the telepathic bond between them couldn't point him in the right direction of her whereabouts. It wasn't like her to not let him know, in one way or another, what was going on, or where she was, and he hadn't picked up any kind of vibes as to her location. He tried to remember their last conversation for clues of some sort. There had to be some kind of hint in what she said that would explain her sudden disappearance. But his memory was vague. All the thoughts of past, present and future weighed so heavily on his mind that his head began to throb.

He barely felt his feet touch the floor as he stumbled to the bathroom, his focus on the BC Powder in the medicine cabinet. As he steered himself through the living room to the bathroom, his eyes caught sight of the blinking light on his answering machine.

"Allie!" he squealed. "That had better be you!" Pressing the play button, he waited to hear what he hoped would be Allie's voice.

"Derrick, it's Tim. He was here . . . Gary was here. He's gone totally mad! If you talk to Allie, you need to warn her. I just hope that she's OK. Call me if you need me, man. Bye."

With that, Derrick bolted out the door, only to return to change out of his pajamas.

Although it was well into mid-morning, almost approaching noon, the inside of the dark dingy dungeon Gary called home emulated light. With the curtains still tightly drawn, the only hint of daylight could be seen in the kitchen where rays filtered through the narrow blinds, rays that faded as clouds maneuvered above.

As hard as the floor felt, Gary awoke thinking it was the first real sleep he'd had in a while, but also the worst hangover. With his lips still pressed against the carpet, he slowly canvassed the room to assure himself that he was still in his own domain. He recognized the lock position on the front door, praising himself for at least remembering that. Then he spotted the empty bottle of bourbon on the floor next to the recliner. Judging from the smell, he gathered he had dropped it and whatever was left in the bottle had seeped into the carpet. The ashtrays, all three, were overflowing with butts. The smell of smoke lingered with the stench of bourbon-drenched carpet, enough to make him heave. But then, the urge to raise a window and allow some air in somehow became overpowered by the urge to urinate.

At least I have some dignity left, no urine stains anywhere, he thought. But his first effort in abandoning the comfort of his carpet proved difficult. His head begged for relief, while his bladder did the same. Never had he experienced a hangover so bad that he couldn't get up.

"I'll laugh about this later," he muttered. "Meanwhile, I need to find the toilet and the tabs."

His second attempt to his feet left him reeling. This time, the urge to throw up overcame the other two needs. He raced toward the bathroom, where he nearly missed the bowl. Once his head was bowed down inside the commode, there was no stopping. What was it about the first regurgitation that kept it coming? He couldn't even remember eating anything the night before but whatever it was came up, along with lunch and breakfast from that morning, and maybe even the contents of the day before.

At long last, he felt relief when he could no longer empty what he had inside. Perspiring, he rested his head on the side of the toilet. *Funny,* he thought, *I don't remember the last time my butt was here, much less, my face. Oh man, never again. I have got to get a grip on things.*

Sweat continued to replace the heat on his forehead as he slowly reached for the handle on the toilet. Hearing the flush of the toilet added an irony to his thoughts, not that he could think too well anyhow, after tossing up all that was left in his gut.

"I'm flushing my life down the toilet," he said. How did I get to this point? Why can't I just let go? I can't keep screwing up like this."

Sore from all the vomiting and heaving, he grimaced, trying to stand up, then eagerly relieved his bladder, while at the same time, reached inside his medicine cabinet for the aspirin. As he did, his knuckles scrubbed against the prescription pills that had remained there untouched for several days, pills that had kept him on an even keel after losing his wife, so short a marriage . . . pills that might have prevented him from losing his job and maybe even losing Allie. But he tossed that up as water under the bridge. The damage had been done and there was no turning back.

Taking the aspirin, he closed the cabinet door.

"Leave the crutch in the hutch," he said, referring to his prescription pills. He wasn't sure if his bout with throwing up was over with and if not, the pills were of no use.

"Oh, how a cup of coffee would taste right now," he said, then remembered he hadn't cleaned the pot from two weeks ago. "That's OK," he decided. "If I can handle the stench from this morning's puke, I can certainly handle a moldy coffee pot."

Derrick drove up Tim's driveway only to discover he wasn't there, or at least his truck wasn't. He knew Tim, on occasions, partied too much, but wisely opted to take a cab or accept an offer to be driven home. And then there was the more likely scenario that he met up with a girl and crashed at her place. Whatever the case, Derrick didn't want to leave without checking the house out first. He tried the front door, which, not surprisingly, was locked. He then meandered to the back door and discovered it was locked as well.

As a last thought, he decided to peek inside one of the windows on the chance he did get home without his vehicle. Cupping his hands against the glass pane of the living room window, he saw no signs of his friend being there. The room was immaculate, for Tim, as well as the kitchen, or what he could see of the kitchen. There was no sound of stirring around, no TV or radio blaring.

"The little devil pulled an all-nighter with some gal," he said, trying to convince himself. But thinking back on the message on the recorder, he quickly dismissed his suspicions. Tim wouldn't leave a frantic message, then dive into a sweltering night of partying or playing Don Juan.

As Derrick turned from the window and headed toward his vehicle, it hit him. *Oh crap, the shop . . . he called from the shop.* Within a matter of seconds,

Derrick was behind the wheel and headed towards Tim's garage. Images of Tim raced through his head. Tim lying on the floor, bleeding, Tim tied to a chair, Tim pinned down beneath a car that fell off the racks, accidentally . . . or not.

"The crazy fool was at Tim's shop," he shouted to himself, "and I missed him! Why can't I ever time things right? Blast it!"

Out of frustration, he slammed the steering wheel so hard, it vibrated. That brought to memory Allie's subtle accusations toward him regarding his temper.

I swear, brother, sometimes you have a short fuse, he remembered her saying. But in the end, she would be laughing. It took a lot to get him riled no matter how much Allie egged him on. On the same token, he could never ruffle her feathers. They seemed to have shared the same genetic type of temperament.

Derrick spotted Tim's truck at the shop as soon as he rounded the corner on the winding highway. His heart picked up speed as his accelerator slowed down. Tim had called from the shop yesterday, and seeing his truck there today, on Sunday morning, was almost like he never left. The images he had before of Tim in trouble came back in rapid succession but with an added frame or two . . . him staring down the barrel of a gun with Gary at the other end. The thought made him shutter, but to abandon his friend, not knowing whether he was dead or alive, was unethical.

As he crept slowly through the lot, his vehicle now parked beside Tim's truck, he visually searched the premises, straining to see anything that looked out of place. From all appearances, the outside gave no hint of any kind of disturbance. But it was what might lie inside that he feared the most. He tried to peek through the windows, but what windows there were seemed of little use. Even if you could see beyond the dirt and grease, the vision was limited with all the equipment and vehicles inside. Derrick elected to simply try the door to see if it was unlocked and hoped no one saw him pull up, and even more, that he was pulling on the handle of a business, closed for the day.

As he meticulously turned the knob, squinting at the squeak it produced, he cracked open the door, which squeaked as well.

Boy works in a garage and don't have a can of WD-40 around here. He found the thought amusing. Peering through the narrow slit he had cracked open, he let his eyes dart from one end of the building to the other as far as he could see. Although the lights were on, the building seemed to be vacant. The urge to back out now consumed him but it was the concern for his friend that willed him on.

Edging the door open a little more, he could feel the intensity of the moment creeping upon him. The silence, beyond the creaking of the door, unnerved him.

Why is it you never hear a door creak at any other time? he thought. But he knew the answer almost as soon as he asked himself the question. You don't hear creaks when you're with people in the midst of your normal activities.

He suddenly feared being alone and wished he had brought along some rein-forcement. Too late to rehash another plan, he pressed forward, ever so vigilant of his surroundings. Perspiration dampened his forehead and slowly descended down upon his face, his eyes catching some of it, blurring his vision. As he wiped his eyes with the back of his hand, another image came to him. What if Tim was all right and startled him by sneaking up on him? That would more than likely shred his dignity as he began to feel the need to pee. Struggling to find his voice, he managed to call out to Tim, his name reverberating throughout the building.

"Tim?" No answer as he inched in further.

"Tim?" he called again, this time louder, but still, no answer. He then noticed the office door ajar so he tiptoed quietly in that direction. Upon looking inside, though, all he found was a desk cluttered with massive amounts of paperwork and greasy desk items, such as a stapler, pens, pencils and paper clips. Oddly, there were no pictures, but Tim wasn't married and he had no family to speak of. It reminded Derrick of his own life, empty except for Allie, with no wife or children, not that he was looking for matrimony and the cargo that came later. He'd seen some of his friends walk down the aisle too soon and it not work out. Now as he pondered, he wondered if he was making excuses for himself or was he really afraid of commit-ment.

"Caught ya!"

Derrick jumped at the sound of Tim's voice, then was glad of the fact he hadn't wet himself.

"Gee whiz, Tim, you trying to kill my ticker? Where were you and what hap-pened to your jaw?" Derrick noticed Tim's bruised and swollen jaw.

"I guess you got my message. Our ole pal Gary paid me a visit and gave me a present," Tim said, pointing to his jaw. "Guess I must have said something to piss him off. At least I still have my teeth."

"Did you stay here all night?" Derrick asked, confused.

"No, no, no. I just came in early this morning to catch up on some work. After that punch in the jaw yesterday, I didn't feel like doing much of anything else so I went home earlier than planned."

"Did ya call the cops?"

"What for? By the time I got my senses back, he was long gone."

"Allie, that's what for! I still haven't talked to her and that nut may be behind her sudden disappearance! Sometimes I wonder where your brain is, Tim! On second thought, I know where it is. It's in your pants!"

"Hey, don't get mad at me! I called and warned you, remember? Where were you?"

"Never mind. I have to find Allie." Derrick started to walk away, then turned back. "Better put some ice on that."

Tim felt his jaw while Derrick turned to leave. The lump seemed to have gotten bigger but at least the throbbing had subsided. Walking over to one of the vehicles in his shop, he bent down and checked himself through the car's side mirror, still rubbing his jaw.

"Nope," he muttered, "think I'll just keep this as a souvenir."

Chapter 19

"One little, two little, three little pine cones . . ." Izzy sang while bagging pine cones in her front yard, ". . . four little, five little, six little pine cones, seven little, eight little, nine little pine cones . . ."

"And one nut picking them up," Richard chimed in.

Izzy quickly turned and spotted Richard leaning against a tree.

"Oh, you talking to me now?" she asked, pretending not to be startled by his sneaking up on her.

"Just came by to give you your mail. Mailman dropped it in my box by mistake yesterday. Funny, looks like your handwriting. You writing to yourself again, Izzy?"

"Yeah. To remind myself what a nosy butthole neighbor I have. Give me that." Izzy snatched the letter from him and put it in her back pocket. "Make yourself useful and hold that bag open. Let's see, where was I? Oh yeah . . . ten, twelve, fourteen, sixteen . . ."

"Oh brother," Richard muttered.

"Shhh, you're making me lose count."

"How many of these babies can you fit into one bag?" Richard asked, trying to trip her up. Izzy ignored him and kept counting.

"How many's in those bags over there?" he asked, pointing behind her. Still ignoring him, she kept her pace. "You know, if you can't get a whole bagful, I got plenty in my yard."

"Richard! Shut up!" Exasperated, Izzy grabbed the bag and turned it upside down, spilling out the few cones collected. "I'm not getting anywhere with you flapping your trap!"

"Just trying to help . . . your countess."

"Well, you're getting on my nerves."

"What do ya know? We got something in common."

"You mean you admit that you get on your nerves, too?" Izzy chuckled.

"You know what I mean, smarty britches."

Izzy pulled off her gloves and threw them on the ground.

"I'm getting hungry. Wanna join me for a pepperoni sandwich?"

"A pepperoni sandwich?"

"Yeah. Or I could fix you a pork 'n' bean sandwich . . . sorry, don't have any grits made or I'd make you a fried grit sandwich."

"I'll take the pepperoni," he said, twitching his nose.

Richard followed her up the steps, ducking his head to avoid hitting her hanging baskets. Sometimes, he wondered if she intentionally moved them around so he wouldn't get used to where they hung, thus sometimes bumping his head on them.

Izzy shooed the cats off the table while Richard helped himself to a glass of water.

"I'll take my pepperoni minus the hairball," he joked.

Izzy turned and gave him a devious grin. While she prepared the sandwiches, the cats entertained Richard by jumping back on the table, expecting him to rub their backs, then turning to proudly display their "litter box" ends. *Nice appetizer before lunch,* he mused to himself.

Izzy walked over with the sandwiches, ordering Claude, Clifton and Clyde off the table.

"Here you are. A 'P' sandwich for you and a 'P & B' for me." Richard grimaced. The thought of pork and beans between two slices of bread repulsed him.

"You have some strange taste buds, Izzy."

"I prefer the word 'exotic.' My taste buds scream out to me, 'Give me something different!' Know what I like for breakfast sometimes?"

"I'm afraid to ask."

"Hotdogs and molasses. I don't know what it is about that combo and why it's so good first thing in the morning, but it works for me. There's some tea in the fridge. Help yourself."

Richard finished his glass of water then went over to the refrigerator for the tea. As he started to grab the pitcher of tea, he noticed two mason jars filled with sauces of some sort. One was yellow and the other red.

"What's in those two jars?"

"One's ketchup and the other's mustard."

"Dare I ask?"

"You know how they always give you more condiments than you'll use when you go through the fast food joints? Well, I save them. I guess I squeezed out about fifty or more of them into those jars. Can't see throwing them away. I mean, it saves me money on buying ketchup and mustard at the store."

Richard shook his head, amazed to keep discovering some of Izzy's quirky habits.

"That's an awful lot of trouble. Why don't you just leave them in the packs and use them as you need them?"

"I kinda like it better in jars, not as junky looking as scattered packs of ketchup and mustard. Oh, and speaking of fast food joints, you ever look down at the drive-thru window and see all that change people drop? It's just laying there waiting for somebody to pick it up. So while I'm waiting for them to fetch my order, I collect what people leave behind. Got a jug full back there in my room of dropped coins."

"A squeezer and a miser. I'm surprised you don't halve an egg before you cook it," Richard teased. Izzy stared at him sternly, her expression clearly saying it all. "I was just joking, Izzy. You really halved an egg?"

"Yeah, I've halved an egg before. One time. I just wanted a little bit to hold some batter together so I used half an egg and fried the other half for breakfast. But that one experiment broke me. You know how hard it is to divide a raw egg?"

Richard looked so serious, with his mouth agape, that she had to laugh, hyena style.

"Some things really aren't worth the trouble of saving a penny or two, Richard. Even I'll admit that. Sit down and eat your pepperoni sandwich before the cats do."

Richard closed the refrigerator and, with his glass of tea, joined Izzy at the table. As she took a bite of her pork 'n' bean sandwich, he thought how easy she made it look like a delicacy. What some might have taken as a joke, Richard knew this was no joke. This was the real Izzy and she didn't try to hide who she was.

As Richard lunged into his own sandwich, chewing and swallowing before actually tasting it, he learned too late what Izzy's version of a pepperoni sandwich was. He thought his mouth was on fire and the burning sensation continued on down to his stomach. Running to the trashcan, he spit out what was still in his mouth. With his eyes watering and his hand fanning his mouth, he hurried back to the table and turned his glass of tea up until it was empty, then went back to the refrigerator for more. When he could finally speak, he didn't hold back his anger.

"You trying to kill me? What did you put in that sandwich?" Not waiting for an answer, he slowly peeled back the remaining slices of bread and peered in between, gasping at what he saw. There nestled between the slices, was a wad of macaroni and cheese, topped with chunks of hot pepper.

Izzy eyed the contents along with Richard, then looked up at him. "Oops," she uttered, almost apologetic like.

"What is this . . . a joke?"

"It's a pepperoni sandwich, my version of a pepperoni sandwich. Macaroni and cheese with hot peppers. I forget my taste buds don't jive with everybody else's. I'm sorry, Richard. Really, I am."

Izzy looked too sincere for Richard to think she'd done it on purpose. As bad as he wanted to choke her at the moment, he let out a long sigh and sat down.

"Forget it. If nothing else, it cleared my sinuses."

"Tell you what, beanpole. I'll make it up to you. Your birthday's Tuesday, ain't it? I'll wine and dine you at Possum Height's finest restaurant. All on me, of course."

Richard grinned, still retaining a sliver of macaroni in between two of his teeth.

"And I get to order anything off the menu? And none of that sharing stuff? And the tip, you do the tip?" He recalled the last time they dined together, she came up short when it came to the tip.

"That's right, birthday boy."

"It's a date then."

"OK, flagpole. I'll pick you up around six o'clock Tuesday."

"Fine. By the way, you have twenty-week-old eggs in the fridge. Might want to get rid of them before they hatch."

As Richard started out the door, Izzy couldn't resist the urge to take a parting poke at him, as she often did.

"Hey Richard! Got any Vaseline?"

"No . . . why?"

"You're gonna need it when that piece of pepperoni sandwich comes out," she laughed, letting loose the hyena.

Chapter 20

"I don't know what the big deal is. You have sausage, egg and biscuit. I simply ask that you don't put it all in one package. I want it separated. I want a platter of egg, sausage and a biscuit, separated, not lumped into a smorgasbord."

"Izzy, we've been through this before," the girl behind the counter patiently explained. "This is a fast food restaurant, not Denny's. We only do biscuits for breakfast. You can have a ham, sausage or bacon biscuit with or without egg and cheese. If you want it separated, you do it."

"Geez, that's the problem with the world today. Everybody's in such a hurry, they've got to have their food all lumped into a biscuit, can't take the time to sit and enjoy the best meal of the day at the table, separated, not squeezed together . . . all right, just give me two of 'em, and a couple of coffees," she sighed.

Izzy made sure she had everything prepared before Allie arrived. Her initial intentions were to cook breakfast herself but ran short of time by oversleeping. Clare and Chloe were stretched out on the wicker sofa in the foyer while Cleo nibbled on the artificial plant on the table. The others were either still napping in her bed, unaware she'd sneaked out to the Biscuit Hut down the road, or catnapping in other areas of the house.

It was eight-thirty. Allie would be there in half an hour. She was glad they would be having a sit-down breakfast in her kitchen, even if she had the job of separating the sausages and eggs from the biscuits. She felt the atmosphere would be more comfortable should Allie want to confide in Izzy about certain things, like her true identity. She just hoped she didn't slip without giving Allie a chance to talk.

With the two plates set out, opposite each other, and utensils on either side, Izzy took out the contents of the Biscuit Hut bag that she had warmed over in the microwave. Within a matter of minutes, she had the biscuits, sausages and eggs separated and placed upon the plates. *Not a gourmet breakfast without the grits,* she thought, *but it'll do.* She checked her watch, then re-heated the coffee in the microwave as well. Just as she was placing the coffee on the table, the doorbell rang. Not accustomed to company, especially that early in the morning, Clare and Chloe scampered from their wicker beds and ran toward the back bedroom where some of their other siblings lay snoozing. Cleo paused long enough to see if the bell would sound again, then continued nibbling on the plastic plant.

"Wussies," Izzy mumbled, watching Clare and Chloe seek out a hiding place.

Izzy eased the door open while Allie started in, then stopped. Her eyes scanned Izzy's garb. She was clad in a white, woven, crinkle-cotton V-neck shirt. The sleeves were long and bell-shaped at the ends. A multicolor needlepoint pattern of flowers adorned the front and the V-neck and bell-shaped sleeves were trimmed with lace. Embracing her neck was a large "peace" emblem, a well known relic from the late sixties and early seventies, and completing the fashion statement was a headband secured tightly around her head. The faded jeans and canvas shoes could be passé or modern. Her attire was very similar to what she had on the first time they met.

Catching Allie's puzzled gaze, Izzy found herself on the receiving end of wonder and curiosity.

"What's wrong?" she asked.

"Ah, nothing," Allie said, shaking her head. "I hope I'm not too early."

"Right on time, sug. C'mon in and have a seat at the table. I have our breakfast prepared. It's not exactly homemade but the Biscuit Hut is the next best thing, I suppose."

Allie reached down and slid off her shoes, leaving them at the entrance just like before. Surveying the spread on the kitchen table, she again appeared perplexed.

"I know I haven't been in this town long, but don't the Biscuit Hut just do . . . well, biscuits?"

"Yeah," Izzy laughed. "They do, but I don't. Here, sit down."

As Izzy pulled out a chair for her, Allie was still staring at the food on the table. *I can't believe she dissected the biscuits,* she thought.

"Cream and sugar for your coffee?" Izzy asked.

"No, thank you. Black, please."

"Woman of my own heart," Izzy said, patting her on the shoulder. "Never did like to cover up the taste of my coffee. Like to smell it, like to taste it. Like to taste the smell of it."

"Yeah, me too. I just love your nook. I know I've raved on it before but it's just so endearing. I've always wanted a breakfast nook. To sit there, have breakfast, drink my coffee and read the morning paper while taking in the three-dimensional view of life outside first thing in the morning. I know, sounds corny, but I've always appreciated the simple things in life."

"No, Jenny, it doesn't sound corny at all." Izzy praised herself for using Allie's alias. "I added on the nook years after I'd been living here. It just seemed to enhance the whole house. This is where I do my deepest thinking," Izzy said, "second only to sitting on the throne."

Allie laughed. "I guess we differ there. When I go to the toilet, I like to do my business and get out as quickly as possible."

From where Izzy sat, the sun shone at a perfect angle across her face. For the first time, Allie got a close up shot of her and saw the beginnings of wrinkles around her eyes and mouth. She was still somewhat attractive with her dark eyes, high cheekbones and lightly suntanned skin. With just subtle hints of slivers of gray in her hair here and there, no one would probably have guessed she was in her late forties or early fifties, save the hippie attire she cloned from the late sixties. More than ten years apart in age, Allie couldn't help but see the youth in her eyes, if you could overlook the crow's feet.

Her mysterious gaze out the window heightened Allie's curiosity of the eccentric world of the woman sitting before her. The hippie clothes, the brass personality and the compulsive behavior certainly added to the mystery. She began to feel an overwhelming urge to get inside the mind of this ruthless, yet kind-hearted woman. Little did she know that Izzy was trying to do the same. Her thoughts were interrupted when Izzy spoke, her eyes still focused on the outside world.

"Ever wonder why bad things happen to good people, Jenny?"

For a moment, Allie almost forgot her alias, but didn't let on to Izzy. Without waiting for an answer, Izzy continued.

"Back about a century ago, or so it seems, when I first started at the diner, back in the good ole days, when Sam was at the helm, we had some of the best customers, not that the patrons who waltz through there now are any less, but you just don't forget the ones early on. There were the regulars who came in on Friday nights. You could almost set your watch by it. The same ones, the same time and the same smiles. But whether it was the Friday night frequenters or the occasional drop-ins, one thing they all had in common was that they were your friends. They cared about you as if you were a part of their family, wanting to know how you're doing and telling you to call them if you ever needed anything and then shook your hand when they left the diner. And it was contagious, the hospitality, that is. Rarely, did you come across someone who left their amenities at home." Izzy took a sip of her semi-hot coffee, then proceeded on with her story, returning to the view outside the window.

"There was this particular family that frequented the diner that I'll never forget. Nice looking couple with two adorable kids. I enjoyed talking to them whenever I could break away from the kitchen. The girl was just a toddler, just learning to walk and talk. The boy was in his early teens. He had the sweetest smile and brightest eyes. You'd never know anything was wrong with him. That is, until he got up to walk. In his early years, around the age of five, he was diagnosed with muscular dystrophy. Now, at thirteen years of age, he could still walk on his own, but wobbly. It broke my heart to see this boy who was so young, so cute, and so full of life, to be living on borrowed time.

"What I would have given to see his body healed of this debilitating malady, to have his whole future to look forward to. I really got attached to him. I think he was attached to me, too. He'd call me Miss Izzy and offered a hug whenever I walked over. I remember secretly wishing that one day one of my hugs had the power to heal his body. Ridiculous as it sounded, I didn't care because my heart ached for him.

"Over the years, he had to rely on a wheelchair to get around. But nothing ever changed about that sweet smile and those beautiful bright eyes and what became known to both him and me as the 'love hug.' His embrace had weakened with his deteriorating muscles, but never his heart.

"After a while, the family stopped coming to the diner altogether. He was, by now, confined to the bed. I made it a point to go see him every chance I got. And then one day I got the news, the news I'd hoped I'd never hear in the ongoing search for a cure. He left this world at the tender age of twenty-one. All I could do for the longest time was ask, 'Why?'

"When I look back now, I reflect on his strength and courage and that un-wavering positive attitude. And although his life was cut so drastically short, he left behind a legacy of true inspiration." Izzy paused, trying to maintain control over her emotions, then continued.

"His younger sister grew up and went on to college. She, too, was an inspiration as she bravely stood by her brother in his final days. I don't see her as much now that she's away at college but I do see her parents every now and then." Izzy seemed sapped of energy as she concluded her story to the outside world, only occasionally glancing at Allie. "You know, few memories stir my heart the way that little guy did."

Allie noticed a tremble in Izzy's lips. This was a side of her hidden until now. She never would have guessed her to have a heart three days ago. It moved her in such a way that she found herself at a loss for words. But seeing her so vulnerable and sad gave her the courage to try and extend some type of consolation.

"Izzy." Allie placed a hand on Izzy's cheek and gently forced her to look her way. She could see the tears glistening in her eyes and it moved her even more. "This boy was destined to have you as a friend. You helped to make his last hours on earth a little brighter. I know he saw in you what I see now, a true, honest-to-goodness friend. And that's something you can't put a price tag on."

Izzy forced a smile to the surface and wiped her eyes. "That's kind of you to say. That really means a lot to me, Jenny."

Allie winced at hearing her fabricated name again. She felt guilt and deceit creep into her consciousness but couldn't bring herself to confess her secret identity . . . not yet, anyway, and especially not after hearing Izzy's touching story.

"Well," she said, changing the subject. "I guess we better eat before the food gets colder."

"Yeah," Allie agreed. Glancing at her plate with the scattered parts of a biscuit, she commented without looking up. "You know, I would've eaten the biscuit the way it was. You didn't have to separate it."

"Yes. I suppose I shouldn't have done that. I guess I wasn't thinking. Just one of my silly little quirks. Sorry."

Allie felt herself going through the motions as she started on her breakfast, cold, but not really caring. She didn't even hear Izzy's response about the biscuit. Her mind was more centered on when and how she was going to reveal the truth to Izzy. She wished she had given her real name to begin with and wondered now why she didn't. It wasn't like she wasn't going to find out anyhow. The desk clerk knew. How long would it take before the whole town knew, especially being such a small town? This seemed to be an opportune time, despite her earlier misgivings. Perhaps if she explained to Izzy, she'd understand and might even offer up some much needed advice on how to handle Gary. But no matter how many times she scripted the words in her head, she knew it wouldn't sound the same from her mouth.

Allie fidgeted with her empty cup and ultimately decided it would be up to her to proceed with their original mission.

"Ready to pick up Barney?"

"Yeah, sure. Let me just get these dishes in the sink. I'll wash them when I get back."

"Ain't gonna let Caesar clean them?" Allie laughed.

"No, not this time."

"The silverware looks new. All clean and shiny. Let me guess, Caesar cleaned that."

"Nope," Izzy laughed, sitting the plates in the sink. "Caesar can't take credit for that. Not this time. It was his brother, Claude."

With a smile and a wink, Izzy headed for the door and opened it, signaling for Allie to precede her so she could lock it. While Izzy, true to her three-turn technique, locked the door, Allie wondered what kind of germs a cat's tongue had.

Chapter 21

Izzy insisted on driving her backup vehicle to pick up Barney, while Allie seemed to have reservations as they approached the jeep.

"Look, I don't mind us going in your vehicle, Izzy, but you know that means I have to drive one of them back."

Izzy slid down what she called her "driving glasses" to the tip of her nose, so she was peering at Allie just above the lenses.

"It's just a piece of machinery, honey. I trust you." But as Allie hesitated, she sensed her friend was having a déjà vu with their first encounter on the road.

"Hop in," she said, peering across the top of the jeep. Allie slid into the passenger seat while Izzy got in behind the wheel.

"You know, some people think I get my panties all in a wad over nothing sometimes, but these same people know me enough to just ignore it. It ain't your fault my Barney stalled, so just put that thought out of your pretty little head, OK?"

"You were pretty teed with me," Allie reminded her.

"No," Izzy laughed, restraining the hyena. "I was teed with Barney. You just happened to be in the wrong place, and in my opinion, at the right time. I didn't mean to take it out on you. I love my Barney. I've had him a long time. I used to have a Pinto Bean and upgraded to a Beetle Bug."

That's an upgrade? Allie thought.

"And of course, there was the Mustang. It was sweet. It was a Shelby GT, candy apple red, four-barrel carburetor. Seeing yours brings back memories."

"Mine is one barrel, but it's great on gas."

"Well, today, great gas mileage takes precedence over horse power. Years ago, I would've said the opposite. But you grow up, along with your brain cells. OK, Jenny, fasten your seatbelt. Let's go get Barney."

Allie had a hard time hearing Izzy addressing her by the name she'd falsely given her. And hearing her say she'd been in the wrong place at the right time just added to her increasingly guilty conscience.

But as she fumbled with her seatbelt, she exchanged a smile with Izzy and hoped at some point before it was too late, she'd be able to express to her new friend who she really was and hoped she'd understand.

Izzy, wise beyond her years, decided to play along. She could feel her distance at times and knew when to pull back. But she also knew how to put her at ease. As she would casually glance over from time to time, she decided that maybe just keeping her mouth shut for a change would do just that. But as they drove quietly for the next few minutes, it was Allie that broke the silence.

"So, tell me. How did Possum Heights get its name, dare I ask?"

"Because Cathedral Heights was taken," Izzy answered, looking serious. Allie, confused, waited to hear the rest of the story.

"Just kidding," Izzy laughed, once more retraining the hyena. "I really don't know, to tell you the truth. Rumor has it, the town was saturated with possums, but if you ask me, I think someone just had a warped sense of humor. Personally, I don't have anything against possums. Number one, they don't hurt cats, at least not to my knowledge. Number two, they don't carry rabies. And number three, they're not finicky eaters. They eat whatever's left over. Possums . . . well, possums get a bad rep, you know. Just 'cause some people think they're ugly, with their long snouts and furless tails, that shouldn't label them as outcasts. Personally, I think they're kinda cute. But then again, I'm a little prejudiced. I once had a pet possum. Yep, sure did, uh-huh. Even tried to get him neutered. But they laughed at me, laughed me right out of the animal hospital."

Allie raised her eyebrows in disbelief while Izzy continued, never cracking a smile, but laughing all the way on the inside.

"Fat little rascal, he was. And then, it happened one day. He crossed the road . . . and became road kill."

Allie wasn't sure if she should remain stoic, laugh or extend a handkerchief. She felt at a complete loss for words. Responding the only way she knew how, she decided on the remorseful approach.

"Sorry." She had just expressed sympathy for her new friend's dead possum. How weird was that? Uncomfortable with this odd conversation, Allie changed the subject. "You know what really caught my eye the first time I came to Possum

Heights?" An immediate image of the "possum busts" outside the gates to the town entered her head. Ignoring that image, she continued. "Frank's Diner . . . that's what really drew me in. It's so nostalgic. It reminds me of the dime store back home when I was a little girl."

"You don't look old enough to remember that," Izzy observed.

Allie blushed. She wasn't sure if that was a compliment or not, but decided to treat it as one. While Allie basked in the moment, Izzy was on her own trip down memory lane.

"I'll do ya one better. The outhouse. Bet ya can't relate to that. I can remember when I thought outhouses were luxuries. Yeah, all our neighbors had one, some even had two, and I was so jealous. We just had the slop jar, or chamber pot, as some called it, a technical term I reckon. Whatever you considered the proper name, it was a step up from the paint can."

Allie, in disbelief over Izzy's comment on the paint can, was more curious about the chamber pot.

"I saw the chamber pots at the grocery store here! I can't believe stores still sell them or even more, that people still use them."

"Well, I don't know that people really buy them for that purpose anymore. I 'spect some people just like to have 'em for souvenirs. Of course, I did hear old Mattie May down the road say they're good for cooking collards in." Allie grew up on collards, being a southern gal as well, but after the image Izzy just gave, she would have to resist her urge to taste anybody's collards in Possum Heights.

"Ah, but never mind that. That's how rumors get started. So you really remember the good ole days, with the old fashioned grills, huh?"

"Yeah. The diner kinda took me back to those days, with the malt machines and the whole display. Even the smell brought back the memories of those good ole days. Makes me feel so . . . old."

Izzy laughed, hyena in tow.

"Sounds like you were on the edge of the good ole days. You ain't old, Missy. Just wait till you have to change your drawers cause you coughed or laughed or sneezed."

Allie couldn't help but chuckle. She'd never know anyone so brazen as Izzy.

Izzy, on the other hand, still hand her own agenda. She was laying the groundwork for putting Allie at ease. Her curiosity and concern were equally matched when it came to getting to know Allie. She'd actually become quite fond of Allie in such a short time, surprising even herself. She didn't really need Allie to drop her off at the house following her resignation from the diner, and especially didn't need her to take her to pick up Barney, as several people had already offered to do so. But from the moment she confronted her at the stop sign, which only escalated to their encounter at the diner, she knew their destiny had a purpose. This stranger had a story and she was going to unravel it.

As they drove along the narrow highway, Izzy's tires catching a pothole or two along the way, the small trivial talk continued on. Izzy could see the evolution of Allie's mental behavior taking shape. The more she talked, the more confident she seemed to be. This made the doors of opportunity even broader for Izzy, who strove even harder to obtain Allie's trust.

With the garage looming up ahead, Izzy purposely slowed her jeep, wanting to keep the momentum going between them, prolonging the ride as long as possible. She felt once they were separated at the garage, she may never get this chance again. Allie would go her own way once she dropped off one of Izzy's vehicles at the house and that would be the end of it, unless by some other chance meeting—highly unlikely. No, this was prime time, and if she didn't seize it now, she may never get the opportunity again.

Izzy pulled over to the side of the road and shut the engine off. Allie, who had been ranting on about the many ways to cook squash, suddenly seemed to coil in fear.

"What's wrong? Why did you pull over? Something wrong with the jeep? Is it running hot or something?"

Izzy removed her glasses and faced her, her eyes more serious than Allie ever remembered seeing them, even as she faced her in the restaurant after the incident at the crossroads. It was those daunting eyes that made it even scarier.

Izzy, on the other hand, knew to take caution. She had to be careful and make sure that Allie's steps taken forward would not, in her effort to confide, be reversed. "No, sug, the jeep's fine. I just wanted to take this time and opportunity to talk to you about something. OK?"

Allie nodded, but reluctantly. Had she done something to make Izzy mad, other than the road rage incident? Was she going to insist on her paying for Barney's "hospital" bills, even though she said it wasn't her fault? Why would she just decide that she wanted to talk to her here, along side the road, a few hundred yards from the repair shop? Her eyes reflected confusion and fear but Izzy was quick to offer her a reassuring smile.

"Look, honey, I don't know if you're in some kind of trouble or whatnot but if you are, I hope you know you can trust and confide in me. I didn't just fall off the turnip truck. I know when things are amiss. Could it be someone hurt you, like a boyfriend? Or did someone you love pass on? Or could it be that you're running from someone, someone who you think may try to hurt you? Am I in the ballpark . . . hmm?"

Allie eyed her with uncertainty, not knowing what to say or how to react. This was, after all, some crazy lady she had first come in contact with along the highway and then ran into inside her former place of employment. She didn't really know who she was, but then again, Izzy was trusting her, allowing her to see where she lived and about to let her drive her jeep back, or Barney.

Sensing Allie's resurfacing insecurities, Izzy sighed and leaned back in her seat. "I'm sorry. I'm not trying to pry into your business, OK? I just happen to care, that's all. You don't have to divulge anything. It's your business. I'm just saying that if you feel like talking, you can trust me."

Izzy then had a spontaneous idea but gave Allie the impression that she had been mulling it over before now. "Oh, listen to me, I'm rambling on. Let me get to the point." Izzy paused and released a long sigh before continuing. "I think you're overpaying at that high price roach motel beside the diner. Now, I have plenty of room at the house, free of charge . . . well, I may ask you to scoop poop once in a while, but anyway, what I'm driving at; it don't make any sense, you staying at that flea bag motel when I got a whole house with all the amenities that go with it. So, what do ya say . . . Allison?"

Allie felt the blood drain from her face. She was too stunned to form any kind of words. She was already reeling from Izzy's generous proposal, to move in with her, but the mention of her name, her real name, sent chills cascading down her spine. Confusion mixed with fear masked her face as Izzy quickly realized that she probably shouldn't have said her real name.

"I'm sorry, Allison, that was being too abrupt—"

"Allie," she interrupted. "People call me Allie. It's OK. You did catch me off guard and I've been wanting to tell you. I just didn't know you already knew."

"Don't get mad at me but I tricked the desk clerk into telling me who you were. I suspected Jenny wasn't your real name and I figured in time you'd tell me, but I guess I got a little overzealous, and anyway," Izzy cleared her throat, "like I said, you're more than welcome to stay at my house. I don't know what your plans are and all or what's going on with you. It's really none of my business unless you want to tell me."

Allie had turned and was gazing out the window.

"Look, Allie, I know you haven't known me that long, but I assure you, I'm very trustworthy. I give you my word on that. I know you have your reasons for not telling me your real name, and I'll respect your privacy if you don't want to tell me why. I'll even continue to call you Jenny, if you prefer."

Allie still focused on the outside of the car window, as if letting Izzy see her face would reveal too much.

Izzy sensed her reluctance and had an idea. "Hey, tell you what. Why don't you come to church with me on Sunday? Don't know what your denomination is or if you even have one, but that's beside the point. I'd love to have you come with me and we could drop your name, whichever name you choose, in the prayer basket. I mean, God knows who you are and that's all that matters."

Izzy noticed Allie's shoulders beginning to shake and she leaned forward, trying to catch a glimpse of her eyes, which, from the side, seemed to be glazed over with tears. "I'm sorry," Izzy said, "I didn't mean to upset you." But when Allie turned around, Izzy realized she wasn't crying, she was laughing. "Not to be the cynical one here, but what the heck is so funny?"

"No, no, I'm sorry," Allie said, still laughing. "It's just that I didn't peg you for the church-going type."

"Well, excuse me!" Izzy barked, appearing offended. "What exactly do you consider the church-going type? Wait a minute; don't tell me. Let me guess. I'm supposed to be adorned in one of them frilly 'church-going' dresses, real proper like, something the other women can gawk at and remember more than they can remember the sermon. Is that the church-going type you talking about?"

Allie felt she had struck a nerve with Izzy. She was aware of her tough outer layer, but beneath that, she discovered a cream puff. She liked that soft, gentle layer beneath, but oddly enough, it was the tougher side that had won her over. "I . . . don't . . . really know what the church-going type is. I guess that was a dumb thing to say. I'm sorry if I offended you."

Izzy stared at her while tapping the wheel with her index finger, giving Allie time to squirm. After a few seconds of silence, she reminded her of the invitation. "I'm still waiting for an answer, about accompanying me to church."

Allie still had tears of laughter in her eyes, but now they mingled with tears of other emotions. "Yes, I would like to go with you. Thank you, not just for the invite, but for your discretion with my identity. I was wondering who would be the first to learn my real identity, not counting the desk clerk, of course. Fancy that, it was you. And yes, I know you must have questions and you deserve some answers. . . . " Allie hesitated, recalling Izzy's earlier offer "Were you serious about me staying with you?"

"Of course I was," she laughed. "I think it'd be great for both of us!"

"Well, to be honest, I don't know how long I'll be here. I'm kinda on an unexpected vacation."

This increased Izzy's curiosity but she was careful not to let it show.

"That's OK. You can tell me about it later if you want. In the meantime, I know where there's a temporary job opening if you're interested. I know that sounds silly if you're on vacation. But it has the potential of becoming permanent should you decide to stay."

"Thank you. It's certainly something to think about . . ." Allie paused, suddenly remembering that Izzy had lost her job. ". . . but what about you? Don't you need a job?"

"No, I think I've about decided to retire. I have enough at the house to keep me busy."

Allie didn't think Izzy looked old enough to retire but decided that maybe she had a past job with a pension. "I think I will take you up on that offer, of moving in. My motel bill is paid up till the day after tomorrow. So, if it's all right with you, I'll get my things together tomorrow and take them to your house."

Izzy grinned, feeling triumphant. She reached over into her glove compartment and produced an extra key.

"Here. It's a spare key. I have some errands to run tomorrow, and tomorrow night, I have a dinner engagement with my idiot neighbor, Richard. It's his birthday and I'm taking the ole buzzard out. I shouldn't be long, though, especially if I get lucky and get on his nerves." Allie wondered why she even bothered treating him with a night out if she felt that way about him. "Your bedroom is downstairs at the end of the hallway to the left," she continued. "We'll go over the rules later, if there are any. OK? Well, that's settled. Let's go pick up Barney. Don't want ole John coming by trying to tow the jeep," she laughed.

Then unexpectedly, she reached over and placed a hand on Allie's wrist. "It's gonna be fine, I promise. We'll fix whatever it is . . . all right?"

Allie thought to herself, *You can't fix this*, but she managed to force a smile and nodded as Izzy put the jeep back on the road and in the direction of the garage where her beloved Barney awaited her.

A police car was parked in front of A.J. Realty to the confusion of passersby. There was no crime scene tape, no CSI mobile unit, no ATF squads. There was nothing visual to indicate to the steady flow of onlookers that anything had happened in the vicinity of the realty, save the one cop car out front.

Inside, Lieutenant Mims sat across the desk from Amber while Derrick paced the floor nonstop. Tess and Frieda sat nearby, more concerned than ever over where their boss could be.

"So you guys haven't heard from Gary any more?"

They all shook their heads, but Amber relayed to Mims the story of Gary and Tim's encounter. "He went to see Tim. I'll let Derrick tell you about that."

Lieutenant Mims turned his attention to Derrick, whose pacing seemed to be keeping with the wall clock's ticking. "Oh, when did this happen?"

"Saturday. He came in the shop and was acting really weird, according to Tim. Tim said something to piss him off and he punched him."

"What did he say?"

"He told him to let go of her, to move on."

"And then he punched . . . Derrick, sit down. You're making me dizzy." Derrick complied and sat next to Tess. "So he punches Tim, then what?"

"He leaves and no one's seen him since."

"Why didn't Tim call the police?"

"I asked him the same thing. I guess he didn't think it was important enough."

"And no one has an inkling of where he lives?"

Derrick, even more infuriated with Tim for not having a file of some kind on Gary, bowed his head and replied without looking up. "No."

"OK. Beside the fact that he punched Tim, which really doesn't account for anything, I have no legal cause to arrest him. You mentioned earlier that he called the realty asking to speak to Allie. At that time, she was already presumed missing. I mean, why would he bother calling, asking to talk to her and then show up at the garage a day later, just to take a swing at Tim?"

"Because it makes him look less suspicious! Don't you get it, Detective?" Derrick shouted, no longer looking down, but straight into Lieutenant Mims' eyes. "He may be crazy, but he's not stupid!"

"That's enough!" Mims roared, jumping from his seat and accidentally knocking over whatever his hands made contact with. Pens, pencils and paper clips scattered everywhere.

Amber scrambled to the floor to help retrieve the runaway objects. Some had rolled beneath the credenza but within easy reach of Amber's tiny hand. As she grasped one of the pens, she also found in her clutches a piece of paper. Slowly sliding it out, she immediately recognized the handwriting. "Oh my word!" she gasped, reading with intensity.

"What? What?" Tess asked, while everyone else anxiously looked on.

"Lieutenant Mims, maybe you better read this." She passed the note to him, while he searched in his front pocket for a pair of reading glasses, then quickly slid them on.

As he began to read aloud, the rest of the room froze. "Hey guys, I know this is short notice and I apologize for relaying it to you this way, but I have decided that this would be a good time to take a vacation. I don't know where I'm going yet or for how long, but I trust you three can keep the business going until I get back. I don't mean to be so vague but I'm anxious to get going. Maybe Gary's obsession with me will be passé by the time I return. Don't worry about me and please tell Derrick not to worry. I'll be fine. You guys, especially Amber, inspired me to take the leap and that's what I'm doing. I will be in touch once I've settled at my vacation destination but don't worry if I don't call right away. Understandably so, I'd like to remain in the shadows as much as possible. Keep up the good work, and Derrick . . . love you, big bro! Later gators, Allie."

Lieutenant Mims slowly removed his glasses then handed the letter back to Amber. For the first few seconds, only the wall clock resonated any type of sound. The stunned gazes from the faces around the room said it all. Only Mims retained his rigid composure. He simply moved his chair to the side and stood up, then placed his hat upon his head. He scanned his audience of four as if he had wandered into a room full of nuts.

"Well, this certainly has been interesting. I think the note pretty much clears up her sudden disappearance. If you'll excuse me."

As the detective walked out, Derrick still appeared stunned. He saw the handwriting. There was no question regarding the authenticity of the letter. No doubt it was Allie's. And even though he felt some relief after hearing the contents of the note, something else seemed to be bothering him, but he wasn't prepared to divulge it just yet. Instead, he savored the moment, watching his sister's friends and colleagues rejoice at this new revelation, that Allie was safe, hopefully.

The note certainly brought relief but it also brought concern. It wasn't like Allie to be spontaneous. The mere mention of Gary in her letter was too obvious a reason for leaving on impulse. Something didn't feel right.

Maybe she'll call soon, he thought. *Maybe then, I can put my suspicions aside.*

Chapter 22

June was the first to see Izzy as she casually strolled into the diner and her reaction brought attention to everyone within earshot.

"Oh my word! Look what the cat drug in! Come here, girlfriend!" she squealed, embracing her once she got close enough.

"Hey kiddo. Good to see you, too. And you as well, Henry," she said, nodding toward the longtime patron. "Where's the warden?"

"Oh, he's out back trying to train the new fry cook. 'Tween you and me, I think he really misses you."

"Yeah," Henry butted in, "ain't nobody been able to do anything right since you've been gone, according to Frank."

A lady who had been sitting at a nearby table approached her from behind and hugged her.

"Please come back, Izzy. It ain't the same without you."

Izzy, a little perplexed at not knowing who she was, turned and hugged her all the same. She glared at June, who just shrugged her shoulders, also unfamiliar with the friendly patron.

"I'm flattered, I really am," Izzy commented, not quite feeling deserving of all the attention. "However, I'm not here to try and get my job back. I just need to talk to Frank about something. I'll explain later. If you'll excuse me," she said, anxious to get down to business.

June and Henry exchanged puzzled looks as Izzy waltzed into the kitchen area with a pleasant sort of arrogance. Although it had only been a few days, the minute Izzy stepped into the kitchen, she experienced an overwhelming sense of déjà vu seeing Frank tutoring his bumbling trainee. She recalled years ago being taught the ropes of running the whole kitchen with Sam as her guide. Although Izzy was quick to learn, she'd watched many come and go under Frank's insolent guidance, failing to grasp the simplest of tasks. But when the boss is a tyrant, learning can be a very unpleasant experience. Where his patience lacked, he made up for in temper.

Sam, on the other hand, had amazing stamina with his rookies and was tireless when it came to teaching his many apprentices the art and skill of the culinary world. His resolve was to instill within them the confidence that they could master anything by making the effort to try. Thus, through his skillful nurturing, Sam cultivated some great employees. Where Sam could convert a clumsy, inept, inexperienced, run of the mill, average street person into a top-notch maître d', Frank lacked the patience, the compassion and most of all, the brains to teach someone to do something as simple as pour a cup of coffee.

Now, as Izzy, back from déjà vu, stood watching Frank rant loudly, flapping his hands up and down like a baby bird first learning to fly, she felt profound pity for the timid young lady holding a fry basket like it was a snake. *This is insane,* she thought. *He's gonna scar that girl for life.*

Strutting into the kitchen like she'd never left, she grabbed the basket from the stunned recruit and stared directly into Frank's eyes. "Gee whiz, Frank," she scoffed. "Why don't you just beat her upside the hand with a spatula? Is this your latest victim? Nothing ever changes!" Looking at the startled girl, by now on the verge of tears, she asked, "What's your name, honey?"

"Tanya," she answered quietly.

"Well, Tanya, let a real pro show you how it's done. Follow me."

Izzy escorted her young protégée to the vat and after a few consoling words of confidence and some brief moments of coaching, she returned to where Frank still stood with his mouth agape.

"You see, Frank, there's a right way, and then there's your way. Your way doesn't work. It's about seeing the potential in a person and working with that potential, not destroying it. Am I making sense to you or did it fly right over that bald head of yours?" Izzy fluttered her hand over her head to stress her point.

"I oughta have you arrested for being back here since you don't work here anymore. What are you doing here anyhow?"

"I came to see you, Frank."

Frank fought to maintain his composure for as angry and resentful as he felt at that moment, he also felt desperation. He wanted Izzy back and hoped that was the motive of her visit. But pride would not allow him to convey this to her. The thought of her begging and crawling had more of an appeal. This moment, it seemed, was his to enjoy.

"Oh, I see. You came to eat crow. You decided that I was right after all, and you were wrong and you've come to apologize. And in appreciation, you just took on the horrendous burden of teaching Miss Dumb Wit over there how to master the fry machine! And I, in turn, am supposed to be gracious and forgiving and invite you back into my humble establishment. Am I right, huh?"

Izzy stepped forward, her eyes glaring with rage. Her first impulse was to thrust a punch at his arrogant face, but instead, she reached up and grabbed him by the collar, pulling him toward her so that they were on the same eye level.

"You listen to me, you jerk! I don't care what you think of me, but you have no right to treat Tanya, or anyone else here, the way you do. I have the goods on you and if I have to, I'll use them to see that you lose this humble establishment. You hear me?"

Frank felt his face flush, wondering exactly what and how much Izzy knew. There were some issues with his taxes that Uncle Sam might be interested in and maybe some not so legal activities in the past.

Whatever she held over him magically worked in her favor. But the truth was, Izzy didn't know anything. Her bluff worked and Frank suddenly humbled himself before her.

"You're right," he said, as he gently removed her hands from his collar. "I have been a jerk, and I'm truly sorry." Embarrassed, Frank glanced around to see how much attention Izzy had drawn his way. Fortunately, it was early and the dining area was nearly vacated, except for a handful of diners, including Izzy's mysterious hugger. And their view was limited, obstructed by part of the diner's décor. But he wasn't without some humiliation, for most of the diner's staff was treated to a front row seat. Despite the absence of cheers and encores for Izzy's performance, he could almost hear the laughter and praise behind their façade. Now faced with the threat of Izzy uncorking his past, he knew the tables had turned. For a moment, he thought maybe jail wouldn't be so bad compared to the image of Izzy gloating. But then, the diner was all he had and if it meant losing the rest of his dignity, so be it.

"You, ah, want a cup of coffee?" he asked.

"Yeah, I could use a cup."

Frank poured them both a cup, after which she followed him to his office. "Izzy, I admit I have my faults," he began, easing himself behind the desk, "and sometimes, it takes someone like you to help bring it to light."

Keep the butter coming, Izzy thought. *I like both sides of my bread buttered.*

"I don't have an excuse for my behavior so I'm not going to make one up. I'm not Sam and I'll never be Sam. But I can work on being a better Frank."

Izzy, bored, sat sipping her coffee, wondering when he was going to stop rambling on and get to what was really on his mind. She could sense that he was still occupied with the delusion that she had him over a barrel, which added to her enjoyment, but this also raised her curiosity about what he was hiding.

"I guess what I'm trying to say, Izzy, is that I want to be a better person, a better boss, a better friend."

"That's mighty noble of you, Frank," she told him, resisting the urge to yawn, "but seeing is believing. Too bad I'm not here to see it."

"Which brings me to something else I want to talk about."

Finally, she thought, *guess I had to provide the ammo.*

"I felt bad about the way you left and I felt particularly bad about the way I acted. I had no right to jump all over you like that. It was a stupid impulse and I'm sorry. Would you, ah . . . ah . . ."

"Would I what, Frank?" Izzy basked in the moment. The desperation was starting to seep into his voice.

"Would you consider, you know, coming back? Please?"

"Hmmmm. Let's get this straight. I was right and you were wrong and you're apologizing to me. And you want me back in your humble establishment. So, who's eating crow now?"

"OK, I deserved that. The truth is, I need you. The staff, the customers, they're all brooding over you being gone and I'm getting the bulk of the blame. There are more cold shoulders in the kitchen and dining area than in the freezer. If you come back, I'll give you a raise and I'll let you pick your own hours. C'mon, what do you say?"

Izzy pretended to be considering his offer, relishing the sight of Frank begging. She enjoyed it so much, she waited a whole minute before answering.

"No . . . no," she finally said, rather casually.

"No?" Frank echoed, unable to conceal the disappointment in his eyes.

"As much as I miss the people and your charming personality, I don't want to come back. I've been thinking of fully retiring for a while."

Frank didn't expect her to completely dash his hopes. He felt confident that she would at least give it some thought. But it was as if she had planned this moment, to see him at her mercy, just to turn him down. It also occurred to him that she had said "retiring." He wondered how she could manage that when she wasn't even close to retirement age.

"I would like to ask a favor of you, though," she said, impeding his thoughts. "I know you have a temp job opening in the office. I just happen to know someone who would be perfect for that. She's experienced, ambitious and smart. I think you ought to talk to her."

Frank, no longer feeling humble, started to reject Izzy's request, then remembered the "thing" Izzy had knowledge of. "Yeah, sure. I'll talk to her. Tell her to come see me around nine Wednesday morning."

"Thanks, Frank. I knew you had a heart in there somewhere." Frank, in turn, made a last ditch effort. "Will you at least think about what I said? I don't care if it's just part-time."

"I'll consider, but I've pretty much made up my mind. If it makes you feel any better, though, I think I'm actually gonna miss you." Izzy offered him a slight smile, then turned and walked away.

As she made her way through the diner, waving at June along the way, Frank realized she had neglected to give him the potential temp's name. "Wait, Izzy! You didn't tell me this girl's name!"

But Izzy was already out the door. She couldn't give him a name; she didn't know which one to give.

Allie wandered around what she had considered her home for the past week, making sure she hadn't neglected any of her belongings, though there were few. This really had started to feel like home to her, a haven of some sort . . . but a short-term haven. She couldn't live her life out in a motel room, as cozy and safe as it had made her feel.

Satisfied she had packed everything, her eyes made contact with the phone. Her biggest concern was Derrick. She wished she could've let him know her plans before she left, but there was no time. She did, however, take consolation in knowing her staff would inform him once they had read her note. She knew Frieda would be the one to take charge until she returned, since she was the broker and knew everything about the business. Frieda had been with her for years and there wasn't anything she couldn't do. She'd left her in charge many times, and Frieda had done an excellent job in her absence, but this was the first time she had more or less passed the baton to her so abruptly, leaving only a note for them to see in the morning.

Although she felt she'd covered all her bases, she couldn't shake this uneasy feeling in the pit of her stomach. Then it hit her. She'd somehow overlooked the possibility that they would really have no way of knowing if she was truly on vacation, or if she'd been kidnapped, and the note had possibly been written under duress, assuming they found the note.

She moved toward the bed, then sat down, her hand reaching for the receiver. After a few seconds of hesitation, she picked it up, but just as quick, put it back down. Not knowing how resourceful Gary was in tracking her was enough to remind her to take all precautions. But the more she thought about her brother and how worried he probably was, the more determined she was to call. *This is crazy,* she thought. *I'm just being paranoid.*

She picked up the receiver again, this time dialing the number and using her calling card. Allie felt a wave of disappointment when the answering machine picked up. Any other time, he'd be right there, practically sitting on the phone, she mused. She started to leave a message at the beep and thought better of it. Instead, she returned the receiver to its cradle and resolved to try again, perhaps at a payphone, concluding that might be safer. Rethinking that last thought, she retrieved her calling card once again. She decided to make two more calls. She knew somebody would be at the realty. It was never left unattended, unlike Derrick's business. He often left the answering machine on when he and his salesman was out on the lot making a sale.

After hearing the first ring, Amber's less-than-chipper voice suddenly came on.

"A.J. Realty. This is Amber. How can I help you?"

"Well, how about you guys making a close on two or three homes today?"

"Allie! How are you? Where are you? We have been so worried about you!"

"I'm OK. I'm sorry about the sudden departure, but I felt I had to go. I assume you got my note?"

"Yeah, we did." Amber decided not to mention how they found it, nor the fact that the police had read it as well.

"And to answer your second question, I'll tell you. But please, just keep it between you, Tess and Frieda. Oh, and Derrick, if you see him. I plan on calling him later. Anyway, I'm staying in a little town called Possum Heights."

"Blossom Heights?"

"No, Possum, with a 'P'." She could hear Amber giggling on the other end.

"You're staying in a town named after a possum?"

"It wasn't planned. It's just where I ended up," Allie said, trying to defend herself.

"Oh, OK. I believe you."

"I'm actually moving out of the motel and in with someone I met here. She offered me a place to stay and I took her up on it. And to tell you the truth, it's kinda nice having someone else around." Allie refrained from giving Amber any details or descriptions of her new friend. *Too much, too soon.*

"You think Gary's looking for you?"

"I don't think so. Have you seen him lurking around?"

"No, but he did call here, Allie, right after you left."

"What did he say?" Allie asked, feeling her heart beat louder.

"He just said he wanted to speak to you and then he uttered the strangest thing."

"What?"

"Miami . . . he just said Miami, and that was the end of the conversation."

Allie felt her skin crawl as she recalled the early morning hours when she left her office and Gary surprised her in the parking lot. His final word was "Miami."

"Allie. Allie! You still there?"

"That's what he said to me, the morning I left."

"What?"

"Never mind, I'll explain later. Just be careful, Amber. This guy's not playing with a full deck. If he shows up there, call the cops."

Hope I don't have to, Amber thought. *Lieutenant Mims already thinks we're nuts.* "All right. I will. And Allie, you be careful."

Allie hung up and immediately made her second call.

"Tim's Garage."

"Tim . . . hey, it's me, Allie."

"Allie! Hey, good to hear your voice. We've all been worried about you."

"I know and I'm sorry. I just had to get away. But I'm OK. Look, I just wanted you to tell Derrick if you see him that I'm all right and I'm staying in a little town called Possum Heights. I told Amber to keep this between her and the girls and I want you to do the same. I'll try to call Derrick later but if you should happen to see him, just give him this info and I'd appreciate it."

"I'll do better than that, Allie. I'll go tell him personally."

"Would you? I appreciate that, Tim. You're a dear."

"No problem. Are you really OK? I know this thing with Gary got out of hand. I feel bad 'cause if I'd never hired him, you probably wouldn't be up there in . . . where did you say?"

"Possum Heights, and don't ask. I don't know how it got its name. And listen, don't feel bad about anything. It's not your fault."

"Allie. There is something you need to know."

"What is it, Tim?" She instantly knew from Tim's tone of voice that Gary had contacted him, in addition to her business.

"He showed up here Saturday. Looked and smelled terrible. Said, 'I miss her. What did I do to deserve this?' I tried to tell him in a nice way to let go, to move on with his life. He didn't take that too well. He punched me, knocking me on the floor. He started to hit me again but changed his mind and left. I called Derrick and left him a message that you needed to be warned. At least I know you're OK."

"Did you call the police?"

"No, I should have, but it happened so quickly."

Allie didn't have to second-guess their breakup any more; she was convinced now that he was really stupid. "I appreciate you telling me this, Tim. It makes me even more positive that I made the right decision coming here. Maybe time and distance will cure his obsession."

"I hope so. He turned out to be a real nut case."

"Well, I better go. And thanks again for informing Derrick. Bye."

As she glanced around the barren room one last time, she softly closed the door to her haven. Her new haven would be in the big white house with the wraparound porch inside the white picket fence, not to mention the furry little felines within.

Tim stared at the piece of paper where he'd written "Allie—Possum Heights." He could only imagine what Derrick's reaction would be when he learned his sister was vacationing in a town named after road kill.

Smiling, he took the piece of paper and tacked it to his corkboard in the office, along with the other important memos he kept. Noting the time on the wall, he locked the office, then the rest of the shop, humming an old Frank Sinatra tune along the way: "Strangers in the Night." Then he was on the road to Jones' Auto Sales.

Chapter 23

Richard, a creature of habit, grew increasingly irritated when Izzy didn't show up at six o'clock to pick him up for his birthday dinner. His first thought was that it had to be intentional. She knew his pet peeves, that everything had to be on time. If the plumber was scheduled to be at his house at nine in the morning, he expected to see him by nine. To be a minute late was downright rude and discourteous, a direct insult to the one waiting.

Glancing out his back window, he could still make out her jeep in the backyard. This irritated him all the more, knowing she'd left it there for him to see and to make him wonder when she was going to get in it and drive the two seconds over to his driveway. Shaking his head, he decided to make one last trip to the bathroom. But before he even reached the bathroom door, he heard the familiar putter of a Volkswagen Beetle creeping up his driveway.

"She didn't," he muttered. "I know she didn't just drive up my driveway in that pregnant roller skate." Deciding that it was her turn to wait on him, he went on to the bathroom.

Tiptoeing back down the hallway and peering out the window, he grunted. Richard had nothing against Barney or VW's in general. He just had a hard time trying to squeeze in it because of his height . . . and Izzy knew it.

She did this on purpose, he thought. Adding insult to injury, she honked the horn, not a regular horn either, but an "ah-oooo-ga" horn. Richard decided not to give her the satisfaction of seeing how peeved he was. He opted to play along. This was, after all, his birthday, and he wasn't going to let a little thing like being scrunched up in an "igloo on wheels" bother him. She was thirty minutes late and came over in Barney. What else could she possibly irritate him with?

Taking a deep breath, he flung the door open and hoped she couldn't see through his happy disguise. "I see you got the insect on wheels out of the shop. Nice."

"Bug," Izzy corrected. "Barney's a beetle bug."

"Insect, bug, whatever . . . how's the ole Barn' doing?"

"Running like a charm. Ollie did a complete physical on him, including a tune up, so he's fit for another hundred-thousand miles."

"You treat that thing better than you treat yourself."

"We gonna stand here and gab or we gonna go chow down?" Izzy flared back.

"OK, OK. But why don't I drive?" he asked, hoping it didn't sound like a plea.

"No, I'll drive. It's your birthday. Besides, Barney needs to get out after being cooped up in that ole grease pit."

Richard shook his head again as he locked the door and started toward the car. Izzy watched him, amused, as he struggled to position himself in the passenger side of the car, his knees almost touching his nose once he got all the way in.

"What?" he asked, visibly peeved as she stood beside the car grinning.

"Oh, nothing." But as she made her way to the other side, she muttered, "Looks like a praying mantis."

"I heard that!" Richard shouted between his knees.

Izzy struggled to keep a straight face as she and Richard started down the road. She knew he had to be uncomfortable but he never complained. He was adamant about not giving in to Izzy's mind games.

Maybe, he thought, *a little reverse psychology would deprive her of this silly little pleasure.*

But no matter what Richard thought and kept to himself, Izzy still relished the idea that she always managed to have the upper hand and could always count on hitting just the right nerve where Richard was concerned. She knew he wouldn't complain, at least not verbally. Inwardly, he had to be raging.

When they pulled into the driveway of the Steak and Seafood Tavern, her right wheel missed the turn, hitting the shallow ditch and bouncing the car, causing Richard to bump his head on the roof of the car.

"Where's your glasses?" Richard asked, again trying to hide his annoyance.

"They're on my face," Izzy said, pointing to her eyes.

"No, I mean the glasses you can see out of. How could you not see that ditch? I'm telling you, you need to get those peepers of yours checked and get some new specs."

"My specs are just fine, thank you. I just couldn't see the ditch through your knees."

"Noooo . . . you need . . . to check . . . your . . . eyes!"

"I'm renewing my license soon, Einstein. I'll prove to you that my eyes and my glasses are just fine. As a matter of fact, I'm not even restricted to glasses. I can drive without them. But I prefer to drive with them."

Once they had parked, Izzy calmly got out and started toward the door, keenly aware that Richard wasn't following.

"Hey! Hey!" he shouted. "Where's the fire? Can't you see I'm stuck?"

Izzy looked back, smiling devilishly as Richard struggled to free his limbs, thinking that must be how it feels to be inside a cocoon.

"I'm hungry!" she yelled back. "With or without you, I'm going in!"

Richard finally managed to become untangled and extricated himself from the VW. He was stiff and sore but tried to mask it as he quickly caught up with Izzy, his long legs being an advantage. "Ya know, if you really wanted to torture me, you could've chained me to the bumper . . . on second thought, that might have been more comfortable." Richard gave up on trying to feign contentment.

Izzy, as usual, had won. "Whatever are you talking about, Richard?" she asked innocently. "Look, we're here to celebrate your birthday. Try to act happy and be positive, for once."

"Oh, I'm positive. I'm positive your mission is to torment me. But you know what? You're losing your touch. I'm glad you drove the bug. It actually helped to limber me up, kinda like yoga."

Izzy rolled her eyes. Did he really think she was that gullible?

Inside the restaurant, Richard breathed in deeply, taking in the tantalizing aroma. This was one of his favorite dining places, not only for the savory entrees on the menu, but for the elaborate ocean décor that graced every wall. It was one of the nice things he could say about Izzy, that she treated him well, when it came to dining out. But he knew, too, that she was treating herself as well so it wasn't too much of a sacrifice.

The hostess escorted them to a secluded booth, where Izzy quickly confirmed hers and Richard's relationship.

"He ain't my boyfriend, just my friend . . . and neighbor." The hostess smiled and seemed to share some of Richard's embarrassment.

As she walked away, he eyed Izzy with contempt. "Do you really think she cares? Or are you embarrassed to be seen with somebody normal?"

"If you don't mind, birthday boy, I gotta go to the little girls' room," she said, ignoring Richard's questions.

"OK. And while you're gone, I'll try and think of something nice to say about you."

Izzy, once again, ignored Richard's sarcasm and headed for the bathroom while Richard played with the cardboard fixture on the table, displaying the different mixed drinks. His arms and legs still felt a little stiff from the ride over but he was thankful to at least get his circulation back.

"Sir." Richard jumped at the voice of the waitress who had just approached the booth.

"Oh, hi. I was just looking over the drink specials." Then, struck with an idea, he grinned. "How about a bottle of your most expensive champagne?"

"Well, sir, your friend, whom I just ran into going to the bathroom, has already ordered the drinks. She ordered the house wine." *Cheapskate,* Richard thought. His idea had floundered.

"OK," he sighed.

"Here's your menus. I'll be back later to take your order . . . and bring your drinks."

Although the waitress was seemingly polite enough, he felt she was acting out a role in a play she didn't want to be in to start with . . . the role of a waitress.

Allie had put away what few belongings she had brought with her and proceeded to explore her new surroundings. It still seemed surreal to her to be staying in what she had always imagined her dream home to be. Every room had its own personalized décor. But what amazed her the most was the actual structure itself. All of it appeared to be original. She knew this by being in the real estate business and seeing so many houses, old and new, but nothing compared to this house. It was a far cry from anything she'd ever seen. Even though her financial status was certainly secure, she would easily pass over a newly-built house for an older one such as this. It had the old pine knot paneling, the narrow slabs of hardwood flooring.

But her favorite feature by far was the wraparound porch that encased three sides of the house. On each side perched several white wooden rockers and on the front side hung an old fashioned swing dangling from rusty-but-sturdy chains. The rarity of seeing old houses like this, especially in such mint condition, intrigued her all the more.

She found herself dreamingly pacing the porch from one end to the other, then finally collapsing onto the swing, where one of the cats lounged, curled up in a ball.

"Hey . . . Claude, Clyde, Cleo, Caesar, whichever one you are. Mind if I sit here with you?"

The huge fur ball briefly opened his eyes, then continued on with his nap, unfazed by his new house guest. Swinging gently, so as not to disturb his slumber, Allie passed the time gazing up at the stars and reminiscing of years long gone but etched in her memories. She could hear the familiar sound of the whippoorwill off in the distance, while lightning bugs frolicked in the sweet smelling air, a scent Allie recognized as honeysuckle. She suddenly felt glad to have taken this unplanned trip, regardless of how it came to be. She just knew that this moment felt right and that was all that mattered.

Leaning back on the hard wooden bench, Izzy made faces while watching Richard consume his order of escargot. He hadn't planned to order the French delicacy, especially since he had never had it before, but seeing the price and remembering Izzy's promise to pay for the entire meal, he couldn't resist the temptation. Once he got past the initial repulsion, he was surprised to discover they were actually very tasty.

"Yuck! How can you eat that? It's disgusting!"

"You like shrimp, don't you? Snails don't look much different than shrimp and quite frankly, I think they have more flavor."

"Yeah, but I don't see shrimp crawling up the side of my pump house, either."

"You won't try escargot, but you eat sardine sandwiches."

"I hate sardines."

"OK, so maybe I got the fish wrong. I know it comes out of a can."

"That's mackerel, you nincompoop."

"Mackerel sandwiches, then. It's still repulsive. Changing the subject, as stimulating and educational as it is, I want to hear more about this mystery woman you've got moving in with you."

"That's none of your business, Rich."

"C'mon, Iz, this here's your ole buddy, Richard, your neighbor, your friend."

"Buddy," Izzy huffed.

"OK. Neighbor, at least."

"Just 'cause it's your birthday don't mean I gotta indulge you. Besides, I don't know any more than I've already told you."

"You ain't worried she's some deranged killer or maybe some escapee from the nuthouse?"

"I've already got somebody from the nuthouse living next door. So why would that worry me? Look, Richard," she said, leaning closer. "I know enough to trust her in my house with my cats, so let's just leave it at that."

"OK, OK. I was just concerned, that's all."

"You ready to go?" Izzy asked, sharply, visibly annoyed with Richard.

"Whenever you are. But we haven't gotten the bill yet," Richard said, proud his part was the most expensive. He wondered if Izzy had already figured it up in her head.

"Oh yeah. What is it with that waitress anyway? She's got the personality of a doorknob."

"I had a sense about her, too, when she first came to the table with the menus. And what little she's been over here since, she's been a real crab."

"Here comes ole happy drawers now," Izzy said.

As the sullen waitress approached the table, Richard braced for whatever might gush from Izzy's mouth.

"Look, honey, we're done here. Could you bring us the tab please?"

Richard, proud of Izzy's cool temperament, gave the waitress a smile, hoping to evoke one in return, but her gaze hinted that she was in no mood to be friendly. Rather, she nodded and walked off, without even asking how they enjoyed their meal. When she returned, her expression remained unchanged, and again, no words. After slapping the bill down upon the table, she quickly marched toward the kitchen.

"Well! How do ya like that? She ain't got any business waiting tables!" Richard raved.

"You're absolutely right. She *ain't* got any business waiting tables. Just the same, think I'll leave her a tip." Izzy pulled out a ten-dollar bill and placed it on the table while Richard stared in disbelief.

"You can't be serious, are you? Leaving her a tip, ten dollars at that?"

"Relax. It's counterfeit. Been trying to get rid of it for months."

The waitress, seeing the odd couple exchanging high fives as she came from the kitchen, delivered two plates at a nearby table. A quick glance over revealed the generous ten-dollar tip, evoking a tinge of remorse from the horrible waitress.

Chapter 24

A faint light illuminated the house as Izzy pulled into her driveway. It was so faint, she imagined it was coming from the hallway where she had placed a nightlight. It was still early, barely turning dark, but she assumed Allie must have already turned in with what appeared to be just the nightlight glowing. It felt odd coming home and seeing this bright red Mustang parked in her yard, having lived alone so long, but it was kind of nice, too. Allie needed a friend in this strange town, someone she could place confidence in. And what better way to do that than to welcome her into her home? It would be good for her as well. She'd have someone to vent to whenever Richard grated on her nerves.

As she started to unlock the door, she suddenly found herself hesitating. What if Richard was right? What if she was a deranged killer or an escapee from the nuthouse? Her heart and instinct had invited her here, but now her mind was questioning her actions. Had she been too hasty? Aside from the absurd possibilities Richard had rendered, she alluded to her own. Was she neat? Would she not leave dishes in the sink? Would she make up her bed every day? Would she not junk up the fridge? To some, this might have seemed trivial, but not to Izzy. It was a very big deal. Had she compromised the order of her domain?

Her nerves tensed as she rotated the door handle. She'd already envisioned her house in disarray. She'd made light of going over the rules, "if there were any," when she'd invited her to move in and now those words made her cringe. Despite having multiple cats, she managed to keep the house immaculate. Had she mentioned that to Allie? Or maybe she didn't have to say anything. Surely, she had observed for herself. Then she recalled Allie's own dainty appearance. Anyone who took the pains of looking her best the way she did, surely kept a clean surrounding. She suddenly felt stupid for having such silly and negative thoughts.

Cracking the door ajar, she noticed the nightlight was indeed on in the hallway, as she had predicted. Although dim and limited to its illumination, she could still make out the spotless condition of the floor. She also quickly got a glimpse of Allie's shoes placed neatly beside the wicker chair, where Claude lay taking a bath.

"Good girl," she whispered. Smiling, she entered and closed the door. Maybe her instincts were right all along. Maybe Allie would make a compatible roomie, for however long. Pulling off her own shoes and setting them next to Allie's, she continued on down the foyer, tiptoeing, so as not to disturb her. As she started past the kitchen, a voice startled her.

"Hi. How was the birthday dinner?"

"Allie? What are you doing in the dark?" Izzy gasped.

"I couldn't find the light switch. And I wanted some tea. Just made a pot. Hope that was OK. Oh, and I used a flashlight you had sitting next to the toaster."

"The light switch . . . it's behind the toaster," Izzy said, reaching behind the toaster and flipping it on.

"Well, I'll be doggone. Boy, do I ever feel stupid. Would you like some tea?" Allie asked, trying to mask her embarrassment.

"Sure."

While Allie prepared another cup of tea, Izzy scanned the kitchen, looking for anything that might be out of place. To her amazement and immense satisfaction, everything was exactly as she had left it; the floors, the countertops, everything was neat and in its place. There was no longer any second-guessing. She knew her instincts had been right all along.

"I'll clean the pot when we're finished with our tea," Allie assured her, almost as if reading her mind.

"No, no. Don't worry about that. You made the tea. I'll clean the pot. So, did you find the room suitable?"

"Are you kidding me? It's great. Thank you. You're a wonderful hostess."

"Well, that's kind of you to say. But I do need to tell you that the cats may go in there. They pretty much have their roam of the house. You don't mind that, do ya?"

"Of course not. I love cats. I had cats growing up."

"Well, these will vie for your attention. I think my lap is the most coveted seat in the house. But as the rule goes, first come, first served. Well, enough about them. Have you eaten anything?"

"I had a bagel earlier."

"A bagel? That's all? I think we can come up with something else to put on your stomach."

Allie grimaced. The thought of what Izzy might cook up nauseated her. After all, this was a woman accustomed to fried grit sandwiches.

As if reading her thoughts, Izzy quickly made a suggestion. "How about a ham and Swiss cheese sandwich? Won't take but a minute to put one together and while you're eating, I can go slip into something a little more comfortable. These pants are riding me something fierce."

"OK, a ham and cheese sandwich sounds good. Thanks."

While Izzy prepped her new friend a sandwich, Allie engaged in small conversation, as well as inconspicuously monitoring her at work.

"You never did answer my question earlier. How was the birthday dinner?"

"Oh, the food was great. The waitress sucked. Other than that, I think Richard enjoyed his birthday."

"So, what's he like?" Allie said, peeking around Izzy's elbow as she spread what she hoped was mayonnaise or mustard on the slices of bread.

"Richard and I go back a long ways. It's a love, hate type thing. No, actually, hate's too strong a word. I know some people don't like him, but that's because they don't know him. He talks like he's mad at the world sometimes, but deep down, he's just a pussy cat. I'm one of the few people that can make him purr, as well as hiss."

"You two see each other, I mean, like romantically?"

Izzy released the hyena, startling Allie. *I'll never get used to that,* she thought.

"Mercy, no. We're just neighbors, and sometimes, friends. He's pretty much a homebody, stays to himself a lot. But when he does go out, you can't miss him in a crowd. He's tall and lanky and if you ask me, a little on the feminine side. But Richard, well, he's all right." Izzy placed the sandwich on the table in front of Izzy.

"Here you go, sweetie. Got some chips to go with it if you want."

"No thanks; this is fine." Caution glowed in her eyes as she stared up at Izzy, then back at the sandwich.

"Go ahead, inspect it if you want. All that's on there is ham, Swiss cheese and a little mayo. No grits, I promise."

Allie slowly separated the slices, then leaned over to sniff, much to Izzy's amusement.

"See, I told you," she laughed.

Satisfied the sandwich was really ham and cheese, Allie rejoined the slices, then took a large bite.

"Mmmm, delicious. Thank you, Izzy."

"You're welcome." Izzy smiled, glad to see Allie was gaining her trust. "Well, if you'll excuse me, I'm going to change into something else and when I come back, maybe we can treat ourselves to a little nightcap, perhaps sample a little of that merlot we bought, huh?"

Allie nodded as Izzy left the kitchen with five cats trailing her. Her first night here, she felt ill-prepared to confide in Izzy, but it appeared the mood was being set. Ready or not, she suspected Izzy was anxious to crack her shell, and considering she took her in, she felt obligated to hand over the hammer.

When Izzy returned, Allie had two glasses of Merlot placed on the table. She laughed, but left the hyena behind.

"I propose a toast."

"To what?" Allie asked.

"To fate. I think it was fate that we kept running into each other . . . at the stop sign, at the diner, at the grocery store. There must be a reason why we kept bumping into each other. So to whatever it is that wants us bonded, so to speak, here's to us."

"Nice toast. Here's to us."

Allie clinked her glass with Izzy's and for the first time, genuinely felt a bond. Despite her eccentricities, she was starting to perceive her in a much different light, a light illuminated by kindness and compassion. *Ironic*, she thought, considering their initial encounter was fueled by rage.

Izzy watched her take a sip, then two, obviously taking pleasure in her pick of the vineyard, once again winning her trust.

"Mmm, good. You were right," Allie admitted. "Not only a bargain, but very pleasing to the palate. Glad I heeded your advice."

"Some more advice. Save the cheaper wines for cooking. Your palate won't know the difference."

"I'll drink to that," she laughed, once more clinking her glass with Izzy's.

"So, tell me something, kiddo." Izzy's gaze took on one of austerity. "Why an alias? What are you running from? Whatever it is, I want to emphasize complete confidentiality and I will not compromise that for your safety. Don't be afraid to tell me what's going on. The more I know, the better I'm able to help you." Izzy leaned forward and grabbed her hands, which were tightly nestled around her wine glass.

"Now, I don't mean to be presumptuous, but I do have the feeling that you're running from someone. Am I right?"

Allie swallowed hard and closed her eyes as if the weight she carried could finally be shifted. She had no reason to not trust Izzy after she'd opened her home to her, to mingle among her precious furry companions. Was that her way of proving her point, that trust should be a mutual thing? This seemed to be the opportune time to relay her story, especially with the knowledge that Gary could and probably would find her in the sanctity of this new haven. That thought suddenly rendered her terrified as she opened her eyes and exposed the fear now clutching her heart.

"Oh, Izzy!" she cried. "I shouldn't be here! I'm afraid . . . I'm afraid I might have put you in danger!"

"Whoa, girlfriend, slow down a bit here. Take it easy. Seems like you just skipped over the whole story and went straight for the end. Now, tell me exactly what's going on and why you feel I might be in danger."

Allie took a deep breath then somberly related her story to Izzy, from the moment she first encountered Gary to that terrible night in the parking lot at her business, where he witnessed her drive away into the night, hopefully, she added, without a trail. She mentioned his strange rantings of "Miami" and wondered what that could have meant. Izzy listened with fascination and concluded that this character was indeed a nut.

"So you see," she said, her voice slightly quivering, "that's why I think I might have put you in jeopardy. This may not have been a good idea after all, I mean, me staying here."

"Nonsense!" Izzy quickly blurted out. "There is no way on God's green earth he can track you here. He doesn't even know what town you're in. I think he's just got you paranoid and rightly so, after what you just told me. Now, don't you worry that pretty little head of yours. You're not going anywhere, ya hear? Mi casa, su casa. Comprende?"

Allie, touched by Izzy's much-needed assurance, wiped the tears that were seeping down along her cheeks and laughed with relief.

"Comprende, senorita. Gracias. I really needed to hear that tonight."

"My pleasure. And since you've been open and honest with me tonight, and wise, I might add, I'll open the gateway for you. You must have some questions in regards to myself. So . . . fire away."

Allie giggled at the prospect of being able to finally probe into the mind of this eccentric woman before her. But even with this unique opportunity at hand, she found herself at a loss of where to begin. All the questions she had harbored within seemed to have collided and picking one from the basket, so to speak, was harder than she anticipated, almost like trying to decide which present to open first on Christmas morning. Although odd behavior was at the top of her list, she decided to focus on something less peculiar: her house.

"This house, it's so enormous and picturesque. Forgive me if I'm being too personal, but how can you afford it? I mean, you were a cook at the diner and now you're out of a job. How is it possible to keep and maintain a place like this on a fry cook's salary and now, none at all?"

Izzy laughed, but softly. "It's an inheritance and with it came, well . . . a little money. But I also made my own money. I had a landscaping and nursery business at one time, which I sold a while back. It was very prosperous, but the opportunity came along to relinquish it and I earned a sizable profit from the sale. Besides, it was getting tougher to handle with my arthritis."

"Oh, sorry. Didn't know you had arthritis."

"It's not that bad. Only flares up now and then."

"But why did you work at the diner? Sounds like you didn't have to," Allie continued.

"No, I didn't. But, I love to cook and I love people and I love to stay busy. Not even ole Frank knows my story about the house or my former businesses. He's not from here originally, so he wouldn't know, unless someone told him, which I seriously doubt. Oh goodness, that reminds me, I almost forgot. Remember that temp job I mentioned? Well, it's at the diner, working in the office. I talked with Frank and he said to come see him tomorrow at nine o'clock, that is, if you're interested."

"Tomorrow?"

"Yeah, sorry it's such short notice. But, like I said, if you're interested, it'll at least give you something to do; ain't much going on in Possum Heights and it'll also give you a little spending money. Plus, like I said before, should you decide to stay . . . look, I know it can't compare to a Realtor's salary—"

"OK, OK," Allie interrupted. "I'll go since you went through the trouble of setting it up. Um, did you perchance tell him my name?"

"No, honey, I didn't know which one to use."

"Thanks," Allie laughed.

"Sure."

"No, I mean truly thanks, for everything. For letting me stay here, for the talk, and of course, the job opportunity. You really are a true friend."

"So are you. Now what do ya say we just put these glasses in the sink and turn in for the night?"

The two women rose from the table with a renewed respect and admiration for one another. Their deepest conversation thus far had erased the tensions beneath the surface, allowing them more freedom to carry on.

"You get a good night's rest, sunshine. See ya in the morning," Izzy said, as she flicked the kitchen light off and started down the hallway to her bedroom.

"Yeah, you, too."

Allie took one final look around before heading to bed herself. *Must be nice,* she thought. *Must be nice.*

Chapter 25

As Derrick lay stretched out on the sofa in his modest, yet orderly living room area, he felt an overwhelming sense of relief. Hearing Amber say she'd talked to Allie and that she was OK had lifted his spirits considerably. And with Tim's unexpected appearance at work earlier re-confirming the same message, he felt doubly relieved. He only wished he'd been near the phone when she'd tried to contact him. But just knowing she'd called and was all right eased his anxiety. *Hopefully, she'll call again,* he thought, *preferably tonight, here at home, where I'll be near the phone, and there'll be no interruptions.*

Half asleep, half awake, he was startled by the sound of a phone ringing, so soft, he wondered if he had heard it at all. Still lying on the sofa, he fumbled beyond his head and grasped the receiver, bringing it blindly to his ear.

"Hello. Hello?"

The phone kept ringing even as he gripped the receiver. Through droopy eyes, he watched a woman on TV pick up her phone as well, bringing the rings to an end. The rings he heard weren't resonating from his phone, he realized, but from the TV.

Frustrated, he returned the receiver to its cradle and grabbed the remote control. Hitting the power button, the TV went blank. His mind on Allie, he knew it'd be hard to fall back asleep. He contemplated going to bed but the comfort of the sofa seemed to lure him to stay. He also knew if he got up to go to bed, he'd only toss and turn. Oftentimes, he wondered why he even bothered to sleep in the bedroom when the sofa was so much more comfortable.

Derrick, in his drowsy state of mind, drifted in his thoughts. It seemed like only yesterday that he and Allie were sitting here on this very sofa having a cup of coffee on one of their usual Friday morning visits, harmlessly ribbing each other. *Funny how you miss the little things in life.* With the exception of the past two Fridays, he couldn't remember when they had not done that, not counting the times she was out of town, which was rare. It had accidentally become a tradition, a part of their weekly routine. Yet, as this Friday loomed closer, it appeared he would be sipping his coffee alone again.

A noise from outside shattered the silence, jolting him upright, unaware he had even fallen asleep. He sat almost paralyzed for the next few moments, searching in his mind for what he might have heard. Unlike before, when he heard the phone ringing, he couldn't relate it back to the TV, since it was turned off. Maybe it was a dream. Yes, that's what it was, he decided. He'd been awakened many times before by crazy dreams, although, oddly, he could never remember the events within that forced him awake.

Lying back down, he closed his eyes and tried to renew his dormancy when a metal clash of some sort sounded, once again stirring his conscious state of mind. This time, he knew it wasn't a dream.

Springing up from the sofa and grabbing a flashlight nearby, he tiptoed to the back door, not wanting to frighten the intruder away without first getting a good glimpse of him. At the same time, he hoped there was nothing to see. Bracing himself, he counted to three, then with one swift motion, unlocked and swung the back door open with one hand, while flipping the outside switch on with the other, and amazingly, all while still holding the flashlight. But to his disappointment, which was somewhat mixed with relief, there was no one there, nor any sign of anyone being there. He was sure that was where the noise originated from but if he was wrong, the phantom of the night was more than likely gone by now, perhaps startled by the door slinging open and the light switched on.

Derrick scanned the yard with the beam from his flashlight, catching the images of his vehicle, the shed, a large oak tree, a picnic table and a trash barrel full of trash. Seeing the trash reminded him that it could have been an animal he heard, perhaps a raccoon or possum nosing around in the yard for something to eat. He remembered throwing out some scraps earlier near the shed amidst some junk he'd put to the side to haul off to the dump, the junk being mostly layers of rusted tin. He concluded that whatever found the scraps stumbled upon the tin, making the noise.

He focused the flashlight closer to the shed and sure enough, he saw two possums scampering away into some nearby trees. He started to laugh for he suddenly remembered hearing the town where Allie was staying, a town called Possum Heights. He couldn't wait to tease her about this. *Possum Heights*, he thought, *wonder if it's close to Raccoon Ravine.*

Satisfied he'd located the source of the racket, Derrick closed and locked the door, then turned in for the night, this time shuffling past the sofa, yawning widely, to the bedroom.

"Possum Heights," he chuckled, then crawled into bed.

Izzy squinted, first one eye, then the other, as the examiner patiently waited for her to read the numbers through the eyepiece of the eye-examining machine. Taking her eyes from the lens and peeping around at the examiner, she repeated her question from earlier.

"Which line did you say read?"

"Third from the bottom," he said, glancing at his watch.

Izzy peered through the lens again and then back at the examiner.

"Are you sure?"

The examiner nodded as Izzy again studied the blurry dots before her.

"An ant couldn't make this out," she mumbled.

"Excuse me?" the examiner asked, wishing he'd taken the day off.

"Nothing. Well . . . looks like 18, 42 . . . 21 . . ."

"What?"

The examiner quickly turned the machine around and peeked through the lens himself. Turning it back toward her, he said, in a calmer voice, "Read it again."

"Look, I have glasses," Izzy chirped. "I wear them for driving, even though I'm not restricted."

"Well, pleeeease, put them on," he stressed, observing the growing line behind her.

Izzy fished for her glasses in her oversized pocketbook. Upon extracting them, she positioned the hippie style lenses upon her face. Gazing back through the eyepiece, she clearly saw that there were no double digits.

"Oh, this is much better. I can even read the bottom line now."

"That won't be necessary, ma'am," the examiner said, wiping his brow. "You definitely need glasses to drive . . . restrictive glasses."

"I've never been restricted before," Izzy protested.

"Well, you are now. Take this over to the next station to have your mug taken," he instructed, relieved to be done with her.

Izzy couldn't help but think how Richard would gloat when he found out she was restricted to glasses while driving. It'd be the first thing he'd ask when he saw her. But then again, maybe he didn't have to know.

Still pouting over her newly-acquired restricted license, Izzy left the DMV and crossed the parking lot toward her car. She paused to watch a group of kids playing on a field nearby. Something in that blurry distance caught her eye. Realizing she needed her glasses to get a better view—*OK, Mr. Eye Examiner, you were right*—she dug them out of her purse. Peering through the lens, she could see the kids actively engaged in a ball game while one kid sat quietly on the bleachers.

Stowing her glasses, she abandoned her car and walked toward the field to get a closer look. As she drew nearer, she noticed that the kid on the bleachers was a little girl, who looked to be about eleven or twelve years old. She had her head partially hidden in her arms on her lap and appeared to be crying profusely. Izzy's heart melted as she approached the raggedy benches and sat beside her. At first, the little girl didn't acknowledge her presence, and then Izzy cleared her throat. The little girl raised her head, startled, her eyes red and her face streaked with tears.

"Wanna tell me what's wrong, sweetie?" Izzy asked, already suspecting she knew. She wasn't dressed or groomed as well as the other kids and Izzy knew kids that age could be cruel if you're different.

"They won't let me play with them," she sobbed. "They called me names and laughed at me."

"Is that so?"

The little girl nodded and fought to keep herself from crying again.

"You know, sweetie, some people, or kids, are going to say or do things in life to make you feel real good, and then there are those who will do their best to make you feel bad. The important thing is, you have to show them that you're better than that, that you're above it. Don't take their words to heart. Their words are meaningless. What's your name, sweetie?"

"Lila," she said, sobbing less now.

"That's a pretty name. I'm Izzy. Do you still wanna play ball, Lila?"

"They won't let me," she started to protest.

"You let me worry about that. Do you wanna play?"

"Yes," Lila shyly answered.

"OK, then. You wait right here. I'll be back."

Lila watched Izzy as she boldly strutted out to the field in her cotton crinkled top and faded jeans. "Hey, you kids!" she shouted. "Mind if I take a swing at it?"

Without waiting for an answer, she grabbed the bat from a stunned ballplayer who had just stepped up to the plate.

"All right, hot shot!" she shouted to the pitcher. "Show me what you got!"

Izzy readied herself by swiveling her posterior end from side to side while those in the dugout chuckled. The pitcher looked around at his playmates, who showed no objection to this intruder on the field. No one seemed to be coming to his aid. He realized it was going to be up to him to meet her challenge or order her off the field. He quickly decided on the former.

"OK, lady! Let's see you hit this!"

Watching as he sliced the ball through the air and low to the ground, Izzy realized it wasn't going to count.

"Foul ball!" the miniature umpire shouted.

"That the best you can do, Mr. Pitcher?" Izzy shouted, then laughed, releasing the hyena.

The catcher threw the ball back to the boy on the mound. This time, he took a more concentrated look at Izzy and the bat tightly gripped in her palms. He didn't appreciate the weirdly-dressed woman taunting him in front of his friends. He had to strike her out. Drawing his arm back, he thrust the ball forward, hoping she'd take a swing and miss. But the ball went exactly where she needed it to go. The loud pop of ball against wood echoed across the field as eyes all over followed the soaring object, flying higher and further away. By the time one of the players had retrieved it, all the runners had completed their way around the bases and there was no one left to send home. Izzy herself had scored a home run. All those watching in the dugout ran to her side in celebration while the opposing team cried foul.

"She's not on the team so this doesn't count!" the pitcher shouted.

"You're right," Izzy agreed, trying to catch her breath. "It doesn't count. But neither does having one side short a player. Yeah, that's right. I counted both sides. You need to even it up." Izzy didn't really know the rules of the game. She just didn't like odd numbers. "Take that little girl over there, Lila. I'll just bet she could hit that ball as far as I did."

"We ain't puttin' no hobo on our team!" one of the kids shouted. "Look at the way she's dressed!"

Izzy strutted her way to the boisterous lad and grabbed him by the ear, as he squealed in pain.

"I don't care if she's wearing a toe sack!" she hollered back. "What she's got on ain't got nothing to do with how she plays ball!" As Izzy let go of his ear, the boy stumbled backwards, nearly falling. He reached up and felt the side of his head as if to make sure his ear was still attached.

"Now, I'm gonna call her over and y'all are gonna be real nice to her or I'm gonna be out here every day, making all of your lives miserable. Ya hear?"

None of the kids dared challenge Izzy for fear she'd make good on her threat. Instead, they maintained silence while she called Lila over.

"Lila's my girl. You better treat her with respect because if you don't, you'll have to deal with me. And believe me, you don't want to do that." Izzy looked down at Lila, who was smiling and no longer tear-faced.

"OK, Lila, you show 'em what you got. I know you can do it. I have all the confidence in the world in you." Then she whispered in her ear.

As Izzy stepped away and the team returned to their original positions from before Izzy waltzed over, one of the boys handed Lila a bat. Lila took her place at the batter's mound, aware that all eyes were transfixed upon her. But in her mind, they weren't there, only Izzy.

As the pitcher prepared to throw the ball, Lila eyed him with intensity. Her first ball, like Izzy's, was no good. Lila glanced back at her new friend, who returned a smile. She decided to imitate Izzy with a wiggle of her butt, stirring laughter in the dugout again. The tension broken, Lila felt more at ease, but she still tuned out the players and focused on Izzy's whispered words.

The second ball whirled towards her as she prepared to swing. With that familiar crack of the bat, Izzy yelled with excitement. None of the players in outfield were prepared to catch such a high-flying rubber orb. As a matter of fact, the outfield had moved in closer, anticipating a weak hit, or none at all. They all struggled to chase the ball, one of them tripping as he ran, while Lila easily sprinted to first, second, third and finally home plate. She'd hit a perfect home run, just as Izzy had done. Her team had won the ballgame. Izzy watched as they all surrounded Lila, celebrating their win and making her a permanent part of their team. Izzy winked when Lila's eyes met hers and she smiled, grateful she had come along, Lila decided Izzy had to be her guardian angel, though somewhat funny-dressed.

One of the girls on the team, in a moment of curiosity, asked Lila what Izzy had whispered to her. She smiled and pointed to the pitcher's mound.

"She just said to imagine the pitcher wearing nothing but purple polka-dotted boxers. And you know . . . it really worked!

Chapter 26

Allie was stunned that Frank hired her right on the spot, considering he knew nothing about her credentials, temp job or not. She was even more stunned that he wanted her to start the same day. It brought to mind how Tim had hired Gary. He hadn't done a background check either and hired him on the spot, even letting him start work the same day. She supposed the difference was that Frank trusted Izzy's judgment, even if they didn't see eye-to-eye on matters within the kitchen.

Much to Frank's delight, Allie agreed to start work right away. He was eager to have someone catch up on the paperwork so he could concentrate on the rest of the staff and their duties. The job was relatively simple, but time consuming, as Frank had fallen way behind in his paperwork. Allie dug in immediately once Frank explained her job. She was astounded by the amount of work left unattended but assumed that was to be expected from someone who juggled his time on the floor with the office. By the time she left the diner, she was ready to go to her new home and collapse.

Climbing the stoop to Izzy's house, she thought she heard the faint sound of music. Once she stepped inside, the unmistakable sound of the Mamas & the Papas filled the air. Slowly and quietly, she removed her shoes at the door and stepped lightly down the hallway. As she neared the entrance to the den, she located the source of the music. There in the den, Izzy seemed caught up in the rhythm of Mama Cass, moving from side to side, her arms swaying above her head. She had on her familiar crinkle top shirt and faded jeans, along with a headband.

Allie, amused and forgetting her original idea of collapsing, decided to join her as she swayed along with Izzy. Oblivious that anyone had joined her on the floor, Izzy continued to dance with her eyes closed until she accidentally bumped into Allie. Startled, she rushed over to turn the stereo off.

"You scared me! I didn't even hear you come home!"

"I guess not," Allie laughed. "You were caught up in the Mamas and Papas."

"Yeah, how embarrassing."

"Don't be. I thought you were terrific."

"Yeah, that's it. Inflate my ego. So, how did the interview go? Did ya get the job?"

"I not only got the job, I had my first day of work."

"You're kidding!"

"No, he was eager for me to dig in and after seeing his mess, I understood why. I guess this works out for both of us. He needed a temp and I only want temporary work. Like you said, it'll give me a little extra spending money while I'm here. I didn't exactly start my vacation prepared."

"Good! Glad it worked out."

"So, what did you do today?" Allie was curious as to how Izzy spent her time now that she no longer worked at the diner.

"Well, I got my license renewed. I'm also restricted to glasses now. But please, let's keep that between us. If Richard ever got wind of it, I'd never hear the end of it."

Confused, Allie nonetheless vowed to secrecy.

"Say, what are you doing Saturday?"

"I . . . well, I hadn't officially planned anything. Why?" Allie asked, leary of what Izzy had in mind.

"It's the town's annual 'Possum Run.' Thought you might like to come, maybe even join in. It's an informal event. You know, most every town has some kind of festival. That's ours."

Allie, amused by the irony of the title, since you rarely see a possum run, maybe scamper, was also nearly speechless by her invitation.

"Uh . . . OK. Sounds like fun," she lied. *I will leave this part out when I get back to Regal Woods,* she thought.

Allie fiddled with the phone cord, twisting, then untwisting it around her fingers as she listened to the ringing on the other end. She had tried to allow enough time for Derrick to leave work, get home and have supper before she called. But as the rings continued, she realized it was going to be another case of bad timing. Upon hearing the fourth ring, she started to hang up when a voice came on the line.

"Hello."

"Derrick? Hey, it's me, Allie."

"Allie! Oh you have no idea how good it is to hear your voice! Are you OK?"

"Yeah, I'm fine. I tried to call you before and couldn't get you, but I did talk to Amber and Tim and they said they would relay my call."

"Yeah, I talked to both but I'm just glad to hear you personally. If I ever get my hands on that jerk, Gary—"

"Whoa, now, big brother. Don't do anything stupid. Yes, I admit Gary sorta pushed me to get away, but I'm actually enjoying myself, believe it or not." Hesitating, but needing to know, she asked, "You haven't by any chance seen him around, have you?"

"No, I haven't. I don't think he's got the nerve to show himself to me. Tell me something, Allie. You have any idea why he keeps mentioning 'Miami'? Amber said he uttered it over the phone and that he said it to you, too, as you were leaving the realty."

"No, I don't. It's weird. The few times I went out with him, he never mentioned Miami. I don't know what's going on with him. It's almost like Dr. Jekyll and Mr. Hyde."

"You ask me, I don't think he's rowing with both oars."

"Yeah, but then again, he seemed so normal when we first met and it's like he all of a sudden became somebody else when I broke it off. And odder still was the fact that we hadn't even dated that long, not long enough to grow that attached. I can only imagine how he would have reacted if we had been in a long relationship."

"Well, I have a feeling that this will blow over. Your time away will lessen his hold on you, although we do miss you around here. I'm missing our Friday morning coffee hour."

"Ditto. I think I miss that the most."

Derrick suddenly thought about last night when he saw the possums in his yard and relished this opportunity to poke a little fun.

"What's with the name 'Possum Town'? Is it more glamorous than Regal Woods?"

"Possum Heights, not Possum Town, dummy. I didn't plan on ending up in a town named after road kill. And I have no idea how it got its name. I don't think the residents do either. By the way, I met someone here and we've become friends. She even invited me to stay with her as long as I needed to so I took her up on it. Oh, and you should see the house, Derrick. It's huge, with a wraparound porch. She even got me a temp job while I'm here."

"Does she have a name?"

"Izzy, short for Isabelle. She's a little on the eccentric side, but she kinda grows on you. I'll give you the phone number, just in case of an emergency. I'm sure that'll be OK with her."

"Hopefully, I won't have to use it," Derrick assured her.

After relaying the phone number to her brother, Allie once again stressed the importance of using it only if he had to. He also needed to keep the number to himself. The less anyone else knew, the more secure she felt.

Derrick stared at the phone for a long time after he hung up, his hand still resting on the receiver. An overwhelming sense of relief rushed over him, like a cool breeze on a hot summer day. It was that moment that something awakened inside him. All he had taken for granted before now had new meaning. Without his sister, he realized how bleak his world would be. They might have been rivaling siblings at one time, but today, they were best friends.

Gary's last image of Allie haunted him as he faced the reality of the past few weeks. He not only lost a job, he lost a friend in Allie, and potentially much more. Would the past keep hindering his future, he wondered, and keep him from finding true happiness?

As he lay on the bed, his eyes fixed upon the ceiling, he couldn't stop the projection of thoughts, recent, and not so recent, from playing out in his head. There was his wife, who had shared so little of his life, and then Allie, who he was just beginning to know. The images of both women seemed to be competing with each other as he savored the memories of one, then the other. Unlike a movie projector, he couldn't turn it off, no matter how hard he blinked. There was no escaping the reality he had helped create. Not even sleep provided a way out with the dreams that alternated between the two women, each once a part of his life.

Reaching out to the nightstand beside his bed, he grasped the bottle of pills that were never far from his reach. These pills, he knew, had kept him on an even keel for a long time. It was the only thing that had kept him out of the asylum, and his futile attempt at ceasing his daily dosage was sure to send him right there, adorned in a straight jacket.

Uncapping the bottle, he reluctantly tapped it so that a pill fell out into his palm. He stared at it for a few seconds, wondering what kind of magic it possessed, then calmly popped it into his mouth, followed by a sip of water. Closing his eyes, he waited for the anguish to pass, for the pill to work its magic, aligning the hormones to where they all should be. The images would eventually fade and the projector could be shut off at his command.

Unaware he had dozed off, he awoke with an odd sense of urgency.

"Allie," he whispered in the eerie silence of his bedroom. He needed to see her, but now for different reasons. A revelation had occurred upon awakening and propelled a need for him to find her, by whatever means.

Bolting out of bed, he grabbed a duffle bag and packed a few changes of clothes and some toiletries. He didn't know where Allie went but he had an idea of where to start. It might take a few days, even weeks, but he vowed he'd look until he found her. There was certainly nothing to keep him here anymore.

Pausing to look around, he grabbed his bag and left everything else behind, heading for an unknown destination, just as Allie had done days ago. Realistically, he had little to leave behind, nothing of real value, save a class ring he could no longer wear on his fatter finger . . . and a bottle of prescription pills on the nightstand, forgotten in the sudden dash out the door.

Chapter 27

The flash of car lights through the blinds seemed to fall in rhythm with the tunes on the radio, like being at a disco club, except there was no disco crowd, no disco ball and no John Travolta wannabes, just the lights from the street and the poor reception of otherwise good tunes.

Gary wondered in his tired state of mind what Allie was doing at this very moment as he strained to hear the fading beat of the Bee Gees . . . night fever, night fever . . . that's how he felt, like he had a night fever. The two-and-a-half hour drive into the wee morning hours proved to be more intense than he had imagined. The initial rush of adrenaline had sustained him for much of the way, but toward the end of the journey, he was met with fatigue. Fortunately, he came upon a motel just outside the city limits. It was only after he'd checked himself in that he realized he'd left his pills behind. A minor inconvenience, he had decided. He wasn't going back for a bunch of pills.

Gary smiled as he lay on the bed, toying with a key on his chain, a key that Tim never thought to ask for when he'd fired him. It made it all that much easier to sneak into his shop and into his office, where he remembered Tim kept a corkboard, pinned with all kind of important notes. That was the only way he knew that he'd even have a clue in where to begin looking for Allie. Tim's carelessness was Gary's good fortune. Although he still had yet to find her, he praised himself for having come this far. It was sheer luck having worked for someone as irresponsible as Tim, neglecting to fill out the proper forms, forgetting to get the spare keys back. Both oversights proved to work in Gary's favor as he recalled the events that led up to now. First, there was the stop for gas, then a stop at Tim's Garage. There'd be no one around at that time of night, especially on such a desolate road. There was no alarm system either, which made it even more vulnerable.

Tim's office, by chance, had been unlocked. After scanning the corkboard near the desk, Gary had easily found what he was looking for, Allie's name with the town scribbled beneath. Ironically, he knew where Possum Heights was, adding to the ease of his mission.

Gary felt oddly suspended between the need for sleep and the desire to stay awake. He felt the adrenaline still coursing through his veins thinking of his sudden flight, leaving his comfortable haven behind, yet the weight of his eyelids beckoned him to sleep. It would be the latter to eventually win him over and for the first time in a long time, it'd be a night of total rest.

Allie paused in front of the mirror in the bathroom arguing with herself, frustrated for not cooking up some excuse to get out of the Possum Run event. She couldn't use work as an excuse since most businesses, including the diner, opted to close for this silly tradition.

It was eight-thirty in the morning. She could hear Izzy in the kitchen singing, or trying to sing, as she brewed a pot of coffee and prepared some sort of breakfast. She seemed too exuberant to disappoint at the last minute but it didn't curtail Allie from desperately seeking a way out of it.

"Think, think, think," she whispered loudly, subconsciously pounding her head on the mirror. "It's a possum parade. How hard can it be to get out of this?"

She then remembered that she was going to see about getting her car aligned after hitting that deep mud hole in Izzy's driveway the week before. Surely, the garage would be open for business. She would simply convey her regrets to Izzy for not being able to attend this exciting festival, but it couldn't be helped. She needed to have this done soon, or it would wear on her tires.

"Can't," Izzy quickly told Allie as she mentioned her plans at breakfast.

"Can't? What do you mean I can't?"

"The garage is closed today, as are all businesses in Possum Heights, I suspect."

"I would have thought that the garage would at least be opened."

"Nope. Most people do their vehicle maintenance during the week anyhow." Izzy studied her for a moment while buttering her bread. "Why the sudden urgency? I have the jeep and Barney if you don't want to drive your car until it's been serviced. Or . . . could it be that you're trying to dodge the biggest thing this town has to offer?"

"No, of course not." Allie protested, but just as quickly, realized that Izzy was no fool. She was wise beyond her years and saw through Allie's façade. "Oh, all right, yeah, you got me there. No offense, but I just don't see myself wasting a Saturday on such a, for lack of a better word, stupid festival. Come on, really, what fun can you possibly have at this thing?"

Izzy stared her down, not sure of whether to unload all of her verbal ammunition or take the calmer approach. Allie, on the other hand, was weighing her own options, to run or brace for a slap across the jaw. But Izzy's reaction decided for her.

"OK," she smiled. "I respect that. You don't have to waste your Saturday watching the stupid Annual Possum Run."

"Oh, good," Allie sighed with relief. "I'm so glad you understand."

"The key word is 'watch.' Actually, I planned for you to be in it."

"What? Are you nuts?"

"I need a toe sack partner."

"Come again?"

"Richard and I usually team up but he can't this year. I was really counting on you to be his replacement."

"You mean there's going to be a toe sack race, and you want me and you to share a toe sack?"

"Yep."

"When were you going to tell me this?"

"Probably when we got there. I was afraid you wouldn't come if I told you beforehand. I just hadn't anticipated you not wanting to come at all."

"Forget it! I'm not jumping around in a toe sack looking like an idiot, no way!"

"But you won't be by yourself. There'll be twenty or more other idiots jumping around in toe sacks."

"You're not helping your case, you know. . . ." Allie paused, hearing a knock at the door. "I'll get it," she said, pulling her chair back from the table. "You expecting someone this early in the morning?"

Izzy shrugged her shoulders as Allie continued on to the door. She was still simmering over Izzy's preposterous notion of making her part of the festival. A float, now that might not be so bad, but a toe sack?

Grasping the knob, she yanked the door open, unprepared for the sight on the other side. Screaming, she slammed the door shut and ran back into the kitchen.

"There's some kind of beast on your front step!"

"Did it have a long snout and short ears and was it grayish in color?"

Allie crinkled her forehead, staring oddly at Izzy. "Yeah, how did you know?"

"I'll let it in. It's probably Richard."

Richard was still standing on the porch, scratching his furry behind when Izzy opened the door.

"Oh, that's classy," Izzy said, seeing him scratch his itch.

"Maybe I should've trimmed my whiskers. Didn't mean to scare her," he said, feeling his snout with his other hand.

"I forgot. You two haven't met. Richard, this is Allie. Allie, this is Richard, also King Possum this year, which is why he can't be my toe sack partner. He's got the most important role in the whole festival."

"Wow, what an honor," Allie beamed. Izzy ignored her sarcasm and leaned over toward Richard, whispering loudly in his fake ears.

"She doesn't want to be in the toe sack with me."

Richard removed his genuine looking possum head and wisely decided not to make any cracks on Izzy's comment, as wide open as she left it. "Nice to finally meet you, Allie. Mind if I appeal to your good nature? I know to an outsider, it sounds kinda ridiculous, but it's all in good fun. There's more to it than just toe sack races and me walking around in a possum suit. It's good food, an assortment of entertainment. Don't let the title of this festivity fool you. I know you'll have a good time. Besides, I'm the one that's gonna look ridiculous."

Richard put his disguise back on then wiggled from side to side.

"That's called the Possum Dance."

Allie smiled, then laughed alongside Izzy, her hyena drowning her out.

"So, will you come and be Izzy's partner?" he asked.

Allie glanced at Izzy, then turned back to Richard. "Yeah, why not."

"Great! We were just finishing up on breakfast. Let me put the dishes in the sink," Izzy said.

"All right, Iz, but hurry. The festivities start in about an hour."

As the three of them walked off the porch, Izzy insisted on driving. She chose the jeep, to Richard's relief. "I think it's against the law to have a possum behind the wheel," Izzy said.

"You're real funny, Izzy Bell."

Izzy instructed Allie to sit up front with her. "And as for you, road kill, you sit in the back."

"I'd stick out my tongue but you can't see it."

"Then please, keep your snout on," Izzy laughed.

Allie was taken aback by the sights and sounds and aromas at the festival. It was more than she had envisioned, making her glad she had come after all. There were rides and games and exhibits, just like the State Fair. There were also numerous booths that served everything from corn dogs, hotdogs and sausage dogs to cotton candy, caramel apples and funnel cakes. Looking around, Allie surmised that the whole town had showed up for this event, and probably some out-of-towners as well.

Richard walked around proudly shaking "paws" with the crowd while Allie and Izzy strolled through the rows of endless activities. Izzy particularly liked the tobacco exhibit as she stopped and watched a trio of laborers handing tobacco to an older lady, who skillfully and quickly tied it to a stick. Then, once the stick was filled to capacity with bundles of tobacco leaves, she carefully tied off the string while a man in overalls removed the heavy bundle and placed it in a pile of tobacco already tied.

"This takes me back," Izzy pondered wistfully. "I guess you've never seen this."

"No," Allie replied. "I came onto the scene when everything was converting over to harvesters."

Izzy turned her gaze to Allie, surprise in her eyes. "You worked in tobacco?"

Allie laughed. "Don't let the fancy clothes fool ya. Yeah, I worked one summer on my uncle's farm. He had a harvester. I actually enjoyed it."

"Well, bless your heart. I never would've thought you for a farm girl in a million years."

"Well, one summer doesn't exactly qualify me as being a farm girl."

"But still . . . you just surprised me, that's all. I guess we have more in common than what I thought." Izzy glanced down at her watch. "Time to saddle up. The sack race is about to get underway. Follow me."

Allie trailed close behind Izzy through the dense crowd of people, trying to sort out the mixture of tantalizing aromas along the way. She vowed to have a taste of something before she left.

The participants were just beginning to line up to be "tagged and bagged," as the old pros called it. Allie and Izzy received their nametags and toe sack, then followed the others to the start line on the so-called track. It was actually five wide lanes of turf marked off by white spray paint with streamers draped across the ends of the lanes. The referee explained the rules as the participants each fitted a leg into their toe sack. There were to be two sets of races, five pairs of participants per set to begin with. And if there were enough volunteers, it would continue throughout the day.

Izzy turned to Allie and winked.

"We're gonna knock 'em dead, kid."

"You know, we should've practiced first."

"Naw, once we get going, we'll get into each other's rhythm."

From up in the stands, a large possum loomed, waving and cheering loudly, to the amusement of the kids below. Allie and Izzy waved back.

"On your mark!" the referee shouted. "Get set . . . and . . . go!"

Izzy started but Allie was slow on the draw and she took them both down. Izzy got up and helped Allie to her feet.

"OK, a little quicker this time. On the count of one . . . one!"

This time, they started in unison, catching up quickly with the other sackers. Two pairs tumbled, making it three in an almost perfect lineup.

"This is it; give it all you got!" Izzy shouted above the cheering.

Holding onto the rhythm and jumping harder than ever, they reached the end and broke the streamers first to the roar of the crowd. The two remaining sackers closed in behind.

"Whooooo!" Izzy shouted, struggling to get out of the sack. In her excitement, she stumbled and brought Allie down, causing her to hit her head on the post where the streamers were tied.

"Oh no! Allie, you all right?"

Richard, seeing her fall and hit her head, rushed down from the bleachers and hovered over her, opposite of Izzy. Allie seemed to be knocked out cold. Izzy leaned in closer and gently patted her cheeks while Richard, forgetting he had his suit on, moved closer as well, his snout brushing her cleavage. In a spontaneous gesture, Izzy slapped his snout.

"Do you mind?"

"That was an accident. You're showing too much cleavage anyway. I can see all the way down Mount Everest."

"Will you just go get me a wet rag, you perverted possum?"

Allie, still flat on the ground, started chuckling. Sitting up, she burst into laughter.

"You faker!" Izzy chided. "You scared us to death!"

"I'm sorry. I really am."

"C'mon. Let me help you to your feet," Richard said as he hoisted her up. The small crowd that had gathered began to disperse at seeing she was OK.

"Congratulations, girls. You won. Let's go pick up your medals."

"Great. Afterwards, what do you say we go grab some grub from one of the booths?" Izzy volunteered. "I've worked up an appetite."

"Just what I had in mind," Allie agreed. Thinking back to the moment she stared in the mirror in the bathroom seeking a way out, she was glad it turned out this way. Richard was right. She did end up having a good time. She felt destined to be in this town, regardless of the circumstances.

As the three of them chattered away, seeking a common booth for food, a little girl rushed up to Izzy, hugging her.

"I'm so glad I got to see you again, Ms. Izzy." Izzy recognized her from the ball field. She was impressed that she remembered her name. "I wanted to thank you for what you did at the ball game. You were a really big help."

"Oh, Lila, was it?" The little girl nodded. "I want you to meet my friends here. This is Allie and the possum next to her is Richard."

"King Possum," Richard corrected. "So Lila, what's this talk about the ball game? What did Ms. Izzy do that you're so grateful for?"

"Well, she got the players out there to let me play ball with them but I was nervous I wouldn't be able to hit the ball. She told me to imagine the pitcher in a pair of purple polka-dotted boxers. So I did. And it worked! The picture in my head was so funny, I forgot about being nervous and I ended up hitting a home run!"

"Well, how about that," Richard said. Izzy could almost feel him glaring at her through his possum head.

"Well, I just wanted to thank you again, Ms. Izzy. And congratulations on the toe sack win. See ya around!"

Izzy waved goodbye, still feeling Richard's stare through his disguise. "Well, it was the first thing that came to my mind, OK?" she said, defending herself. "It ain't like you wear the only purple polka-dotted drawers in the world."

"I won't even ask," Allie said as they wandered over to a booth selling hotdogs and sausage dogs. She wondered why Izzy never mentioned the little girl to her. Some people would've bragged about that, but apparently not Izzy. Her respect and admiration for Izzy continued to grow. She wondered what else lay beneath that tough exterior.

"You made a big difference in that little girl's life," Allie said, smiling.

"No, I think it's the other way around," Izzy said, as she watched Lila join some friends, friends with familiar faces from that fated day.

Chapter 28

Allie couldn't remember the last time she had experienced so much fun, and cried so hard from laughing. Between Izzy and Richard, she didn't know who was the zaniest. But she ultimately understood, after spending time with both of them, why they bonded so well, even through all the bickering and insults. Their years of communing with one another had, on the surface, formulated a kind of sibling bond, unlike the kind she and Derrick shared. Perhaps it was the absence of a sibling in Izzy's life that drew her closer, somewhat, to Richard. Yet, the similarities were obvious, the love and compassion for one another. But love and compassion took many forms. In Izzy and Richard's case, it was an unspoken mutual admiration for the years cemented between them, years engraved into their memories, as old neighbors, and better yet, as friends.

"Don't take this the wrong way, Rich," Izzy said, getting out of the jeep, "but I'm glad you weren't in my sack today. You really do make a better possum."

"I'll try to take that as a compliment, coming from you, Izzy. And as much as I'd like to stay and bask with you on your toe sack victory, I need to go shed some fur. I'm starting to break out in hives."

"That's right. Leave while you have a shred of dignity intact," Izzy teased.

"Haha . . . Allie, enjoyed having you along and a strong word of advice: do not let Izzy make you a pepperoni sandwich. Goodnight, girls!"

As Richard blew them a kiss from the end of his "snout," Allie blew one back, then turned to face Izzy. With her arms crossed and her head tilted, she questioned Richard's comment. "What did he mean by that, don't let you make me a pepperoni sandwich?"

"I don't have the faintest notion of what he's talking about," Izzy said, smiling.

"Uh, um . . . I bet," Allie said, nodding.

"Oh, almost forgot. You've got the keys to the house."

"Oh yeah, that's right. Gotta dish 'em out of my pocket here. Be patient."

Allie managed to retrieve the keys, while trying to balance the load in her arms—goodies bought at the festival—without dropping it. Feeling a need to reshift her load, she clinched the keys between her teeth and grabbed a firmer hold on the bag. She glanced at Izzy just in time to see her squinting her eyes.

"What is it?" she asked, still holding the keys in her mouth.

"Oh, nothing. You might want to brush your teeth, though."

"What's wrong with my teeth?" Allied asked, laughing irritably.

"Well, it's just that I dropped the keys in the litter box earlier," she said, raising her eyebrows.

After several tumultuous rounds of spitting, then reluctantly picking up the tainted keys dropped at Izzy's candid revelation, Allie turned to her, her eyes glaring with disgust. "Thanks for telling me. I'll probably be picking kitty litter out of my teeth for the next week or so."

"Aw, don't worry. Could've been worse. It missed the poop by a hair."

Allie suddenly felt queasy. The image of kitty feces near the set of keys she once clinched between her teeth repulsed her worse than the cats cleaning the dishes. She now found herself seriously wondering how many were cleaned by the dishwasher and how many were cleaned by Claude or Caesar or whomever.

"Thanks for that picture. I think I'm gonna turn in for the night . . . after I brush the litter from between my teeth. Today wore me out, but you know, Izzy, truthfully, I'm glad I came. I really enjoyed it."

"I'm glad you came, too," Izzy said as she closed and locked the door, three times, as was her habit. "You still plan on going to church with me tomorrow?"

"Tomorrow?"

"Yeah, tomorrow. It's Sunday, you know. You haven't forgotten already, have you?"

"No, well, yeah. I kinda lost count of the days. But yeah, I'm still going." *I can't be any more surprised than I have been already*, she thought. *Besides, this is church. What could possibly go wrong?*

"Good. Richard will be by here around ten-thirty to pick us up. We usually go together . . . saves gas," she added.

"He's a nice guy. I like Richard."

"Yeah, Richard's all right. We tuffle now and then, but it's all in good fun. He's just a long scrawny teddy bear, truth be known, but don't tell him I said that. It'll go to his head."

"Oh, that'll be our little secret," she whispered. "Well, goodnight, Izzy."

"Goodnight, Allie Cat."

As Izzy watched her make her way down the hallway to her room, she noticed several furry tails trailing behind. *How quickly she's won them over,* she thought.

Glancing back at the locked door, she felt an overwhelming compulsion. Reaching out for the lock, she turned it once, then twice, and finally a third time. Although she knew that this had already been done, she needed absolute assurance for her own peace of mind. *I would love to know for just once,* she thought, *what it felt like locking a door with one turn of the latch, and never worrying about it again for the rest of the night.*

As she switched off the lights en route to her bedroom, she was keenly aware of the absence of tiny footsteps that usually kept pace with her when she turned in. But a casual glance in Allie's quarters confirmed that her four-leggers had adopted her new friend. It appeared that all of them were sprawled out on the bed, each vying for her attention.

"Normally, I'd be jealous," Izzy said, as Allie rolled over in bed to face her, "but I kinda take this as a good sign. They warmed up to you pretty quick. That must mean you're a really good person, or you got some tuna hiding beneath the sheets."

"Cats are smart. What can I say?" Allie smiled.

"Yep. It's the tuna."

"Goodnight again, Izzy," Allie said, waving her on.

As Izzy faded out of sight, Allie cuddled her new feline friends.

"No, my little furry bedfellows, it wasn't the tuna, it was the sausage dog," she whispered, unveiling a leftover piece of food from the festival.

A large oak tree stood between him and the white house with the wraparound porch amidst a scenic view of azaleas and crepe myrtles and off to one side, an aromatic magnolia tree just beginning to bloom. *A Monet picture,* he thought, *with a Mona Lisa inside.* How easy it had been to trace her steps, her every move since he'd learned of where she'd gone. And now, he knew where she spent her evenings, dining with that crazy hippie from the sixties, with a repugnant laugh, and on this night, accompanied by a beast with a snout.

Then at night, when the beatnik turned in, he envisioned the Mona Lisa gazing at her beautiful image in the mirror, dabbing cream on her delicate cheeks, then brushing her shiny locks of auburn tresses, and finally, slipping beneath the covers of sheets scented with her own perfume.

The voyeur lifted his binoculars to his eyes to catch a glimpse of what lay beyond the window of this picturesque house, but the curtains proved too dark a barrier to penetrate. It would be a blind endeavor without a visual layout, helpful, but not necessary, he decided. The primary source of concern, population, had easily resolved itself once he canvassed the secluded neighborhood. Few houses, and far between, the closest one belonging to a degenerate in what appeared to be a possum suit. Although he'd never seen him outside the costume, he was certain he could recognize him by voice again, feminine and a bit articulate. The temps were perfect this time of year being the early months of spring with lingering chills of winter. It had to be that stupid festival they held each year.

As night transcended into full bloom, with the moon hovering high above, and the creatures emulating each other, the stalker quietly left his post by the tree and retreated to his own haven for the night. It was only a matter of time now. All he had suppressed would soon spew forth with a vengeance.

"Goodnight, sweet Allie. I will see you soon."

Chapter 29

"Come on, Izzy! Granny was slow but she was old, and wore panty bloomers!" Richard hollered from the den, irritated as he glanced at his watch for the third time. "What's taking you so long? We're gonna be late!"

The distinct sound of pots and pans rattled throughout the kitchen, peaking Richard's curiosity.

"What the . . ." he mumbled loudly before getting up to follow the noise. Peeking his head through the door, he gasped as Izzy continued tearing the kitchen apart, cluttering the counter tops and floors with cookware of all sorts.

"What in Sam Hill are you doing? This is no time to do spring cleaning! We're gonna be late for church!"

"I can't find my water bottle!"

"I have a milk bottle at the house. You can fill that up with water."

"I need my water bottle," Izzy stressed, ignoring Richard's sarcasm. "You know how I start coughing in church and can't stop. The air is so dry."

"Why don't you use cough drops like everyone else?"

"That don't help a dry throat, you nincompoop. Now, are you gonna help me look for it or not?"

"I declare, you and your obsessions," he said, barely audible.

"What's that?"

"Nothing. Can't you just forget it this one time? Allie's out there in the van probably getting wrinkles and gray hair by now.

"Just get on out of here!" Izzy snapped. "You're not helping matters at all. I reckon I'll just have to substitute another bottle of some kind."

"Fine!" Richard snapped back, throwing his hands up and walking out.

Izzy spotted a basket beneath her island and quickly deposited the contents on top of the counter. She remembered a gift someone had given her a few years ago, and not knowing what it was or what to do with it, she'd simply tossed it in the basket, along with other items she had little use for. Now, she realized that perhaps it could serve a purpose. Sifting through the vast collection of forgotten gadgets, she finally located the abandoned object.

"Aha! There you are, my beautiful . . . well, whatever you are. This is perfect, just perfect!" she said, kissing her new "water bottle." She fingered the engraved initials on the front of the six-ounce, stainless steel flask that signified it was her very own bottle. Dashing toward the kitchen sink, she filled the flask with water then capped it and buried it deep inside her purse.

After checking the burners on the stove three times, as well as the coffee pot, the toaster and anything with a cord and a plug, she started for the door, but not without looking back one more time for something she might have missed. Satisfied with her thorough inspection, she closed the door and locked it, skipping her routine three turn method, but pulling it several times to assure it was secure.

"Finally!" Richard grumbled, seeing Izzy approach the van. "Did you find your water bottle?"

"No," she proudly smiled. "I found something better."

Richard apologized to Allie on behalf of Izzy as they finally got underway. Izzy, snuggled in the back seat, grunted in resentment.

"It's OK," Allie said.

"Maybe next time, you need to get a two-hour head start," Richard suggested to Izzy.

"Nice van," Allie intervened, hoping to intercept an ensuing argument.

"Thanks," Richard beamed. "I like sitting up high, plus it has a lot of leg room and head room," he said, waving his hand above him.

"He hates Barney," Izzy said, snickering from behind.

"I don't hate Barney. He just ain't that comfortable to ride in. If I had short legs like you, it'd be different."

"You calling me Shorty, now?"

"Like you don't call me names like Beanpole, Flagpole, Giraffe, Ostrich . . ."

"OK, you guys. We're on our way to church," Allie reminded them.

"Hey . . . pull over!" Izzy suddenly shouted. "I just saw a stray cat!"

"What? We're on our way to church! What are you gonna do with him if we catch him?"

"C'mon! He may not be there later! The poor fellow's probably starving. Besides, we're not running late. You're always too early. You need to get that clock in your head fixed. I've got time to nab him and take him back to the house and feed him."

"All right, all right, anything to shut you up."

Richard pulled over to the side of the road. As he did, he spotted the gray tabby in the rearview mirror just a few feet behind, walking alongside the shallow ditch. Just as Izzy slid the side door open, the cat ran further up the road.

"Doggone it! Drive a little further, Rich!"

Richard rolled his eyes but consented to Izzy's wishes, inching the van a few more feet along the side of the road.

"Stop! I think I can catch him now." Izzy stepped one foot out of the van but the cat sensed her intentions and ran again.

"We keep this up, he may beat us to church," Richard said.

"I ain't giving up," Izzy vowed. "Move up some more."

Richard continued to cruise alongside the highway, but every time they stopped, the cat would take off running. He secretly hoped that no one would recognize him as they bounced along the edge of the road, knowing how weird it must look to drivers passing by. Then, having a change of heart, he decided to make the most of the situation by making faces at the curious onlookers. Allie was privy to his antics, but Izzy kept her eyes on the cat. After several starts and stops riding along side the highway in an attempt to capture the stubborn feline, Allie had had enough.

"Izzy, we're getting an awful lot of attention. People are breaking their necks staring at us going by . . ." Then looking over at Richard, she said, "This ain't the most inconspicuous vehicle for cruising along side the road."

"I'm sorry, Allie," Richard said, feeling guilty for relenting to Izzy's demands. "I didn't know we were going to be in high pursuit of a fur ball on the way to church."

"He keeps looking back like he wants us to rescue him," Izzy whined, leaning partly out the door.

"He keeps looking back 'cause he thinks you're an idiot!" Richard scoffed. "Look, he just ran off into the woods. He doesn't want to be caught. Slide the door closed; I'm getting back on the road."

As Izzy slammed the side door shut, Richard eased the van back onto the road.

"Probably end up road kill," she muttered. Richard glanced at her through the rearview mirror, willing to let her have the last word in order to keep the peace.

Many of Possum Heights' rooted citizens were starting to file into the church for the eleven o'clock service as the trio arrived. Hoping to blend in with the crowd and perhaps slip into a pew near the back, Allie eagerly led the way. But Izzy grabbed her by the arm before she could go further into the small sanctuary, ignoring Allie's gesture toward the perfect pew, the last pew in the back, completely vacant.

"Look, whatever you do, " Izzy advised, "don't ask that lady over there how she's doing." Izzy pointed to an older woman with cat-eye glasses and a beehive hairdo, long gone out of style. The heavy rouge and lipstick only added to a bygone era but probably helped to conceal her true age.

"Why not?" Allie asked, puzzled.

"Because . . . she'll tell you."

"What's so bad about that?" Allie laughed.

"Shhh, here she comes."

"Well, hello, Izzy. Nice to see you, as always. And who's our lovely guest?"

"Mamie, this is Allie."

"Pleased to meet you, dear," the older woman said, taking Allie's hand in her own. "Glad to have you with us on this fine Sunday morning. And how are you today, my dear?"

"Oh, I'm just fine. And you?"

Izzy made a face and Alllie realized her mistake too late. Mamie began to rant on and on about all her ailments while Allie listened to excruciating details of her flare-ups with arthritis, bursitis, bronchitis, until it ended up with constipation. Her jaw was agape, amazed that one person could suffer from so many disorders. Izzy, unable to hide her irritation, decided it was time to intervene and grabbed Allie by the elbow.

"We need to go if we're gonna get good seats. Nice to see you, Mamie." Izzy whispered in Allie's ear, "I warned you."

"She tricked me," Allie said.

Izzy located Richard seated about midway of the church. He had turned around and was motioning them to his pew. Allie was a little disappointed they weren't taking advantage of the pew in the back. All the same, she slid in behind Izzy while Richard held his spot at the end next to the middle aisle.

"She met Mamie," Izzy leaned over Allie and told Richard.

"Did she—"

"Yep, she did," Izzy said before Richard could finish his question.

"You poor kid," Richard said to Allie.

"Thanks," Allie said. "It was quite an experience."

"Oh, no," Izzy blurted. "Here comes Lester and his cow."

"Izzy!" Richard reprimanded her, evoking some leers surrounding them. "That's horrible," he said more quietly.

"Why are you calling her a cow?" Allie asked. "She's scrawny."

"It ain't about her weight. Just watch her when she pulls out a stick of gum and starts chewing it. Looks like a cow chewing cud."

"Are you serious?" Allied laughed.

"Don't tell me you ain't never seen a cow working them jaws. I think ole Elsie here's got it down to a science, 'cept the cow does it with more grace."

"Shhh," Richard cut in, waving his hand for Izzy to shut up. Reverend Barnes had just approached the pulpit. Everyone rose to their feet as the reverend led them in the morning benediction. Izzy watched from the corner of her eye as Lester stopped at the other end of their pew and motioned for his wife to slide in first.

"Great," Izzy whispered to Allie and Richard. "My worst nightmare just came true."

She faked a smile at Harriet, Lester's wife, and continued to sing the benediction. Once they were seated, she observed Harriet fumbling around in her pocketbook, and to her bitter disappointment, produce a piece of gum. Politely declining her offer of a piece of gum, Izzy tried to focus on Reverend Barnes. Harriett decided to put both pieces in her mouth, crumpling the empty holder.

My first Sunday here with a guest and I have to sit next to Elsie the cow, Izzy thought. As if reading her thoughts, Richard leaned over with pleading eyes. She knew what that look meant. She had known him long enough to interpret his glare and he had known her long enough to know anything was possible with Izzy, even in church.

Reverend Barnes was quick to observe the newcomer seated beside Izzy as he proceeded with the morning announcements and prayer concerns.

"We want to welcome everybody here, especially you visitors," he said, smiling at Allie. Allie nervously returned the smile and glanced towards Izzy, who was now preoccupied with Harriet and the wad in her mouth. Allie nudged her and she immediately turned her focus back towards Reverend Barnes. She admitted to herself that Izzy was right, that it was hard not to notice the jaw-working woman seated next to Izzy. She chewed like there was no tomorrow, smacking and popping and causing heads to turn. The distraction even carried to the back of the church, where members were craning their necks to see where the irritable noise was coming from. Allie mimicked Richard's concern as she leaned into him and whispered.

"I think Izzy's fixing to do something."

"I know," he whispered back. "I only wish I'd sat on the other side."

"Please remember Mabel in your prayers," the reverend announced. "She just had hip surgery. Thomas Owens is recuperating from gall bladder surgery. Please keep him in your prayers. And for all of those on our prayer list . . ." From somewhere a few pews back, a member of the congregation was grossly clearing her throat. ". . . oh, and ah, let us continue to keep Ms. Mamie in our prayers for . . . let's just keep her in our prayers. Now, let us all bow our heads please," he concluded.

"Hypochondriac, that's what she is," Izzy whispered to Allie.

"Shhh!" Richard hissed. Allie smiled as she watched the two of them flay at each other. It was odd, but she found herself growing fond of this little town, its people, the laid back life, and the quaint little shops, the diner, and now, this simple country church. But she especially enjoyed the company of Izzy and Richard, who seemed to be bonding with her as well.

As Reverend Barnes began the morning service, Allie was enthralled. His words seemed to hit home. His message seemed to embrace her heart and lift her spirits. It was as if the whole weight of the world had magically disappeared as she sat upright in the pew, her eyes glued to the reverend, who delivered his message with ease, dividing his attention across both sides of the aisle.

"Friends, God does not want us to be anybody but ourselves. He doesn't want us parading around, pretending to be something we're not. He wants us to be ourselves and to use our God-given talent, whatever that may be, to serve Him. Not everybody is cut out to be a minister or a Sunday School teacher or a missionary. But we all have a purpose in life; whether it be large or small, we have a purpose. You may not think a small act of kindness can make a difference, but friends, take my word, it can and it does. It can oftentimes make a huge difference. Everything you do or say can make the difference in someone's life. Think about it. Pray about it. Pray for guidance and strength to fulfill His purpose. Say, 'Lord, use me, whatever Your will is for me, so let it be.'"

Izzy struggled to maintain the tickle in her throat but as Reverend Barnes delved deeper into his sermon, she found it increasingly harder to restrain from coughing. It was then that she silently praised herself for finding her new gem of a water bottle and felt this was the time to break it in. She would deal with the cow next to her later.

Reaching deep into her purse, Izzy grasped her replacement bottle and proudly held it with both hands, kissing it graciously, as Richard and Allie stared straight ahead, mesmerized by the reverend's sermon. Harriet, she noticed, gazed up front as well, pretending to be all ears, but to Izzy, she was all jaws. She suddenly felt appreciative for all the Sundays before, when she had successfully guarded her pew. Sure, she could still hear, if not see, Harriet the Sundays before, working those mandibles—the whole congregation could—but at least she wasn't in her ear the way she was now. The heifer had invaded her pew.

Harriet kept pace with her noisy and obnoxious chewing and occasional popping, oblivious to Izzy and her flask. As much as Harriet was grating on her nerves, Izzy's priority at the moment was stifling the cough creeping into her throat. She pressed the miniature canteen against her skin, enjoying the cool texture. She could almost taste and feel the water as it would slide down her irritated throat, soothing it along the way. She again praised herself for not discarding this odd contraption and finally finding some use for it, this thing given to her years ago by someone, though she couldn't remember who. How clever she was to have kept it. It was perfect, even better than her old plastic bottle.

Tilting it forward, she saw the familiar words engraved beneath, "Made in China." *What's not made in China?* she thought. Tilting it back up, she slowly and quietly unscrewed the top of her new water bottle, the cap resembling a short, fat bolt. It looked vaguely familiar to her, like something she'd seen on her mower perhaps. Or maybe it was like a car engine bolt. But this bolt was special. It was attached to a kind of bracket that was also attached to the portable vessel. *I guess that's so you don't lose the bolt,* Izzy thought.

Moving the bolt to the side, she stifled one last cough, then turned the flask up for a much-needed drink of water. The more she drank, the more she tilted the flask until it was straight up in the air.

The reverend was the first to notice the flask attached to Izzy's mouth and stumbled in mid-sentence. Others in the church followed his gaze and some, the ones with a clearer view, even gasped. Richard looked dumbfoundly around, trying to see what had aroused the congregation, only to discover they were staring his way. Only when he turned to whisper something to Allie did he see the flask, fully exposed, bottom end up, on Izzy's mouth. Harriet got a ringside view of the awkward scene the same time as Richard and ended up swallowing her gum.

Richard instantly reached across Allie and forced Izzy's hand down, splattering water on the ones seated in the pews in front of them. "Sorry," he muttered, when they looked back in surprise.

Izzy was visibly furious but also a bit puzzled. She'd been taking water to church for years, so what was the big deal now?

Reverend Barnes stuttered as he struggled to maintain his momentum with the service, unable to avert his eyes from Izzy and her flask. Much of the congregation peered over and around their neighbors to catch a glimpse of the reverend's distraction.

"Izzy!" Richard whispered loudly. "What's gotten into you? Put that thing away!"

Izzy, still confused and unaware of the cause for all the commotion, returned the flask to her purse, without bothering to screw the top. Sensing her confusion, Richard scribbled something on a piece of paper and passed it to Izzy. It simply read, "It's a flask," which meant absolutely nothing to Izzy. Incredibly, she had no idea what a flask was. She still couldn't comprehend what Richard was trying to convey. Allie, meanwhile, fidgeted with her church program. She gave up on trying to hide her embarrassment, knowing everyone within view could see her scarlet-red cheeks. Leaning into Izzy, she whispered so only she could hear. "What . . . you couldn't wait till we at least got out of church?"

"I don't understand!" she whispered back. "What's with you two? You got the whole congregation staring at us!"

"You don't know? You really don't know?" Richard asked, leaning over Allie. "What's in that flask anyway?"

"Do you have amnesia? I told you this morning I lost my water bottle. Then I came across this little gem."

"That's not a water bottle, you ignoramus. It's a flask . . . for holding whiskey!"

"Oh, shi—" Izzy slapped her hand across her mouth, suddenly realizing where she was. "Why didn't you tell me?"

"I didn't know you had brought it to church!" Richard whispered loudly.

Reverend Barnes, having found his composure, cleared his throat, cueing them to silence. Allie took the hint.

"Both of y'all, shut up," she said through clinched teeth.

Harriet jeered at all three of them as she reached down to get her purse. Izzy felt her nerves on edge again as she watched her dig through the clutter of makeup and Kleenexes and other personal items. She'd hoped the gum she'd swallowed was the last in her purse. But to Izzy's horror, she pulled out a whole new pack of Juicy Fruit. Eyeing her with intensity as she unfoiled the pack, Harriet again opted on two pieces of gum, cramming them eagerly in her jaw. Izzy hoped for a short sermon, at the same time feeling guilty for having such a thought.

Reverend Barnes was just gearing up for the climax of his message despite the earlier distraction among Izzy's pew. He, too, found it difficult to ignore Harriet's over-the-top performance with her love of gum. Coughing and sneezing, baby cries, even snoring, he was used to, but Harriet had introduced a unique kind of turbulence, one which he had no prior experience dealing with. This, he couldn't recall covering in Divinity School, so this was definitely new terrain.

It wasn't that he objected to gum, for he sometimes enjoyed a stick of Wrigley's. But this was a matter of tact. How do you approach a member of the congregation and tell them that they're an absolute nuisance when the gospel is being preached? It was an awkward predicament to say the least. It was even brought up casually and jokingly before the board, but no one had an answer. In short, no one had the gumption to approach the source of the problem.

Izzy, seemingly over the water bottle/flask incident, retreated to her earlier self, pretending the "cow" wasn't sitting next to her, but grazing in a pasture far away. Allie exchanged a smile with her, mending their tensed moods earlier, but Richard wasn't so sympathetic. He eyed her with caution, as if she were a bomb, due to explode at any moment. Not even Izzy's angelic demeanor could sway Richard's feelings. Her eyes always told the truth, no matter how hard she tried to disguise it.

"I say we all need to pray and ask God, 'What is my purpose? Use me,'" the reverend stressed, holding out his Bible. As habit, he focused on one side of the congregation, then on the other. "What will you have me to do?"

Izzy smiled, almost mischievously, as Reverend Barnes gazed toward her side of the church. She seemed absorbed with his words and compelled by their meaning, while Harriet enjoyed her double dose of Juicy Fruit, working double time in her jaw and beyond. Perhaps it was the beyond, when the massive wad produced bubbles unbecoming in a sanctified gathering, that stirred Izzy and pushed her over the edge, or maybe it was simply an opportunity waiting in the wings. Whatever the case, Izzy grasped the opportunity, repeating in her mind the words of Reverend Barnes. *What is my purpose? Use me.*

Smiling and nodding as the reverend slowly faced the other side, Izzy seized the moment. Harriet proudly displayed her biggest bubble yet and Izzy was prepared. A pop, much like the sound of a cap gun, resonated throughout the sanctuary, but no one seemed to know its origin, not even Richard or Allie. The sound seemed to have echoed off all four walls, and left everyone scanning the room for the cause. Reverend Barnes, instinctively, cast a gaze toward the other side, where Izzy sat grinning like a Cheshire cat. Harriet appeared stupefied, her mouth wide open, but no gum in between. A single strand of the gooey substance hung off her nose, but the rest had magically disappeared.

Richard and Allie glanced at each other and simultaneously bowed their foreheads into their hands. Reverend Barnes locked eyes with Izzy and winked, his face aglow.

Even Lester, Harriet's husband, had a hard time holding back. After the morning service, he felt compelled to express his gratitude to Izzy for her bold performance. When Harriet's eyes were diverted, he smiled and discreetly shook her hand. Izzy nodded as if understanding his intentions but at the same time thought, *What a wimp.* She thought it was his responsibility as a spouse to defuse the problem. *Good ole Lester, trying to dodge the bullet.*

"You put on quite a show this morning, Izzy," the reverend said as she trickled out with the rest of the congregation. "I won't even ask what you had in that flask." Izzy blushed, at a loss for words to explain. "Fact is," he continued, without giving her a chance to respond, "you may have started out as a distraction, but actually got rid of one." He nodded toward Harriet, who chattered wildly with those still inside the sanctuary. "I would say you were listening to my sermon and putting it to use. Nice redemption."

Izzy smiled, knowing he was referring to the flask. "Thank you, Reverend," she said, squeezing his hand, exchanging remnants of Harriet's Juicy Fruit. "Sorry, still got a little gum on my hand. And for the record, it was water, not alcohol, in the, ah, flask. I'm truly sorry. I didn't know . . . ." Reverend Barnes held his hand up, and shook his head.

"You don't have to explain. I understand," he said, then leaned over and whispered in her ear. "If Harriet hadn't invited me over for dinner one Sunday, I wouldn't have known what it was either." Then he added, "She kept it next to a bottle of Jim Beam."

Chapter 30

The town had an odd sense of familiarity. He could remember being here in one sense and in another, he couldn't. Gary's memories of Possum Heights came in bits and pieces, many of them blurred. He certainly didn't recall the DMV building as he ventured on foot, nor the ball field close by, or had that been there all along? Years had a funny way of losing touch with memory. His mind strained to remember the past as he scratched his chin, feeling the stubbles, a reminder that he hadn't shaved in days. It would be his disguise, although, realistically, he knew he didn't need one. He hadn't roamed these streets in years. Chances were that no one would know who he was, except for Allie, provided she could recognize him behind the five o'clock shadow.

Just past noon, the town seemed to stir a little, people driving or walking by in their Sunday best. Those who he passed on the street stopped chattering and eyed him with curiosity as they continued on down the sidewalk, staring behind them. His feeling of alienation was heightened with each passerby. The townspeople were obviously curious as to the identity of this stranger who had suddenly taken it upon himself to explore their town. *So much for small town hospitality*, he thought. He was starting to wish he had driven through rather than parked his car in a vacant lot just on the inner skirts of the town. But walking provided a better view, a chance to take in all there was to see, including Allie, should she cross his path.

As he strolled along the way, he entertained the possibility of meeting Allie, and although he felt ill prepared, he was willing to risk such an endeavor. There were things she had to know and it couldn't wait until her return, provided she had planned to return at all, to the stability of her own hometown and realty business.

Suddenly, the aroma of food filled the air and his stomach growled ferociously, long void of any kind of substance. The last thing he remembered eating was a pack of stale nabs about this time yesterday. Food, it seemed, hadn't been a prime priority then, but now the savory delights filling the air lured him closer to its origin.

Nearing the end of the block, his memory finally captured a glimpse from the past . . . the old motel, and next to it, the diner and gas station. The years in between had faded, but somehow, he had managed to retain this image. He'd have to do the psychology later on. Right now, he was ravished and the diner was most appealing as he observed the "Open" sign lit up for business.

As he wandered in and took a seat at the counter, June strolled over with her pad and pencil. As usual, she could spot an out-of-towner.

"Hey, sweetie. New in town, aren't ya?"

"Yeah, just passing through," Gary quickly obliged.

"What'll ya have, honey? The special today is meatloaf," she said, pointing to the board behind her.

"I'll just have a burger with everything on it and fries."

"And to drink?"

"Coffee, please."

"Okie dokie. It'll just be a few minutes. You timed it right. The Sunday crowd'll soon be pouring in."

Gary smiled. He liked the waitress. She reminded him of another waitress he'd seen on some TV sitcom. But he couldn't remember her name, nor the name of the sitcom. He chalked it up to getting older.

As she poured his cup of coffee, he felt her eyes trying to penetrate his mind, which he chalked off as being paranoid.

"Here's your coffee, darling, and there's some cream and sugar there on the counter. Say, ah, you look kinda familiar. You sure you ain't from around here?"

"Yeah. Just passing through, like I said."

"Well, OK. Guess I'm just having one of them moments of déjà vu."

"Yeah, guess so," Gary said, wishing she'd leave him alone.

June, knowing her limits, wiggled her way to the other end of the counter where another customer had seated himself. Gary, meanwhile, tried his best to keep from locking eyes with anyone around him as he scanned the inside of the diner. Except for the name, Frank's Diner, everything appeared to be the same as he remembered it, with the fifties and sixties nostalgia décor. He had even toyed with the idea of opening a joint similar to this one many years ago but decided it would be too time-consuming, not to mention the hassle of hiring and keeping help, as turnovers could be frequent in the restaurant business, if you didn't have the right staff.

As promised, it was just a matter of minutes when June was back with his burger and fries.

"Bon appetit," she cheerfully said, placing the food before him.

Gary quickly grasped the burger and took a huge bite, savoring the char-grilled delicacy with each chew. He was beginning to regret not ordering two burgers but he still had the fries. Maybe that would satisfy him until dinner.

Unaware he was being watched, he finished his burger without bothering to wash it down with any liquid, but rather continued on with the fries. The fries were prepared just the way he liked them, fat and crinkly. Soon, the fries had disappeared as well. It took several gulps of coffee to get the lump out of his throat where he'd eaten too fast. The customer at the end of the counter was on alert, prepared at any moment to implement the Heimlich maneuver, if necessary. Fortunately, it wasn't. Gary finally found relief when the lump in his throat dissipated. *That was stupid*, he thought. *I'll be chewing on Tums the rest of the day.*

Gary looked around, suddenly aware of the attention he had attracted, and felt beads of sweat pop out on his forehead. *This is no time to go crazy*, he thought. His pills were miles away on his nightstand, and that thought made him perspire even more. The diner was starting to get packed and he began to fear the worst, a debut performance before a packed house, or in this case, a packed diner. There was nothing left to do but pay the bill and hope he could leave with his dignity.

Sliding off the stool, he nervously approached the register where a nauseatingly cheerful cashier took his bill and began ringing up his order.

"And how was everything, sugar?" she asked, her smile stretched from ear to ear. Gary was reminded of that expression "grinning like a possum" and thought, *Well, this is Possum Heights. And what is it with these dames calling everybody honey, darling and sugar?*

"Fine, just fine," he said, suddenly starting to feel the world close in on him. His face filled with blood and sweat seemed to seep through every pore in his body. He began to sway on his feet and the cashier's voice became a distant echo.

"Sir, sir! Are you all right?"

Still holding onto his wallet, Gary felt himself collapse to the floor, keenly aware of the room full of eyes witnessing his tumble to the floor. It had happened, his ultimate fear, cracking up in front of a complete audience of strangers.

"Somebody call an ambulance!" he heard the cashier say from inside a barrel. He wanted to scream out "No!" but he couldn't. He'd lost his voice. He closed his eyes, wishing his dilemma away, while a cold wet towel made contact with his forehead. The coolness of its touch felt good to his skin, but he still seemed dazed. Patrons of the diner huddled close by as he tried to form words.

"Mi-mi-mi . . . am . . . i."

"What's he saying?" June asked.

"Mi . . . am . . . I," he repeated.

"Miami," June said, answering her own question. "I heard that clear as a bell. Is the ambulance on the way? I think he's had a concussion." *Maybe he's not from here . . . must be from Miami,* she thought.

"Mi . . . am . . . i," Gary said softly, then even softer, "Allie," before passing out.

Izzy felt the need to take her mind off the escapades at the church earlier, and what better way to do that than to do a good deed? She felt no need to inform Allie of her plans and good intentions. Although she had weighed the idea of her tagging along, she quickly dismissed it, feeling this was something she needed to do alone.

"I'll be back in a couple of hours. Maybe I'll pick up a bucket of chicken for supper. Say, do you mind rolling the trash barrel out to the end of the road?"

"But Izzy, there's nothing in it," Allie said, having peered in it earlier.

"I'm paying a quarterly fee. I wanna get my money's worth," Izzy insisted. "Whether there's anything in it or not."

"You must drive the trash people crazy," Allie laughed.

"Here. If it'll make you feel any better, Allie Cat, here's a plastic cup. Throw that in there," she said, thrusting a cup at her.

"Why don't I just bag up what you have in the trashcan in the kitchen and throw that in?"

"It's only half full. That'd be a total waste of garbage bags."

Allie, shaking her head, reluctantly took the cup Izzy held out and threw it in the garbage container beside the house.

"I'll be back shortly," Izzy yelled out as she slid on her tinted glasses and cranked up Barney.

That is one loony person, Allie thought as she wheeled the almost-empty container to the end of her driveway.

Izzy pulled into the crowded parking lot of Hayden Memorial Hospital, thankful to have found a parking spot close to the entrance. She felt slightly apprehensive about her mission this afternoon, given the fiasco inside the church, but pressed on with an outer layer of confidence. She prayed for strength and words of wisdom as she came upon the large sliding glass doors and entered the lobby. She started to bypass the receptionist's desk, as she often did in the past, but was stopped when the new attendant motioned her to the station.

"What patient did you wish to see, ma'am?"

Izzy smiled, and without hesitation, answered her.

"All of them."

As the bewildered lady dropped her jaw, Izzy began her mission with the first floor.

Izzy had covered two floors and was taking the elevator to the third floor when she began to have regrets about not asking Allie to come along. *She would have enjoyed this,* she thought, knowing of Allie's compassionate side. *Maybe next time,* she promised herself.

Stepping out of the elevator, she moved from room to room, not knowing what she would encounter, but prepared all the same. There were elderly patients she held hands with and listened to as they reminisced of being younger and independent. There were the younger ones who defied the odds of surviving horrendous accidents of one nature or another. Some were there for minor surgeries, others, major. But they all had stories to tell, many with heavy hearts. Izzy embraced each story and amazingly found the wisdom in words when she spoke. Oh, how she wanted to eliminate their pain!

By the end of the long but rewarding afternoon, she had visited everybody in the modest three-story hospital, except for one. And his was a special case. He had been brought in that day and was heavily sedated until the doctors could identify his mystery illness. Izzy respected the nurses and avoided his room altogether. She was just elated that she'd accomplished ninety-nine percent of her mission. Maybe next time, if the mystery patient was still there, she'd visit him.

Officer Russell Banks, a rookie with the Possum Heights Police Department, having been on the force for only two weeks, patrolled the desolate town, seeking action, anything to break the monotony of his routine. The whole town appeared to be asleep, as if it rolled up the sidewalk after dark. At first, it excited him to be assigned to the graveyard shift, where the goons came out at night, where he could proudly show his passion for the law and single handedly bring in the thieves, the drunkards, the wife abusers, the vandals. This was his shining moment, to prove to his older peers that he could work the beat at night, and keep the citizens of Possum Heights feeling safe in their own homes.

But after two weeks of patrolling the streets, he only received two calls from dispatch. One was to investigate a store alarm accidentally set off by a careless employee who had left a window partially opened, sending a breeze through the vacant shop and causing the curtains to sway inward, therefore setting off the motion detectors and triggering the alarm. The other call involved a theft. Again, the same store left the window open, but the alarm off. A passerby heard noises in the shop and called 911.

Banks canvassed the store and discovered the register untouched, but bags of chips and packs of nabs littered the floor, opened and devoured. The intruder had a bad case of the munchies. There also seemed to be a trail of miniature poop. Following the tiny droppings, he located the source of the thievery. High on a shelf, munching on a bag of Fritos, perched a brazen fat squirrel. The squirrel was chased throughout the store with a broom and finally dove out the way it came in, leaving behind a massive mess in its wake.

Officer Banks was pondering his possibilities of being relieved of this shift, regressing back to those calls, when he happened upon an immobile vehicle in a vacant lot across town. Pulling up beside it, he shined his flashlight at the car, checking for life inside. Although it appeared abandoned, Banks decided to get a closer look. Getting out of his patrol car, he cautiously edged closer to the Honda Accord, peering in with his flashlight. Empty. Somebody must have run out of gas, he decided. As routine, though, it was standard to report an abandoned vehicle to be sure it wasn't stolen property. He was excited to finally get to show off his knowledge of the police codes he'd studied up on, and hopefully impress the dispatcher. Leaning into the patrol car and grabbing his mic, he nervously keyed it.

"Ah, dispatcher, Unit 3 . . . I ah, have an 11-12 and could you do a 10-27 and ah, also a 10-32? Over."

Banks smiled as he proudly and patiently waited for Carla to respond. When she did, a minute later, he was flushed with embarrassment.

"Unit 3, let me get this straight. You want me to check on any outstanding warrants on a dead animal and also provide an Intoxilyzer?"

He could detect that she'd been laughing her butt off while he'd been waiting for a response, she and all the other two-way radio users listening in.

"Shi—" He stopped, realizing he had prematurely keyed his mic. "No, no," he corrected. "I mean I have an abandoned vehicle here and I need the registration checked to see if it's stolen." *How could I have gotten the codes screwed up? They'll never let me live this one down.*

A couple of minutes later, the dispatcher called back to him after running the VIN number Russell gave them. "Unit 3, the vehicle is registered to a Gary Carter. He's from out of town. It's not been reported stolen so your guess is as good as mine."

"10-4. Thanks."

"Oh, and for the record, it's, 'You have an 11-24 and need a 10-28 and 10-29.' Got it?" Carla boomed into the mic. Banks felt angry and humiliated but managed to keep his temper under control.

"Right," he responded.

Unable to resist her impish mood, Carla wanted to take one more crack at him. "You mind if I do a 10-112 on you?"

"What's that?" Banks foolishly asked, unfamiliar with the code.

"Impersonating a police officer," she answered, bursting out laughing as she keyed off the mic.

Banks wisely decided not to respond. He'd continue on his patrol and at the end of his shift, if the car was still there, he'd seek its owner.

Chapter 31

Gary fidgeted with the remote control draped over the handrails. He had flipped through all four or five channels and nothing seemed of interest, not that he really cared. His mind was on other matters. When the doctor burst into the room, he quickly switched the TV off, anxious to get on with his release.

"You're looking much better today, Gary," Dr. Hart commented as he walked to the other side of the bed where Gary lay quietly. "Do you remember any of what you said when you came in yesterday?"

"No, not really."

"You apparently had a nervous breakdown. I'm speculating that maybe something has happened to you recently, or even not so recently, that triggered the attack at the diner. Bits and pieces of what I could gather from your conversation told me of an underlying depression. You also seemed to be regressing back to your past, perhaps trying to make amends of something that happened or didn't happen. Now, you say you're not taking anything now, correct?"

"No." He didn't feel he was lying, because he had left his pills behind. And he didn't want anyone, not even the doctor, to know his battle with depression. But even more, he was too weary to divulge his pain within. At the moment, he just wanted to be out of there.

"Well, I'm going to prescribe some Chlorpromazine. This will get you on an even kilter, so to speak. I'm also referring you to a psychiatrist . . ."

Gary did his best to look attentive but the words of Dr. Hart faded as fast as he spoke them. His mind and his heart were in another place. He'd come to this town with a purpose in mind and nothing, including what the doctor had to say, was going to prevent him from doing what he'd come to do.

". . . so unless you have some questions, I'll go ahead and fill out the discharge papers. Good luck to you."

The doctor shook his hand as Gary meekly thanked him. Discharge papers, that's the only thing he wanted to hear. He was relieved to finally be discharged but then the thoughts of where he'd left his vehicle plagued his mind. He knew he'd have to call a cab to take him to it. Hopefully, it would still be in the same spot where he had left it.

Chief Bradley peered through the open blinds of his office, agitated that his rookie officer was late off his graveyard shift. He had tried several times to contact him by radio but there was no answer. If something bad had happened, he felt he'd have known by now. Different scenarios played out in his head of what could have delayed Officer Banks, all of which just made him angrier. He was less concerned with his safety and more occupied with the idea that just maybe his young rookie cop was goofing off.

As he gazed through the window, he heard the unmistakable sound of a Volkswagen Beetle coming up the street, its rear engine getting louder as it approached. It slowly cruised past his line of vision, then rumbled on down the street, its distinct VW engine fading further into the distance.

"Dang hippie," he muttered.

"Now, now, Chief," Carla reprimanded. "You need to honor your badge." She had a keen sense of hearing, even from way across the room.

"That don't mean I can't call her names behind her back," the chief snorted.

Carla respected her boss but she liked Izzy better and didn't care for his unmerited insults, and she was quick to make it known. In truth, she liked Russell, too, but felt he was a little green beneath the gills. She felt it her duty to break him in, as she did all the new recruits, even if it involved a little teasing now and then.

The door suddenly swung open and Russell, reluctantly, stepped in, appearing haggard and forlorn.

"Banks! Where have you been?" Chief Bradley yelled, then he stopped and wrinkled his nose. He took a few cautious sniffs before backing up, as Banks looked visibly nervous just coming off his shift. "And what is that smell?"

"I had a last minute call from dispatch, sir, a potential home invasion. You ought to know that, Carla. You called it in to me," he said, glaring at Carla.

"Yeah, but that was over two hours ago. I tried calling you and I called the house where the alleged invasion occurred, and they said you'd already left," the chief barked.

"I know, sir. I told them not to elaborate on the situation, should you or anyone call."

"What situation? This better be good."

Russell canvassed the room, taking in the reactions of his peers, some pretending to be preoccupied with what they were doing, others gawking at him with intense curiosity.

"You see, I went to the premises of the reported incidence and sought out the intruder that was still inside the house. Well . . . it turns out . . . it was a skunk." Giggles exploded in some areas of the room.

"I see. That certainly answers my second question."

"I had to go home and take a shower and put on fresh clothes." More snickers could be heard from all around but Chief Bradley remained stoic.

"I still smell you."

"He got me good, sir. I was clearly downwind from him. I can't seem to get rid of the scent."

The chief almost felt a bit of pity for him, knowing he was out there doing his job, unaware the intruder packed such an offensive weapon.

"OK. Next time, son, call in, will ya? Is that clear?" he said, easing himself behind the desk.

"Yes sir," Russell answered meekly, feeling humiliated all over again. He had previously decided not to broadcast his dilemma over the two-way radio for the entire department to hear. But this futile attempt at discretion made him a laughing stock after all.

"All right, now that we have that out of the way, I understand you reported an abandoned vehicle."

"Yes sir. I meant to go back at the end of my shift to see if it was still there, but then, well, this other thing happened." Again, more snickers.

"Yes, of course. Well, I'll send one of my men here over there to check it out. Meanwhile, since you're not on duty till tomorrow night, that'll give you a chance to wash all the skunk away. Now . . . go home. We don't want you stinking up the whole precinct. And please, take a long hot shower with a fresh bar of soap before you come in tomorrow night."

"Yes sir." Russell left feeling mildly degraded, but not defeated. His determination to succeed was even greater. He supposed every rookie cop, at one time or another, was subjected to the same type of taunting, maybe to test their stamina. *But this rookie's tough,* he thought, *let 'em have their fun while they can.*

As soon as Russell left the office, Chief Bradley made a gesture with his right hand.

"Somebody. Please open some windows!" he yelled.

Just as the windows went up, Izzy cruised by again, this time her beetle backfiring, just as the chief took a sip of his coffee. The noise, much like a gunshot, caused him to spill coffee into his lap, while some of the others in the room ducked, a reflex response.

"Dang hippie! And I don't care who hears me!"

Gary tipped the cab driver as he stepped out onto the vacant lot, thrilled his car was still there where he'd left it. He feared it might have been vandalized, towed, or even worse, stolen. But there it was, waiting for him, seemingly undetected by anyone since he had abandoned it yesterday.

Guiding the car out of the lot and onto the road, he decided to search for a motel as obscure as possible nearby. The one near the diner provided the best view but the worst disguise. By now, he was positive everyone in Possum Heights had heard about the stranger who had freaked out at the diner, the motel clerk next door for sure. No, he couldn't risk staying where he could easily be recognized.

As luck would have it, he did find an exclusive inn a few miles further down. It was far enough out where he could stay hidden, yet close enough to where he could navigate the town in secrecy.

Cutting the hospital band from his wrist, he grabbed a change of clothes from his duffle bag, along with some toiletries. A nice hot shower would help alleviate some of the tension. A hot shower and a cold drink. Maybe he'd venture over to the convenience store after his shower for a six-pack. It was still early. Maybe a drive was just what he needed.

About midway through his shower, he started to feel the effects of the Chlorpromazine. Taken an hour earlier, he had skimmed over the list of side effects, drowsiness being one of them. But he chose to overlook it in favor of the "even kilter" the doctor had mentioned. The lithium he had left back home on his nightstand didn't have the same effect, but he'd also been on it for a while, having adjusted to any side effects it may have caused. This drug would probably work the same way but he couldn't spare the time to find out.

Grabbing a towel nearby, he carefully emerged from the shower, drying himself while fighting to stay alert. He felt a swagger as he walked, his head dizzy with each step. Stumbling to the bed with his change of clothes, he realized he'd have to sleep it off tonight, letting the drug run its course. When it was out of his system, he could continue with his mission.

Donning a fresh T-shirt and pajama bottoms, he crawled into bed beneath the warm covers and quickly fell asleep.

Chapter 32

Allie had barely sat down and was enjoying a sip of her first cup of coffee in her tiny quarters of the diner when Jean waltzed in.

"We missed you yesterday, sweetie. Glad to have you back."

"Nice to be back. Frank was kind enough to let me have Monday off to get my vehicle maintenance done. I'd planned to do it Saturday but I didn't realize the whole town shuts down for a possum celebration." Her real purpose for taking off was to do a little clothes shopping since the majority of her wardrobe was back in Regal Woods, but she didn't want to divulge that to Jean.

"Oh, it's a silly tradition, I suppose, but it's a lot of fun. Looked like you were having fun." Allie raised her eyebrows. "The toe sack race," Jean clarified.

"Oh, you saw that?"

"Are you kidding? That's my favorite part of the festival. By the way, congratulations."

"Thanks," Allie said, not really sure if a toe sack race carried much merit.

"Say, did you hear about what happened at the diner Sunday?"

"No," Allie replied, grabbing a tissue to wipe up some coffee she'd just spilled onto her desk.

"This guy came in, some stranger from out of town, and had lunch at the counter. Then when he went to pay his bill, he collapsed. I mean right there at the cash register. I went and got a wet rag to put on his forehead and he came to a bit but when he spoke, he wasn't making much sense."

"What do you mean," Allie asked, still wiping her desk.

"Well, he kept repeating 'Miami' and was mumbling something else, but . . . well, it was too soft for me to decipher. But I definitely heard 'Miami.'"

Allie felt her blood run cold as she tried to hide her panic. Gary had found her. But how? And how long had he been trailing her? Had he been watching her every move, absorbing everything she did? The thought chilled her to the bone as she struggled to remain calm while Jean continued on.

"Then he passed out and we had an ambulance take him to the hospital. Is that not wild or what?"

"Did . . . anyone find out the guy's name, or anything about him?" Allie asked, hoping Jean couldn't detect the nervousness in her voice.

"No, but I guess the hospital knows by now. Poor guy. Must have been from Miami. Long way from home to have something like this happen to him."

"Yeah, I'll say."

"Well, I'll let you get back to work. Just wanted to chat a little since I missed you yesterday."

Allie waited till Jean left her office, then made a frantic call to Izzy's house. *Please be there,* she prayed.

Izzy removed her straw hat and wiped her brow. Only nine o'clock in the morning, the sun barely in the sky, and she was starting to sweat. She couldn't believe just three days ago how cool the temperature was, which was to Richard's advantage, prancing around in a possum suit. But this time of year was often unpredictable. If Saturday had even been close to this morning's sudden heat wave, Richard would have forgone the suit and just worn the headpiece.

Izzy gazed over the rows of assorted vegetables planted just a few weeks ago. The long hours of tilling the ground and removing grass and weeds and sculpturing the rows had paid off. She just hoped and prayed that no sprouts would emerge until the danger of the frost had passed. At least she had remembered to mark the rows this year. Last year she forgot and had to wait until the vegetables started poking out of the ground before she could figure out what was what. As always, she reserved the front row for tomatoes, which was what she'd be working on all morning. Planted all down the row was a mixture of Better Boys, Beef Masters and cherry tomatoes, twelve plants in all.

Putting her straw hat back on, she started to ground stakes into the soil for support as the vines would grow bigger in the weeks ahead. She would also run twine around each stake as added support for her future tomatoes.

Whistling beneath her breath, she hammered the stakes in one by one, the sound echoing off into the trees. It was also drowning out the sound of her phone ringing at the house. By luck, Richard happened to be coming over with a garden sprinkler when he heard the phone.

"Hey Iz, your phone's ringing!"

"You mind getting it? You're closer to it!" she hollered back.

"All right!"

Izzy then remembered she'd waxed the kitchen floor that morning.

"But be careful! I just waxed the floor and it's a bit slippery!"

Richard was already in the kitchen and on his rear end when Izzy relayed the warning.

"Crazy hippie. Who waxes the floor anymore?" he mumbled, struggling to get up. When he finally got to his feet, he quickly, but carefully, tiptoed the rest of the way to the living room and picked up the phone just in time.

"Hello," he said, panting.

"Hey . . . who's this?"

"This is Richard, Izzy's neighbor. Who's this?"

"Oh, hey Richard. It's Allie. Is Izzy there? I need to talk to her. It's urgent."

"She's in the garden. I'll go get her."

Allie's mind was in a whirl as she waited for Izzy to pick up the phone. She was certain Gary had found her out of desperation and had used all sorts of tactics to accomplish it. He'd actually been in the diner, where she could have easily been had she not requested Sundays off. The thought made her shiver as she imagined the scene Jean had described. She then jumped at hearing Izzy's voice on the other end of the line.

"Hey, kiddo, what's up?"

"He's here, Izzy! He's found me!"

"He who?"

"Gary! The guy who's obsessed with me! He was in the diner Sunday! I don't know how he found me or what I'm gonna do!"

"You went to the diner and saw him?"

"No. Jean said a stranger came in here Sunday and ate. Then he had a spell of some sort and collapsed. When they brought him to, he repeated the word 'Miami' several times. It's definitely him!"

"OK, OK. Calm down. I doubt he knows where you're at. And I'll make a few phone calls to make sure he doesn't find out. I'll alert the cops and they'll keep an eye out for him." *At least I hope*, she said to herself, realizing that her and Chief Bradley weren't the best of friends.

"You think that's gonna stop him? Even if I get a restraining order, it'd be a worthless piece of paper."

"Allie, you can't keep running. This is where it stops. Trust me. I know what I'm doing. Now you just come on home, but make sure you're not being followed."

"Well, hopefully he's still in the hospital."

"You're kidding," Izzy said, almost to herself. Allie had neglected to mention that the stranger had been taken to the hospital. This was ironic, him being there at the same time Izzy was visiting patients. She remembered the one patient she wasn't allowed to see and wondered if that was the stranger. She decided not to mention this to Allie, not yet. The name on the mystery patient's door simply said "John Doe," but surely by now, the staff knew his true identity.

"Maybe I can find out if he's still there and if so, we'll alert the cops."

"Good luck with that. They probably can't do anything with him till he tries to hurt me."

"We'll see about that. Now, in the event he's out of the hospital, you need to be on your best guard. He may be lurking around the corner . . . probably not, but just in case."

"Hey Izzy, I am so sorry about all this. I didn't know my troubles would be following me."

"This isn't your fault, Allie. Ya hear? Don't worry. It'll be all right. You'll see."

Izzy had such a reassuring confidence about her that made Allie feel safe again. She wondered, though, if and when all this would be over. She wondered if maybe it would have been better to have stayed in Regal Woods and face the problem head on rather than run and have it chase her down. And now, someone innocent was involved, her new friend Izzy.

When Izzy got off the phone, she gave Richard a dumbfounded look, as he stared back. Suddenly realizing he was holding the sprinkler, he handed it over to her.

"Thanks. I'll try not to run over this one with the mower. I'm still picking up remnants out there from the last one I destroyed."

"Wanna tell me what's going on?" Richard asked, trying to read her face.

"No, not really. But you're gonna find out eventually. Some nut's stalking Allie. That's why she's here, in this town, but apparently, he's found her."

"Oh my . . . what are y'all gonna do?"

"I'm working on that. But for starters, do me a favor. You see anything suspicious around my house, you let me know."

Richard nodded, concerned for Izzy and their new friend. He wondered just how obsessed this guy was to have followed Allie here and even more, how far he'd go to prove his point.

Allie sat at the table, her head in her hands, more concerned for Izzy than herself as she sobbed, remorseful of having her friend exposed to this relentless stalker.

"I am so sorry. I had no idea he would go this far. All I've done is put you in danger. I never should have come here—"

"Stop it! Stop! Stop it!" Izzy interrupted. "You are underestimating yourself, and me. He hasn't won! And he's not going to!" Izzy sat down beside her and took her hand. "I'm not exactly a rookie, you know. I can handle guys like that. Trust me. OK?" She pulled out a Kleenex from her pocket and wiped the tears off Allie's cheeks. "Listen to me. I'm gonna give you a little something to calm your nerves and then I'm gonna make a couple of phone calls. All right?"

Allie nodded and managed to smile but her smile merely hid how she really felt.

Izzy placed a shot of brandy in front of her, then grabbed the phonebook off the counter. Any other time, she would be able to recall the number to the hospital, but with the drama unfolding before her eyes, her memory had faded somewhat. Snatching the receiver from the phone, she quickly dialed the number beneath her forefinger.

"Yes, I need some information, please."

Izzy explained who she was and that she had just been up there two days ago visiting all the patients. However, her good Samaritan nature did nothing to persuade the operator to cooperate with her. She wasn't surprised that the mysterious patient had been discharged, but she was disappointed and even angry that the hospital refused to release any information, including his name, age, description, citing privacy laws, even when Izzy stressed her reasons for needing to know.

The lady who took Izzy's call sympathized with her predicament, but the hospital rules were strict and meant to be followed at all times. After all, she didn't know Izzy. For all she knew, *she* could be the real lunatic. But she didn't dare say this to the irate woman at the other end of the line, rather choosing to commend her for her kindly act of visiting the patients, although she was not on duty Sunday to verify Izzy's claims. She thought it was a kind and selfless thing to do, but still insisted that the policy would not allow exceptions to the rules.

"Well thanks for nothing! And don't be surprised if he ends up back in the hospital . . . if that was John Doe!"

Izzy slammed down the phone. Glancing back at Allie, she realized she had to maintain control, for Allie's sake. Allie, however, seemed unfazed, nursing her brandy.

"Well, that was a useless call. But no big deal. Guess I better call the police." This was the call she dreaded more. But she wasn't going to let her personality conflict with Chief Bradley deter her from what needed to be done. With a calmer demeanor, she dialed the police department. This call, although more informative, induced the same frustration.

"You mean to tell me there was an abandoned car on the outskirts of town registered to Gary Carter and now it's gone?" Izzy squeezed the receiver of the phone as if it might slip from her fingers. She listened intently as the party on the other end explained the intricacies of the matter.

Allie, not use to anything stronger than what came out of a vineyard, leaned back in the chair, slouched to one side, with a smirk across her face. The brandy seemed to have served its purpose. Izzy glanced back at her, shaking her head, at the same time taking in the conversation on the other end of the line.

"Yeah, yeah. I understand . . . you didn't know. But putting that aside, we still have a problem. He could be lurking around the corner of my house as we speak. This nut seems to have a strong obsession with Allie. I just don't want to see anyone get hurt. With that in mind, you tell Chief Bradley I'm giving fair warning. I have a revolver. If this guy in so much as enters a hair into my house, I'll blow his brains out. That's called self-defense. I, as a law-abiding citizen, or hippie, if that's what the chief prefers to label me, have the right to protect my property and everything and everyone on it."

"Yes, ma'am," the voice agreed. "You do indeed. But your first line of defense is to call us."

"Before or after we're dead?" Izzy yelled into the phone. Allie snickered from behind.

"Calm down, ma'am, I wasn't finished," the operator said, trying to remain calm. "If he poses a real threat and you feel the need to use force, then by all means, you have no choice but to defend yourself, in whatever matter deemed necessary. But . . . you shouldn't have to worry about that. We have his name and the make of vehicle he's driving and we'll be on the lookout for him. In the meantime, if you see or hear anything suspicious, dial 911 right away."

"Right." Izzy hung up the phone, less convinced than ever that the police would be of any help. At least Allie was relaxed, too relaxed, after three shots of brandy, two of which Izzy didn't see her pour.

"Oh, for Pete's sake, you're snookered, girl. Let me get you to bed. At least you've had supper. I just hope you can keep it down."

Allie reached up and put an arm around Izzy's neck, then slowly pushed herself to a standing position.

"I'm not . . . ussssed to this," she slurred.

"I know. My mistake. I left you alone with the brandy bottle. At least you should be able to sleep. And you'll have all the little 'furry blankets' to keep you warm."

Izzy guided her to the bedroom and laid her down.

"Oh, Izzzzzy, you have been soooo good to me. I don't know how to thank you."

"I do. You can shut up and go to sleep. There's a trashcan next to the bed if you have to puke. Now lie down, pull up a cat, and go to sleep."

Allie chuckled. "Imagine . . . a week ago, I was driving you to the repair shop to pick up your . . . Baaaarney. And a week later, here I am, camping out with you, the lady I first encoun . . . encoun . . . the lady I first met on the road. Is this fate or what?" Allie laughed, then on a somber note, added, "I'm really sorry, Iz. I didn't mean to put your life in jeop . . . jeop . . . ah, danger because of some deranged S.O.B. I can be outta here first thing in the morning. If he was at the diner Sunday, how long do you think it's gonna take him to find out where I'm staying?"

"You're not going anywhere," Izzy snapped. "I told you to trust me. I don't give in to psychos, and you're not going to either. Now please, close your eyes and get some sleep. We'll figure this thing out tomorrow."

"OK," Allie said, yawning, already succumbing to the soothing effects of the brandy. "I'll see you in the morning. Goodnight."

"Goodnight," Izzy said, watching her as she drifted off. Then she realized that didn't sound quite right with it still being light outside. "Good day, I mean," she whispered.

As she tiptoed backwards out of the room, she thought she heard a bump of some sort and stalled to listen. After a few seconds of straining her ears, she decided it had to be one of the cats, perhaps Chloe, jumping on top of the cabinet, as she sometimes did. Not feeling the urgency to check the source of the noise, she staggered into her own bedroom and shed her hippie attire for a loud pair of pajamas, also a replica from the sixties. It was still early in the evening, but the past few days convinced her body that she needed to forego any more constructive activities and retire for the night. There was nothing she liked better than curling up in bed and reading a good novel. Tonight, however, fatigue would prevent her from getting beyond the page marked from last night.

Gary found a sack of corn to lay his head on in the cluttered barn. The mile-and-a-half walk from the motel tired him immensely. He felt it his good fortune that he'd gone to the convenience store that afternoon and overheard a conversation involving Allie. It was the contents of that exchange that revealed to him her whereabouts. Although it had been over a decade, possibly two, since he'd been in Possum Heights, he knew the road the townsperson had mentioned. He even thought he knew the house with the wraparound porch. With the new information he had obtained at the convenience store, he forgot the nature of his trip and embarked on his original mission . . . to find Allie.

Not wanting to risk his car being recognized, he left it where it was, at the rear of the motel, and set off down the rural highway to find the house with the wrap-around porch. Although few vehicles traveled this lonesome road, he found it easy to dodge them by ducking into the woods. The last thing he needed on this night was to attract attention in such a small town.

Although weary and sore from the hike, he found it difficult to relax. After the evening before, he decided to leave the pills alone. He wondered now if he had made a mistake. Despite the cool evening breeze, he felt his body rising in temperature. The familiar sweat and disorientation were taking control again. He closed his eyes, wishing it away.

"Oh, no. Please . . . not here, not now," he pleaded to himself.

.

Chapter 33

When Allie awoke from her brandy-induced slumber, her eyes searched the room for something familiar. She took on the demeanor of a comatose patient, suddenly awakening, unaware of her surroundings, not knowing where she was, or how long she'd been here. After a few seconds had elapsed, she regained control over her senses, with the aid of one of Izzy's "tuxes." She figured it was Clare, the mother of the other seven. Although she still couldn't attach the right names to the right cats, Clare stood out with her "mustache" face. She lay stretched out across her chest, purring long and loud. But it was Izzy's snoring next door that helped to remind her where she was.

Other than Clare's purring and the various renditions of her children's purrs, and of course Izzy sawing logs next door, the house was an eerie calm. She suddenly wasn't convinced that she awoke on her own. The soothing effect of the brandy long gone, she found herself wide awake and oddly afraid. Just before her eyes popped open, she thought she heard a noise. But could that have been part of a dream? Sometimes dreams have a way of mocking reality. But this thought did little to ease her fear. If Gary was desperate enough to track her down miles away from home, he just might be desperate enough to find his way into the house and maybe even harm her or Izzy.

Sliding Clare to the side, Allie sat up, swinging her feet to the side of the bed. Reaching over to where the blinds were tightly closed, she slowly parted a slat to catch a glimpse of the night outside. A full moon enhanced the sky, lighting the world beneath with its glow. As beautiful as it was, she couldn't help but remember hearing how crimes peaked during full moons. Maybe it was the effect of the stellar world that heightened man's criminal behavior or perhaps it was that they simply could see better on full moon nights, thus using this to their advantage. Whatever the case, she hoped it wasn't true, not here anyway.

Returning the slat to where it was, she slowly eased off the bed, hoping the cats would stay behind. Any human headed toward the kitchen was an automatic signal for a feline feast; it didn't matter what time of day or night it happened to be, or if they were just fed five minutes ago. Much to her relief, all of Izzy's furry friends chose to go on snoozing, even Clare, who quickly went back to sleep.

A quick glance at the clock revealed it was just past midnight. As she made her way into the kitchen, using the nightlight in the hallway as her guide, she cautiously peered out the window, jumping when she saw her own reflection. Letting go of a nervous laugh, she peered out again and this time surveyed the entire yard, but could see nothing out of place. Breathing a sigh of relief, she turned to go back when she felt a hunger pang. Her stomach was reminding her that she hadn't eaten since early afternoon and was very much in need of a mid-night snack.

Scouring the kitchen cabinets, she wasn't surprised to see all the cans and boxes and bottles neatly stacked and labels out front. It was the first time she'd ever thought about looking in the cabinets, since she either ate at the diner or indulged in meals prepared by Izzy, which actually were very good, considering her love of fried grit sandwiches. She may have had her peculiar culinary ways, but with Allie, she knew how to separate the two.

Seeing a lone can of Chef Boyardee's spaghetti, she grabbed it just before a clamor of some sort, even louder than before, froze her in her tracks.

Russell beamed as he started patrol. Vowing he wouldn't repeat his mistake from the other night, he'd studied all the police codes and nearly had them memo-rized. As a precaution, though, he had inserted a copy into his pocket, just in case the smart aleck dispatcher decided to toy with him again.

Seeing the full moon, as bright and high in the sky as it was, made him hungry for love. The nightshift hours made it difficult, if not impossible, to date. And even if he did meet someone, the question always loomed in his head. Could she accept his devotion to working the beat at night?

"Unit 3, you got a copy?" the radio crackled, intercepting his thoughts.

"10-4; go ahead."

"Seen any more pole cats?"

Russell anticipated Carla's jabs and was prepared. "Not since I left the presence of your company . . . Ms. Pepe Le Pew." Russell laughed, pleased he had a comeback. When Carla failed to respond, he transmitted again. "What's the matter . . . skunk got your tongue?"

He could tell the dispatcher was frantically searching for something smarter to say, but after a few seconds, she aired her defeat. "No comment, Unit 3."

Didn't think so, Russell mused. He wished he had been this savvy growing up. His size and shy demeanor allured the attention of bullies waiting in the wings at every turn he made. Whether at school or canvassing the neighborhood or even in Sunday School, Russell endured the endless taunts of his peers, who knew no boundaries. He watched them grow taller and stronger as his own body stayed the same, creating a hole of deep despair, which he sunk deeper and deeper within. His father, keenly aware of his son's sadness and frustration, approached him one evening as he sat on the stoop of their paint-chipped house. Taking a seat beside him, he removed his cap, placing it in his lap. He knew his pain first hand, a seemingly genetic trait.

"You know, Russ, I remember a time when I thought I'd never grow."

Russell met his father's eyes, surprised. His father was six-foot-two. It was hard to envision him short. "You were small, like me?"

"Yeah. I was the same age and I thought I'd be small forever. But a year later, I sprouted and even surpassed boys my age in size. Things have a way of surprising you. You'll see. And even if you don't grow taller or bigger than those your age, you'll soon find out that what's important in life is not the outside, but the inside. You're tougher than you know, son."

Russell smiled, thinking of that moment and how a year later, he did indeed catch up with his taunters. The teasing and bullying subsided, and despite the pain it had caused him, it had a positive impact on his future. It was the first time he considered a career in law enforcement. Ironically, he never expected to be taunted all over again, as a rookie, by his peers, but fortunately, the early years of his life had taught him how to rise above and beyond.

With so many hours laying ahead on his shift and so little action, Russell had plenty of time to think. He reflected upon the chief's comments earlier, to be on the lookout for Gary Carter. He couldn't help but sense the apathy in Chief Bradley's voice. Maybe Izzy tiptoed on his ego, ruffling his feathers just a tab. Maybe he was just plain grumpy from a lack of sleep. Maybe he and his wife, a match not made in Heaven—or so he heard—had exchanged some cross words before he came to work. Regardless, Russell thrived by instinct. He chose this career not by some egotistical aspiration, but of a deep-rooted need to serve and protect. It was his heart that guided him to this milestone in his life and he knew his heart never lied.

His heart also told him that he was wasting his time canvassing the same territory night after night when he needed to be somewhere else. Despite Bradley being his superior, he vowed he would adhere to the reasoning of his heart, which brought him here to start with. His intents on this night seemed to override his appointed post.

Only a short few weeks into his internship as a police officer, he had faced his first potential obstacle: the chief. But the words of his father—"What's important in life is not the outside, but the inside," and "You're tougher than you think"— ultimately gave him the push he needed. He wasn't sure if that meant defying the boss's orders, but he quickly decided it didn't matter.

Russell left the confines of the usual cruise around town and ventured toward the highway where Izzy's house stood nestled off the beaten path. He, like Allie, had admired this house many times over, but tonight, he wouldn't be there just to admire it. He'd be guarding it.

"Izzy! Izzy! Wake up!"

Allie had to poke her several times to get her to open her eyes. Even when she did open them, she was far from being coherent.

"Izzy! Wake up! I hear something outside!"

Allie shook her and then watched in despair as she snorted and rolled over. She then realized if she was going to get her up, she'd have to get more creative, maybe even think like Izzy.

"Izzy! Wake your hippie butt up! Somebody stole Barney!"

It worked. Izzy found her senses and jumped out of bed, then raced toward the door and out onto the lawn in her psychedelic pajamas. Much to her relief, and confusion, she found her beloved Beetle parked just where she left it. Allie had followed her to the doorway, trying to stop her, afraid of what might be lurking outside after the noise she'd heard earlier. She figured whoever or whatever it was could still be watching them close by. On the other hand, they could be long gone with Izzy's frantic rush out of the house wearing those ridiculous pajamas.

Izzy, puzzled and out of breath, turned and looked at Allie.

"Barney . . ." she panted, ". . . he's still here. What . . . what's going on?"

"I'm sorry," Allie said. "I was desperate. I was just trying to get you up."

"So Barney's OK? Nobody . . . nobody tried to steal him?"

"Yeah. The little guy's fine. But we may not be. You need to come back inside, like, now!"

Izzy, on the verge of losing her temper like on the day she and Allie had their first encounter, managed to gain control when she saw the terror in Allie's eyes. Still panting, she hobbled back up the steps and into the house, switching the kitchen light on to override the nightlight in the hallway. Allie watched her as she turned to lock the door. As predicted, she turned the lock three times. To Izzy, it was peace of mind, but to Allie, it was irritating. She insisted she could have locked it once and got the same results.

Izzy, ignoring Allie's sarcasm, calmly but firmly demanded an explanation on why she was alerted out of her bed and into the yard only to find Barney safe and sound. Exhausted from her sprint out the door, she took a seat at the table while Allie took a seat beside her.

"I thought I heard something in my sleep. But when I awoke, I wasn't sure if it was real or not. So I went to the kitchen to see if I could see anything out the window, but I didn't see anything. That's when I decided it must have been my imagination. While I was in the kitchen, I felt my stomach growling, so I raided your cabinets, hope you didn't mind, and found a can of spaghetti. As I grabbed it from the shelf, I heard a noise, a distinct noise this time, somewhere close by. This time, I knew I wasn't dreaming."

Izzy remembered the noise she heard as well before going to bed, but thought it best not to mention it to Allie. It would only rouse her suspicions and cause her unnecessary alarm. After all, Izzy was accustomed to hearing all sorts of bumps in the night being in the country where critters of several species roamed around at night.

"Maybe we should call the police," Allie suggested, "just to be on the safe side."

"Ha!" Izzy blurted. "I'd rather call the tooth fairy."

"You have something against the police department?" Allie asked.

"No . . . just Chief Bradley."

"Why?" Allie was eager to hear her story.

"Call it a personality conflict. He grew up in the same era as I did, the hippie movement, Woodstock and all that jazz. But he automatically thinks that anybody who dresses the way I do is a drug addict or even worse, a Manson follower. How shallow is that? Anyway, you know how shy I am about speaking my mind." Allie grinned, knowing Izzy was teasing with her. "He made some smart comment to me one day at the diner, thinking it would embarrass me, being in a public place. But I came back swinging and it took him for a loop. I told him, where everybody could hear it, that if he'd lay off the way I dressed, I wouldn't tell anybody how he liked to cross dress."

"You're kidding! You really said that to the police chief?"

"Indeed, I did. It shut him up, too. He never taunted me after that, but it didn't improve our relationship with one another either. He had to deal with damage control after my comment, but the way I look at it, he had it coming."

"Wow, now that's a story. Nonetheless, Izzy, the law is there to protect us. If we can't rely on the police department to do that, what good are they?"

Without waiting for an answer, Allie wandered over to the phone. Reaching down to pick it up, she froze when she saw the light blinking on the answering machine.

"Did you check the messages before we went to bed?"

"Yeah. There were none. Why?"

"Someone must've called while we were asleep."

Izzy walked over to the machine and hit the "Play" button.

Russell had discreetly camouflaged his patrol car in some overgrown brushes near the highway, then walked silently and cautiously toward Izzy's house. Until now, he'd only seen her house from the highway, but now as he edged closer, he couldn't help but marvel at its grandeur. He felt a slight tinge of envy for the owner of this one-of-a-kind house with the wraparound porch, encased inside a beautiful white picket fence, and wondered if he would have to wait until he was that old, as old as Izzy, to be able to afford something as enormous and picturesque as this.

Although he didn't know Izzy that well, being a rookie cop and a newcomer to Possum Heights, he remembered meeting her for the first time at the diner when he was being considered for the job on the police force. The chief had treated him to lunch after a tour of showing him around, which pretty much took all of twenty minutes or less, since Possum Heights only extended from one corner to the next, or so it seemed. Although Izzy worked in the kitchen, it was obvious she liked to mingle with the crowd every chance she got.

She spotted Russell right away as they took a seat near the window and immediately came over to greet him. He was touched by her kindness in taking the time to welcome him to the community and even offered him a complimentary slice of pie. But after she walked away, the chief produced a sour face and mumbled a few derogatory remarks. Puzzled, Russell questioned Bradley's ill feelings toward Izzy. But Chief Bradley was all too vague. So what if she dressed like a hippie? What business was that of his? Despite his potential boss casting her in a negative light, he liked Izzy, who seemed to have a magnetic personality. In fact, he found it hard to believe anyone could dislike her, even if she might be a little eccentric. This personal opinion of the chief's, he decided, would not cloud his thinking. He'd grown up around the likes of his kind and would not join the ranks of the same idiotic mentality.

As Russell came within yards of the house, he could see shadows through the kitchen window. Two figures seemed to be moving about, chatting with one another, then they moved out of sight. Seconds later, he heard a man's voice, like a recording. It then occurred to him that they were playing a message on the answering machine . . . but this late at night? His curiosity peaked as he decided to move in closer. Easing onto the porch, he crouched and placed an ear against the side of the house.

Allie and Izzy stared at the answering machine, then at each other, as Derrick's voice played back to them.

"Allie, this is Derrick. I know I ain't supposed to call there unless it's important. But I thought you ought to know. Tim is missing. He's not showed up at work and he's not home. It's odd 'cause we spoke just last Friday and he never mentioned going anywhere and it's not like him to up and leave his business without letting someone know, especially his customers. Look . . . there might just be the possibility that Gary had something to do with this. After that tuffle they had at his shop, who knows what else could've happened? Call me first chance you get, OK? Love you! Bye!"

Russell strained to hear the message on the machine as he continued to hug the outside of the house, but it was too muffled. The noise of the frogs doing their nightly serenade didn't help the effort. It made him wonder if the old trick of listening through a drinking glass really worked, since he'd never actually tried it.

Suddenly, he heard the crackle of leaves close by, possibly around the corner or the back of the house. Quickly grabbing his revolver, he turned and backed against the wall. Hopefully, the girls hadn't heard what he did and come running out the door, ruining the chance of capture, or worse; someone could get hurt if the intruder happened to be armed.

Easing bit by bit against the wall, he reached the corner of the house, then took a deep breath before turning and pointing his gun. To his relief, there was no one on or near the porch. Quietly climbing over the rails, he sidestepped to the back corner, his revolver aimed straight forward. Repeating his earlier move, he rounded the corner and once again, prepared to fire, if necessary. But again, nothing. Approaching the last corner, he paused. Although the night air was rather cool, he could taste the perspiration from his forehead as it dripped to the corners of his mouth, leaving a salty aftertaste. Some of it had seeped into the corners of his eyes, stinging them as he blinked.

Silently, counting to three, he turned the final corner, aiming at nothing but a tree. He suddenly felt foolish prancing around outside Izzy's house with his revolver, chasing what was probably a squirrel or a rabbit. *Maybe he didn't even hear anything at all*, he decided.

Placing his revolver back into the holster, he turned to walk the path back to his car and nearly tripped over a ladder propped against the house. He thought that maybe Izzy was doing some sort of repairs or maybe some painting and had just left the ladder there. Then a moan in the distance took his attention away from the ladder. Once again retrieving his revolver, he followed the sound of someone in distress. It led him to the barn out back where, in the bright light of the moon, he thought he detected some movement.

"What the . . ."

"Mi-am-i," Gary moaned.

"Yeah, buddy, wouldn't we all love to be in Miami. I think you're soused. You can't be crashing here. This is private property. I'm gonna have to haul you in so you can sleep it off. Can you tell me your name?"

"Look . . . out be . . ."

"Luke Altbee? Your name's Luke Altbee—" The echo of the shovel hitting Russell's head penetrated the air and resonated into the woods nearby as he fell to the ground. He never sensed someone sneaking up from behind, and the blow to his head made sure he wouldn't turn around and see his attacker.

"Well, hello, Gary. Fancy running into you."

The attacker jeered down at Gary with menacing eyes as he still held his grip on the shovel.

"I can see you're more or less incapacitated . . . of some sort, soooooo . . . I'll just get back to you later. Right now, my friend, I have other things on my agenda. See ya in a little bit, ole buddy."

Gary lay gazing at the thug who knocked the young rookie cop out cold. It wasn't until the attacker walked away that he managed to utter the words Russell misunderstood.

"Look . . . out . . . behind . . . you," then he added, "you dumbass."

Chapter 34

Allie studied the phone for a moment. Something didn't feel right about Derrick's call, something besides Tim being missing. Images of the events that led her here raced through her mind like a tape being fast-forwarded, from her first encounter with Gary at Tim's garage, to the last sight of him at her office as she was leaving town. And then there was the news that someone fitting his description had been at the diner, passing out on the floor and being taken to the hospital.

Tim, on the other hand, had spoken with Derrick Friday. But where was he on the weekend? All she really knew for sure was that Gary was still in the hospital Monday. If it wasn't for that puzzling word he uttered at the diner, the word "Miami," she might have doubted it was Gary, but it was too much of a coincidence for it not to be.

Allie reached down and hit the "Play" button again, eager to dissect the message in hopes of hearing something she'd missed. But there was nothing to interpret. Derrick had felt it important enough to call her here, but the mystery of Tim's sudden disappearance and Gary's whereabouts was no closer to being solved.

While Allie and Izzy talked incessantly by the phone, they noticed some of the cats, who had snuck into the kitchen, now scrambled to get out.

"What in the world's gotten into them?" Izzy asked, silently aware of their keener senses.

The voice that answered back didn't come from Allie, but from someone in the hallway. "Guess cats are more in tune to noises," the voice said. When they turned to face the intruder, they froze with fear. Fixing his gaze on Allie, he smiled. "Wow! You are more beautiful than ever!"

"Tim! What are you doing here? How did you get in?"

She knew Izzy's obsessions with locks and was sure he couldn't have come in through a door or even a window, as the windows were secured as well. Izzy, just vaguely learning his identity through the message on the answering machine, shifted her eyes from Allie to Tim, then back to Allie, her mouth agape. She was also mystified as to how this stranger snuck into her house.

"Surprised to see me? You know, Allie, Derrick was right. Gary does have something to do with my disappearance, but not in the sense he means it. Seeing you that day in my shop when you brought your car to me, the way you looked, the way you smelled, the way you smiled, it just nearly took my breath away. It brought back memories. I realized I still had feelings for you, that I never truly got over you. Then along comes Gary to deprive me of that chance with you again.

"I couldn't let that happen. Even when you broke it off with him because of what he did, I knew you two still carried a torch for each other, that y'all would make up in time. I wasn't about to sit on the sideline and watch him steal you from me. Don't you see? It was fate you came by that day." Tim sighed, then continued. "I love you, Allie. I have always loved you. I had to do something to steer you away from Gary. He was going to ruin my plans, Allie."

"The manure in my car, the flowers at my house, at my business, that was you?" Allied asked, suddenly enraged.

Tim ignored the question and continued on. "I see you have made a couple of new friends, the hippie beside you and the furry thing with a snout, hard to tell the gender. Regardless, it's just you and the two loony tunes."

"You were spying on us?" Allie asked, feeling her blood begin to boil.

But again, Tim ignored her question, choosing rather to satisfy her much earlier question. "Oh, you wanted to know how I got in. I discovered an opening around the chimney."

Now it was Izzy's turn to seethe as she felt a sudden surge of anger at the crew who had delayed her job on the fireplace. This maniac had not only been spying on them, but knew the boarded hole on the roof existed, apparently seen through the use of his binoculars.

"And the flowers," he said, recalling another of her questions. "Well, I have to plead the fifth on that. And the manure, well, that was an accident. I borrowed, so to speak, a truck that a customer had towed to my shop. Darn stunk up the whole place with that manure on board. But I agreed to fix it, and quick. I took it out for a test drive in the wee morning hours and got to thinking while I was test-driving, what better time to pay you a visit in your lovely neighborhood? I was driving the perfect decoy. Anyway, I should have checked the latches on it and well, you can pretty much guess what happened. Pew! What a smell! Obviously, I couldn't hang around to clean it up. It was an unfortunate and unforeseen event. I would never have intentionally ruined that beautiful car of yours, Allie. You know how I love your Mustang. You have to believe me on that."

"Why should I believe you? You harassed me and made me think it was Gary all along."

"He doesn't deserve you! I can make you happy if you'd just give me the chance. I love you, and we belong together, baby."

Allie was stunned at his blatant revelation and apparent delusion that he could just say what he felt and it would all come together.

"You seem to be forgetting something, Tim. I don't love you!"

Tim reached into the back of his pants and pulled out a pistol, provoking gasps from both Allie and Izzy. "You will. I'm confident in time you'll come to feel for me what I feel for you. Now, say goodbye to your hippie friend and let's go."

Allie thought of her own revolver that lay useless in the nightstand beside the bed. She needed an excuse to go back to the bedroom.

"All right, Tim. You win. I'll go with you. But I need to pack some clothes."

Tim eyed her curiously, sure she had a plan. He wanted to trust her, but knew that was too premature. "OK," he consented. "But you stay here. You go," he said, pointing to Izzy. "Pack her some clothes and make it quick! And don't try anything foolish. Her life is in your hands, you know."

Izzy glared at him with contempt. She knew he wasn't about to harm the woman he loved. What fury she felt for the chimney crew was now aimed toward him. "You may walk out with her, but you won't make it far. Mark my words. The cops are watching this house," she lied. Little did she realize how true this was. "They know Allie's being harassed."

"Shut up!" Tim yelled, waving the pistol at her.

But Izzy seemed unfazed, locking her eyes upon him. "I'm in my own house, butthead! I'll talk if I feel like it!"

Allie felt more tense than ever. Izzy's brazen personality knew no boundaries, not even in the face of danger.

"Yes, this is your own house. But I'm in charge now. And yes, I know the man in blue is watching you. But he made the mistake of turning his back, and now he's taking a little break."

Izzy wondered if he was bluffing just to lessen her feeling of security. If he was, he sure made it convincing. She searched Allie's face for an answer.

"I know what you're thinking," he said. "I couldn't possibly harm Allie. Maybe not. But I have no reservations about shooting you! Now go, before I really lose my patience!"

"Oh, Izzy, could you also get my makeup out of the nightstand?" Allie asked, knowing Izzy would see the gun inside.

Izzy nodded, picking up on the hint.

As she brushed past Tim and down the hallway, he called her name. "Oh Izzy Bell, just in case you're looking for something other than clothes, you won't find it." Tim pulled another weapon out of the back of his pants. It was Allie's revolver. Allie froze at the sight of her own gun in the hands of this deranged villain.

Izzy, keeping her composure, shook her head and continued on to the bedroom. Minutes later, she reemerged, toting a suitcase and calmly placing it down at the entrance to the hallway. He and Allie were now standing near the door.

"Good. Very good. How about bringing it here?"

Izzy picked up the case and brought it to him, sitting it at his feet with a thud.

"Thank you," Tim said, sincerity lacking in his voice. As he turned to unlock the door, Izzy stepped a little closer and quickly shoved a revolver to his back, while Allie appeared horrified. Izzy had her own revolver, secretly stashed away. If he had rummaged through her drawer of hippie attire, he'd have found it.

"Drop the guns or I'll blow a hole straight through you!" she commanded.

Heeding to her demand, he let the pistols fall to the floor, while Izzy kicked them both over to Allie. Allie quickly picked them up, placing her own revolver inside her pocketbook nearby. She then checked the chambers of Tim's weapon.

"There's no bullets in there!" she shrieked.

Izzy foolishly diverted her attention away from Tim and toward Allie, giving him the perfect opportunity to jerk himself around and grab Izzy's revolver.

"No, but I bet this one has!" he yelled, triumphantly.

"Does it?" Allie squeaked.

"Yeah," Izzy said, shamefully nodding her head.

"Don't bother to pull it out," he told Allie, seeing her reach for the gun she'd just placed in her purse. "I emptied the bullets in yours as well. I didn't think I'd need any, but looks like that's changed. Now . . . I'm starting to get a little impatient. Allie, open the door," he said, waving the gun from her to the door.

Allie timidly walked the few steps to the door and embraced the knob, turning it ever so slowly while watching Tim from the corner of her eye. As she cracked it partially open, she caught sight of a uniformed cop hugging the side of the house. His shirt was stained with grass and dirt and there appeared to be a small amount of blood on his hand. Oddly, his head and face seemed to be soaked with water.

Catching eye contact with her, he placed a finger to his lips, signaling her to keep quiet. As she proceeded to walk through the door, with Tim close behind, Officer Banks seized the moment. With one swift motion, he knocked the revolver from Tim's grip, then grabbed him and pushed him to the ground. Too surprised to react, Tim grimaced as Russell snapped the handcuffs on behind his back.

"You have the right, you S.O.B., to remain silent. Anything you say can and will be used against you in a court of law. You have the right to an attorney . . ."

While Russell was reading Tim his Miranda rights, Allie grabbed Izzy and squeezed her tightly.

"Do you understand these rights as I have read them to you?" Russell asked.

Tim appeared defeated as he acknowledged with a nod. Russell pulled him off the ground, and made a gesture toward the road.

"I'll be back, ladies, my car's near the highway. I need to get this scumbag secured inside."

Izzy stepped inside to take a shot or two of brandy while Allie waited outside for Banks to return. It wasn't long before she saw the flashing blue light atop of the car coming toward the house. She could see Tim in the back gazing at her as the car stopped a few feet from the porch. As Russell got out of the car, Allie approached him, puzzled at his impeccable timing, being at the house at just the right time.

"How did you know?" she asked.

"Well, ma'am, call it instinct. I know I'm just a rookie but even rookies sense when something ain't right."

"Whatever it was, I'm just thankful you were on duty tonight, Officer . . ."

"Banks. Russell Banks. Oh, and I can't take full credit for this. Will you ladies follow me?" he asked, as Izzy joined them outside.

Feeling a little flushed from the shot of brandy, she, along with Allie, followed Russell out to the barn. Through the bright light of the full moon, they recognized Richard, kneeling just inside the barn, hunched over what appeared to be the form of a man curled up inside, his head resting upon a sack of corn.

Richard looked up, hearing them approach.

"He keeps mumbling something. I can't understand him."

Puzzled, they stared at Richard, then back at the body. Although the uninvited guest seemed to be asleep, he was mumbling, just like Richard said. As they inched closer to the two, Russell flicked on his flashlight, careful not to target the stranger's eyes. Although his face and hair were drenched with sweat and he had a five o'clock shadow, Allie recognized him immediately.

"Gary!"

Izzy leaned in and also yelled in surprise at who her eyes were beholding.

"Paul!"

"What?" Allie quickly shot a glance at Izzy. Richard and Russell exchanged looks of confusion.

"Mi . . . am . . . i," Gary muttered.

Allie, clearly confused, looked down at Gary, then back at Izzy. "Why does he keep saying 'Miami'? And why did you call him Paul?"

"That's my brother, my half brother, Paul, and he's not saying 'Miami.' He's saying, 'My Emmy.' That was his wife's name, short for Emily. And the fool is off his medication."

Allie felt faint. Her head was reeling from the whole night's events, from learning that Tim was the one stalking her to finding out that Gary was Izzy's brother. How bizarre!

"But . . . you called him Paul," Allie said, her voice shaking.

"Gary Paul. I'm the only one who's ever called him Paul. And Carter's such a common name . . . well, I just didn't connect the dots." Then she consoled her brother. "Paul, everything's gonna be all right. We're gonna get you back on the medication and you'll be good as new." She rubbed his arm, then bent down to kiss his forehead. "I love you, bro."

Weak, but suddenly aware of Izzy's presence, he looked up and smiled. "Long time, no see, sis. Thanks for letting me camp out here," he joked. "I love you, too." His comprehension seemed to be improving. Turning to Allie, he stared, as if seeing her for the first time tonight.

"You OK, Allie?"

"Yes, thanks to Officer Banks. What are you doing here? I'm confused."

"Tim was the one harassing you. I guess you know that by now. I had to find you, to warn you," he quietly said. He was fighting to stay alert even though images of Emily, his deceased wife, floated by.

"Yeah," Banks intervened. "He gave me just enough info to put the pieces together . . . after I came to, that is."

"After you came to?" Izzy asked.

"Yeah, ole Tim conked me in the head with a shovel, knocked me out cold. Next thing I see is Richard here, with an empty bucket in his hand."

"I was watching your house, Izzy, like you asked," Richard reminded her, "and I saw someone toting a ladder. Next thing I knew, he had it propped against the house and was climbing it. I put some clothes on and ran over here as fast as I could. But the guy was gone. The ladder was still propped against the house but the dude was nowhere to be found. That's when I heard something coming from the barn. I eased out to the barn and saw Officer Banks laid out on the ground and Gary—or Paul— halfway unconscious. I filled up a bucket of water and doused Officer Banks with it to wake him up."

"Well, that explains why you're wet," Allie noted.

Russell kneeled beside Gary. "You need to go to the hospital, buddy."

"No, no, no. I'll be fine. I have some medication, not my usual stuff, but it'll do. If I need it, I'll take it."

Russell started to say, "How bad off do you need to be to take it?" but didn't.

"Well, OK, Gary, ah, Paul . . . Mr. Carter. I'd stick around but I gotta go book somebody. Looks like you three have a lot to talk about."

"Thanks again, Officer Banks," Allie said, as he strutted back to the patrol car.

Although she still had a slight tremble in her voice from the shock of it all, Izzy, remarkably, remained calm, perhaps from the effects of the brandy shots earlier. "C'mon, little brother. Let's get you inside the house. A nice hot shower and warm bed'll fix you up."

Richard and Izzy hoisted Gary to his feet. Supporting him on either side, they assisted him back to the house. Allie struggled with a mixture of emotions as she imagined his familiar smile and touch. It was a sensation that sparked old feelings, old feelings from a few weeks ago. She wondered how Gary felt now that she knew what "Miami" meant. "Miami" translated into "My Emmy." And considering what he said, was he still in love with his wife, long passed on? Could he look beyond the pain and see her? What was really on his mind?

With all the events that had intertwined their lives, Izzy's, Allie's, Gary's, she knew that, realistically, it would be a matter of time to sort things through, time for their hearts to heal and their minds to focus. The future, whatever it held, would be there later for them to explore. But for now, they'd enjoy the present and let the future take care of itself.

EPILOGUE

"It's nice and peaceful out here on the porch." Allie savored the serenity as she sat alongside Izzy in the swing, sipping her tea.

"Yeah, just look at the stars out tonight," Izzy agreed, gazing up at the sky. "Such a beautiful night. Who would have thought we'd be sitting here a year later enjoying this?"

"Who would've thought a year later, you'd own the diner?" Allie laughed. Izzy eyed her, then laughed, her hyena echoing in the night air.

"Thanks to you," she said, still laughing. "But I'm glad I did it. I mean Frank, he's a good guy deep down, I guess, but he doesn't, you know . . ."

"Have the personal touch like you?" Allie finished.

"Yeah, something like that."

"Besides, Izzy, let's face it, he had no business sense. You, on the other hand, owned your landscaping and nursery business, so your experience, coupled with your great magnetism toward people, could only add to the success of the diner." Allie thought she detected tears in Izzy's eyes.

"Thank you, Allie. That's one of the nicest things anyone's ever said to me. But I kinda trusted your judgment, being a businesswoman yourself, with the realty and all. It was a good opportunity, like you said. Frank was willing to let it go cheap."

"I know June's happy. She'd much rather have you as boss. But it was also nice of you to keep Frank on. I think he does prefer being more behind the scenes."

"I think making him Employee of the Month went to his head."

"Ah, let him have his moment in the sun. After all, you taught him everything he knows and I'm sure he's grateful to you for that."

"Well, I don't know about grateful, humble maybe."

"Speaking of humble, someone sure is spreading good stuff about you all over town."

"What do you mean?" Izzy asked, curious of her admirer.

"Ex-Chief Bradley. All he does is rave about you. Talking about vinegar turning into sugar! I heard, through the grapevine, that he called you a decent, sensitive, caring and wonderful human being."

"Oh please, you'll make me puke. Not Bradley."

"I'm serious! It's too bad he couldn't have expressed that side of him when he was the chief. But I do commend his choice to succeed him . . . Officer Banks, Chief Banks now."

"Yeah, no one was surprised when Russell was elected almost unanimously. What he did was smart detective work . . . and heroic. He may have been a rookie but that was one smart cookie of a rookie."

"If he hadn't been looking out for us that night, there's no telling what Tim would've done. I shiver when I think what could've happened. I suppose with Tim in the asylum, we can rest a little easier." Allie leaned back in the swing and smiled, reminiscing of the day she moved in with Izzy. "It's really nice being here. Still can't believe it's been a year that I was staying here and all that happened."

"I know Richard's excited that you're back. He's coming over in a little bit. . . ." Izzy stopped when she recognized his familiar lanky form in the shadows, crossing over into her yard. "Well, speak of the devil, there he is."

As he came closer to the steps, she could see he wasn't alone. Falling close behind was Bradley. Richard ducked to avoid one of the potted plants Izzy had hanging off the eaves. The former chief merely walked beneath them, being considerably shorter.

"Hey, girl! It's good to see you!" Richard said, leaning over to plant a peck on Allie's cheek. "And I think you know who this is," he said, gesturing toward Bradley. Izzy was the first to acknowledge his attire, a tie-dye T-shirt and a peace emblem on a chain wrapped around his neck.

"Where's the headband and bell-bottom britches?" she asked.

"Cute, Izzy, I had to work up the nerve just to put this on. I did it just for you."

"Well, I might be a little biased because of the attire but I must say, you do wear it well."

"Thanks, I think."

"I ran into Mr. Bradley earlier, Allie, and told him you were back in town," Richard said. "He told me he needed to see you again. There was something he badly needed to say to you."

"Yes. I just wanted to apologize for not being more aggressive with your situation. And that goes for you, too, Izzy. I'm just thankful Banks was on duty at the time. I commend him and Richard for being vigilant. I think this town will do fine with Banks as chief. Again, my apologies."

"Thank you, Mr. Bradley. That means a lot."

After a moment of awkward silence, Richard chimed in. "Say, Allie, you're really thinking of moving here?"

Allie glanced at Izzy, who in turn looked sharply at Richard. "Blabber-mouth."

"No, no, it's OK, Izzy. Actually, Richard, I have been mulling that idea over with Izzy but it's a lot to think about. I mean, I'm really close to my brother. It's hard to imagine me and Derrick living that far apart from one another. We have our Friday coffee ritual, and I also have the realty to think about. Then there's the house in Regal Woods. There's a lot of things to consider. Besides, I'm not the only one who can make that decision."

The screen door opened at that moment and Allie smiled as she reached for her husband's hand.

"It's up to Paul as well." Paul, as she called him now, leaned over to kiss her. "We're still in the thinking stages right now. But I promise, Richard, you'll be the first to know, besides Izzy, when we decide."

As the five of them laughed and sipped tea by the light of the moon, a possum wandered onto the porch and sniffed along the boards, eventually hitting the jackpot when he located one of the many cat food bowls Izzy had sitting around.

"You know, he's really kinda cute, except for that tail," Allie said.

"Been around Izzy too long," Richard muttered.

"Honey, I can see where you might have compassion for the creature and sympathize with his predicament. I mean, he is, after all, a possum. But why, for Pete's sake, did you have to name him?" Paul teased.

"Ya hear that, Clem? He thinks you should be nameless. Altogether now . . ."

Richard and Izzy took the cue and started singing, with Bradley falling in.

"Oh my darling, oh my darling, oh my dar-ling, Clementine . . . you were lost and gone forever, dreadful sorry, Clementine."

Clem, the possum, ignored their little sing-along and continued to snack, while Paul shook his head, happy to have not only Allie back in his life, but his sister as well, who he'd seen very little of over the years. And better still was the realization that he no longer needed the drugs that had kept him on an even keel. Although he missed Emily and would always love her, he had a new life and a new wife . . . and a possum named Clem.